D0546901

Tangle of Time

Tangle of Time

Maureen Thorpe

Ekstasis Editions

Published in 2018 by:
Ekstasis Editions Canada Ltd.
Box 8474, Main Postal Outlet
Victoria, B.C. V8W 3S1

Ekstasis Editions
Box 571
Banff, Alberta T1L 1E3

LIBRARY AND ARCHIVES CANADA CATALOGUING IN PUBLICATION

Thorpe, Maureen, author
    Tangle of time / Maureen Thorpe.

Issued in print and electronic formats.
ISBN 978-1-77171-305-4 (softcover).--ISBN 978-1-77171-306-1 (ebook)

    I. Title.

PS8639.H6745T35 2018   C813'.6   C2018-904978-2
                                               C2018-904979-0

Canada Council   Conseil des Arts   Funded by the   Canada
for the Arts   du Canada   Government
                                      of Canada

Ekstasis Editions acknowledges financial support for the publication of *Tangle of Time* from the government of Canada through the Canada Book Fund and the Canada Council for the Arts, and from the Province of British Columbia through the Book Publishing Tax Credit.

Printed and bound in Canada.

For Jim
And in memory of Valerie James, my first reader

Man…can go up against gravitation in a balloon, and why should he not hope that ultimately he may be able to stop or accelerate his drift along the Time-Dimension, or even turn about and travel the other way.

~ H. G. WELLS, *The Time Machine*

King Henry: Here, Uncle Exeter, fill this glove with gold crowns and give it to this fellow. Keep it fellow; and wear it for an honour in thy cap.

~ WILLIAM SHAKESPEARE, *King Henry V, Act 4, sc. 8.*

Canonical Hours

In medieval England, time was measured by the canonical hours. The church bells rang out the times for prayer and provided a rhythm for the day.

Matins - daybreak.
Prime - about 6 a.m.
Tierce - about 9 a.m.
Sext - about noon.
Nones - about 3p.m.
Evensong, Vespers - about 6 p.m.
Compline - The curfew bell.

1

Tiny hairs rose, one by one, on the back of Annie Thornton's neck. She shivered.

From across an elegantly laid table, complete with a three-tier cake stand and silver teapot, her friend Mary looked around at people enjoying afternoon tea at the old inn.

"What's wrong, Annie, seen a ghost? You've gone as white as that china cup."

"I don't know. I had a weird sense of all of the people who have passed through the inn, drinking and eating, living their lives throughout the last five hundred years or so, then passing on. We know nothing about their lives and it'll be the same for us. We're born, we live and we die: that sort of thing."

"My God, Annie. We're here to celebrate my job promotion. This High Tea is costing a fortune. Don't be so damn gloomy. Still, I wish I had your imagination. We'd be celebrating the release of my first novel, not me becoming boring number-cruncher two on the insurance company's highway to glory."

"Sorry, Mary. I didn't mean to sound gloomy; just an eerie feeling, that's all. But please don't start again about being a writer. I've been hearing you say it for years but you never do the writing. Your skill is with numbers—hence the promotion. Let this novel stuff go."

Mary's shoulders stiffened and she placed her teacup carefully back onto its saucer. "That is not a nice thing to say to your best friend, especially when we are out enjoying ourselves. Just because you've never had a dream doesn't mean I can't."

"How do you know I've never had a dream? Because I don't talk about it all the time, doesn't mean I don't have one."

Was she being mean to her friend? Annie pretended to sip her Earl Grey. It was simply irritating, this business of Mary wanting to be a famous writer because Mary didn't write or couldn't write—just talked about writing, on and on and on.

And it wasn't true about Annie not having a dream. Of course, graduating as a midwife had been amazing but her yearning to graduate as a witch—now if that happened…

First she'd have to get over the fear of opening The Book of Spells. Stuffed at the back of a clothes closet it may be, but her skin tingled whenever she passed the door.

What if opening The Book would be like opening Pandora's Box? What if she tried spell-making and somebody died? What if people found out? No, best keep her mouth shut; ignore the call of The Book and focus on mothers and babies.

Forcing her attention back to the plate stand of custard eclairs, orange madeleines, jam and clotted cream scones, Annie tried to make up for her earlier irascibility. She changed the subject to 'The King's Glove' new venture of special events.

Walking back to Hallamby Village from the inn took about fifteen minutes and the two friends ambled along quite contentedly until Mary exploded. "Annie, I know—I mean I really know—I am meant to write a novel. Do you remember being in detention after school and we had to write an essay with a prompt from Miss Taylor about a circus clown and she chose my story for publication in the school rag that year? Well, that proves to me I've got the stuff it takes."

Annie sighed. "So, why aren't you writing?"

"I can't get started. Like, the opening sentence isn't coming to me. Once I get that down, I know I'll be off and runni—"

Shut up. Shut up about the writing. Seal your mouth. The familiar tingling Annie felt on passing the clothes closet surged up her spine.

Silence. Blessed silence.

A quick look at Mary showed her lips firmly pressed together and an appearance of utter surprise on her face.

What have I done? What did I say? Shut up. I said seal your mouth—and she has! I really am a hereditary witch. The power is in me—not The Book. Oh My God. What do I do now?

Annie and Mary carried on walking—in silence: Annie frozen in a strange mixture of fear and excitement.

There must be a way to break the spell—if it was a spell. But it must be, Mary hadn't said a word. Okay, Mary; You can speak now; your mouth is unsealed.

"Mary, I was thinking, what if I help you to get started on your novel?"

"How can you do that? Do you know any magic spells?" Mary laughed at her own joke and kept walking.

2

Late November 1415, Hallamby, Yorkshire

"Not long now, Jack, before we reach the inn. The landlord at the last place said once we crossed the ferry on the Derwent it'd be less than a mile."

Will Boucher's feet throbbed and his belly rumbled: the rumble a familiar sound from the long marches in France. At least now, his belly wasn't cramping from dysentery. He and his mate, Jack Fletcher, had walked for days along the remains of the old Roman road called Ermine Street, running as straight as an arrow, north from London to York and beyond.

"Aye, and it's our last stop before York, thanks be to God. We'll be home by the morrow." Jack stopped and stretched his back muscles, his dark hair, and beard making him almost invisible in the November night.

"At least the weather is calmer tonight." Will pointed his staff at the heavens. "The storm we suffered through yesterday soaked everything. My boots still feel damp. We must get off this road now darkness has arrived. The Lord only knows how many villains are lurking in the forest. We're two fat pheasants waiting to have our throats cut."

The outline of a building loomed in the murk as an even darker, solid block.

Will sighed. "At last; I can't wait to taste a bowl of steaming pottage and fall into a soft bed."

"Something's not right." Jack reached out to halt his friend. "It's odd there are no lights though it is past curfew. The innkeeper must have doused the fire and closed up. He appears not to be interested in late night travellers."

The inn's cracked wooden sign creaked in the gentle breeze. Will could barely make out the hostelry's name, painted in fading letters on the wood—'The King's Head'.

Jack walked through an archway into the pitch-black courtyard. Peering around, he found it difficult to locate a door against the blackness of the building. Following a wall by feel, hand over hand, a large door materialised on the left side of the building and he banged hard, using the hilt of his dagger. Will, hand on his knife, kept watch.

The moon broke from behind a cloud, lighting up Will's blond hair and casting shadows at the feet of the frustrated men. The effect of heavy wool cloaks covering their bows and backpacks gave their shadows the appearance of grotesque hunchbacks.

Will cursed. He was tired and hungry, although happy to be back on English soil. He and Jack were a long way from France and King Henry; even so, the memory of the events at Agincourt remained fresh in his mind.

"Now what?" Jack turned to his friend and brother-in-arms.

Will walked out of the courtyard. The moon still offered some illumination and he spotted a wooden post, ten paces from the entrance to the inn. Curious, he peered at the carved letters: 'Hallamby Village'. As Will read the name, goosebumps blossomed on his skin and his spine tingled. He shivered.

* * *

"One," Mistress Wistowe said to her cat, Bea.

* * *

"Are you alright, mate?" Jack grasped his friend's arm.

Will shrugged off Jack's hand. "I'm fine; a goose walked over my grave. Perhaps my empty belly is affecting me. We'll follow this sign. The village must be close by. At least we'll be off this damned road and safer for it."

They turned off the road and began following a well-worn path.

"Did the sign say how far this Hallamby is?"

"No," Will shook his head, "but it won't be far, not like in France. That's a big country and I swear we covered a lot of it following King Henry."

Jack turned to his friend. "I thank The Lord that I'm off that ship from Calais. I can't believe how much I offered to the sea."

Will laughed. "It's all behind us now. I wish that moon would stay out. It's hard to see the path when it goes behind the clouds."

They walked on, watching intently for signs that they were close to Hallamby.

"At last." Jack pointed to the dark bulk of a large stone building. "Looks like the village church."

The church sat at the top of a gentle rise. From there the path opened out onto a broad main street with the shadowy shapes of dwellings lining either side. The tired men trudged through the quiet village.

"Keep an eye out for an outbuilding where we can bed down. Looks like a night without supper," Will grumbled.

Once again, the moon broke through the barrier of clouds, illuminating the silent, darkened cottages. Will blinked. Was that a plume of smoke writhing out of a cottage window? He rubbed his tired eyes. Yes, it was smoke and—by the Virgin, he must be tired— he could see letters swirling through the plume. He alerted Jack and they hurried toward the cottage. Will pushed at the sturdy door, which opened to his touch. The pair stumbled through the opening and found a long room full of smoke. Dropping to their knees, they were able to see along the ground from the light of the hearth fire embers. A youth lay on the floor. He appeared unconscious. A cat lay beside him, also unmoving. Jack and Will lifted the slight young man and carried him outside, laying him gently on the road. Jack went back for the cat.

Will peered down at the unconscious youth, but something was wrong. Yes, he was wearing men's clothes but this body had the face and shape of a girl.

He looked closely at the face. It *was* a girl and she was comely. Curling black hair and arching eyebrows offered a stark contrast to her pale face. Will experienced a peculiar ache in his heart and drew in his breath as he appreciated her vulnerability: he knew with certainty he would protect her with his life.

* * *

"Two," Mistress Wistowe counted, nodding at Bea, her familiar.

* * *

Will shook his head. Why did he think that—he had enough to do searching for an inn. The girl opened her eyes: grey eyes framed by long black lashes.

"Who, w-hat, w-w-where am I?" she whispered.

"It's alright, you're safe," he reassured her. "We've pulled you from your cottage. We saw smoke pouring from the window."

"God's Britches," roared Jack. "The damned cat just scratched me, some thanks for rescuing it."

A blood-curdling yowl filled the air as the animal took off into the bushes. Will went back into the cottage. Visibility had improved although the room had grown cold from the open door. Will sniffed. He sniffed again. That was not smoke he had seen, but steam coming from a heavy iron pot hanging on a hook over the now slumbering hearth fire. Swinging the pot away, he set it beside the open hearth.

The two young men helped the young woman into the cottage and sat her on a stool at a table of boards set on a trestle. Will found a candle stub and lit it with embers from the dying fire. The light from the flickering flame played upon the dazed face of their new acquaintance.

3

Annie looked around in bewilderment. This was not the cottage she knew and loved. What had happened to her flagstone floor with its scattered rugs? Rushes covered the ground, and, sweet smelling though they might be, that was a dirt floor underneath. Familiar looking herbs hung from the ceiling rafters but her sink and Rangemaster cooker (the jewel of her kitchen), had vanished. Instead, a stone hearth in the centre of the dark room held a smouldering fire; the smoke made her cough. A large iron pot sat on a trivet at the side of the hearth. Two young men, apparently her rescuers, stared at her, both bearded, one dark, one fair, wearing some kind of fancy dress: hose, tunics, and heavy wool cloaks.

Annie took a big breath. What had she done? Last thing she remembered was being in her kitchen, stirring the pot on the cooker. Cooking something? Shaking her head to clear the cobwebs, an image grew. She was reaching for a heavy book sitting on the counter. The book was key—but to what?

The image vanished and she gasped as another picture formed. Annie's mother held out the same book. "Don't blame me for this. I am obliged to hand on this Book of Spells on your eighteenth birthday. You've inherited The Family Curse, I'm afraid. I don't want to have anything to do with it."

"Mum, what are you talking about?"

"You come from a long line of witches. What you do with this knowledge is up to you. I won't mention it again."

Annie had been overwhelmed with relief, having believed she was different in some way. She chose not to share her sense of 'weirdness' with her friends, including Mary Bradley, her best friend. She remained unremarkable, looking in from the outside and mimicking her peers' obsessions—boys, pimples, and diet.

One of the men threw some sticks on the fire. Like an elderly man on a cold morning, the fire grumbled to life, its flames illuminating the surroundings of the long room. Herbs hung from the roof rafters and above the rafters, straw. A hole in the straw roof seemed to be the only way the smoke from the fire could escape although a couple of wood-shuttered openings in the walls provided ventilation. Two stools, a table, and a weaving loom were be the only furniture apart from a mattress and blanket in a corner. It all looked like stuff from a museum. The walls were of rough plaster, brown coloured, and wooden shelving supported some bowls, cups, and jugs. A carved wooden chest sat next to the mattress.

Annie stared into the flickering flames. She remembered what she had been doing in the kitchen—making a creativity spell for Mary. After returning home from the High Tea incident, she'd been overwhelmed with guilt for sealing Mary's mouth. Reparation had to be made. Realizing she really did have magic power—witch power — Annie's fear of The Book of Spells dissipated and she released it from its prison.

"Creativity spells, Rosamund," she had muttered as she carefully turned the heavy vellum pages. "Here's one, it is perfect: 'A Scribe's Enhancement.'"

Pausing to review the ancient script, she reached for the dried herbs and read the ingredients out loud.

> "A pinch of yarrow to give courage,
> add myrtle for a fertile imagination,
> lavender for contentment,
> ginger to make the endeavour successful.
> Sage for wisdom,
> seeds to produce growth and,
> most important, salt and soil."

Dusting off her hands, the novice witch had mixed the herbs in a large pot, covered them with water, and turned up the gas flame. Taking a small torch, she went into the now dark garden to dig up soil to sprinkle around the outside base of the pot.

"I have two of the main elements, Rosamund; earth, and water. I'll use my Himalayan sea salt. Given the price of it, it will be more powerful than table salt."

The mixture was boiling and filling the room with steam. After nervously clearing her throat, patting her flushed cheeks with a tea towel and crossing her fingers, Annie had chanted her incantation:

> *Powers of air, of beginnings and light*
> *Descend upon me and bless this rite*
> *Send to Mary the power to know*
> *And let her creativity grow*
> *Fill her head and let her be*
> *A wealth of creativity.*

Rosamund, her inky black cat, had remained beneath the kitchen table, twitching her tail and purring an accompaniment to Annie's words.

Annie fervently wanted Mary to let her imagination fly; develop a spellbinding plot; create strong characters; write flowing senten— **darkness has fallen.**

Where did those words come from? She had stared in amazement as the words she heard in her head became visible, forming a chain, moving through the steam. The chain of words grew longer and began twisting around and around, creating a vortex inside the vessel. *Darkness has fallen…darkness has fallen.* The words turned into sound, the sound becoming louder and louder, filling the small kitchen with a pulsating beat. The last thing she had remembered was falling to the flagstone floor with her hands over her ears and hearing Rosamund yowling.

"We found a cat with you, mistress," said the dark-haired man, wiping the blood from a scratch on his hand. "It took off outside."

How long had she been sitting, lost in the past? "That's my Rosamund, I must go find her. She'll be frightened." Annie jumped up. Her vision blurred; the walls wavered. She sat abruptly.

The fair-haired man was watching her with concern. "Mistress, my name is Will Boucher and this is my mate Jack Fletcher. We are longbowmen returning home from the French Wars and plan to be in York tomorrow. Do you have anyone we can fetch to help you?"

Annie shook her head, stifling a sob. She didn't even know where she was, never mind who she might know. Jack offered to go look for the cat, but he sounded half-hearted. He looked across at his friend and rubbed his belly.

"What's in the pot?" asked Will. "We would dearly love a bowl of pottage. It's a long time since we ate."

"No!" Annie cried. The men looked startled. "I mean no good for eating. Let me see what I can find. You saved us, it's the least I can do."

Looking automatically for her fridge and, realizing her mistake, Annie explored the contents of the shelves. Carrots, onions, and a round lump resembling a turnip sat in a wooden bowl. A clay jug of water sat beside them. At least the vegetables still looked the same as in her time and they seemed fresh.

"These will make a nourishing soup." Annie walked to the large pot and peered into it. This couldn't be the same pot—could it? If it was, the herbs she had placed in it such a short time ago had vaporized. Annie brought the bowl of vegetables to the table, looked around for a knife and froze when the two men moved to each side of her, and took out their daggers. *God in Heaven,* they were going to rape and kill her! She relaxed when they calmly began chopping up vegetables. As they worked, the man called Will recounted his and his companion's recent adventures in the French Wars.

When Will began the story of the Battle of Agincourt, Annie remembered her school history lessons about the famous battle. She had written an essay about it when studying the Hundred Years' War. The battle gave her a fix on time. Could it be possible she was somewhere in the fifteenth century? King Henry V was seeking the title of King of France in order to regain lands for the English Crown. France and King Henry were a long way from this little village in Yorkshire, although King Henry had a long arm when it came to gathering his taxes.

Annie paused in her chopping. Was she still in Hallamby village where she normally lived? Was she still in Yorkshire, for Heaven's sake! She could be in Timbuktu for all she knew, although the blond haired man did say they planned to be in York tomorrow.

The men had mentioned the inn on the highway. If this was Hallamby—and that was a big if—then 'The King's Glove' on the main highway outside of Hallamby originated in the thirteenth century, and the local church was built after the Norman conquest of 1066. The Manor House, also dating from the thirteenth century, had undergone a metamorphosis many times and was now occupied by an aging rock star and his family.

Annie had found it curious that the name of the 'The King's Glove' at Hallamby didn't appear to follow the traditional naming practice of inns and pubs. Many names had survived the centuries, such as 'The Green Man', reflecting pre-Christian folklore, or 'The Lord Nelson', recalling the exploits of the famous naval officer who saved England from the French. Plenty of pubs had names with royal references: 'The Crown' or 'The King Edward' or 'The Queen's Arms', but she did not know of any other pub or inn in Britain called 'The King's Glove'. What was the history behind the name?

The appetizing smell of simmering soup brought Annie's mind back to the present. No one spoke, just eyed the soup pot as though willing the contents to cook faster. At least the room began warming up. Declaring the broth ready, Annie found some wooden bowls on the shelf and filled them to the brim. A loaf of bread sat beside the bowls. The bread tasted surprisingly fresh but coarse, its grain dark and heavy. The two men gulped down the soup while tearing huge chunks out of the loaf. They both offered apologetic looks at Annie.

"We haven't eaten since Prime," explained Will.

The soup pot emptied in a trice. Jack yawned. "I noticed an outbuilding at the back; do we have your permission to bed down inside?"

"Of course, will you be warm enough?"

"We have our cloaks." Will wrapped his heavy cloak around him.

Annie bid them good night and the men stumbled out, now with full bellies and almost asleep standing up. Annie shook her head with fatigue and stepped outside hoping to entice Rosamund in, to no avail. She banked up the fire and collapsed onto a rustling mattress. She would sort everything out tomorrow.

4

Late November 2015, Hallamby, Yorkshire

Mary Bradley tiptoed upstairs to the spare bedroom she and her husband had converted into an office, not wanting to disturb him snoozing in front of Sunday's football game. Opening her laptop, she stared in frustration at the blank screen then pecked at the keyboard.

'It was the best of times and the worst'—that was no good, she was sure she had read those words somewhere. Deleting the line, she gazed into space then tapped again. 'In the beginning'. After staring at the three words and realising she had just plagiarised the opening words of the Old Testament, Mary turned away from the screen in frustration. If she could only find a beginning for her novel, she knew she would be on her way to fame and fortune.

A small window in the wall above the desk showed her that darkness had fallen; typical November, dark by teatime. Craning her neck sideways, Mary saw the North Star twinkling above her. On the other hand, could it be the space station? She went back to her screen.

What was the expression she had just used? 'Darkness has fallen'; m-m-m, she liked that, and it had a ring to it. Sounded like a good opening for her story. She'd tell Annie she had started her novel. Her friend would be pleased.

Mary typed 'Darkness has fallen'. As she did so, a peculiar feeling like pins and needles started in her toes and crawled up her spine. The tingling stopped. She shrugged her shoulders then paused. Was this how it felt when the muse came to visit?

* * *

"That's three," Mistress Wistowe told her familiar. "It is all coming together. You and I must be off to Selby and leave these young people to do their work."

5

The sound of church bells woke Annie to a room still dark. The dawning realisation that she neither was in her own bed nor in her own time shot her off the straw-filled mattress. A cockerel crowed outside; a dog barked and another dog responded. The village was stirring. Despite the curtailed sleep, she was wide-awake and filled with tension. The villagers would know immediately she was a stranger in their midst and her mind was empty of a rational explanation to give them.

Scratching noises at the door signalled Rosamund had decided to return. She wound herself around Annie's feet.

"You appear to be taking this time travel thing in your stride, Rosamund. Do you know something I don't?"

Rosamund offered a plaintive meow. Food first: the message was clear.

A pitcher of milk sat on a shelf. Struck by guilt; Annie sent a mental apology to whomever had provided the food; she would have to pay them back somehow. She poured milk into a bowl for a grateful Rosamund. How interesting that fresh food was available in the apparently empty cottage, almost as though she—or someone—was expected—or had just left. The cottage certainly looked cared for and smelled sweetly of dried herbs and those freshly cut rushes on the floor.

Annie desperately needed to look for something suitable to wear; her current outfit of jeans and a tee would create too many questions. Poking around in the wooden chest, she found linen shifts and woolen gowns, neatly folded. A strong draught of lavender filled her nostrils as she lifted the exquisitely carved lid. The bright colour of the fabrics was a surprise; she had imagined medieval country people clothed in dull greys and browns.

"I bet they used madder and woad for the dye," Annie murmured as she dressed in a rose coloured gown. A night school course in weaving and dying raw wool with natural plants suddenly came in handy. With any luck, her rescuers hadn't noticed her jeans last night. Once dressed, and making do by combing her fingers through her curls, her only hope was that she would fit in with the locals, whoever they were. Annie shrugged her shoulders; best she could do under the circumstances, yet once again, her pulse raced as realization of her situation flooded her mind.

It was no good panicking, she told herself firmly; meddling with spells had landed her in this predicament and it was up to her, Annie Thornton, to get herself out. Recognizing dried mint amongst the many bunches of herbs hanging from the rafters; she fanned the embers of the fire and boiled water for an infusion, hoping for clarity.

The aroma of mint filled the air as she sipped the hot drink. Thinking back to the scene in the kitchen last evening; she remembered the loud sound the letters made as she was casting her spell, but the words—*darkness has fallen*—where did they come from? Certainly not from her. Evidently, she had made a mistake and now was a long way from home, time-wise if not distance-wise. At least it was England, but exactly where, she had no idea. So many questions and no answers.

Who lived in this cottage? What went wrong with the creativity spell? Perhaps the Himalayan salt substitution caused the glitch, making the spell too powerful. On the plus side, she had retained much of her school history studies, especially the medieval period. Oh, call a spade a spade! She was a witch and came from a long line of witches. She needed to be a more accomplished witch. What did they call it in the nursing profession—best practice? That is what she needed, training in Witches' Best Practice. Someone should write an instruction manual.

Surely, she could find a way back home. As a midwife with a busy practice in rural Yorkshire, people would be missing her. Her friend Mary would definitely notice her absence. Her parents would eventually realize their daughter hadn't been in touch.

In the meantime, caution was paramount. She must not reveal that she was a witch, albeit a poor one, having no desire to burn at the stake; this was the time of witch hunting. Annie's mind whirled with the confusion and fear of her situation. A gentle knocking at the door brought her back to the present and announced the return of her two guests.

"Thank you both again for helping me last night. I didn't introduce myself. I'm Annie Thornton and this is Rosamund. What are your plans?" she asked before they could ask any questions, offering each a bowl of warm milk to break their fast. The only food remaining was the half turnip.

Master Boucher lifted his head from the milk and looked at her, appreciation in his eyes; was it for her or for the milk?

"Jack and I are weary of war," he said, a milk moustache on top of his blond one. "We've served our king well. I am searching for a hostelry to buy, to make my own. My mate Jack here is going help me run it. By the way, we noticed last evening that 'The King's Head' had closed down on the highway. That's why we turned off the road and came into Hallamby village."

Annie sighed with relief on hearing the name of her village. "You must mean 'The King's Glove.'"

"No, I'm sure it was head, not glove."

Jack concurred. "Yes, 'The King's Head," and went back to slurping his milk.

Before Annie could contest them again, another knock came at the door. She hesitated before opening it. Who could be visiting her?

An older woman stood on the doorstep. She looked comfortable in a soft, plump way. To Annie's relief, the woman was dressed in a long gown similar to Annie's, covered with a spanking clean apron. A white bonnet covered most of her grey hair and her eyes peered short-sightedly at Annie.

"'Ow do, Mistress Thornton. A know it's still early but a chanced tha would 'ave arrived today. Thy aunt, Mistress Wistowe, asked me to watch out for thee. As tha knows, she 'ad to go to Selby on business an' she told me tha would tek over while she's gone. Tha looks a lot like 'er, a must say, same grey eyes if ever a saw 'em. A've brought thee sum eggs."

Annie stared at her, her mouth dropping open. The woman knew Annie's name. Her aunt...?" *Do something,* her stunned brain shouted. Ingrained politeness took over. "Please come in."

The woman bustled to the table and sat down on one of the benches, looking curiously at the two men. She waited for them to introduce themselves and when this did not happen, she spoke.

"'Ow do, gentlemen. Am Mistress Davey, widow of this parish. A live just down t'road. Mistress Wistowe mentioned 'er niece might 'ave two companions with 'er."

Will and Jack looked startled, then bewildered.

Mistress Davey paused significantly and waited. Will introduced both himself and Jack, and emphasized they were soldiers returning from the French wars.

"We were planning to stay at 'The King's Head' last night on the way to visit my aunt, not knowing she was away," he nodded at Annie to include her in his rapidly conceived fabrication, "and when we discovered the inn had closed we woke up cousin Annie to claim a bed in the outbuilding."

"Tha cousin, is 'e? Mistress Wistowe didn't mention one of t'men is 'er nephew. Where are they to stay? They can't stay at t'inn, as 'e's reight in what 'e says. It's closed down, and they can't stay with thee: an unwed lass." Mistress Davey looked at Will. "T'inn only closed down yesterday. There's all sorts of stories goin' round, who knows what's true? Sumbody said t'duty officers were 'anging around t'inn, sum talk about where t'innkeeper's been gettin' his wine. Sumbody else said t'innkeeper 'ad tekken off, scared he were goin' to be arrested. A must say," she sniffed, "if we're at war wi' France, and, well, it seems we're always at war wi' France, we shouldn't be trading with t'enemy, although there's sum as think different.

"I 'ave a spare room," she went on, "A cud use extra money and am a good cook. 'Ave lots of fresh eggs as well an' sumtimes a fowl in t'pot." She paused and, tipping her head to one side, she waited.

The two men exchanged glances.

"That sounds perfect," Will smiled. "We're not planning on staying long as we're on our way to York; that's where we grew up. We'll just collect our belongings and be ready to go with you."

Annie sighed with relief once they left; however, she still had more questions than answers. Who was this aunt? What was she, Annie, supposed to 'take over'? How did this mysterious new relative know Annie was coming to visit? How did she know Annie would meet up with the two soldiers? What did this have to do with her assumption that the bungled creativity spell had caused her ride through the centuries? She was reluctant to ask Mistress Davey about her aunt as the woman believed Annie knew of the arrangement. When they left, she would continue to dig deep into her memory to recall what she knew of life in the fifteenth century, not that it would answer her immediate questions.

6

Late November 2015, Hallamby, Yorkshire

Mary stared in amazement at her computer screen as she scrolled down pages, one after the other, filled with writing. She had no memory of creating all those words but did recollect dreaming deeply last night. She remembered the tall, blond man. According to her screen, his name was William Boucher. She must have risen during the night and written down everything she dreamed. "I have to tell Annie," she told the screen. "I've become a writer!" She dashed off to bathe and dress.

Mary lived just down the road from Annie, so it took no time at all to get to her cottage. The next-door neighbour's curtains twitched before the woman, whom Mary knew had the reputation of being the eyes and the ears of the street, came bustling out to meet her.

"Annie must have gone away for a few days," the neighbour pointed at Annie's cottage. "I usually see her goin' to work most mornings. She always gives me a wave. When I didn't see her this morning I knocked on her door t'see if she were all reight but nobody answered. It's odd she didn't tell me she were goin' away; she usually asks me to watch t'house for her, an' her car's still 'ere. Did you know she was goin' away? Anyhow, I expect you have a key, Mary. You can keep an eye on things."

Mary was gobsmacked. Annie had not said anything to her about going away. Checking the time on her phone, she had to be at work by 9 a.m., she decided she might as well check the house, hoping not to find a body and tons of blood. She paused, wishing her imagination could be that vivid when writing.

Mary moved cautiously from room to room in the old cottage. All seemed in order: there were no signs of a struggle, no dead bodies lying around and no blood splatters on the walls. The cosy living room looked peaceful with its overstuffed sofa and armchair. Annie's bedroom showed no signs of violence, the bed neatly made, and Rosemund's basket lay, as usual, in the corner. Speaking of Rosamund, there was no sign of her and Annie would not go away and leave without making some arrangements so the cat must be with her. The kitchen looked reasonably tidy with no dirty dishes in the sink. Milk, yogurt, and salad greens in a container sat in the fridge. Odd that Annie hadn't cleaned out the fridge before leaving. Her car was still in the driveway. Someone must have given her a lift to wherever. Perhaps she went to the coast for a break; unusual that she didn't tell her friend, though.

A large empty pot sat on the kitchen range. Annie had left a mess on the range surface. Pink salt grains were everywhere, mixed in with —she peered closer—soil! What had her friend been doing?

The kitchen table held a large, heavily embossed book. Mary turned the ivory vellum pages, hoping for a message but could see only some almost indecipherable writing about herbs, sketches of flowers and leaves, and recipes. She sighed; Annie couldn't be far away. She would get in touch eventually. In the meantime, her novel was waiting. She could not wait to get back to Will Boucher as soon as the workday was done.

7

Late November 1415, Hallamby, Yorkshire

Mistress Davey led the way down the village street. Will and Jack looked around curiously at the village they had arrived at in the pitch dark. Now, seeing it in the grey half-light of a November morning, Will thought it not unlike the villages they had passed through and destroyed in France. He hung his head for a second, remembering the ragged army's march through the rural landscape. Food was always the main objective, but an army on the move had no scruples. The wide main street offered lots of room for horses and big lumbering carts. Jack laughed as they sidestepped hens scratching in the packed earth and getting underfoot. "We'd have had them in the pot quicksticks in France," unconsciously echoing Will's thoughts.

About thirty wattle and daub cottages with thatched roofs sat along the sides of the road, some looking neat and fresh, others a little run down or in ruin. These cottages comprised the village of Hallamby; a village of about two hundred souls, their guide told them. Two men sat on a roof, repairing the thatch, the sound of their voices floating down. Walking by one cottage, Mistress Davey pointed out a broom handle secured over the front door. "Tha knows t'broom tells thee this 'ouse 'as extra ale for sale. No doubt tha'll find a few men in there of an evenin.'"

The widow chatted on about how, in any village or town, an alewife had to have permission from the authorities to sell her ale, and the reeve or bailiff would taste the ale to ensure it was of the right quality. She would have to give the steward either money or ale for the privilege of being able to sell her brew.

"We can't alus trust water frum t'river so we drink small ale, not as strong as t'stuff tha drinks in t'taverns, even kiddies drink it, but a suppose tha knows that."

They came to a small village green with a little pond at the centre. Mistress Davey explained the villagers' water supply came from the river close by. The village had grown up on the banks of the River Derwent as it made its way to join the River Ouse. The River Ouse flowed through York on its way to the coast and, fortunately for the Hallamby villagers, the Derwent was much cleaner than the Ouse.

"It's a common saying: Ouse by name and ooze by nature," she told them with a smile.

Pointing out the bakehouse—the yeasty smell coming from the smoking chimney made their bellies rumble; and the village smithy —no smoke emerging from its chimney yet.

"Both these buildings belong t'Manor. We 'ave to pay to use 'em; that's more money goin' t'landlord."

The road rose gently and a large square, grey stone church sat on the rise, dwarfing the village cottages. A substantial house sat at the side of the church, with a base of stone and wattle and daub walls.

"That's our priest's 'ouse. Tha saw where t'inn is last night up on t'big road, and t'Manor 'ouse is back behind them oaks."

Narrow strips of cultivated fields surrounded the village. Winter crops pushed their tender sprouts through the soil: others lay fallow. Beyond the fields, sheep grazed on the common pasture as well as on the fallow fields, which retained some stubble. A couple of men, leaning on staffs, kept an eye on the sheep.

"Sum animal pens are over there."

Mistress Davey pointed to a small collection of sheds and pens made of sturdy fencing. The smell drifting over left no doubt that pigs were in residence.

They turned into a small lane and arrived at a two-story house with a neatly thatched roof, its sturdy cruck frame showing on the end wall.

"'Ere we are. Me 'usband, God bless 'im, were a carpenter so everythin' is well-made and me two sons, both married now with bairns of their own, took over from 'im, an' keep things up to scratch."

She continued chatting as she led them into a long, narrow, and dark room with a central hearth. "T'oldest lad moved to York wi' 'is family to find work an' now t'uther un's on about goin' there as well. A'll really miss 'em, 'specially t'bairns."

They climbed up a narrow ladder to a small loft with a tiny, open window covered with wooden shutters. Mistress Davey opened the shutters to let a little grey light into the room.

"There's a chamber pot by the bed and t'privy's out back. Come down when tha's both settled and 'ave some porridge."

She left them and went back downstairs. Jack sat down on the crunchy straw mattress and waited until their new landlady's footsteps had faded.

"What did Mistress Davey mean when she said Mistress Thornton's aunt knew we were expected? We hadn't planned to come here. How did you come up with the cousin idea?"

"I have no idea what she meant. I felt as confounded as you did. I came up with the cousin story to protect Mistress Thornton. She was so kind to let us stay and to feed us, I was worried about her reputation."

Will didn't mention the overwhelming sensation he'd had of needing to safeguard Mistress Thornton forever.

"Well, it's all very mysterious: us finding Mistress Thornton unconscious like that and then, when she came around, looking so lost and scared. Did you see her face when our new landlady knocked on the door? She looked like she was about to be executed. It's a bit like the peculiar business at the inn." Jack dropped his voice. "Think about it, Will. Your plan is to buy an inn somewhere in Yorkshire with the gold the king gave you and here is one sitting empty for some reason. Maybe we ought to stay for a while and look into it."

Will had been mulling the same thought over in his mind. Why would an inn in such a good location close down? 'The King's Head' was on the main London to York road, one of the much-needed network of hostelries available to travellers within a day's travel distance. No sensible traveller wanted to be stuck on the highway after dark. The monasteries provided food and a bed, but church dignitaries and knights of the realm were their regular guests.

"I agree, Jack. This might be an opportunity for us, the location being so close to York. We need to find out who the Lord of the Manor is here. He might tell us who owns the inn. We'll talk to the locals too; they usually know what's going on."

"Make sure," Jack stood, "we have our discharge stamp with us, we don't want to be sent back as deserters." They clumped down the stairs for a welcome bowl of Mistress Davey's porridge before heading out to investigate.

8

Annie pondered the news that her recently-discovered aunt knew both she and the two soldiers would arrive in Hallamby at the same time. Perhaps a bungled spell had not caused her predicament. Why wasn't her mysterious aunt here to answer Annie's questions? What was the purpose behind this travel through time?

Thinking back, the shift in time came when she heard the words 'darkness has fallen'. She must find her way to dwellings where villagers gathered: there lay information. Two locations came to mind immediately: the bakery and the smithy. Both would be warm and busy places and almost sure to have people there. She needed bread anyhow as the hungry young men ate the whole loaf last night. Annie found some coins on the shelf, left there by her new aunt, no doubt. Wrapping a shawl from the clothes chest around her shoulders, she left the cottage, telling a disgruntled Rosamund it was not safe outside for her.

Annie remembered learning the village bakehouse belonged to the Lord of the Manor and villagers paid for the use of it even though the baker baked the bread from their own flour, the barley, and rye grown by them and ground at the mill—for which they also paid. The feudal system certainly ensured the elite flourished on the backs of the peasants.

The strong smell of yeast guided her to the small building easily. The bakehouse, with its warm air and comforting smells, would be a cosy gathering place for locals, especially on a raw November morning.

Entering, Annie immediately felt the heat from the wood-fired domed oven welcoming her. The baker was a small, round man, coated in flour, his face glowing from the heat. Using a large wooden paddle, he removed loaves from the stone-built oven while other prepared loaves were rising in bowls on the shelves. Most of the loaves were a dark colour. Only the rich ate white bread made from wheat. Stacks of evenly cut branches lined the walls ready to feed the fire. An apprentice was kneading a large amount of dough on a table, red-faced from the effort. They must have been at work from an early hour.

Two women watched the activity, each intent, unconsciously, on their own timeless occupation. Both had a distaff, or pole, about three feet long, tucked under one arm. A furry mass of soft, white wool perched at the top of the poles. Their nimble fingers teased out the wool fibres and guided them to gather onto a spinning spindle lower than the pole, the spindle weighted down with a small rock. Annie fingered the soft woolen tunic she was wearing; marvelling that women used yarn spun from wool, flax, or hemp to weave all of their families' clothing.

The women chatted quietly to one another while watching the baker perform and their hands continued to create yarn.

Annie offered a good morrow and the two women welcomed her. Annie struggled a little to understand their strong Yorkshire dialect, which sounded much broader than the dialect spoken in her time.

"Tha's Mistress Wistowe's niece, is tha? She told us tha were cummin' t'village an' that tha were goin' to look after babies an' such while she were away. I'm Mistress Bainbridge." The woman bobbed a curtsey. "Thy aunt delivered all my babbies."

Hallelujah! One question answered. "I haven't seen my aunt for a while," Annie embarked on a fishing trip. "Is she still as busy as ever?"

"Oh, aye, she nivver stops. If i'n't one thing it's another. Babbies keep cummin', old 'uns die, little 'uns as well. She's there for everybody. That's why we were all glad when we 'eard tha were cummin' to tek her place while she's away."

Annie filed the thought that her new aunt appeared to have planned her arrival thoroughly—except for telling her niece.

The two women discussed the state of health of their respective children and moved on to complaining about the weather. Annie smiled to herself, her spirits lifted slightly; nothing had changed over the centuries. She maneuvered the discussion around to the last few days.

"Has anything unusual happened, talking about the weather?" she enquired, thinking of the word 'darkness'.

The other woman, who introduced herself as Mistress Atkins, nudged her friend with her elbow.

"Why, tha wouldn't know, not bein' 'ere," she said. "We 'ad a great storm t'utha night. It were dark by dinnertime. Men 'ad t'cum in frum fields early 'cos they couldn't see an 'and in frunt of their faces. Wind cum up summat shockin' an' brought down trees, blew thatch off a couple of 'ouses. Then we 'ad thunder an' lightnin'; real noisy it were, set me bairns off blubberin'."

"Aye," Mistress Bainbridge agreed. "Me man spent next day choppin' up branches for faggots, wi' say so of our steward; reight mess of branches all over t'place."

"Did anything else unusual come about from the storm?" Annie asked. The women glanced at each other.

"Well," confided Mistress Bainbridge, lowering her voice. "We did 'ear as how yon innkeeper frum t'inn on big road 'adn't bin seen since storm 'it us."

"Can you remember when that happened?"

"Ee, it were only a day back."

Annie chatted with the women a little longer, then she paid for a loaf of bread and left.

She planned to visit the blacksmith next, complimenting herself on being smart for finding another warm place to visit. Possibly, she might see some men there and be able to glean more information.

Entering the warm and smoky smithy, Annie was surprised to see her two new acquaintances warming their hands at the forge. "Good morning,"

"Good morrow, cousin," Will smiled. Jack nodded at her. "We were just talking to Big John Braithwaite here. The reason the inn was closed down last night is because the innkeeper has disappeared, a surprise to everyone."

Big John Braithwaite, justifiably named for his size and width and looking bigger still in his large, leather apron, was working the bellows, the coals glowing a fiery red.

"Aye, true enough," John wiped the sweat from his forehead with a hand as big as Annie's head. "'Ow do, Mistress. Tha must be Mistress Wistowe's kin. I 'eard she'd asked thee to cum an' 'elp 'er." He nodded at Annie. "She's a good'n is Mistress Wistowe. T'village can't do without 'er. Mind you, a dunt 'ear tha cousin were cummin' as well." The smithy nodded at Will. "But as for t'innkeeper—folk are saying t'devil cum and grabbed 'im during t'storm."

"Why t'devil?" asked Will, broadening his Yorkshire speech a little, in the hope it made him more acceptable.

"Ridley weren't a good man. A dunt like t'talk ill o' nobody, but 'e were right mardy, an' a buggar wi' wimmin. A dunt know 'ow 'e did any business up at t'inn."

Annie gathered that the innkeeper had been a miserable curmudgeon as well as a womanizer.

"Any 'ow," continued the smithy, "why's tha bothering wi' it? Tha's just passin' through, right?"

Will smiled. "My mate an' me just want to know why the inn is closed. We'd planned on staying there."

"Aye, well tha said tha's stayin' at Widow Davey's. Tha'll be all reight there. Bloody good cook, she is, an' tek no notice o' what folks round 'ere say; they know nowt, an' best tha knows nowt as well. T'inn's business is nowt to do wi' thee. Anyhow, tha'll be back on t'road t'York sooner than later."

With that pronouncement, he turned his back on them and gave his attention to the bellows.

"Interesting," Jack waited until they were outside the shop, "we've been warned off. Stay away from anything to do with the inn, and get out of the village as soon as you like. I wonder why that would be. What do you think, Will?"

"It just makes me more curious to find out."

"Me too," Annie agreed. "Somebody should find out what happened to the innkeeper, unpleasant as he sounds. People don't disappear without reason." Solving the mystery would occupy her time too, until she could find a way home.

"Let's work together on this, I can tell something's amiss here, even if the innkeeper is a miserable bastard. Oh, sorry, Mistress." Will looked embarrassed.

Annie shook her head; she had heard worse. "Please call me Annie."

"I am pleased to see you looking better today, and you, Annie, shall call us Will and Jack." Will reached out and touched her arm. A flicker of electricity pulsed at the spot where his hand had rested. Looking into Will Boucher's eyes an image of mint leaves floating in a flute of sparkling champagne came into her mind. She shook her head again. Did time travel affect the mind in such a way?

9

Even though Mistress Davey knew how efficiently the village communication system worked, it came as a surprise to the widow when she heard a loud knocking at her door early the next morning. She opened it to see the reeve of the manor standing there.

She had known Thomas Brighouse since he was born. He was a small man and had features strikingly similar to a ferret. The villagers chose him for the job of reeve, and he worked for the manor steward, making sure the villagers stayed in line. She did not trust him, suspecting he was over-zealous in his duties and enjoyed tittle-tattling back to the Manor House about his neighbours. Reeve Brighouse remained at the bottom of the administrative pecking order but he believed himself to be important enough.

"I need t'see yon boarders, Mistress Davey—now!" He puffed out his chest and stood taller.

"Oh, yes Reeve Brig'ouse, please cum in," Mistress Davey's heart beat faster. The reeve did have some power and could cause trouble for the villagers if he wished. "T'men are out back, I'll fetch 'em."

Will and Jack came into the house, taking care to remove the earth from their boots. They had been turning over the soil in the yard behind the house, each cottage having its own vegetable plot. This plot, plus strips of land, often situated in different parts of the manor, provided the means to feed each household.

"Good morrow." Will regarded the visitor. "How can we help you?"

Reeve Brighouse cleared his throat importantly. "I 'ave been informed that tha's been asking questions about yon innkeeper. I'm telling thee to cease and desist and to think about movin' on. Affairs in this village 'ave nowt to do wi' thee. Tha's not wanted 'ere." He stopped abruptly and cleared his throat again.

Mistress Davey's heart rate rose. The silence grew as her two boarders stared at the little man. Finally, Will broke the silence and responded to the reeve.

"You need to know that we are freemen and as such not under orders from you. You also need to know that we have the favour of our King Henry, having just returned from fighting for him and for England. I don't think he would be too pleased to hear we are being threatened."

He and Jack looked down at Master Brighouse.

"I'm not threatenin' thee. I'm only sayin' as what's good for thee."

"Thank you for your message," Will bowed his head. "We'll think about what you said."

Reeve Brighouse attempted to save his dignity. "Aye, see that tha dus," he muttered as he scurried off.

Mistress Davey wiped her hands nervously down her apron. "It dusn't do to upset our steward. 'E's a powerful man and 'e 'as a couple of bullyboys t'do 'is dirty work. It's best to steer clear of 'im and 'is bailiff."

"Please do not distress yourself, Mistress. We've done nothing wrong and we are well used to bully boys."

After that firm statement from Will, the men went back outside to resume their digging.

10

Late November 2015, Hallamby, Yorkshire

It was wonderful! All Mary had to do was sit down in front of her computer, turn it on, flex her fingers and she began writing like a fury. She could not believe the transformation from permanent writer's block to incredibly creative novelist. It seemed strange her friend had a role in the story, but figured it might be because she missed Annie so much. Besides, she had no choice; it was all she could do to keep up with the story of Annie, Will, and Jack flowing from her brain. Having to go to work at her regular job at an insurance company in York was frustrating, and her husband complained he never saw her. None of that meant anything. It was vital she find the time to write.

11

Late November 1415, Hallamby, Yorkshire

Over the next couple of days, it became apparent to Annie silence would meet any enquiries she and her new friends made about the inn or the absent innkeeper. Animated and welcoming faces quickly became flat and guarded: almost fearful, Jack observed at one point. It was obvious the villagers mistrusted outsiders. Even though word had spread that the two strangers were returning longbowmen from the now famous battle of Agincourt, the locals still refused to talk.

No one had, as yet, knocked on Annie's cottage door asking for help, thus limiting her ability to ask questions, so she spent her time familiarizing herself with the contents of the cottage. There seemed to be an impressive supply of herbs stored there as well as containers of vinegar and a box of clean linen rags. Scissors, a sharp knife, and a hook like a crochet hook lay in another box. Little containers of salves offered Annie the opportunity to guess what they were. Jars of honey and salt sat in a basket ready for the next patient. She was delighted to find a birthing stool in a corner and recognised its similarity to modern ones.

Starved of information regarding the missing innkeeper, the three new investigators decided to make their way to the inn one morning. Hoping to be less conspicuous, they went early, the cockerels still crowing as they walked along the main road. Mistress Davey had told them that many of the villagers would be working inside these days. Some were busy threshing the harvested grain crop in the Manor

House barn, both their own and, as part of their rent, that belonging to the Lord of the Manor. Other men stayed inside and mended tools while women worked at their spinning and weaving. Children would be in the forest gathering firewood.

When they came to the large, grey stone church Annie stopped in her tracks and took a deep and shaky breath. This was the same church building in her village, so familiar to her. It had changed little over the centuries. She walked or drove past this building almost every day and occasionally attended special events. The rest of this medieval village was not familiar: primitive cottages built of wattle and daub, dirt roads, and animal pens. This solid, stone building reminded Annie so much of home and how far away she was from her real life; she found it hard to breathe.

Will and Jack looked at her with concern.

"Are you well, Annie?" asked Will. "You look quite pale."

Annie gulped and shook her head. "I must be out of shape; coming up the rise from the cottage took my breath."

"What shape are you out of shape from and what took your breath?" asked Jack, ever curious. Annie shook her head. She couldn't cope with translations right now.

They continued walking along the well-worn path to the inn. An early morning mist covered the ground and muffled sounds; the only exception being when they walked past a rookery located in a stand of leafless elms. A cacophony of noise came from the rooks as they flew into the air, leaving behind their large, untidy nests. Annie smiled to herself, feeling somewhat recovered. A rookery still flourished in her twenty-first-century village—perhaps these birds were the great, great, great ancestors. She returned to Will's conversation.

"…and this is a great location for an inn. There's so much traffic in and out of York and Selby: it's the last stop for travellers before going there."

They walked up to the solitary building warily. Annie could just about make out the wording on the sign 'The King's Head' despite the faded writing and the peeling paint. The standard royal head wearing a crown sat beneath the name. Will pointed out a dried branch tied to the sign.

"They sell wine as well as ale. You don't see that too often."

The men had told the truth about the inn's name. There must be an interesting story about the name change; when did 'Head' become 'Glove' and why? The inn had the same basic shape from her own time and the location remained the same, although this fifteenth-century version was much smaller, lacking the additions of later years.

From a distance, the inn, built of local limestone at the base with dark timber framing above, and the walls plastered and whitewashed, had offered a pleasing aspect, but closer inspection showed grime and green mould marring the white walls. Clumps of dead thistles grew from the base of the limestone and the timber framing showed patches of bare wood.

A graceful stone archway at the front led into a cobbled courtyard. The stables were on the right and a pungent smell from their direction told of old, soiled, and wet straw bedding. In front of the stables were a solid looking pump and horse trough. When they walked through the stables, Annie was relieved to see empty stalls and pinched her nose to avoid the acrid smell of piles of horse manure and stale urine. On the left side of the yard, the entrance to the main building beckoned them. A steeply thatched roof, in need of a thatcher's attention, topped the building. An outside staircase led to the second floor.

The solid wooden door stood ajar. Jack paused. "This door was closed when we came here the other night."

His hand went to his dagger. They entered cautiously, the two men having to duck their heads, and peered around the corner of the doorframe.

In the main hall high walls reached to the arching roof beams. Iron sconces set evenly around the room had darkened the white-washed walls with soot. A substantial stone hearth dominated the centre of the large room with a louvre in the roof to allow the smoke to escape; blackened ceiling beams displayed the smoke's trail. Wooden shutters covered the window openings creating a subdued light.

A long trestle table with benches hugged one side of the hall and a number of half barrels acted as tables. Three-legged stools lay scattered around. Once again, the air smelled sour, this time from old, decaying rushes on the floor. The odour of rotting food soon followed. The trestle table still held moldy bread trenchers, bowls with spoiled pottage, and dried pools of wine and ale.

"It looks like everyone left in a hurry," Will observed.

A substantial kitchen was located behind the main hall. Again, the room gave the appearance of a hurried evacuation. The large hearth featured a deep alcove with a chimney. The stones surrounding the alcove, like the roof beams, showed a thick layer of blackened wood smoke and grease. Part of a pig's carcass remained skewered on a solid iron spit perched over the remnants of the now dead, grey ash-strewn, cooking fire; the dried and cracked skin showing patches of green. At the side of the hearth a large iron pot, filled with an unknown substance, and capped with a bubbling, white skin, provided its own stench. Crusted food and greasy stains embellished a large wooden table. Various iron pots sat on shelves, all looking in need of a vigorous scrub. Fat, late autumn flies buzzed lazily around the feast. Annie tried to block the smell by covering her nose and mouth with her shawl.

"Praise the Lord it's November and not July," she mouthed through the material.

They returned outside and followed the stairs up to the sleeping accommodation on the second floor. Both men kept a hand on their daggers and tucked Annie in between their more substantial bodies.

Two rooms, both narrow and long, occupied the entire floor, each holding a number of beds. Wooden frames strung with rope supported straw mattresses encased in stained canvas covers. Chamber pots, some full to the brim, gave off a pungent smell, strong enough to make their eyes water. Although dirty and unkempt, the rooms showed no signs of a disturbance.

The three investigators descended the wooden staircase and looked for the innkeeper's private quarters on the main level. They found his room at the back of the building, accessed from the kitchen and the only room they had seen so far with a stone-flagged floor. This room told a different story. A mattress lay crookedly on its bed frame and had gaping slashes in a number of places. Straw from the stuffing littered the floor along with clothes dumped out of an elaborately carved oak chest.

"It looks like a search party has been busy," Annie sorted through the straw in frustration.

Will pointed toward the back door. "Time to put our heads together."

They went out to the back of the building where they hoped no prying eyes could see them.

"What I can't understand," Will looked around, "is this is a substantial building. A great deal of money must be invested here, so why is it so run down and neglected?"

Annie nodded her head. "It looks as though the people who worked here just ran away. I imagine they all must live in the village."

"Aye." Jack sounded frustrated. "But as the villagers won't talk to us, what good does that do?"

The trio made their way back to Annie's cottage. The men warmed themselves at the hearth fire and Annie gave them sprigs of dried rosemary to remove the sour smell from their nostrils. She made a bergamot infusion to help their brains work more efficiently.

Rosamund greeted them effusively, particularly her tall, dark friend. Annie looked at her cat with raised eyebrows; her purring sounded like a car engine.

"We must find someone in the village who worked at the inn and is willing to talk to us," Annie proposed.

Will scratched his head. "I think Jack and I have to talk to the head man. The blacksmith told us a manor steward is in charge here. Surely, he knows what has happened at the inn. Are the people who have invested money, and I am presuming some have, not concerned that the inn looks and smells like a midden? And what has become of the innkeeper?" He blew out his breath impatiently.

"I think we should stay in the village until we've solved this mystery. It might prove interesting." Jack looked at his friend, raising his eyebrows.

Will agreed. "The whole picture intrigues me. There is an empty inn sitting there in desperate need of an innkeeper, by the looks of things."

He and Jack drained their drinks.

"We'll be off then, see you on the morrow."

Annie saw them to the door. "Please be careful. The reeve has already warned you."

Sipping the remains of her drink, Annie contemplated the reticence of the villagers. What were they hiding? Perhaps it was time to cast another spell, this one about releasing the truth. She would try raising the vibrations in the room before beginning her incantation. This was a method described in her Spell Book but she had been too afraid to experiment. It seemed such a balance of getting the energy right, not too much, not too little.

Rosamund leaped onto Annie's lap and began purring.

"Can you read my mind, Rosamund?" Annie laughed and began humming in time with the hypnotic purring. She had to find someone willing to talk about the abandoned inn and the disappearance of the innkeeper. The villagers were being close-mouthed and were scared of something or someone. This spell—if it worked—might create transparency and openness.

The spellbinding sound reverberated around all four corners of the cottage. A rush of energy filled the room, ruffling Annie's curls, and making the walls vibrate. From the rafters, the dried herbs rustled against one another and dust motes danced wildly in the air. Annie sent an incantation into the cosmos, the words flowing easily:

Bring light where there is darkness
Bring hope where there is hopelessness
Penetrate the fog of defensiveness

The gloom vanished as spheres of light gathered in the air and merged into a bright beam of light, which began spiralling dizzily around the walls. Annie winced. Had she made a mess of this one as well? It was so hard to get the energy just right. A sharp knock came at the door. Again the knock came. The light died and the vibrations ceased.

12

Annie jumped up abruptly. Rosamund leaped off her lap with an indignant cry. A young boy stood at the door. Tears had created white streaks down his dirty cheeks and his nose needed a good wipe.

"Our mam sent me. Please 'urry up missis. Our Jen's time's 'ere. She's cryin' an' screamin'."

Annie had no problem recognizing this cry for help; a baby was making its way into the world. Quickly, she sorted through the herbs she needed, collected clean rags and a jug of vinegar from the pantry, an apron, the box of instruments and salves, bowls and two candles, and threw them in a large basket. She carried the birthing stool in her other hand. The boy took her to a cottage further down the main street. Loud moans escaped through the shuttered windows.

"Oh, Bless the Lord you're 'ere!" cried the woman who opened the door. "Am Elsie Bagsworth an' the one mekkin' all t'noise is me daughter, Jenet. Am jiggered already, an' she won't shut up."

Mistress Bagsworth was a small woman: she barely came up to Annie's shoulder, and Annie was not tall. Her hair, partly covered with a white coif, still retained some of its fairness from her youth but the hard life she lived showed in her face, making her look older than her years. Although her words made her sound uncaring, her face showed her anxiety.

"I 'ope she's alreight, she's been at it for a few 'ours now. Meke sure tha 'ears 'er confession. God forbid owt 'appens to 'er but we don't want 'er an' babby to go to purgatory."

Annie looked at Mistress Bagsworth blankly. She had no idea what the woman was talking about. It took her a few seconds to locate the source of the moaning. Jenet lay in a corner of the long, dark room. The only illumination came from the hearth fire and a weak light struggling to get through the wooden shutters.

The girl rolled restlessly around on a thin mattress. Her cries of "A'll bloody kill 'im! A'll bloody kill 'im!" resounded throughout the room.

"Jenet's our eldest, fifteen she is an' can't work now," said Mistress Bagsworth, wringing her hands. "This 'as made it really 'ard on us, losin' 'er wages."

Jenet, clad only in a thin wool shift, cradled her distended belly with both hands. Her mother turned to her hapless son hovering by the open door. "Put wood in t'oyle; was tha born in a field?"

The young lad—Annie guessed him to be about nine or ten— closed the cottage door as ordered, beating a retreat as fast as he could. Mistress Bagsworth showed Annie a pot filled with water heating up over the hearth fire. The room felt uncomfortably hot; beads of sweat popped out on her forehead.

"Mistress Wistowe 'ad told us as 'ow tha were cumin' in 'er place. We all luv 'er, she's so good to us."

Annie looked at Mistress Bagshaw. There it was again. Everyone in the village knew she was coming—except her.

She went over to the panicking Jenet. "Hello Jenet. I'm Annie. We'll soon have you sorted."

Jenet became still and looked at Annie with big, frightened eyes.

"I'm just going to check how far along you are, it won't hurt. Take some big breaths for me."

Jenet proceeded to breathe heavily through her mouth. Annie wiped her hands with a clean rag dipped in hot water and vinegar, parted Jenet's legs and inserted two fingers into the birth canal.

"You've quite a way to go, Jenet. Let's have you off the bed and walking around. Mistress Bagsworth, please bring to boil a little of the water and we'll make a raspberry leaf infusion to help Jenet with the labour pains."

Annie assisted Jenet off the mattress and began walking her around the dark room, trying not to bump into the few pieces of furniture and avoiding the less than sanitary space kept for the animals at the far end. She wanted to save the precious candles until the actual birth. Jenet calmed down and offered a wobbly smile.

"By the way, who are you going to kill?"

"That bloody mister at inn," Jenet whispered. "I 'ad a job there in t'kitchen. He were a bugger for youn' uns. He took me soon after I started there. 'E told me I'd lose me job if a telled on 'im, an' we needed t'money at 'ome. A din't know a were in t'family way 'til a were getting' big an' me mam guessed. A were scared me dad would do summat, then e'd get 'urt, like Master Pickless."

"Are you talking about the innkeeper, Jenet?"

"Aye, I am, and I 'ope devil teks 'im. Can I summat t'drink?" she asked. "Am fair clemmed."

Annie gave Jenet a wooden bowl of the raspberry leaf infusion and Jenet leaned against the wall while she sipped.

"Devil may have taken him," Annie said. "He's disappeared, did you know?"

"We knew," whispered Jenet's mam. It 'appened night of t'storm. Jenet weren't there due to 'er being too far gone. Jenet 'ad told me what mister were up to. What could we do, anyway? Me 'usband's not strong enough to give 'im a good thumpin'. Sum of 'is mates would 'ave but they're scared o' bailiff's bullies. Serves 'im reight, if 'e's gone. He were a sneaky bugger, up to all sorts. If it weren't owt to do wi' girls I bet thee it 'ad summat to do wi' smugglin."

Jenet looked with horror at her mam and Mistress Bagsworth's hand came quickly up to her mouth. It was too late though; the words had escaped and hung heavily in the air.

"Did I hear you say 'smuggling'?"

"Nay, nay," denied Mistress Bagsworth, shaking her head vigorously.

"Oh yes, I did. You know the work my aunt and I do, mistress. I'm used to keeping secrets, just like Mistress Wistowe, and in my business, I hear all sorts of secrets."

Mistress Bagsworth and her family had been keeping this secret so long that the floodgates opened. Annie hoped the earlier incantation was working its magic too.

"Smugglin's bin goin' on for years. My Tom's been workin' at it for last few months. It starts reight after shearin' time in t'summer. Fleeces get packed at t'inn then t'men teks 'em t'coast on pack'orses.

Boats tek wool away an' bring wine back frum France. Tom 'elps fetch wine back 'ere t'big 'ouse. He can't work a lot in t'fields anymore on account of 'e 'urt 'is back, so its money cumin' in for us. If we dint 'ave that, as well as coins frum our priest to buy food, we'd starve."

Jenet dropped the bowl, doubling over and yelling, "A'll kill 'im, a will."

Annie had identified one of the cottage salves as fennel so she used this to massage the labouring girl's back and when the contraction ended, helped her to sit down on a bench. The whole story started to come out, and in between Jenet's contractions and cursing, Mistress Bagsworth continued to reveal the village secret.

'The King's Head' was the centre of a smuggling operation involving many of the villagers. Again, Annie's history lessons came in handy as she remembered how King Edward taxed wool nearly a hundred years earlier to pay for the costly campaign against the French at the beginning of the wars. As soon as the crown taxed a product, people found a way to avoid payment. The general population, including respectable businessmen, saw smuggling as a reasonable occupation. The Crown hired duty men to catch the smugglers but there were too few against so many.

Mistress Bagsworth didn't know the details of the business but she did know the fleeces came in from different manors south of York. Women re-packed them into woolsacks at the inn. Packhorses carried them under cover of darkness to Robin Hood's Bay on the east coast of Yorkshire. From there, a boat took the fleeces to France and Holland.

Jenet sipped her tea in between contractions. "Like me Mam says, ships load up wi' French wines. Same packhorses bring t'kegs back to the village. 'Ave seen wine kegs stacked up at t'inn. Sum travellers prefer wine to t'ale and an' don't mind spendin' extra money."

"Why is it such a big secret," asked Annie, "if everybody knows about it?"

"Well, smugglin' *is* against t'law. T'money from taxes is supposed to go t'king as far as I know. Anyhow, we've all bin told time an' again t'keep out mouths shut, an' if we don't, bailiff's bully boys'll mek us keep 'em shut. Tha dun know 'ow scared we all are o' them two buggers.

"Dun't tell anybody a told thee this," whispered Mistress Bagsworth, "but we 'ad a neighbour down t'road, Master Pickless. 'Im an' 'is wife 'ad two girls. She'd 'ad boys but they died. T'oldest lass went to work at t'inn. Came 'ome like our Jen in t'family way. "Master Pickless went crazy. 'E went up t'inn an' thumped Master Ridley. Next thing, Master Pickless 'ad two broken legs: never 'ealed straight. We all knew who did it. Mistress Wistowe did 'er best for 'im. T'ole village did what they could to 'elp but family were starvin'. They 'ad to move to York. Am told 'e works in tannery now, only way 'e can feed 'is family."

Jenet's contractions increased in intensity and frequency. Conversation ceased as Annie worked hard to keep Jenet focused on her baby and not spinning out of control. After a couple more hours of hard work and some vigorous cursing by the young woman, her groans turned to grunts as she began to push. The birthing stool did its job well by adding gravity to Jenet's efforts. Mistress Bagsworth held her daughter's hand and wiped her face with a wet rag. Two of Mistress Bagsworth's neighbours had come in during the labour and the women were observing Annie's administrations with interest and offering suggestions and comments along the way.

The labour ended well with Annie catching a baby boy, all the parts being in the right place. She lay the pink and wrinkled newborn, still covered in his waxy, protective coating, across Jenet's abdomen, covering both mother and baby with a wool cloth. Watching the cord closely, she waited until it stopped pulsing before tying and cutting it. Once Jenet expelled the afterbirth, Annie placed the baby, alert and wide-eyed, into his mother's arms. Mother and baby gazed at each other. Annie always had the urge to sing 'Getting to know you, getting to know all about you' at this point in the birthing process but so far, had managed to refrain. When the baby started rooting for the breast, she helped to guide him to latch and suckle the precious colostrum.

Using the last of the hot water, Annie and Mistress Bagsworth sponged a happy and sleepy Jenet and helped her into a clean shift. She refused to let go of her new son but allowed Annie to cover them both before settling down for a well-earned rest. Annie palpated Jenet's abdomen one last time to ensure her womb was firm and cutting off the large blood vessels at the site of the placenta.

"Isn't tha goin' t'swaddle t'bairn," asked one of the women with a worried expression. "'Is poor little limbs are loose. It'll keep 'em in one place."

"Aye an' Mistress Wistowe rubs 'em with salt to get that waxy stuff off. An' she rubs honey on their gums," the other neighbour chimed in."

Midwifery in medieval times had some unusual procedures.

"We do things different in York," Annie explained. "These are newer ways."

"Baby has fed and they are both ready for a sleep," the tired midwife told the new granny. Mistress Bagsworth looked at Annie with both relief and fear.

"Don't worry," Annie whispered in her ear. "No one in the village will know what you have told me." She considered Will and Jack to be outsiders so they didn't count. "I'll be back in the morning."

Annie returned to her cottage and fed a disgruntled Rosamund who made her feelings obvious: her contribution to the success of secrets shared needed acknowledgement. Annie fussed over a now mollified cat, helped herself to a bowl of pottage and went to bed feeling good about her care of Jenet and the results of her spellmaking even thought it might have been a little too forceful. That was a nasty story about the Pickless family, though. She had lots to share with Will and Jack tomorrow.

13

Jack and Will arose at Prime the next morning and had just finished large bowls of porridge when a sharp rap at the door startled Mistress Davey. She answered the door and once again, Reeve Brighouse stood there.

"Please to cum in, Reeve Brighouse," she whispered, looking worriedly at her two boarders.

The reeve turned to the two men but his eyes remained lowered as he stared at the ground.

"Steward wants to see thee both at t'Manor House, er, at thy convenience."

Will raised his eyebrows at Jack, curious about the change in attitude. "Please tell the steward we will attend shortly,"

After the reeve had gone, they spruced up their clothes and set off to the Manor House with Mistress Davey's advice ringing in their ears.

"E's a bit of a funny un, that steward. 'E's not one of us: not frum round 'ere. Be careful 'ow tha talks to 'im."

Mistress Davey had told them the Manor House sheltered behind some oaks. They could see a large stand of now leafless trees in the distance, with the outline of a substantial building behind.

"It never ceases to amaze me that all this land," Will waved his arm across the fields, "belongs to the Manor House, and the poor villagers have to work it to keep the owner rich."

Will and Jack walked past barns where the wheat and oats were stored, taking the time to observe the pigpen, the cow barn, the dovecote and the dairy. Cows and the ubiquitous sheep littered the landscape, grazing on the thin grass and fertilizing the soil for spring sowing. Horses in a fenced pasture close to the main buildings lifted their heads when they saw the two men and came trotting over to the fence, making snickering noises, looking for a treat.

"Sorry, boys, next visit I'll bring you something." Jack looked around as he patted the horses. "Most pleasant; it all looks well kept, too, unlike the inn."

Arriving at the Manor House, they paused to admire the clean lines of the building, built of mellow Yorkshire limestone with a central door of solid oak. The impressive frontage boasted six mullioned windows, and a large chimney sat at each end of the sloping roof.

Will lifted the heavy iron doorknocker and rapped it hard. They both stared at the doorknocker as though it might provide answers.

"I feel as though we've been brought before the sergeant," Jack grimaced. "I don't think we've done anything wrong but you never know."

The door swung open and an older serving woman stood there, her eyes lowered in her wrinkled face. She stood aside and a man in his middle years waited just beyond the entrance. Tall and bony, with a long narrow face and a long narrow nose to match, he gave an impression of sharp edges. His shoulder length faded blond hair straggled below his floppy wool hat. Dressed in fine woollen robes and soft leather boots, his image proclaimed a man who did not spend his time in hard labour.

"Thank you for seeing me so promptly," he said. It was immediately apparent he did not come from these parts, his dialect being softer than the blunt Yorkshire speech: he rolled his rs, had rounded vowels and a sibilant s.

"We came as soon as we could," said Will, standing tall and speaking resolutely. "We had planned to visit you today so your invitation worked well for us."

"Relinquish your daggers and enter, if you will," the man motioned with his hand, then held it out. "I am the steward of this Manor. I presume you to be our new guests in the village. You have the cut of soldiers. I have been hearing of your activities and understand you have the favour of our good King Henry."

Duly impressed by the man's intelligence gathering, as the steward clearly intended, the two men handed over their daggers before entering the great hall of the Manor House and looked around with interest.

Boards set on trestles lined one wall with benches alongside them. Tapestries hung on white plastered walls with exposed dark, oak beams. Colourfully painted scenes from the Holy Bible adorned other wall space and the high roof displayed a myriad of oak rafters. A stone chimney occupied the western wall, and beneath the chimney, a large open hearth boasted a cracking log fire. The hall proclaimed wealth and power.

"Come, gentlemen, sit with me at the boards. I shall send for ale."

He clapped his hands and the same serving woman entered the hall through an archway at the far end.

"Bring ale, Matilda, and sweetmeats for our guests."

Will was curious as to why this powerful man was being so courteous to them. The steward must have sent the reeve to get rid of them; for some reason he had changed his tactics. Once Matilda served the food and drink and disappeared back through the archway, presumably to the kitchen, the steward spoke again.

"I am Francis Sneed, formerly of areas south of here. I have been steward to Prior Gilbert, who is responsible for the affairs of this village, for over five years. He is Prior of Kirkham Priory, north of York. This village and the land surrounding it belong to the Augustinian Order. The essential business of running the Manor of Hallamby happens from here. We hold the Manorial Courts here, settling local disputes and tenancy issues. The peasants gather in this room quarterly to pay tithes and rents, which belong to Prior Gilbert as Lord of the Manor.

"Again, I thank you for coming to see me." His voice took on a steely note. "What, may I ask, is your interest in the inn?"

Will cleared his throat and took time to swallow some of his ale.

"I am William Boucher of York, lately of France. This is Jack Fletcher, also of York and lately of France. We are newly returned to England from fighting the wars in France with King Henry and are making our way back to York. We came to this village to visit my aunt, Mistress Wistowe, not knowing she was away. Luckily, we found my cousin in residence. We had planned to stay overnight at 'The

King's Head' on our way to York, yet we found the inn closed and the innkeeper missing."

"Thank you for the information." Steward Sneed steepled his fingers and pointed them at Will. "However, it does not explain your insistent interest in the inn."

Will needed to be delicate in how he framed his answer. He took his time again taking a long draught of his ale, and then wiped his moustache. "Jack and I have plans to open our own hostelry. We find ourselves intrigued by the manner in which 'The King's Head' appears abandoned. Although we still plan to move on to York, this mystery interests us. It seems a shame such an impressive building be allowed to deteriorate, and odd a man disappears without a trace." He sat back, glanced at Jack and they awaited a response.

Steward Sneed sat quietly, crumbling a piece of sweetmeat between his fingers. After a long silence, he surprised the men by introducing a completely different topic. He asked them if they knew of the great pestilence that had devastated England over sixty years ago.

"England lost almost half of her population. This village was bigger in those days; it even had a weekly market. You may have noticed the empty cottages. After the pestilence had passed, the manors did not have enough peasants to work on the land. Some of the arable lands became pasture for sheep. We have amassed large numbers of sheep in the whole of Yorkshire. I do believe we have more sheep than people." He laughed at his own wit and took a swallow of ale. "We now encourage outsiders to work for us because of our lack of able-bodied men and women." He paused and poured more ale for his guests.

Will did not know where the man was going with this monologue so he maintained his peace.

"You may know the wool trade is the major market in England, both at home and across the seas. The inn you speak of has been here for over a hundred years. This is a good location as it is a half day's ride to or from York or Selby. As York's main industry is making cloth, the city attracts many travellers from all parts of England and the continent. It has been a struggle to keep enough people working at the inn due to the losses from the pestilence. We are only now beginning to increase our population. Our current, or should I say, recently departed, innkeeper did not help the situation. He did not have a business head even though he, himself, had invested in the inn."

"You talk of him in the past." Jack interrupted the steward's flow, speaking for the first time. Will knew his impatient nature demanded more answers than were forthcoming.

Steward Sneed raised his hands. "I do not know what has happened to Master Ridley. I imagine fathers or brothers of any of the young pregnant girls hereabouts may have had a hand in his disappearance. Master Ridley's wenching habits were common knowledge and contributed a fair number of bastards to the village. It is another reason why he had difficulty in finding workers.

"I have a proposition for you both." The steward paused, looking up, first at Will and then at Jack. "How would you like to take over the running of 'The King's Head'? We can work out the details later but, as you have seen for yourselves—" he looked pointedly at Will as though to emphasise he knew of their visit to the inn, "—it is in immediate need of attention. We are already receiving travelers here at the Manor House looking for accommodation and they are most perturbed when they find out they have to travel on to York."

Will and Jack stared at him in amazement. Will recovered first.

"You seem to take lightly the disappearance of Master Ridley. I am presuming that is the innkeeper's name. Is anyone looking for him at all?"

"Our bailiff has made some enquiries, and he will continue to do so; however, they have come to naught as yet—enough of the innkeeper." Sneed shook his head impatiently. "What do you think of my offer?"

"We are, of course, interested," replied Will. "Please allow us some time to think about it."

The steward acknowledged this comment with a nod and continued. "I am willing to provide workers to clean up the place, and you will have no problem obtaining permanent help as winter is nearly upon us. The field work has ended and villagers will be grateful for the extra income."

Steward Sneed stood, pointedly ending the discussion. He escorted them to the door and handed back their daggers.

"I hope to hear from you soon. We need to bring business back to the inn as soon as we can."

The two young men looked at each other outside of the door and both sets of eyebrows raised in unison. They began walking slowly back to the village. Jack stopped and flung his arms out wide, once again startling the inhabitants of the rookery. The birds rose into the air as one, complaining noisily. He waited until the clamour subsided to speak.

"I am completely baffled. One minute they're trying to get rid of us and the next we're being offered what might yet be a dead man's job?"

Will shook his head. "Calm down, then you can think straight. The question we need to ask is, 'why would he do that?' Moreover, why is everyone ignoring the fact of the missing innkeeper? I do not trust him, for some reason he makes my skin creep."

"I'm with you there. He made your skin creep 'cos he's one creepy steward."

They both laughed and felt the tension ease.

Will wrapped his arm around Jack's shoulders. "Let's call on Annie and bring her up to date on our news."

Unknown to them she had a tale of her own to tell.

14

Mary stopped typing. Picking up her mug of now-cooled tea, she walked in circles around the tiny room. She smiled and wriggled her shoulders, delighted with the progress of her novel. The words flowed easily, characters were developing nicely,—particularly Will—and the steward seemed creepy enough. Annie was a concern, knowing how headstrong her friend could be. As the writer, she'd try to prevent Annie from getting into trouble.

Mary and Annie had been friends since childhood. They went through school together and grew into teenagers sharing their triumphs and angst. Athough at different universities, they'd kept in touch.

Mary considered herself the more stable of the two. Annie had always been impulsive, jumping into situations without considering the alternatives. Whereas, she, Mary, always deliberated on other options, like choosing to study business. It made sense. Commerce drove the world. Annie had pursued health care: a hard way to earn a living, according to Mary.

At university Mary had met her husband, Jonathon, who also studied business. They got on like a house on fire and married as soon as they graduated. Annie was the maid of honour.

Mary pinched herself. She was actually writing. Her dream of becoming an author was materializing at last. She honestly had no idea how she had come up with the story line; Will and Jack just emerged onto the page. She hadn't planned on either of them, and Annie—

why was Annie in her story? Somehow, she sneaked in, and as for Annie being a witch—where had that come from? Mary shook her head. Knowing nothing at all about witches might be a problem. But it seemed to be working. All the stuff she'd read about story and plot, about building characters—rubbish—she didn't need to do any of that work. It was true, what she had told Annie—she was born to be a writer.

Mary would simply go where the creative muse took her. It was all beyond her control.

15

"Steward Sneed did what?" Annie exclaimed as Will recounted his and Jack's visit with Steward Sneed to a fascinated Annie. "He offered you both the innkeeper's job?"

"Correct," said Jack. "What do you make of that?"

"It actually makes total sense to me."

Will and Jack stared at Annie as if she had taken leave of her senses.

It was time to share her news about the smuggling operation.

"Mistress Bagsworth doesn't know who is behind the smuggling, but most of the village is apparently involved one way or another. I imagine the boss, whoever he is, wants to keep the route open. The smuggling operation is one of the reasons people are so fearful around here. It seems Steward Sneed rules by intimidation, or, if *he* doesn't, he allows his bailiff and his henchmen to do what they want. Mistress Bagshaw said they are constantly warned to keep quiet about the smuggling or pay the consequences."

Annie related the story of Master Pickless and his family. "So it's not just threats about the smuggling operation that keeps people cowed. Sneed's needs to open the inn—the fleeces must be stacked in barns somewhere. There's money to be made."

"God's Teeth!" Will erupted. "I can't get involved in smuggling. I'm a soldier, and loyal to the king. I can't buy a hostelry with his money then turn around and cheat him of his taxes."

Annie could see by Jack's face that he considered this might be a bit too honest a view, but he kept quiet.

"Besides," she continued, "this doesn't solve the mystery of the disappearing innkeeper. Somebody dragged him from the inn during that storm and did something to him. It must have been so frightening that the locals ran away and the guests left."

"We'll never find out what happened unless the villagers who were there talk to us. Don't hold your breath waiting for that. As Annie, said, they're intimidated," Jack said. "They all seem scared."

"Look," Will stood, almost knocking the bench over. "I am not going to go along with this. We'll tell creepy Sneedy *no* and we'll be on our way to York. To hell with the fate of the innkeeper; it sounds like he deserved whatever happened to him."

With that pronouncement, Will stalked out of Annie's cottage and left Annie and Jack staring after him. Rosamund remained under the table twitching her tail. She was not a happy cat when her mistress became upset.

Jack apologized to Annie for Will's outburst. "It's usually me who blows up," he explained, as he went to the door to follow Will, stopping to scratch Rosamund's ears. The cat stopped swishing her tail and purred her way around his legs.

Annie watched Rosamund's reaction to Jack's attention. "You like that man, don't you?" she chided after he'd gone. "I believe you were flirting."

Annie sipped an infusion of chamomile to calm down. Then wrapping herself in her unknown aunt's shawl, she went off to visit the Bagsworths.

Mistress Bagsworth greeted her. "Jenet an' t'babby are doing reight good. Babby's feedin' well; he's a greedy little un."

Annie stepped inside the dark room, and when her eyes became used to the gloom, began her examination of the new mother and baby.

Mistress Bagsworth joined them. She leaned over and spoke in a soft voice. "It's luvly to 'ave a babby in t'ouse again. A lost two, tha knows, one after t'uther. It were after Jenet were born, a lad an' a lass; neither lived past a year."

She brought a bowl of warm water and a cloth to Annie. "Funny thing 'appened 'round Matins, Reeve Brig'ouse were 'ere. He were asking me questions about you. 'E wanted to know if you did any chantin' to mek babby slide out easier. I told 'im not t'be so bloody daft, but 'e kept on at me; did a see thee use any magic spells or boil up sum dead animals. Then 'e 'ad a go at our Jenet."

Annie tensed. "Did you say anything, Jenet?"

"Aye, a did. A told 'im tha worked magic on me; everythin' tha did made it all easier."

Annie groaned inside. It sounded as if the reeve was witch hunting, and that remark would not help. She completed her postpartum care of Jenet and was about to leave when Mistress Bagsworth shyly handed her a beautifully woven shawl.

"This'll keep tha shoulders warm," she said. "Tha's a good un, just like thy aunt."

Annie looked at the shawl in awe. The soft blue fabric had a pale yellow diamond pattern woven throughout. Long fringes adorned the ends.

"I dyed t'wool using elderberries and meadow rue."

"Why, Mistress Bagsworth, this is beautiful, you can't afford to give this to me."

"It cost me nowt. I got wool for nowt an' I wove it myself. Am that thankful for what tha's dun for our Jenet. I 'ad intended it for thy aunt but it were thee what delivered babby so…"

The two women hugged and Annie hurried home. She felt afraid. She only stopped looking behind her once she entered her home and barred the door.

Jack did not see Will on the street and when he returned to their lodgings, Will was not there. He began to worry. When Will got on his high horse, he could be unpredictable, as in the incident with King Henry in France. Fretting, his mind cast back to the night before the battle at Agincourt. With a few other longbowmen, they had been sitting around their campfire talking when a man approached wearing a long cloak with a hood. The man introduced himself as a gentleman soldier, strolling around to check on the soldiers' moods prior to conflict. Will, unlike his usual easygoing self, began censuring King Henry's actions, saying it was his fault good Englishmen men were dying. Their argument became heated, and ended when they exchanged gloves, in order to recognize each other after the battle, and pledged to fight.

Jack shook his head at the surprising outcome. Who would have—?

Mistress Davey burst through the door, looking out of breath and red-faced.

"Oh, Master Fletcher, 'ave got terrible news; there's lots o' fuss goin' on in t'forest. Lads were out there wi' pigs, lettin' 'em root for acorns. Well, tha'll not believe it, pigs 'ave rooted up a body!"

16

Will made his way back to the Manor House at a rapid pace. Normally an easy-going man, he felt duped and used and intended to let that sneaky, conniving steward knew how he felt.

Crossing the field, voices floated from the forest at the edge of the Manor lands. He shook his head: it had nothing to do with him. Arriving at the Manor House breathing heavily, Will rapped the iron doorknocker hard, but silence followed. He rapped harder, again, no response. He hesitated, and then began to walk away; frustrated he had not been able to speak his mind. The sound of a sliding bolt brought him hurrying back. Matilda, the same serving woman he saw earlier, stood at the half-open door.

"Nobody's 'ere," she said. "There's summat goin' on in t'forest. Steward Sneed an' Bailiff Crompton are out there."

"It would please me to wait," replied Will, using his most authoritative manner. Matilda muttered something beneath her breath and opened the door wider.

Will paced up and down the great hall. He did not raise his eyes to the arching oak beams supporting the roof. He saw nothing of the tapestries and the paintings and ignored the impressive stone fireplace and chimney. He rehearsed his speech of refusal to Steward Sneed until excited voices broke into his silent soliloquy. Will went to the big oak door and opened it. Villagers, talking loudly and excitedly, carried a bundle wrapped in a large cloth toward the main barn. Steward Sneed and a burly man in a leather jerkin walked behind. Will presumed him to be the bailiff Matilda had mentioned. He followed them and stood at the entrance to the barn, watching as the men dropped the bundle onto the floor. A body rolled out of the cloth. An unpleasant odour filled the air.

"Step back," called the steward in a commanding voice.

The men shuffled backwards, still trying to get a good view of the object.

"Flippin' 'eck, a told thee all it were bloody innkeeper!" shouted a voice from the group.

"An' it looks like sumbody's bashed 'is 'ead in," called another villager.

"Get these men out of here," Sneed snapped at the bailiff.

The barn fell quiet as the man in the leather jacket pushed the men outside and the barn door closed on them. Will joined the group of chattering labourers.

"What happened?" he asked one of the men.

"Eeh by gum, it were a rum un. We 'ad tekken Manor 'ouse pigs into t'forest so they cud forage for acorns an' they were 'appy as 'ell about it. All of a sudden, they got excited and started pushing each uther and squealin' like bloody mad. We went over to see what were up and t'buggers 'ad dug up a body. Truth t'tell," the villager paused to spit, "they'd started to eat it instead of t'acorns."

All the men started talking at once.

"Serves 'im bloody reight," muttered a gray-haired worker, "after wot 'e were doin' t'lasses."

"Shut tha gob," hissed another. "We know nowt."

The men fell silent and Will turned back and rapped on the barn door, which flew open so violently he had to step back quickly to avoid a broken nose. The bailiff stood there and glared at Will and the men.

"I told thee all to leave," he said. "Get back to work. Go collect pigs an' bring 'em back to t'pens; they'll likely be in bloody Lincolnshire by now."

The men took off at a brisk shuffle. Evidently, they had no desire to tangle with the bailiff.

"What does tha want?" he barked at Will.

"I'm here to see Steward Sneed," Will drew back his shoulders and straightened his spine.

"Well, tha can't. Tha can see he's a bit busy, call in on 'im later."

The bailiff slammed the barn door.

Will made his way slowly back to Mistress Davey's. He pondered the discovery of Ridley's body; for a quiet, rural village, there seemed to be a lot going on.

"Thanks be to God you are back," cried Jack. "All hell's broken loose here."

"I know of it," said Will.

They put their heads together and shared the latest developments.

"Did creepy Sneedy say anything?"

Will explained how the bailiff barred his way. "When I had to leave, the corpse lay in the barn with only Sneed and his bailiff there. By the way, the bailiff fits in well with Sneed's style: not one you can trust too much. The innkeeper's body is a mess, a crushed skull, a foot chewed and possibly more chewed bits, and it must have been in the ground for two or three days. It's a good job the temperature is low. Even so, it smelled a bit ripe."

"I wouldn't mind having a look at the body. Perhaps we could see what caused his demise in the first place." Jack scratched his head. "The Lord knows we've seen enough dead bodies on the battlefield."

"Small chance of that," replied Will. "I don't think they will allow anybody near the corpse in case they see something significant. I did hear one man say his head was bashed in."

"Do you believe Sneed had something to do with Ridley's death?"

Will thought about it. "I think we have to consider all the possibilities. Some think a villager killed him because of his wenching. Some think his death had something to do with the smuggling. There's talk that the devil took him. If so, he didn't take him far. I don't trust Sneed, nor do I like him. It'll be interesting to see what they do now they have a body to deal with."

They did not have to wait too long before they found out.

A short time later Mistress Davey came rushing back into the cottage, throwing her arms up in the air and wailing.

"T'bailiff and 'is men have taken Tom Bagsworth. They say 'e killed t'innkeeper on account of 'is Jenet bein' in t'family way from 'im. That man were terrible wi' young uns workin' at inn. Everybody knew what was goin' on but nowt were ever done about it. Tom Bagsworth wouldn't 'urt a fly. Lord bless us, what's 'appening in our village? Summat terrible is goin' on."

Will and Jack tried to comfort her, to no avail.

"Family'll starve."

The men decided to risk going back to the Manor House and find out more. They would insist on seeing the steward, and not take no for an answer. They would ask Annie to support Mistress Davey and Mistress Bagsworth. They accompanied a distraught but determined Mistress Davey, who carried a basket full of eggs, carrots, and onions, to the Bagsworth home.

In the street groups of people stood around, speaking in hushed tones. The feeling of tension was palpable. Seeing Mistress Davey, a few women broke from the clusters and followed her.

Leaving Mistress Davey at the Bagsworth's, Will and Jack walked to Annie's cottage. To their puzzlement, she refused to open the door until they had repeated their names. She sat at the hearth with Rosamund on her knee.

"What's wrong?" asked Will in consternation.

"The reeve is going around the village asking questions about me."

"What sort of questions?"

"Do I use magic spells to deliver babies? I think he's trying to make me out to be a witch. Why, I don't know."

"That's the most ridiculous thing I've ever heard," said Jack.

If he could have translated Rosamund's meow, he would have heard her say, "that's what you think."

Will shared the latest happenings with an increasingly alarmed Annie.

"What *is* going on? The whole village seems to be in an uproar."

Will figured the steward might be manipulating events. "We wondered if you would sit with Mistress Bagsworth but it looks as though you have enough troubles of your own," he said. "We are off to insist on an audience with his stewardship and see if we can get an explanation."

"I'll go see Mistress Bagsworth, if you'll take me and and bring me back." Will and Jack were happy to agree. Taking her new shawl, Annie petted Rosamund goodbye and they hurried down the village street where villagers still loitered. Will and Jack saw Annie safely inside the Bagsworths' cottage, and made their way to see Steward Sneed.

17

As soon as the villagers were out of sight of the barn, Bailiff Crompton went to stand by the side of Steward Sneed. They both contemplated the unpleasant spectacle of Master Ridley.

"Looks like we're rid of Ridley." The bailiff sniggered at his own wit.

"Yes," replied Sneed in a low voice, "and none too soon. We protected him long enough. He outlived his usefulness. I do not know who did this and I do not care. Let's finish what the pigs have started." He turned to his bailiff and lowered his voice even more. "I prefer that Prior Gilbert does not hear of these events, so if there is no body, there can be no evidence. The last thing we want is the Prior or his minions sniffing around here; but," he paused and began walking up and down the barn, making sure to skirt around the very dead corpse, "we have a challenge. If the word does get out about finding the innkeeper's body, we will need a scapegoat to deflect attention. We'll work on that one—"

"—I know just the scapegoat," Crompton grinned.

Sneed hated interruptions at any time so he glared at his bailiff. "—and we need to make this body disappear. I have it! Give the pig-man sufficient coins to take into York to check on litters for next year's pigs. Tell him we need a stronger breed or some such story. Make sure he knows he can stay in York for a few days; with enough coin in his pocket, he can stay drunk for a while. While he's away, ensure the pigs go hungry. Then bring them in here and give them a real treat. I appreciate this is work below your station but we need to keep this between ourselves. Meanwhile, ensure the workers remain busy and away from the barn, and give the men who brought the body here a few pence to keep their mouths shut with the promise of a few broken bones for them and their families if they talk. Begin with that. Get Butts and Cartwright on to it. They're well practiced at scaring people."

18

All appeared quiet outside the Manor House. The pigs were back in the pigpen, rooting around restlessly and squealing loudly at one another.

Jack nudged Will. "They've missed out on a good meal and its making them mad."

Other than the noisy pigs, the whole area appeared tranquil, as though the recent events had never happened. Will stepped up to the big oak door once again and rattled the iron doorknocker hard. After a long wait, Matilda came to the door.

"Tha's 'ere again," she muttered.

"Aye, we are," agreed Will, "and we're not going away. We wish to see the steward if you please."

"I'll see if tha can."

She closed the door on them. After another long wait, she reappeared. "Enter. T'steward'll see thee now. Give tha weapons t'bailiff."

The bailiff stood just beyond the door. He held out his hand for the daggers without saying a word.

"Do come forward," called Steward Sneed. He stood before the great fireplace, warming his narrow, nether regions.

He waved his hand toward his bailiff. "Please meet our manor bailiff, Master Crompton, my right-hand man. Master Crompton is responsible for keeping law and order around here and will *not* tolerate unseemly behaviour."

The heavy emphasis on all his words and the piercing look that came with the statement was not lost on Will. This powerful man meant what he said and aimed the threat at them.

Master Crompton stared straight ahead; they might have been invisible for all he knew or cared. Will noted the bailiff stood a head taller than he did, with shoulders equally as broad. Uncommonly, he wore his hair and beard cut close to his skin, emphasizing the angular shape of his skull, his prominent cheekbones and his flinty blue eyes. This was not a man to tangle without good reason. He reminded Will of some of the hard cases he had come across in the army.

Will and Jack made their way over to the steward.

"I am sorry about not seeing you earlier," Sneed said, now genial and offering an apologetic smile. "As you could see, we were busy. I suppose you have come to reply to my offer?"

Will almost shook his head in disbelief. Did Sneed just ignore the very real dead and nibbled body? "Yes, we have; however, we have just found out you believe Tom Bagsworth to be guilty of killing the innkeeper. Is this true?"

"How quickly word gets around in this village, but you are correct," Sneed nodded his head. "Our bailiff has found witnesses who saw Bagsworth enter the inn and dragged Master Ridley out to his death."

"What will happen to him now?" asked Jack.

"He will remain in jail at York until the next Assizes, possibly in the spring."

"How does an Assize Court work?"

"As you may know, local crimes of a minor nature are tried here at the Manorial Court, but serious crimes like murder go to the Assize Court. Judges appointed by the Crown represent the king and a jury of twelve men is present. The Assize Court travels around the country so we never quite know when it is our turn."

"What about crimes like rape?" demanded Jack, his dark skin looking darker still as the blood rushed into his face and his hands clenched into fists.

Will opened his mouth to soften Jack's words; he did not want them thrown in jail before they'd even got started. However, the bailiff forestalled him.

"If we know of rape we act on it. Sumtimes lasses 'ere are more willin' than they should be, then tell a different story after."

Jack looked at him in disbelief. His mouth opened in preparation to blast the man.

Will stepped in quickly. "The Bagsworth family will suffer badly with Tom in jail."

"'E should 'ave thought of them before 'e killed a man." Bailiff Crompton's voice sounded blunt and uncompromising.

Will picked up the strong Yorkshire dialect. Not from the same place as Sneed then.

"I am tired of hearing about the damned innkeeper business," Sneed snapped. "It has nothing to do with you anyway. What is your decision about the inn? We need to move forward on this."

Will opened his mouth to begin his well-rehearsed speech, when, to his own amazement, he had a complete change of heart.

"Yes, Jack and I shall be pleased to take on the challenge, for a short time anyway." He closed his mouth with a snap and avoided Jack's astonished gaze.

"Excellent. I did not ask before, can you read and write? I must state, you sound like a reasonably educated man."

"We were able to attend grammar school for a number of years because of our fathers' positions as guildsmen."

He explained his father was a butcher in the Shambles in York and Jack's father had been a bowyer. Jack jumped in to tell them of the respect a bowyer's skill in the manufacture of bows, arrows, crossbows, and bolts engendered. He went on to say, with pride, how effective the longbow had proven to be in the battle at Agincourt.

Will continued. "We practiced at the butts every Sunday, as decreed by King Edward, long ago. We became successful in local tournaments. Since completing grammar school, we both worked for our fathers, learning the trades. But it was not for us and we joined King Henry's army as bowmen. We have fought with the king ever since." He saw Steward Sneed's eyes begin to glaze over.

"Then you will be capable of keeping the inn's accounts, and I will be pleased to go over them with you. It is important we show a profit to our investors. Just a little word of warning—my men have reported to me that your cousin, Mistress Thornton, has displayed some disquieting practices."

Both young men opened their mouths to speak and the steward held up both hands to silence them.

"I have the utmost faith in her aunt, Mistress Wistowe; having known her since I arrived here, but Mistress Thornton has me concerned. She is new to the village yet is already building a reputation. She is a spinster and has knowledge of the use of herbs and, perchance, some unnatural substances. We have heard first hand from a labouring woman that Mistress Thornton used magic to ease the pains of her labour. We are all aware these are the ways of witches. A villager passing by saw the walls of her aunt's cottage shaking and an unnatural light shining out of the window. I suspect she was communing with the devil. My reeve informs me she told some village women a big storm caused the outrage at the inn. It all begins to add up. I know, I know—" he held his hands up again to stop the denials from Will and Jack. "—I only mention this as a caution. If all goes smoothly regarding the inn, I will take no action. If things do not go as planned, well, we shall have to look more closely at Mistress Thornton and her seemingly witching habits."

Will could feel his face flushing, and he could see Jack beginning to smoulder once more. He shook his head slightly at his friend.

"Good," Steward Sneed observed the motion. "I am glad to see you have received my message in good faith. Let us agree to meet at the inn at Prime tomorrow. In the meantime, I will recruit some workers."

The bailiff escorted the simmering bowmen, soon to be innkeepers, to the door and handed them their daggers.

"Mark tha listens well to Steward Sneed. "'E's a man of his word." He closed the door on them.

"Dismissed," muttered Jack.

Will and Jack walked slowly across the field in silence until Jack finally erupted like a long-simmering volcano.

"I can't believe what you did in there. Remember when you were on your high horse spouting about your loyalty to the king, what happened? Christ's Fingernails, what about the rubbish he spewed out about rape? Why did we have to keep quiet about Annie? And all the codswallop about witnesses to Tom committing a murder—how convenient, straight after the body was found?" He ran out of steam and stood still, legs akimbo, arms folded, glaring at his best friend.

"I know you must be vexed with me, but as God is my Judge, I don't know what came over me. It's as though someone put the words in my mouth; mayhap because I, too, thought it so convenient to arrest poor Tom Bagsworth. When Sneed threatened us with Annie, I knew we must play his game for a while. Something is going on in this village and in order to sort it out we will have to play by their rules. They have enough power to lock us up and leave us to rot, or kick us out so we'll never get to the bottom of this mystery." He put his arm around his friend's shoulder. "We've been in scrapes before; we'll survive this one and then we'll head off to York, maybe take Annie back with us."

"Do you believe Annie to be a witch?" whispered Jack.

"Never heard such a load of nonsense in my life."

19

Late November 2015, Hallamby, Yorkshire

Mary paused at her keyboard as she gazed off into space. She realized her readers might think Will changing his mind so abruptly about taking the innkeeper job as unlikely, but she had to protect Annie. Keeping the two ex-soldiers close by seemed the only way, until she could bring Annie back home. And what about Tom Bagsworth? She could not allow his family to starve, not the new baby, not any of them. She felt the huge responsibility of writing this novel weighing on her shoulders. She had never had so many people to care for. What would happen if she couldn't look after them all? She, Mary Bradley, might be to blame for the destruction of a whole village. Could she cope with the challenges ahead?

20

Late November 1415, Hallamby, Yorkshire

Will and Jack eventually arrived at Mistress Bagsworth's home. The room was crammed with women talking in hushed voices and shaking their heads. Mistress Bagsworth sat on the rush-covered ground in the middle of the circle of her neighbours, with her pinny over her head and wailing in chorus with the wails of baby Thomas; his distraught mother frantically rocking him. Annie must have seen the two men first because they were only able to locate her by a wildly waving arm in the middle of the throng. They gathered up Annie and took her home.

Once settled with mugs of ale in the blessed peace and quiet of the cottage, both Will and Jack started to tell Annie about the most recent events—at the same time.

"Whoa! One at a time," laughed Annie.

Will was relieved to see her laugh; she had looked so tense since hearing about the reeve's prying. He took over and related the story of the offer from Sneed and how he, Will, unexpectedly changed his mind. Jack jumped in to say how shocked and surprised he had been at his friend's change of heart.

"I felt as though I'd been hit by a well-thrown turnip."

The men had agreed on the walk back to not introduce talk of witches into the conversation they were about to have with Annie.

"So you are both going to run the inn?" Annie looked bewildered. "What about the smuggling? How are you going to deal with it?"

"Oh, we'll cross that bridge when we come to it." Will cleared his throat. "I was thinking about the reeve ferreting around, causing mischief. Be sure you trust who you are speaking to and watch what you do."

"Why are you saying that?" asked Annie, her voice rising and red roses blossoming on her neck.

"Did the steward say anything about me?"

"No, no. Jack and I talked about what you told us and we believe it is best if you keep everything as simple as possible when you are visiting the villagers. You know how quickly people can get the wrong idea. Spend tomorrow with Mistress Davey. Take her with you if you have visits to make. I'm sure she'll enjoy your company. We'll meet you at her home when we're done."

They finished their ale and prepared to leave. This eventful day was coming to a close and cleaning up the mess at the inn on the morrow would not be an easy task.

21

When Will and his friend Jack arrived at the inn in the dark the next morning, the scene that greeted him brought back memories of the chaos of a battlefield. Flaming rushes illuminated the building. The rendered animal fat used to make the rushlights created a smoky stink causing Will's eyes to water. People were everywhere: men, women and children, the latter racing around excitedly and getting under-foot. Women swept, dusted, and scrubbed; spiders and crusted dirt did not stand a chance under their onslaught. Men tended a large fire out back, burning old rushes and rotten food, stable waste and heavens knows what else.

Two men, whom Will and Jack had never seen before, gave orders with loud voices and supervised the frenetic activity. Their appearance did not invite argument. They were both short in stature but stocky, their arms bulky with muscle. Their faces provided maps of previous conflicts. One of the men had a nose that wandered across his face in a disturbing manner. Will and Jack introduced themselves.

"Aye," the one with the interesting nose nodded. "We've 'eard about thee. Am Asne Cartwright and this 'ere is Jobe Butts."

Jobe Butts rolled his heavy shoulders backwards and braced his legs. "I'm tougher than you," his body language signalled. He had a myriad of criss-crossing scars around his eyes and one eyelid drooped, but miraculously, his nose remained in the right place.

"Steward Sneed filled us in about tha tekkin' over King's 'ead frum now on," Cartwright continued. "We 'eard tha's frum York. A suppose tha thinks that meks thee both better than rest of us. Tha best think again. Jobe an' me 'elp out steward now an' then. We'll be seeing lots more o' thee." He smiled and showed teeth resembling leaning, moss covered headstones in a graveyard with space for more graves. Following that enigmatic remark, the two men took off and carried on ordering the workers about.

Will and Jack already felt like a couple of lumpkins standing there doing nothing and the introduction from Sneed's men didn't help.

"Who are these villains?" Jack whispered, "What do they have to with us and the inn?"

"It looks like Sneed isn't taking any chances with us. Those two beauties must be his spies." Will punched his friend lightly on the arm. "We'll just go along with it all for now."

The new innkeepers wandered into the large kitchen, now looking completely different from their last sighting. The busy bees must have started in here. Big iron cooking pots hung on hooks, a damp sheen still showing on their gleaming metal sides. A log fire crackled away, sending smoke and sparks up the chimney and a newly scrubbed spit sat at the side of the hearth waiting for the next roasting pig. The boards used for food preparation still gleamed with wetness from their scouring, and the air smelt clean: a huge improvement on their last visit.

They moved into the late innkeeper's quarters, soon to be their own. They backed out hastily as the room bustled with activity, including two women stuffing a clean-looking mattress with straw. The young women looked up at them with interest, their first view of the new innkeepers. Curiosity and admiration showed in their eyes.

"Put two mattresses in here, if you please," Jack asked with a smile as he left, testing his new authority.

Noticing a narrow corridor leading off from the kitchen, they wandered along it and found another room at the end. This room was bare of furnishings except for more boards placed on trestles down the centre. Piles of sacks lay in one corner and wisps of sheep's wool lay on the yet unswept dirt floor. Narrow beams of early morning sunlight came in from between the wooden slats covering the open windows. Will suspected this room's purpose was for packing the untaxed wool brought in from the outlying manors. He chose not to comment on the room's use, as his new policy towards smuggling was to ignore it. Jack, too, remained unusually silent.

Moving back into the kitchen, an open door displayed a large storage room where shelves lined the walls and earthen storage jars stood on the floor. A large terracotta jar contained coarse salt, a precious commodity for preserving meat. Smaller containers revealed tiny amounts of spices, their pungent smells filling the air, but as Will and Jack knew nothing of these things, neither their noses nor their eyes helped in identifying them. Dried herbs hung from the beams and, like the spices, posed a mystery to them. A shelf held a small stack of round wooden trenchers. Will noticed these with amusement. He and Jack only ever had their meals served on stale bread trenchers in the inns where they had lodged. Wooden, leather, and pewter tankards sat in piles haphazardly on a corner shelf; the pewter, no doubt, like the wooden trenchers, kept for the use of the wealthier traveller.

So the busy day passed, although Will and Jack twiddled their thumbs as the two overseers made no demands on them. Will commented to his mate that standing around trying to look busy was more tiring than if they actually had something to do.

Jobe Butts told them, in a reasonable manner, to go over to the Manor House and see Steward Sneed. Thus, as the Vespers bell rang its message to the people, they made their way back there. Bailiff Crompton was not present. Matilda brought in tankards of ale and more sweetmeats though she kept her head down and did not acknowledge their presence.

A relaxed looking Steward Sneed greeted them affably. "I wish to review the financial side of the business and where you fit into the picture." The steward then pulled a number of leather wrapped rolls of parchment towards the newly minted innkeepers and for a long, long time, went into detail about the finances of running an inn. "The investors expect to see a considerable profit at the following year's end, at least ten pounds."

"I understand the inn makes its money by selling accommodation, food, and drink," Will eyed the columns of numbers. "Are there any other avenues to make money that operate out of the inn?"

"I know of none," replied Sneed, "but by all means, if you come across any, do use your initiative and go ahead."

Will took that to mean the steward knew of the smuggling and had just given them permission to become involved.

"As you are not investing money into this venture at this stage," Sneed continued, "I will arrange for you both to receive wages. You will, of course, be enjoying bed and board so we will take that into consideration. I expect you to move into the inn immediately; to supervise the supplies that will be arriving, and to accommodate the brewster when she arrives, also the cook. They both worked at the inn previously but left and found positions in York. They found it difficult, apparently, working with Master Ridley. They are happy to return to their village and families, yet will live at the inn along with the rest of the workers from the village. You will have met Butts and Cartwright today. They will take on guard duty and generally be responsible for keeping the peace, if fights break out, for example, amongst the guests. Although I am sure you two will be quite able to deal with any ruffians."

By this time, the eyes of the new innkeepers had glazed over: the day had been a long one.

"The sooner we have ale and food, the sooner we can start to make money," Sneed droned on. "I expect your full cooperation, as we have previously discussed. Butts and Cartwright report directly to Bailiff Crompton on a regular basis. I trust you will both be far too busy running the inn to concern yourselves with any other business. That is sufficient for now. I expect to see you in your new positions on the morrow."

They were ushered out of the door and sent on their way, feeling as though they had been in school all day plus a detention on top. When the two men arrived back at Mistress Davey's cottage Annie was waiting impatiently for them. It took a while to fill the two women in on the news of their day and, while Annie appeared interested, Will became conscious of her foot tapping on the rush-strewn floor.

"I have news for you too," she burst out. "I am to take Mistress Bagsworth and her son into York. She will ask to stay with her sister and brother-in-law there. She can provide an income with her weaving and sell the cloth on her brother-in-law's market stall. This means she can take food to her husband at the jail. Meanwhile, her daughter Jenet, and the baby, are to stay with Mistress Davey. Mistress Davey says her son is willing to watch the Bagsworths' home and animals until they all return when Tom has been found not guilty."

Annie had to stop speaking as she had run out of breath.

"It is more than a good half a day's walk to York," Will was concerned. "How will you manage that?"

"It's all arranged. Dick Radcliffe is taking a load of turnips and cabbages into the city. It's a regular run for him. He has a horse and cart. We'll ride in with him and I'll come back with him."

Will experienced a sharp sense of loss at the thought of Annie being away. He mentally shook his head. What was that about?

The men expressed their appreciation of the manner in which the villagers had rallied to help the poor, unfortunate family. It spoke well of the spirit of Hallamby, despite the intrigues of the steward and his cronies. Mistress Davey appeared less agitated than before and said how much she had enjoyed her day with Annie.

"And so to bed," said Jack, looking exhausted. "We will see you on your return. By the way, what will you do about Rosamund?"

"I'll leave her food and water; she shall roam as she will. Sweet dreams to you both."

Will insisted on walking Annie back to her home and Annie nodded her head, not meeting Will's eyes. They did not speak on the way and both stood awkwardly outside her door.

"Well, sweet dreams, again," she whispered and bolted into the cottage.

22

The next morning, after a bowl of hot oatmeal served by a fussing Mistress Davey, Will and Jack rolled up their few possessions, bussed their former landlady's forehead, causing her cheeks to fire up, and headed up the street in the early dawn to start their new adventure. As Will and Jack drew closer to the inn, Will remarked that the outside still required some attention, but as they walked under the stone archway into the courtyard, a pleasantly different face greeted them. The newly swept cobbles led to the horse trough now scrubbed clean of its mat of moss and algae and an aroma of fresh straw wafted from the stables.

Entering the hall both stopped abruptly and looked in amazement at the transformation. The large room was immaculate. The scrubbed boards gleamed and the fresh rushes smelled sweet on the floor; a fire burned cheerfully in the central hearth, the smoke heading upwards to the louvre. Two village girls stood by the long boards, dressed in clean smocks with white linen coifs covering their hair.

When they saw Will and Jack, they both bobbed a curtsey. "I'm Cissie and she's Nettie," Cissie chirped with a cheeky grin. Her mate looked shyly at her own feet.

"We're to serve at t'boards," Cissie explained. "We'll be bringin' food and drink frum t'kitchen, an' any uther jobs tha might 'ave for us."

Both Will and Jack tried valiantly to look like sober innkeepers but it was hard not to smile at such fresh and enthusiastic liveliness.

"Oh," Cissie said, "Master Butts left this for you." She handed Will a sheet of parchment. They both curtsied again and ran off to the kitchen, giggling. The two young men bent their heads over the parchment with curiosity.

Duties and Obligations of an Innkeeper:

A Common innkeeper has made profession of a trade, which is for the public good, and has thereby exposed and vested an interest in all the King's subjects that will employ him of his trade.
To whit:
To greet all travelers with warmth whether liked or not.
To provide shelter, food and protection; the protection to be from threats outside or inside.
Each traveler to be shown to their sleeping accommodation and made aware of sharing a bed.
Travelers with horses to be provided with shelter, grooming, and food for their horses.
If travelling with servants and/or companions, provision of food, shelter and protection also to be provided to them.
A bed for one night to cost one penny, plus two pence for a meal, more if with meat and more again if wine or ale is drunk. Two pence charged for a horse to be fed and looked after. Also charge for bed and board for a servant.

"Well, now we know what to do. It doesn't seem too onerous, does it?" Jack smiled.

"I think we can manage." agreed Will. They headed to their private accommodation and, once again, stared in wonder. Two straw filled mattresses were resting on top of wooden bases, with clean looking wool blankets folded at the base. Two basins sat on top of a long, low cupboard beside a large pitcher of water. The wooden chest they had seen before, some of its contents scattered around the room, now sat empty with the lid open for their use. The air smelled sweet from the rushes strewn over the flagstone floor. A chamber pot sat discreetly in a corner.

"I think I can get used to this," Jack leapt onto one of the beds. "This one's mine."

They deposited their goods and chattels in the chest. Will removed an old, rolled, well-worn hose from around his waist, concealed by his tunic.

"That's a relief," he sighed. I have had these coins wrapped around my middle since we left Agincourt." He looked glanced around the room. "However, I don't know where to hide them in here."

Jack looked up from the chest. "I am still amazed by the king giving you his glove full of gold coins."

"So am I. I thought when he sent for me after the battle he was going to have me executed. Mind you, I didn't know it was the king in disguise when I was calling King Henry names."

"So, instead of putting you to death for treason, he rewarded you for your honesty; this is one crazy world. Still, it gives you the freedom to look for an inn to buy—and here we have an empty one."

Not finding a hiding place for the present, Will rewound the hose around his middle and they went to explore the kitchen.

A scene of orderly tranquility unfolded before them. A small, round woman of indeterminate age stirred the contents of a large iron cooking pot hanging on a hook over the hot coals. She had iron grey hair partially covered with a white coif and her dark eyes observed them intently from above her heated red cheeks.

Two kegs of wine sat at the end of the boards, along with earthenware pitchers. The baker had delivered a pile of stale bread trenchers, perfect for serving up the evening pottage. The perspiring cook greeted her new gaffers.

"'Ello, you must be Master Boucher and Master Fletcher. I'm Agnes Croft—call me Aggie." The young men went over and peered in the pot. Carrots, turnips, onions, and pieces of chicken bobbed around in a savoury smelling stew. Their bellies rumbled, even though they were still full of oatmeal.

"Greetings, Mistress Croft, I think we are going to enjoy working with you," Jack grinned at their new cook. "But please call us Will and Jack. I'm Jack, he's Will."

"Like a said, call me Aggie. Am glad to be back. A trust we'll get on well. How tha findin' things so far?"

"Easy, so far," laughed Will.

Will was to remember those words at the end of another long day. Travelers started appearing soon after the Nones bell rang. From the arrival of the first tired traveler on horseback, the new innkeepers had not stopped except to swallow bowls of excellent chicken pottage whilst on the run. As the day wore on more travelers arrived: some on horseback; some walking; some came in groups and some alone. All expressed pleasure that the inn was in business again.

By early evening, guests were sitting around the boards, mopping up the chicken stew from the bread trenchers. Cissie and Nettie carried the heavy pitchers of wine up and down the table, refilling the wooden goblets. The guests, full of good food and wine, looked overly warm, mopping perspiration frequently from their faces. Torches set in the iron sconces around the room gave out light and heat along with the heat from the hearth fire.

It would be quite a while before Will and Jack could retire. Cissie and Nettie looked a little worse for wear as their hair escaped from their coifs and their legs lost their spring. Jobe Butts stood at the main door, having vetted each traveler before entry; taken charge of an array of weapons, and glowered at all. He would stand guard all night. The stables were full of horses needing grooming and feeding. Will was beginning to realize being an innkeeper was not such a simple job.

The next morning saw everyone up and busy by Prime. The travelers were stirring and heading into the hall, some looking dapper and some worse for wear. Watered wine sufficed for breakfast, along with bowls of porridge. The stable yard rang with the sounds of horses being made ready for the day's travel. Some travelers were heading to York or Selby, some further north. Others were moving southeast towards Lincoln or south to their final destination of London.

Will and Jack went out in the yard to say farewell to their guests, even though their bodies ached from insufficient sleep and their throats hurt from too much talking. The stableboy, Jed, young and full of beans, whistled cheerily as he groomed the horses and appeared to be coping with the hustle and bustle. Breakfast being over, 'Call me Aggie', as Jack now named her, had started peeling and cutting up a pile of vegetables in preparation for the evening meal.

The brewster was due to settle in today and begin the first batch of ale, her brewing room ready and waiting. Women were upstairs sweeping the sleeping rooms, running up and down the stairs to empty the slop pails into the privy and chatting excitedly to each other. No doubt, the enthusiasm would not last as routines became humdrum. When the last guests had gone, Will and Jack went back inside to update the accounts and check stock, both now wiser about the life of an innkeeper.

23

November 2015, Hallamby, Yorkshire

Mary sat in front of her computer screen, gazing off into space. She startled when her husband's voice boomed up the narrow staircase.

"Aren't you ready yet?"

She jumped up, applied some lip-gloss and went downstairs. Jonathon leaned against the front door jamb, jiggling his car keys and showing his irritation.

"I thought we'd agreed to go to 'The Glove' for Sunday lunch," he complained. "There won't be any tables left at this rate. I hope Bob and Janet are quicker off the mark. We'd better take the car."

Mary murmured her apologies and they drove the short distance through the village to the inn. 'The King's Glove' had established quite a reputation for its epicurean efforts. People drove there from the surrounding area, even from York, for a Sunday excursion and fine food.

When they arrived, they found the parking lot full and had to squeeze in next to a stone wall, putting the car's paintwork at risk, adding to Jonathon's ire. Inside the dining room, all the tables appeared occupied, but friends whom they met there regularly waved to them from their table.

"How is it that we live further away but get here before you?" their friend Bob joked, unknowingly increasing Jonathon's ill humour.

Once they settled into the usual Sunday banter Jonathon perked up. They ordered drinks: pints of a local microbrew for the men, Silver Heart IPA, and an Aussie Shiraz for the women. A serious perusal of the menu commenced, although they usually ordered roast beef and Yorkshire pudding.

The sounds of the voices and clinking of china around Mary faded away and once again, she found herself back in another century, only this time she was not writing. She felt goose bumps pop up on her skin and looking around the room she saw—quite clearly—Will! He was walking along the side of the room where the long boards would have been in 1415. He had a pitcher in his hand and smiled at his guests. He looked exactly how she imagined him; tall and broad-shouldered, blond hair tied back.

"Mary," her husband's voice brought her back to the present. "Anyone would think you'd had a spell cast over you, you've been behaving so strangely this past week."

Their friends looked uncomfortable at this little domestic scene, but Mary pulled herself together and relieved the sudden tension by rejoining the group; however, that remark about the spell had set her mind racing furiously. Something was starting to make sense. She risked another glance around, furtively, but Will had vanished. Maybe she wasn't going dotty after all.

The server took their orders. The friends chatted about the latest political gaffe from Westminster until the dinners arrived. The smell of the roast beef was delicious, and the Yorkshire puddings were superb round puffs of golden brown; the craters in the middle filled with onion gravy. Small, perfectly crispy, and browned roast potatoes along with roast parsnips and brussel sprouts accompanied the beef. A dollop of horseradish completed the perfection and silence reigned at the table.

Mary and Jonathon returned home after a dessert of sticky toffee pudding and custard. Jonathon settled down for his usual Sunday afternoon: feet up on the sofa and Sky Sports on the telly. He was snoring within five minutes.

Mary had some serious thinking to do. As she crept upstairs, she remembered her moment of enlightenment at the inn, realizing she could be under a spell placed on her by Annie. Something was driving her to write this story, but what and how?

Mary tried to work it out. She, the writer, created Annie the wannabe witch—right? What if her best friend really was a witch and put a spell on Mary? No, too fantastic.

As bizarre as it seemed, what if what she was writing so furiously was really happening? Annie had travelled to the fifteenth century and would not return to the twenty-first century until the story—Mary's novel—ended. It made total sense; otherwise, how did she, Mary know what to write? Seeing Will at the inn during lunch meant she too might move between the thin veils of time.

She must not share these thoughts with her husband; he'd have her put away! So many unanswered questions. Mary's head ached, but she felt compelled to write, whatever the cost, whatever the pain.

24

Late November 1415, York, Yorkshire

Dick Radcliffe's cart, filled with cabbages, turnips, and passengers, rumbled its way slowly toward the great city of York. The busy road bustled with people and animals: walkers carrying their goods on their backs; travellers on horseback; traders with strings of pack-horses; mules or horses pulling carts of every description, each one filled with produce from the surrounding countryside, or materials needed by the voracious city folk. Not everyone was English. Dick pointed out prosperous-looking wool merchants wearing clothes cut of a different fashion and speaking in a different language. These people rode on sturdy horses followed by their family and servants.

The travellers talked to each other, sometimes shouting across the wide road. Annie caught snatches of local gossip: who was pregnant and who was not, of insults called with smiling faces and accompanied by rude gestures. Evidently, travelling to York created a social occasion as well as work. Tension only arose when an occasional party of well-dressed horsemen, usually knights and their escorts, moved arrogantly through the crowd. People would obediently move to the side of the road, but not without casting resentful glances from under their lowered heads.

One time, the leader of a group of ten riders demanded passage. The horses wore elaborate saddlecloths and intricate bridles. Various bits of metal attached to their harnesses jiggled musically. A couple of older travellers, a man and woman, both bent over with large packs on their backs, were slow to move out of the way. The lead rider, on a huge black horse, moved forward and snapped a whip over their heads. The crowd reacted with a communal gasp but the riders moved through the space created by the already dusty people, creating more layers of dust. In the centre of the riders, a grey horse, carrying a woman gracefully mounted side-saddle, her features hidden by a heavy veil over her face, trotted on, in total disregard of the people around her.

Annie, sitting in the back of the cart with Mistress Bagshaw, rose, her mouth opening to protest. A large, gnarled hand landed firmly on her shoulder and she sat abruptly.

"Nowt to do wi' us, lass. Keep tha gob shut."

Clouds of dust continued filling the air, making breathing uncomfortable. The road now followed the River Ouse so the overriding smell was of sewage and decay. In spite of the smell and the impact of the iron-rimmed wheels rolling over remnants of the old Roman road, Annie dozed. Mistress Bagsworth leaned against her and nodded off. Her son lay curled around the turnips and slept the sleep of a baby.

As Annie moved in and out of consciousness Will's face kept popping up in her mind. She found it curious as she wasn't trying to think of him and it became a little irritating. *Go away,* she admonished him, but back he came. She tried thinking of Rosamund instead, but no, Will's face, smiling at her in that warm way he had, his green eyes sparkling, kept filling her vision.

The day wore on. Dick Radcliffe proved a taciturn man; he preferred grunting to speaking. Annie could not guess his age: somewhere between forty and sixty, she estimated. His hair and eyebrows were a grizzled, non-descript colour and his ears seemed overlarge for his head, perhaps he had great hearing to make up for his lack of speech. The reins were steady in his hands as he sat hunched over on his seat. He told Annie his horse was called 'Arry'—after our young King 'Enry."

Annie smiled. She understood the name change. In her time, the twenty-first century, a popular member of the British Royal Family was Prince Harry, baptised 'Henry'.

As the journey continued, Annie and her companions nibbled on crusty black rye bread and sipped weak ale from a leather container.

She continued to be amazed at the busy-ness of the road, having no idea people travelled so much in medieval times.

"Did you have any dealings with the innkeeper?" Annie abruptly asked the driver. She had been contemplating whether to risk asking him the question for the last few miles. He could just grunt at her if he didn't want to talk. Dick turned his head and looked back at her.

"An' why might tha be askin' questions about that bugger, missus?"

"I'm not sure Tom Bagsworth killed him. Perhaps he upset someone else."

Dick spit onto the road. "There'd be a bloody big queue for that job, 'e could upset most folk soon as look at 'em."

"Who's your best wager?"

"Way as I 'eard it, two men pushed their way into t'inn on night o' big storm. They 'ad bloody big swords in their 'ands. Lad guardin' door 'ad no chance of stopping 'em. They grabbed t'innkeeper an' dragged 'im out in t'storm. That were last any bugger saw of 'im. Workers left reight away and travelers left in t'morning. Don't know who t'men were."

He said that with finality so Annie knew she would not get any more information, but on thinking about what Dick inferred, 'two men and strangers', surely that let Tom off the hook. Silence descended again, on the cart, anyway.

The travellers crossed the Ouse on the ferry at Bishopthorpe, the traffic backing up as the travellers waited to board. The long queue created an opportunity for another social occasion with much chatter and laughter as people waited their turn to cross; the resentment caused by the incident with the riders apparently left behind for now.

The Bagsworth boy looked thrilled at being on the flat barge and watching the ferryman and his helper maneuver his vessel across the calm water with heavy poles. Dick had to pay the ferryman a farthing, a fact that he grumbled about under his breath, for at least the next mile.

Annie dozed again and awoke when Dick grunted louder than usual and pointed into the distance. The defensive walls surrounding York came into view. As they came closer, Annie began to distinguish the crenellations on top of the walls. The cart followed the walls around until arriving at the imposing Micklegate Bar—Dick called it the Micklelith Bar—joining the queue outside. As Dick put it succinctly, "we 'ave t'pay for t'privilege of feeding t'city buggers."

Annie and Mistress Bagsworth gasped with shock as they looked up at the top of the Bar. A head impaled on a spike crowned the gateway! Birds had pecked the eyes out. Hair attached to the skull stirred gently in the slight breeze and clumps of grey and blackened flesh were still visible on the bony cheeks. The boy viewed the head with relish.

"That's what tha gets for conspirin' t'kill King 'Enry," Dick spat over the side of the cart again and earned a glare from a matron standing close by. "That's Baron Scrope, that is, 'e's been up there since t'summer." He explained the king liked to display the severed heads of traitors.

"Supposed t'stop t'uthers frum doin' same."

Annie shuddered. To see a spiked head in the flesh, rather than reading about it, *was* gruesome.

She remembered from her history classes that Micklegate Bar had been the entry into York used by the ruling monarch when visiting the city, who had to ask permission from the Lord Mayor to enter. This act alone symbolized the power that York represented in England.

Annie was familiar with Micklegate Bar, as she had grown up in York, but she had never seen it like this—the masons were still building it. The bottom part was Roman; of a reddish brick, (she *was* familiar with that). The barbican she could now see at the front, solid and defensible, was no longer there in Annie's time. The two top stories with the elegant towers had men hanging off them, secured by ropes, carving into the limestone, creating the arrow slits.

Dick paid the toll and they passed through the arch, thankfully leaving the head of poor Baron Scrope behind, and the cart travelled along Micklegate. Annie loved York, and, like all true Tykes— someone born in Yorkshire—believed it to be the centre of the universe. She knew its history well. This city had known, and had been a part of, much of the history of England. The Romans built a fort at the joining of two rivers, the Ouse and the Foss, naming it Eboracum. The Anglo-Saxons moved in and renamed it Eoforwic when the Legions left Britain. When the Danes attacked and colonized most of what would become Yorkshire and Northumberland, Eoforwic became their capital city and, because they had difficulty saying the name, they renamed it Jorvik. York had retained much of its Danish ancestry through language: 'Gate' meant street and 'bar' designated an entry into the city. Mickle was Old Norse for 'great' so Micklegate meant 'Great Street'. Annie remembered the excitement when archeologists discovered a Danish settlement locked in the mud of the Ouse in the 1980's, now recreated as Jorvic, a Viking centre.

York was a thriving city when William the Conqueror arrived in England in 1066 from Normandy. Once he had established his authority in the south, he came north and took over the city. William was determined to stamp his authority on the whole area because unrest and rebellion were rampant. He laid waste to the north and built a castle in York, followed by a second one shortly thereafter. Other than London, York became the only place in the country with two castles. As in the rest of the country, William's barons took over all of the northern lands on their king's behalf and imposed the feudal system on the defeated English.

The memory of the incident on the road with the aristocratic woman and her escort with the whip brought home to Annie the harshness of the feudal system: it existed solely for the benefit of the ruling classes. Men who had supported the king in battle by supplying resources, such as arms, men, and money, were given the title of baron, which came with huge tracts of land as a reward. They did not own the land: only the king owned land. They held it in tenure. Their job was to continue to provide support to the king. The brunt of this service lay on the shoulders of the common man and his family who toiled for long hours in the fields for little reward, while the so-called 'landowners' enjoyed a completely different life.

Annie had gathered from Will that Hallamby was not under the control of a baron, but the Church, although in Hallamby's case, it was a religious Order, the Augustinians, headed by a Prior. Even so, the village would have to pay its dues to the Prior rather than the king, which did not make too much difference to the poor villagers who hardly scraped by with what they had.

Annie brought her attention back to the city. It felt strange to see this 'early' York when she was familiar with the 'later' city. As this was a working day, she wondered if she might bump into Mary. She smiled at the thought; there were a few veils of time between them.

Mistress Bagsworth and her grimy son were gazing around, their faces reflecting a mixture of fear and wonder. Neither had left their village until now.

"Where's tha' sister live?" asked Dick, his longest sentence for a while.

"Just off big church. Our Edith's lived there for years. If tha can drop us off there, I'll ask for 'er. Sumbody'll know 'er."

"What are your plans, Master Radcliffe?" Annie asked.

"When a get t'market a'll unload me goods. Then me an' 'Arry'll find a quiet spot t'kip down. We'll be off back 'ome early t'morra."

The light, such as it was, was beginning to fade. Annie would have dearly loved to explore medieval York but couldn't risk it on her own.

"I would like to find you after I've seen Mistress Bagsworth settled; please watch for me. Is that alright?"

Dick Radcliffe grunted.

They made their way slowly along Micklegate, a busy and noisy street. The cart lumbered by clusters of monks; traders touting their wares; craftsmen carrying their tools; women with baskets clutched in their arms or bairns hanging on their skirts; knights on horseback with their retinues taking up too much road; piles of stinking garbage; and always, overriding everything, the smell of the Ouse. Annie longed for a sprig of rosemary to waft under her nose.

The cart crossed the Ouse again, this time over a stone bridge. Dick—surprisingly—volunteered that there was a prison on each side of the bridge as well as five more in York. "Even t'Minster 'as its own prison. Locals call all t'prisons kidcotes."

Having turned into a tour guide, he seemed to like the job, as he didn't stop talking until they reached the courtyard beside York Minster. The Minster offered an amazing sight. Annie's two companions gasped at their first sight of the building with its soaring buttresses and towers, seemingly reaching up to touch the sky. The many stained glass windows offered a warm glow to counteract the November gloom. Annie puzzled at her view of the great Gothic cathedral. Something was missing. Then she noticed scaffolding in the central area of the roof. The masons were just in the process of building the large square central tower, a fixture in her York landscape.

Dick parked his cart on the cobbles by the beautifully-arched western entrance. Saint Peter and two saints looked down on them from above the cusp of the stone arch. The black-garbed clerics busily moving around and in and out of the great oak doors reminded Annie of ants scurrying around a disturbed anthill. Her dark feelings about the harshness of the feudal system had soured her thrill of witnessing history.

Annie, Mistress Bagsworth, and her boy climbed stiffly off the cart.

"You'll find me at t'market, that's on Market Street." Dick turned his horse around and rumbled off over the cobblestones.

The tired trio walked across the cobbles, turning right into a ginnel that opened onto a narrow lane. Small, mean looking houses crowded together under the shadow of 't'big church' as her companion described it. They knocked at the first door they came to. As Mistress Bagsworth had predicted, the woman who came to the door knew her sister and directed them further down the lane. Mistress Bagsworth's sister opened the door and cried out with surprise to see her younger sister and nephew standing there. After the two sisters had thrown their arms around one another and had a good cry, Annie felt safe to leave them. They would have to find out in which of the seven prisons, or kidcotes, poor Tom was languishing, and visit in the morning.

Having delivered her charges, Annie set off for Market Street, heading along Low Petergate. The layout of the streets had not changed in centuries so the route was familiar. The roads were still crowded with people, hurrying to do whatever they had to do before darkness and the curfew claimed the city, so she didn't feel apprehensive about being on her own.

Annie smelled the street called The Shambles before seeing it. She peered down the street of butchers. It was so narrow: the second stories of the houses were almost touching. Big, burly men were in the process of taking down meat that had been hanging on hooks outside and rotting meat was lying in the central channel of the cobbled road. Will told her his father owned a shop in The Shambles. Annie was familiar with the Shambles in her century. It was one of the most visited streets in Europe, famous for its original architecture and boutique shopping, very different from its origins.

Walking briskly, she turned onto the street called Pavement, named from it being one of the first paved streets in York. Passing the point where Mark's and Spenser's stood in the twenty-first century, she came to the Church of All Saint's; the pale yellow limestone blocks looking newly quarried. Annie thrilled to see a light glowing at the top of the tower before she turned toward Market Street. Familiar with the venerable and ancient church in her time but having no knowledge of the light; the tower reminded her of a lighthouse. Crossing the road still busy with carts and people, the street she sought appeared before her, the stallholders calling to one another in the gathering dusk as they packed up their stalls for the day. She located Dick's horse, free of the shafts and hobbled next to the cart, tucking into some hay.

"Master Radcliffe, why is there a light burning at the top of All Saints Church?"

"Ee, lass, A thought tha'd know that, bein' frum these parts." Dick peered at her, his eyes sharp under his sprouting salt and pepper eyebrows. "It's t'guide travellers in frum t'north o' city. Wolf infested forest up there."

After delivering this further travel guide information, he unexpectedly brought her some cheese and bread from a market stall and then disappeared into a tavern.

Following a night best forgotten, having spent it wrapped up in her cloak under the wooden cart beside a loudly snoring, frequently farting companion, Annie went off to find a privy. When she returned she was surprised to see the cart piled high with plump sacks. 'Arry was already hitched up to the loaded cart and Dick paced up and down, anxious to be off. As they began their journey back to Hallamby, Annie hoped her driver would revert to his previously silent self, allowing her to rest. Climbing on top of the sacks, she collapsed thankfully into their softness and slept most of the way home.

25

As Mary drove through Micklegate Bar on her way to work, a tingle climbed up her spine and goose bumps rose on her skin; Annie's presence was close by. The sensation was so strong her arm raised of its own volition to reach out and touch her friend. She shook her head at her suddenly fanciful imagination.

Mary was still puzzling over this business in her story of Annie being a witch. If—and it was a big if—Annie really was a witch, why hadn't she told her best and closest friend, Mary, before.

If it were true, and not something from Mary's imagination, she felt a little piqued that Annie had kept that secret from her; they could have had such fun playing with magic, maybe putting spells on the teachers, or making love potions for their friends.

Arriving at the insurance building on Feasgate, around the corner from Market Street, her sense of Annie's presence remained strong; so strong that Mary drove around the parking lot and went out onto Market street, looking closely at all of the people as they walked to work. Finally shrugging her shoulders and laughing self-consciously, Mary parked her car and walked into the building, her mind still reflecting on their friendship.

She and Annie were so different: one blond, one dark. Different in temperament too, now she came to think about it. Annie was quick to action, whereas she, Mary, was more deliberate. Well, maybe deliberate was the wrong word to describe herself; she could be a little slow to action. Actually, her school reports had often implied she could do more if she really tried; 'somewhat of a plodder' she had overheard one of her teacher say.

Enough of that train of thought. It was important to focus on her day's work; she'd been making a number of errors recently and the area manager had called her in. The dressing down she received in the manager's office had not been pleasant. All she wanted to do was write and being nagged at by both her manager and her husband wasn't helping. They didn't appear to understand she had a whole village to care for.

26

Late November 1415, Hallamby, Yorkshire

Rosamund sensed *she who shared her life* would soon be home. While she waited, she would take a stroll to the inn. She had be on high alert in case any of the village dogs were around, but they were no match for her. Rosamund had a number of ruses in her repertoire capable of scaring off the most aggressive dog. One of them was to make herself look twice as big and, at the same time, send a subliminal message to the animal that she relished dog meat even more than mice. It worked every time.

She completed her morning's grooming and set off. Padding without incident along the village street, a couple of opportunities to chase birds and mice arose but she ignored her hunting urge; a much more important task lay ahead. Filled with a sense of self-righteousness, the cat held her head high as she approached the inn. There would be barn cats in the area, retained to keep vermin down. Rosamund was ready to send a warning hiss should one of the mangy things approach. The plan was to see Jack, just to say hello.

The inn and its surroundings looked peaceful. Rosamund could hear someone whistling in the stables, otherwise the courtyard was empty. She settled down to wait, cats having an abundance of patience. Eventually, a girl came out of the main door to fetch water from the pump. Rosamund streaked through the open door. She headed for the boards and sat under them; her tail primly curled around her feet and observed the situation. No humans were in this large room, either. She took the time to enjoy the fresh smell from the floor-covering. It reminded her of hunting for mice in a grassy meadow. Thinking of mice, she couldn't smell any—not that she had time to go hunting. The girl came back from the pump, carrying a now heavy-looking pail of water and disappeared into the kitchen. The sound of voices arose. Rosamund padded over to the kitchen door and listened.

"So you were 'ere t'night of storm?"

"Aye, a were, real scary it were. T'gaffer were in kitchen, shoutin' at cook for sum reason or another. Nowt new about that, regular show it were. We 'eard shoutin' from big 'all and three big bloody men burst inter kitchen. They were wavin' daggers around, niver seen 'em before."

"What 'appened then?"

"They grabbed t'gaffer and dragged 'im out of t'kitchen. We were rooted t'spot so I dunt know what 'appened after that."

"As tha telled anybody?"

"Nay, nobody's asked me but am tellin' thee."

Silence reigned. Rosamund washed her face. Her cat antennae picked up notes of falsehood and deception. She knew *she who shared her life* would be interested in that conversation. Now where might Jack be? She eventually found him in his room, fast asleep. He had survived one and a half days as an innkeeper and had finally collapsed.

"My poorrr Jack," Rosamund purred and jumped on the mattress to curl up beside him.

* * *

When Annie returned home, she found Rosamund sitting outside the door assiduously grooming her black fur, a smug look on her face. Annie gave her lots of attention then lit the hearth fire and prepared water to boil for a mint infusion and a good wash. She had thanked Dick profusely when he dropped her off at her cottage.

"What's in the sacks," she asked as she jumped down, "that they were so comfy to lie on?"

"Niver thee mind, nowt to do w'thee," and then he winked at her. She stood and watched him and 'Arry rumble up the street and was surprised to feel a warm glow of affection inside her for the grumpy cart driver and his horse.

27

Dick continued up the street, making his way to the inn. Stopping his horse outside one of the cottages, he whistled softly. A whistle responded from inside the cottage and two men came out and clambered onto the back of the cart. Dick clicked at 'Arry to walk on. The cart arrived at the back of the inn as dusk softened the edges of the building and the smell of wood smoke reminded Dick he had yet to eat his supper. The two men hopped off the cart and began unloading the sacks, ready to transfer them into the room at the back.

"Ave a good trip t'city then?"

"Aye, fair t'middlin'. Good crop there, though."

Dick was familiar with the routine that would begin once he had delivered the goods. The same tasks were repeated month after month. Light spilled out from the small, shuttered window. He climbed stiffly from the cart and popped his head in the door to nod hello. Two women from the village were unpacking the rolled fleeces and repacking them into regulation woolsacks ready for the packhorses; another woman was sewing the woolsacks closed.

"Be as quick as tha can," called one of the men to the women. "Orses will be 'ere afor Matins."

* * *

Jack woke up and went out to the back of the building to use the privy. He was on his way back to the main hall when he first heard, and then saw the activity. It was dark and secluded at this side of the building. He slipped quietly into the room while the men were busy around the cart.

The women looked up, startled, then fearful. Jack placed his finger on his lips and smiled as he stepped to the back of the room and squatted down on his haunches. He had thought long and hard about the smuggling operation; who was running it and into whose pockets did the profits disappear? He figured the only way to find out was to become one of the smugglers. The women watched the new innkeeper warily then the woman sewing the woolsacks closed shrugged her shoulders and signaled the other two to keep doing what they were doing. One of the men came back into the room carrying a sack on his shoulder and dropped it quickly when he saw Jack.

"Good eventide," Jack greeted him. "I'm one of the new innkeepers. Jack Fletcher's the name." He paused and waited a beat for the man to introduce himself. He did not. "I can see that what you're all doing is going to provide income for the inn so I'm in full favour. I would even like to go out to the coast with the horses, maybe on the next run."

"Nowt to do wi' us," growled the man. "Tha would 'ave to ask t'gaffer."

"Oh, who is that?"

"We dunt know," interceded one of the women quickly. "We just do as we're told."

The second man had entered the room during the exchange.

"'Ell fire!" he swore. "What's tha doin' 'ere? Is tha tryin' t'cause trouble for us? T'utha innkeeper knew what were goin' on but thee an' tha mate are new."

"That's not a problem," Jack tried to sound reassuring. "We don't want to change anything. As a matter of fact, Steward Sneed trusts us completely."

He had thrown that gambit out to see what happened and waited for the result. Silence. Over the last few days, he and Will had learned to recognize that particular silence. He realized that no further information would be forthcoming.

"I'm sorry to hear about Master Ridley's disappearance. Was he a good man to work for? How did he treat you?"

"'E were all reight," muttered the second man. "We 'ave to get on, beggin' tha pardon."

As he and his mate went out for more sacks of wool, Jack turned to the women. He didn't have much time before the men came back.

"I heard he could be somewhat forceful with the girls?"

"Niver bothered us."

Jack appreciated he was dealing with experts at withholding information. He offered them a good evening, walked around to the front of the inn and went back into the hall, where a bad-tempered Will asked him where in the name of 'All that's Holy' he had been. Jack spent five minutes placating his friend without mentioning the activity in the back of the building then resumed his legitimate duties as an innkeeper. He figured he would hear from someone soon about becoming a smuggler.

The next morning no sign remained of the wool packing activity, nor of any horses, so Jack imagined them now crossing the moors, single file, heading for the sea, and he with them.

28

The next day was Sunday, and Will and Jack escorted Annie to church for the obligatory day of church attendance. Families made their way to the big stone church along the broad road. It took Annie a few minutes to see why the people she was now recognizing looked different in some way. Then the penny dropped. They looked clean and their clothing had a freshness, not quite a newness, but noticeably their Sunday Best. Faces lifted to the sun, the villagers celebrated a rare event in November—sunshine, weak, but still sunshine—a welcome change from the normal grey light and misty drizzle.

Seeing the church for the first time had given Annie a jolt. Now, she was able to view the building with a sense of belonging rather than loss. She knew, from the pamphlets given out by the Ladies' Guild in her own time that the Norman stone church had replaced a wood and plaster building from the twelfth century. Like most English Norman churches, its large square tower held the bell that rang out the canonical hours and was ringing now to call the people to worship. The graveyard was around the side and back of the big grey building and she could see sheep grazing between the gravestones. Round stone arches graced the tops of the windows and entrance. Carvings of fantastical animals and flowers decorated the stones forming the arches, weaving in and out of one another and telling a story. The oaken door, adorned with heavy looking iron hinges and a doorknocker, led into a small porch and on into a wide nave; the roof supported by two long rows of pillars, which created side aisles.

Annie looked around and, without thinking, blurted, "Where are the pews?"

Villagers stood around in groups in the wide-open nave, talking earnestly to one another. Children were playing hide and seek around the pillars. The elderly had perched their posteriors on the base of the pillars to rest their legs. It looked to Annie more like a social occasion rather than a solemn church service.

"What's a pews?" Jack, his face alive with interest, waited for her response.

Thinking furiously, Annie replied, "Oh, in York now, some of the churches have seats for people, made of wood, often in rows. They're called pews."

She wandered off to recover from her gaff and studied the stone font at the entrance, also carved with entwined and intricate flowers. Annie could feel the cold emanating from the stone walls and flagstones; her breath arose in a soft mist. Wrapping her beautiful new shawl more securely around her shoulders, she watched Mistress Davey take her leave from a woman who resembled her to greet Will and Jack. Annie moved down the nave to join them.

The pillars in the nave branched into graceful arches displaying more carvings. Grotesque faces, each one different, stared down at them. Colourfully painted walls depicted scenes of the life of Christ. A compelling mural occupied the space above the stone chancel arch, beautifully carved and leading the way to the altar. The painting portrayed Jesus sitting in judgment, the people on his right climbing the stairs to heaven and the people on his left descending into hell. Annie smiled to herself: the message was clear. The villagers knew they had to lead a good Christian life in order to avoid hellfire and that included going to church on Sundays and feast days. They were required to pay their tithes and rents quarterly to the steward, who collected on behalf of Prior Gilbert and the Order of the Augustinians.

Beyond the chancel arch, Annie could see the back of Steward Sneed's head as he sat in a large and elaborately studded chair, his bailiff standing by his side, both staring into space. No doubt examining the state of their souls, she thought, and then chided herself—she was in church.

"That fancy chair's reserved for our Prior or any other visitin' 'igh ups, or for t'steward," Mistress Davey whispered. "Rest of us get to stand."

The chancel itself occupied a small space and, with the addition of a wooden screen, protected the altar from the gaze of the common people. A thick slab of stone resting on a smaller block formed the altar. The priest stood before it reading the Mass in Latin. His voice droned on, only becoming louder as he intoned a prayer. Murmurs of conversation arose from the worshipers as they caught up on the gossip and business of the village as most could not hear, nor understand, what the priest was saying. The varied stories about the missing innkeeper and poor Tom Bagsworth's misfortunes produced the most comments from the villagers.

Mistress Davey nodded in the direction of the priest. "That's Father John. Born an' brought up in t'village, 'e were. 'E were blessed. Prior Gilbert got to 'ear about 'ow smart 'e were frum t'old priest who showed 'im 'ow to do 'is letters an' numbers. Prior Gilbert sent 'im to York for more learning an' now 'e's our priest. Looks after us too, best 'e can."

"He might be a good person to talk to about the village affairs," Will murmured to Jack. "We could bring up the subject of the newly departed innkeeper, just to see what he might divulge."

The service ended eventually and the priest stood at the door greeting and blessing his parishioners; no doubt noting who attended and who did not. He paid particular attention to his new attendees but Annie could read nothing on his face.

After the service, Will and Jack walked Annie back to her cottage. To Annie's consternation, she found she could not look at Will without blushing and feeling shy. On the way they met Jenet, walking up the street with the baby tucked into a cloth wrapped around her body. Jenet had cleaned up well under the care of Mistress Davey; her long fair hair covered with a red coif and her clear complexion glowing.

Looking delighted to see Annie and being introduced to Will and Jack, Jenet explained that Church Laws required her to remain secluded inside her home for a short time following the birth, after which she would participate in a churching cleansing ceremony. "A were going crazy fastened up in t'cottage, even though Mistress Davey is bein' ever so good t'me."

They all admired her baby, and Jack appeared to admire Jenet, observed Annie with an inward smile and a sense of relief at the tension between Will and herself being released by Jenet's presence.

The group said their goodbyes and went their different ways. Even Sunday required home visits and Annie had a number of families to visit as chest infections and aching joints were becoming more common as winter approached. Will and Jack, on the other hand, were going off to play.

29

Before Will and Jack could return to work, they had business to attend to on the village green. A small group of older boys and men had already arrived. The men had set up the big straw butts waiting eagerly for their first archery practice session with the two professional archers.

An English law requiring all men between the ages of fifteen to sixty to own a bow and arrows and practice on Sundays had been in effect for a few hundred years. Kings depended on being able to draw from a large group of highly trained archers when going off to fight a war. The first King Henry even decreed a man should be absolved of murder if he killed someone during archery practice.

The men gathered eagerly around Will and Jack, reaching out to touch their longbows: the longbows and their bowmen now being famous from their use at the recent Battle of Agincourt and, prior to that, the Battle of Crecy, some sixty before.

These particular bows stood over six feet high and were made from yew, the bowstrings from hemp. The wood shone from a rub of wax, resin, and fine tallow. The arrows brought by Will and Jack were three feet long, the tips bulbous, nocked to prevent the arrow going too deep into the butts. The younger boys had bows and arrows made for their respective sizes and eagerly awaited their turn to aim at the straw butts, hoping to hit the bull's eye.

Soon the cries of 'Ready your bows!' 'Nock!' 'Mark!' 'Draw!' 'Loose!' carried across the green and sweat began to pour off the archers. The practice quickly turned into a fierce competition as boasting rights would last until next week's practice. The light became poor as low clouds dominated the scene and the November day drew in quickly. Will decreed the low light created a danger and ended the practice.

The archery training over, the longbowmen-turned-innkeepers, having thoroughly enjoyed stretching the long bows and feeling the familiar ache in their shoulders, made their way back to the inn. They and the servants had to catch up with the work they had been neglecting.

Will left Jack to settle into their private quarters with the inn's account records. These were not the same ones they had seen when Steward Sneed had reviewed them. These roles belonged to the inn but, like the manorial roles, they consisted of sheets of parchment neatly stitched together and wrapped in leather. Jack had discovered an aptitude for numbers as a schoolboy and he explained to Will that he wanted to get a better grasp on the state of the inn's finances. Will went into the kitchen, poured himself an ale and stood idly, listening to 'call me Aggie', who was plucking an old hen, unfortunately beyond her egg-laying days.

"...so that kitchen helper, Lisbet, the one who only lasted 'ere two days, told me about t'night that t'innkeeper vanished... "

Feathers flew everywhere, including up Will's nose. After a couple of enormous sneezes, he turned his attention back to the continuing monologue.

"...an' four 'uge men, armed with daggers and cudgels, came chargin' into t'kitchen and cut 'is throat there and then. There were blood all over!"

Will listened to this version with skepticism as he had seen the kitchen prior to the big clean up and saw no bloodstains, but he didn't voice this to 'call me Aggie' who was enjoying telling the story with great relish.

"Why did Lisbet only stay here for a couple of days?"

"'Er mam came to the inn and made her go 'ome, said as how the family had changed their minds about 'er being 'ere."

"Odd," reflected Will, "you would think they'd be glad of the extra money." He cut himself a chunk of bread and a wedge of cheese and wandered off to check on Jack.

He found his friend with his focus still deep into the accounts. As

Will, who never had any interest in rows of numbers, could not comprehend Jack's pleasure in this particular past-time. It puzzled him in school that Jack, the one with the restless energy and only happy when released from the confines of his desk, could settle down and focus on a knotty math problem.

Jack explained that some of the account roles were quite old and maintained by previous innkeepers over many years. Each role recorded wages paid to servants and skilled staff members. Lists of furniture, kitchen equipment, and other sundry items bought and sold over the years filled the pages. Ridley's entries had begun about five years ago and his small, crabbed penmanship meticulously listed all amounts in various columns. The second role tracked food supplies, wine and ale expenditures, and stable maintenance costs.

"You are not going to believe this; someone has been creative with these numbers. It is in the columns for the wine—it is cleverly hidden but at least two to three percent is not accounted for every month. I can find no account of the wine merchant yet the innkeeper pays out substantial sums for the inn's wine."

"Who would have kept the accounts?"

"Well, it had to be the innkeeper as these are the inn's charges and discharges.

"There's another interesting thing," continued Jack. "Ridley had listed all of his credits and debits and used initials to label various suppliers. I'm guessing that B for is baker, M for the miller, and so on. But," he paused and held out a folded piece of parchment to Will, "I found this tucked in the centre of the role."

Two heads leaned over the tightly creased sheet of parchment: one dark, and one blond. A list of figures going back about four and a half years trailed down the page. The amounts of money grew increasingly larger as the years went by. The handwriting was the same as Ridley's cramped scribble seen on the other sheets. The identifying initial was always the same.

"It's a C," said Will.

30

Will made his way to the house at the side of the church the following day. He timed his visit as early as possible, hoping to catch the priest before he went out on his rounds, although November did allow for a longer stay in bed due to the short days and long nights.

The priest answered the door looking like any ordinary villager without his black robe of office. Will observed him carefully, as he had not been able to study him well in church on Sunday. Father John was not a tall man, he barely came up to Will's chin, but he was squarely built, his broad shoulders emphasizing his peasant stock rather than a priestly bearing. He had penetrating blue eyes, looking decidedly cool right now. His nose appeared a little too large for his walnut wrinkled face, and his grey, sparse tonsure ringed his scalp.

"Yes?"

"My name is William Boucher of York. I am the new innkeeper at 'The King's Head', as you may know. I'm hoping to have a few words with you."

The priest opened the door wider allowing Will to enter the house. Once Will's eyes had become used to the gloom, he looked around with interest. The church house was bigger than the other homes in the village. It had several rooms plus a loft. Will had taken notice of outbuildings and a vegetable garden behind the house. There were winter cabbages still looking green and healthy and, growing beside them, what looked like feathery carrot tops.

The priest took him to the main living area. A small fire burned on the hearthstone, making the room warm and comfortable. Smoke from the fire made its way straight up to escape from the opening in the roof. The two men sat across from each other at a trestle table.

"I am Father John, priest of this parish. I saw you yesterday in church with another tall young man and the dark haired young woman. What can I do for you?"

"As Jack and I—he's the dark haired one you saw and Mistress Thornton is my cousin—are partners in running the inn, we thought it would be helpful to know more about the village and how it functions, as quite a number of villagers are working for us. Perhaps you can start with yourself, as you have such an important position in the village?"

Father John offered Will a questioning look.

"It sounds like you should be speaking with Steward Sneed rather than me. He is the main man around here."

"You are familiar with Steward Sneed, are you not?" asked Will.

At this, Father John allowed a tiny smile to appear and just as quickly disappear. He spread out his hands in a gesture of acquiescence. "I have been parish priest here for twenty years. My father was a freeman on the Manor House farm. Father Septimus, the priest in our village, taught me to read and write. Prior Gilbert had just become Prior of Kirkham. He favoured me and sent me to the Church school in York where I learned Latin and the rites of the Church. Being a village priest is not an easy position, as I have to work my land as well or pay someone to work it for me. I receive a tithe from the villagers on behalf of the Augustine order, shared between the Order and my church here. They complain about it, but it prevents me from starving. They provide me with some grains, eggs, and flour, and, if I'm lucky, the odd chicken or pig."

As the Father talked, Will could hear someone moving around in one of the other rooms. Father John saw Will's head turn to the sound and explained the presence of his housekeeper.

"I expect you knew the innkeeper, Master Ridley?" Will enquired.

The priest's face darkened. "Yes, I knew him. He was, unfortunately, a man of sinful habits. He caused many problems for the young girls and their families in the village. I believed him to be untrustworthy. I do not wish to speak ill of the missing but we are better off without him."

"You use the past tense, Father when you speak of him. Do you think he is dead? On the other hand, do you have any thoughts on who might have been involved with his disappearance? It seems strange to me that a man can vanish so mysteriously."

"I only speak in the past tense because the innkeeper is missing. I have no thoughts on the causes. I do; however, pray for his soul, alive or dead."

Will watched with interest as Father John mopped his face with a large rag. The room was warm—but not that warm.

"I do not believe for one moment a villager had been involved. I know Tom well. He is a good man; he cares for his family. I pray constantly for him and his wife and children. Life has been a struggle for him since he hurt his back. I try to help the family as best I can." The priest paused, "Mayhap it was an outsider who had been cheated by Ridley?"

"I have met Mistress Bagsworth and Jenet," Will said, "and I too, feel for them. It would be good, therefore, if we can track down this person or persons. There are so many different stories going around the village, it's almost as if someone is attempting to confuse us."

Father John jumped to his feet.

"I can spare you no more time. Please leave, and 'twere best if you did not interfere with village matters."

Following the abrupt ending to the meeting, Will found himself back outside of the door. What had caused such a change of attitude from being helpful to being warned off—again?

He decided to walk up the street and visit Mistress Davey. She appeared to know quite a lot about the parish priest, at least from what she had said in church. He arrived at his old lodgings and his former landlady greeted him with obvious pleasure. She bent over a pot sitting at the side of the hearth and scooped out some porridge into a bowl.

"Am sure tha can manage a bit of porridge? Jenet's still sleeping with t'babby," she spoke in a whisper. "She's up a lot during t'night to feed 'im."

Will took the hint and lowered his voice. "I've just visited with Father John, and he was quite informative about his role in the village. Do you know his housekeeper?"

"Aye, that'd be Florrie Ridley, as was. She's his 'earth-mate, lived with 'im for a few years now. Funny thing, she came into these parts with t'innkeeper. I dunt know where they came frum, but that bugger weren't good to 'er. Everybody knew what were goin' on. She often turned up in church wi' a black eye, poor soul. Anyway, she finally 'ad enough and ran t'church 'ouse. Father took 'er in an' she's been with 'im ever since."

"What do you mean by a hearth-mate?"

"Well, as tha knows, priests can't marry, and, as they are but men with the same needs as other men," Mistress Davey paused and blushed, "often they'll 'ave a mate in t'house. T'Church won't allow 'em to be called wives so they're called 'earth-mates.'"

"Sharing the same woman; now that's an interesting connection to the innkeeper," mused Will. "I imagine there was a lot of tension between Master Ridley and Father John?"

"It were reight tricky. Ridley 'ad to go to church at least once a week like rest of us, but 'e would just nip in and out. "'E never talked to nobody, just showed 'is face and left."

"I believe Father John is worth keeping an eye on. Maybe he knows more about this murder than it seems. I will be obliged if you keep this conversation to yourself, mistress."

Will bussed Mistress Davey, making her round face blush again and took his leave to return to the inn. As he walked back past the church he imagined a large spider web with Father John as the big, black spider in the middle, trapping his victims before he ate them.

31

Late November 2015, Hallamby, Yorkshire

Mary leaned back from her laptop and laughed. Will could not know that she, the writer, wove the spider web—not Father John. She held the power. Events were becoming more complex in Hallamby village, and it was up to her to define who the bad people were. She needed to look more closely at Annie's role, and this growing attraction between Annie and Will—well, it would never do—Annie would be coming back home.

Jonathon had gone down to the pub. She couldn't understand what was wrong with him; he was so grumpy these days. She'd brought home fish and chips as a treat—they had made a change from the ready-made dinners she'd got into the habit of picking up after work. He had stormed out, saying he'd get a proper meal at the pub. It couldn't be helped. Writing this story was her priority; cooking and housework could wait. Jonathon forgotten already, Mary went into the kitchen to steep some tea and ponder her next chapter.

32

Late November 1514, Hallamby, Yorkshire

Annie looked around at her adopted home. The surroundings reflected her mood: dark and desolate. She had no idea what she was doing here. It was important to remember she had another life if only she could get back to it. Who was this aunt who knew her so well? How could the woman do this to her? What was her purpose in bringing Annie here and disappearing herself?

Annie lifted Rosamund onto her lap and looked into her deep green eyes.

"It's not just that, Rosamund. What am I to do? I feel so attracted to Will. This can't happen, I'll return to my other life at some point. I just can't afford to get involved with a man from a different century."

Rosamund purred in sympathy. She looked back into Annie's eyes and focused her gaze, sharpening her oval pupils. Energy began to pass between the two of them, external sounds faded, and time became suspended.

Annie emerged from her meditative state. "My God, Rosamund, if I didn't know any better, I would swear you can read my mind. I have thought of a solution. I shall solve the mystery of the death of the innkeeper by myself—at least I will have accomplished something —and then we'll find a way to return to our own time. I'll forget about Will. And this unknown aunt—well—the hell with her."

After making this emphatic statement, Annie spoiled the effect by bursting into tears and missing the gentle tap at the door. Rosamund leapt off her lap and moved to the entrance. Annie tried to dry her tears as a woman she had never seen before came in to the cottage, followed by a cat, the mirror image of Rosamund.

"Hello, my sweet. Oh, you are crying, let me comfort you."

The woman gathered a startled Annie into her arms. When Annie pulled back in alarm, she cupped Annie's blotchy, tearstained face into her hands. "I am your Aunt Meg. This is my home. I was visiting friends in Selby but I sensed your distress and realized you needed some moral support, so here I am."

Annie glared at the unknown woman who said she was her aunt. "So it's you, you who brought me here without telling me why. Do you have any idea how awful it's been, not knowing, yet all the village knows more than me. I have to go home. I don't belong here."

"Let's have a hot drink and get to know one another. All will become clear." Aunt Meg removed her shawl and moved quietly around the room while Annie sat sniffing.

As they sipped their fragrant drinks, Annie told her newly found Aunt Meg all that had happened. The arrival of the two ex-soldiers at the same time as herself; the decrepit state of the inn; the vanishing innkeeper; the different stories going around the village regarding what had happened the night of the storm...

"...Then the pigs dug up a body in the forest—turned out to be the missing innkeeper. We heard the nibbled corpse finished up in the steward's barn, never seen again. Then, straight after that, the bailiff arrested Tom Bagsworth and dragged him off to York. You must know that family; the innkeeper made his daughter Jenet pregnant. I delivered her baby—I'll tell you all about that later. Then I went to York to take Mistress Bagsworth and her son to be with her sister."

Annie forbore to mention her growing attraction toward Will; that was none of her new aunt's business.

"Oh, my," cried her aunt, "what a series of events. It is a good job you are here to help sort it all out."

"Why me? Why am I here?" a puzzled Annie shook her head. "I have no special skills as a detective."

"What is a detective?" asked Meg, "I've never heard the word before."

"A detective is a person who is able to follow clues, to look for

motive, means and opportunity in order to find the guilty person."
Annie stopped abruptly. She must have absorbed such knowledge
subliminally, probably from watching too many BBC television murder mysteries.

"It sounds to me as though you come well equipped to sort out
this murder business, which is what I had hoped. I believe you have
a concern regarding Will. You have omitted to tell me about that."

Annie blinked: this woman could read her thoughts. "Aunt Meg,
how did Rosamund and I come back here through time? I mean, how
could you know I would arrive here? And, what did the storm have
to do with it? And—"

"Oh, child," Meg laughed, "I know you are a witch, albeit a novice.
I too have the Calling. We are both wild women; wise women. We
are women of Mother Earth. We have inherited her natural powers
of birth, transformation, healing, and rebirth. We have the ability to
call on the elements of nature to help us: air, fire, earth, and water. I
use the energy from these elements to weave my spells. I do believe,
from what you have told me, you try to do the same. We have the
guidance and protection of the Mother Goddess. We have knowledge
of medicines that come from the earth. We have the assistance of our
spirit guides: our familiars.

"Some men fear us because of our power. The Church, in particular, finds us to be a threat and seeks us out. Cursing people or their
livestock, as many accuse us, is not our way. Neither do we call on
the devil to help us. We do not inflict the pestilence onto our people.
Our practice is to do good work and always try to help our neighbours. Our knowledge of herbs and remedies for diseases may differ
from that of the male establishment and that makes us vulnerable,
as they fear our power.

"I do hope you are aware Rosamund is your familiar: your spirit
guide. Do you remember finding her, a tiny black kitten, outside of
the door of your cottage when you moved in? I sent her to you. I am
aware your heart's desire is to follow your heritage and I plan to help
you in that regard. I believe that devilry is at work here in Hallamby,
and we need to uncover and destroy it for the sake of the villagers.
My reason for bringing you here offers an answer to both. I used a
storm as the precursor of the energy required to get you here. I now

realize that I should not have left you alone for as long as I did, but I thought my absence created a good reason for you to take my place."

Annie sat with her mouth open. Her mother would have said she was catching flies. She tried hard to absorb all that her aunt told her.

"Rosamund is my *familiar*? What does that mean?"

"She is your spirit guide and well able to assist you with spell-making. She has telepathic powers: able to read your mind and send you messages."

"I knew she was special! I didn't realize how special. Where do Will Boucher and Jack Fletcher fit into your plans?"

"They too, are—what word did you use—detectives, but, more importantly, their main purpose is to protect you. They will deal, as men, with the steward and men of his ilk. I am hoping you can go about your business in the village as a caring woman, keeping your eyes and ears open, yet you must not appear to be inquisitive by asking pointed questions. No, your job is to work as quietly as possible."

"Are you saying you arranged for them to come here too? But why me? I'm nobody special, to be chosen to come all this way to solve a village mystery?"

Meg tilted her head sideways to look at Annie and, with a little smile on her lips, said, "I confess my initial reason was selfish. I wanted to meet you and get to know you better. We really are related and I feel our kinship strongly, even throughout all of the centuries. Rosamund has been a strong ally in keeping us connected, even if you were not aware of it. As you know, your mother chose not to be a practicing witch and I was concerned you would not be able to come into your full power as a witch without a teacher."

Annie shook her head at her newly-acquired aunt. "I always knew I was different from my friends. When I became a teenager, I used to have dreams. They were always the same; women dressed in old-fashioned clothing; of heat, flames, and crowds screaming. Once, in school—even now, I break out in a sweat when I think of it—it was a hot day in June. I was in a math class and the teacher droned on and on, writing incomprehensible numbers on the blackboard. A fly buzzed around the room. Its sound became stuck in my head. I remember I was doodling a parade of icebergs on my notebook and chanting 'ice, ice, ice' under my breath. The teacher dropped her chalk with an audible gasp. It shattered into numerous ice pellets and all the kids ran up to the front to grab them. I never told anybody. It wasn't 'til my mother gave me The Book that I realized it came from my witch's power. It scared me to have that kind of power, especially as I didn't know how to use it. It's all starting to make sense now, and I think you're telling me I'm not here because I bungled a creativity spell." Annie sighed with relief. "But what about Will and how I'm beginning to feel about him?"

Aunt Meg held up her hand. "What is this about a creativity spell? I am not aware you had gone so far."

"That's what I was trying to do when you brought me here. My friend, Mary aspires to be an author and can't write to save—"

"—I know of Mary and of her writing ambition. Back to what you were saying about Will. You will be returning to your time, so I do not recommend any entanglements of the heart."

"Aunt Meg, did you never marry? Have you ever been in love?"

Mistress Wistowe smiled a sad smile. She reached out and held Annie's hand. "My childhood sweetheart and I planned to marry in York, many years ago. He went to be a soldier for King Richard. He had the urge to visit new lands before he settled down. He died at the battle of Najera in France. Many men died that day and the French claimed the victory. So silly, all of this fighting over land. I could not bear to stay in York so I came here. I knew of this little village from traders who came into York for the markets. I resolved to dedicate my life to the villagers. It was then I began to realize I had special powers which I use sparingly and carefully. The villagers lead such a hard life; I do all I can to ease their way through."

Meg patted Annie's knee. "I do hope you forgive me for not being here for you. Now, let's enjoy another chamomile infusion; it's been a busy day."

33

Jack had been thinking—hard. It seemed logical to him that a document existed somewhere in the inn with an account of the smuggled wool trade. The innkeeper had been most particular about keeping lists of everything. He promised himself he would have a good look around; such a record would contain valuable information.

Having completed his tasks for the morning, he walked to the village for some fresh air. It was a normal November day with low grey clouds and a soft drizzle of rain, so fine and gentle it could be mistaken for mist. Even the rooks were subdued, trying to keep dry in their nests, the black and twiggy shapes standing out in the bare tree branches.

The sheep were busily performing their usual activity of eating grass and fertilizing the fallow fields. When he reached the main street of the village, he passed men filling in holes in the dirt road. The same two men he saw the other day were working on another roof, replacing thatch. The ale-stake had moved from its previous doorway to another one down the street denoting a change in the local tavern for the evening. Everything looked as usual. He thought he might call in on Mistress Davey, just to say hello and, maybe say hello to Jenet, ask about the baby, not that it was Jenet he planned to see…

Jack awoke from his reverie hearing a 'psst' coming from the door of one of the cottages. Startled, he swung his head around and touched his chest.

"Me?"

"Get over 'ere an' be quick about it."

Jack entered the cottage. Two men stood inside the door. When his eyes became used to the gloom he recognized them as the ones who had helped unload Dick's cart of fleeces the other evening but it was still too dark to make out their features.

"'Ere, sup this." A mug of ale found its way into his hand.

Jack considered his options. Either they were friendly or they meant to poison him. Notwithstanding the latter thought, he supped.

"Tha needs to understand we make t'trips t'Bay when moon's reight," said one man, who identified himself as Sam and his mate as Red Rob. "We can be a bit picky now, this late in t'year. In summer, after t'shearing, we go as often as we can. Not too bright and not too dull is what we want. We can't 'elp it if it's cloudy, we manage as best we can then."

Jack experienced a quiver of excitement in his belly. They were telling him he was going on their next trip to the coast with the fleeces.

"How long does it take to get to the sea?"

"Depends on t'weather, usually a night an' a bit, but we're crossin' moors so it's single file, an' there's boggy bits to watch for. It's great if we dunt meet any 'orses travellin' t'utha way. Then o'course, we 'ave to return wi' wine so we sleep sum durin' day and set off back at dusk."

"Do you ever have trouble with the duty men?"

"Ain't dun yet, alus a first time, though."

"When do you expect to go?"

"A week 'til moon's reight. Dick'll go t'market in York t'pick up fleeces and then we're off. We'll let tha know. Not a word t'anybody; tha knows that dunt tha?"

"My lips are sealed." Jack's heart thumped with excitement, and then he remembered why he wanted to make the trip. "Who said I could go?"

"Niver thee mind, nowt to t'do wi' thee. Now bugger off!"

Jack wanted to skip up the street as he did as a boy but managed to calm down and sedately made his way to Mistress Davey's home. He hid his elation and chatted quietly with Mistress Davey and to Jenet, who looked appealingly tousle-haired and sleepy. She sat on a bench feeding her baby. Jack thought she looked like a painting of the Madonna. He sat contentedly; just looking at her seemed to ease the ache in his heart that he'd carried around since he lost his own family to cholera before he and Will went overseas.

When Jack returned to the inn, the welcoming smell of malt greeted him. The brewster must have set up shop. He rubbed his hands in anticipation of a draught of strong ale. He found Will in the kitchen, munching on bread and cheese.

"Been down to the village?" asked his friend.

"Aye. I stopped in to pay my regards to Mistress Davey." Jack thought it best not to mention his meeting with the smugglers.

"And how is our fair Jenet," Will asked with a grin on his face.

"Oh, Jenet. She's fine."

"Come off it, Jack; it's obvious you like her."

"I've only known her for a short while." Jack's neck grew warm. Damn the man.

"She looks like a good lass to me." Will finished chewing on his bread. "Not her fault she's got a bairn to take care of all on her own." He walked out of the kitchen, leaving Jack to contemplate the bread-crumbs left on the table.

34

Florrie Ridley finally found the nerve to approach Father John. She had tossed and turned all night in the bed she shared with him and thought she would burst from the worry of it all. He was in the quiet and empty church.

"What did that man want?" she inquired.

"He introduced himself. He is just getting to know about the village." Father John paused in his contemplations and turned to her. "It had nothing to do with us. He's the new innkeeper. Steward Sneed asked him and his friend to take over the inn. I'm sure it's only temporary, but it's important to keep the route operating for the wool shipments, and they are the best and quickest choice."

"Aye, but what about Ridley?"

"It's all dealt with, we won't hear any more on that matter."

Florrie seated herself at her loom, not too convinced that John was right. The rhythmical action of weaving her shuttle between the weft then battening down the thread soothed her. She had been lucky to find Father John. Yes, he was a simple man and viewed the world differently than she, but he was good to her—unlike that misbegotten bastard, Ridley. How she had hated him. He didn't treat her too badly before they moved up here to Hallamby, but they'd lived with her brother in Sheffield and he wouldn't have put up with Ridley's temper. Once she and Ridley were on their own at the inn, he used her as a punch bag whenever he felt like it. He was always sorry afterwards, told her she was still his sweetheart even when she was nursing a black eye or bruised ribs.

Florrie's action with the shuttle and batton grew jerkier as she thought back to the last time he'd had a go at her. She'd complained about his lecherous behaviour with the girls. She didn't give a damn what he did with them, it kept him away from her, but they couldn't keep staff and all the work fell on her shoulders.

He'd knocked her sideways in their bedroom; she'd bounced off the wall. After kicking her in the ribs, he left her sobbing on the floor and took off to get drunk in the wool packing room; his usual practice. She stopped crying, disgusted with herself.

That had been it. She'd reached the end of her tether; never again would that bastard touch her. As painful as it was, it took no time at all to grab her only other gown and shift, and shakily make her way to the church house. Father John knew her situation. He'd seen her bruises in church and, no doubt heard the village gossip. He took her in and nursed her back to health. Ridley came banging at the door a few times but the Father saw him off. Now, John took care of her needs and she took care of his; a simple business arrangement that suited them both and be buggered what the nosy villagers thought.

She stopped and looked down at her weaving. It looked like something a six year old might have done. The whole damn lot would have to be re-done.

35

Steward Sneed was reviewing the manorial rolls. His face held a self-satisfied smile. Master Crompton stood at his right hand.

"I am pleased that the wool shipments are to resume," Sneed commented. "It is astonishing that there is still so much raw wool, over and above the taxed fleeces going to Calais. Of course, Calais, which praise the Lord, is in English hands, is the central destination for all the wool from England before it's shipped to other parts of France, Holland and Belgium."

Sneed paused to savour his wine. "Just consider the size of the flocks owned by the abbeys and manor houses. The king realizes huge sums of money from taxing the wool. That money has kept this war with France going for almost a hundred years. It's only fair and reasonable that we get to share in the bounty."

The bailiff had heard this story frequently from the steward: it was his favorite topic. Sneed could hold forth for a long time. He no longer listened, having learned to nod and shake his head at random while invested in his own thoughts. Sneed's voice faded away and Crompton found himself back in his hometown of Sheffield.

Like the rest of England, the population of his small, south Yorkshire town had suffered during the pestilence on its last visit. His mother was the only survivor of her family, a young girl at the time, so she told him, left alone to find her own way in the world. He still remembered being a snotty-nosed brat in the tavern where his mother worked. He experienced an ongoing succession of 'fathers', most of whom thought nothing of giving him a clout around the ear whenever they felt like it. One of the fathers contributed to the addition of his sister, Florence, three years after his own birth. To his surprise, he loved her fiercely, perhaps because she was the only person in the world who loved him. He became her protector as she grew up and *nobody* messed with him.

He learned early the art of filching a crust of bread or a few coins from under the nodding head of a drunken diner and always made sure Florrie had something to eat. He had fond memories of tear-arsing around the streets and alleyways with his mates, tormenting cats, jeering and nipping at any poor soul who crossed their path and tripping up unwary travellers who blundered into the maze of slums. Crompton smiled. Strangers could report the theft of their money as much as they wanted. The local watchman received his few coins regularly to keep his mouth shut.

Although not a big town, Sheffield was involved in the wool trade and becoming known for its manufacture of cutlery. So, even though the majority of its inhabitants were farmers, there were sufficient numbers of workers around to have a few extra coins jingling in their purses. The weekly market and annual fair provided great pickings for an enterprising lad. When older, he and Ridley set up a profitable business: a hovel, rented cheap, consisting of three local lasses for hire and ale on tap. Florrie became the brewer and that's how she met Ridley. He wasn't too happy when Ridley and Florrie hooked up. He knew of Ridley's reputation with women, but his plain-faced and scrawny sister's choices were limited.

The three of them fled Sheffield when some even tougher boys moved into their patch. Talk about being in the right place at the right time: they arrived in Hallamby when Sneed needed a bailiff and the inn needed an innkeeper. The money he and Ridley brought from Sheffield secured them a share in the inn and Florrie kept him informed of Ridley's doings. He was upset when she ran to the mealy mouthed priest but even that turned out all right, as she reported her new employer's activities to him regularly.

Crompton had come a long way from the slums of Sheffield and planned to keep this easy billet. When he realized the job meant 'keeping the peace' in Hallamby Manor, a trip down to his old haunts secured two mates, Butts and Cartwright—brainless but loyal—who maintained a high level of compliance amongst the villagers.

Ridley had been a mistake. The innkeeper knew too much of Bailiff Crompton's past and present business and he had used that knowledge to make sure the bailiff didn't interfere with his own way of life.

God's Breeches! The man was still droning on. The bailiff sighed and reluctantly tuned back into Sneed's monologue.

"...I agreed with the suggestion that Jack Fletcher could go with the next wool shipment because I believe he could be an asset to us. I perceived he was not averse to the idea of smuggling, just like most people, and he still seems to have a sense of adventure, unlike that stiff-necked Boucher."

"Aye, but 'e needs to know to keep his gob shut—or else."

"I believe he has been warned about that by Rob and Sam. We will keep an eye on him and send a stronger message through Asne Cartwright that we are watching Annie Thornton; she is unquestionably their weak spot. Our share of the wool and wine profits is too plentiful to risk losing it with an ill-advised word in the wrong ear. You know, Bailiff," at this point Sneed actually looked embarrassed, an unusual occurrence. "I always appreciate being able to talk to you."

* * *

Sneed gave his bailiff permission to leave to do his rounds and bestirred himself to throw a log on the fire. He called for Matilda to bring him wine and settled back in his chair to contemplate life.

When he had left Kent abruptly five years earlier, he left behind any assets he had accumulated as leader of a smuggling gang in the Romney marshes. By the Blood of Christ, life had been fun then. The fleeces were no sooner off the sheep's backs than they were bundled into woolsacks and taken to the beaches at night. 'Owlers' they were called—wool smugglers. He'd choose a different beach each trip to fool the small number of customs officers. The ships would be waiting and off the wool would sail to France. Unfortunately, life became a little too precarious; it was time to move on and stay away from towns and cities. His name was on a list somewhere, easy to change a name, though. Imagine his amazement when he landed this steward position and found himself in the middle of another wool smuggling treasure trove. He missed Kent but this life had a few compensations. With that thought, the steward poured himself a goblet of good Burgundy wine, smuggled, of course.

36

Will and Jack were taking a break from their chores and discussing the ongoing mystery of the innkeeper's demise.

"I'm sure the priest is involved in some way," said Will, using his finger to wipe the ale froth from his moustache.

"With the murder or with the sm…" Jack stopped himself just in time; he had nearly acknowledged the reality of the unmentionable.

Will carried on, ignoring the slip. "Of course with the murder, what else would we be talking about? Perhaps Father John is in league with Sneedy but the only connection I have found so far is that the Father's hearth-mate, as Mistress Davey calls his housekeeper, was the wife or companion of our dead innkeeper. According to Mistress Davey, Ridley was a brute toward his wife, fond of knocking her around. She finally had enough and sought refuge at the church. Father John took her in and she became his housekeeper. The priest certainly looks angry when he talks about Ridley."

After asking Will what he meant by a hearth-mate, Jack raised a questioning finger in the air.

"What if Ridley was holding the esteemed Father to ransom for something or other? That would give the priest a reason to get rid of him."

"Good thinking. It gives us something to work on in our spare time, that which we actually do not appear to have. I'm off to talk to 'call me Aggie' about buying an old sheep. The travellers will enjoy some mutton stew now the cold weather's here."

Life at the inn had now become a more settled routine: almost operating with military precision. The rigour of army life had enabled a couple of ex-soldiers to transform their army skills into innkeeper proficiency.

Jack went into their private quarters. He was on a hunt for a record of the inn's wool smuggling business. He did not know for sure that one existed, but he couldn't believe that one did not. He presumed that if Sneed was involved in the wool and wine smuggling, he would certainly be keeping an account, but that was Sneed's business. Ridley's records had proved to Jack the innkeeper was a detail man who loved to keep lists so, logically, there had to be a reckoning somewhere of his own fiddling.

There were limited opportunities for hiding a document in the room; Will still chose to carry his coins around his waist. Jack tapped each flagstone, listening for a hollow sound. His eyes followed the line where the walls joined the floor looking for irregularities. He swept the rushes to one side and looked for disturbances in the flagstones.

"Found it!"

Heart thumping, he saw a large stone slab slightly askew in one corner of the room, with one edge raised a tiny amount from its neighbour. He would need something with which to lever the slab.

Jack made his way to the stable, it being the most likely place to find an iron bar. Young Jeb, the stableboy, was mucking out the stalls, aimlessly whistling as usual, and paid him no heed. Floating dust and debris from the straw swirled around Jack, making him cough. He felt a tap on his shoulder. Expecting to see Jeb, he was surprised when Asne Cartwright stood there.

"Ow's tha doin?" said Asne, with what passed as a smile on his face and showing the remains of his crooked and blackened teeth. Jack had not had much to do with Asne. He knew his mate, Jobe, a little better and trusted neither.

"I'm fine, Asne, I'd like to talk but I'm in a bit of a hurry right now."

"Nay, lad, tha can spare a minute or two. I 'ear tha's off on a trip to t'coast soon, is that reight?"

Jack froze; he struggled not to nod his head. *How did he know?*

"Well, all I wanted to say is keep tha gob shut about it, 'cos if tha dunt, Mistress Thornton might feel sum 'eat, if tha gets me meanin."

Jack felt a strong urge to smash the clod's face in and make his nose travel in the opposite direction. He contained himself with a huge effort.

"Leave Mistress Thornton out of this," he muttered between his teeth.

"Aye, a will, but that's up t'thee. We'll be keeping an eye on young Jenet, too. We all know she likes a bit o' fun."

Jack didn't think—he drew back his fist and smashed it into Asne's face. Blood spurted from the bully's nose and he staggered backwards. He recovered quickly and retaliated with a blow to Jack's head. Jack dodged the rapidly moving fist and it caught him on his shoulder. He heard Jed shout but all he could see was Asne's ugly and blooded face—one more good swing and he'd have him. His body swelled with rage. Reaching his right arm back, fist clenched, he aimed at the skewed nose. His own head exploded. Asne's face vanished.

Rough arms pulled him away and, as he struggled to throw another punch, a wave of cold water hit him in the face.

Will's face swam into view. Something was wrong with his vision. He could only see his friend out of one eye.

"What the hell is going on?" Will shouted.

Asne wiped his bleeding nose on his already soiled tunic sleeve. He winked at Jack, tapped the side of his much-abused proboscis, and pointed. The threat was implicit. He swaggered off, leaving Jack shaking with anger.

"Jack, what happened?"

Jack looked at his friend with his one open eye. "I had to shut him up; it's as simple as that." He turned away and went out to the pump in the yard to wash himself off.

Will followed him. "You'd better put something cold on that eye," he said as he headed back into the inn. "It's going to be a real shiner."

Jack stayed out in the yard until he calmed down. He relived the moment when he smashed his fist into Asne's face. It felt good. He stuck his head under the pump again, no mean feat as he pulled the pump handle up and down.

He remembered why he had gone into the stables in the first place and went back to find a lever of some sort. Jed was back at his work but turned around when he heard Jack.

"Tha'd better watch tha back wi' them buggers. They'd as soon kill thee as not."

Jack acknowledged this sage advice with a nod, which didn't help his thumping head. He found the shaft of a spade and headed to his room, hoping not to bump into Will.

Ignoring his dripping clothes, Jack began to lever the heavy stone up, then manhandled it against the wall. A package lay in a shallow depression, scooped out for that purpose. He reached down to retrieve the bundle, his hands shaking. He felt exhausted from the effects of the fight and the effort required moving the stone. His eye throbbed. He must be getting soft now his army days were done.

The package, coated in soil but protected by a tightly woven wool cloth, housed a role of leather-covered parchment, undamaged; the sheep fat in the wool had kept out any soil or damp. He unrolled the parchment, the leather still supple.

Column after column, line after line, page after page of meticulously kept records lined the sheets. It would take time to go through it all to discover Master Ridley's affairs.

37

Meg gave her niece a hug before Annie departed on her rounds. They had agreed that sticking to the normal routine would provide the best chance of Annie learning something new. Today's plan was to visit Jenet and two other pregnant women. A mother whose one-year-old daughter had died—a common enough occurrence but nonetheless tragic—was also on the list. Then there was Master Stubbs, an old man with a persistent chest cough, and possibly Father John. They had been unable to come up with a health reason for visiting him but he might be able to help them regarding Tom Bagsworth.

After Annie left, Meg sat down with a bowl of bergamot infusion. Inhaling the aromatic steam, she contemplated the progress of her carefully-laid plans. She looked forward to meeting Will and Jack. According to Annie, they were steadfast young men. Her niece described Will as mature for his age, with amazing eyes, caring and considerate. Annie portrayed Jack as the opposite of Will; mischievous, impatient, wanting answers for everything—quite the contrast.

Although Meg Wistowe had become familiar with Steward Sneed since he arrived in the village, he was a difficult man to like. He projected a coldness that warned 'hands off', yet he appeared to do his job efficiently enough most of the time and she presumed Prior Gilbert must trust him; however, she did not care for Bailiff Crompton, nor his methods. There were never any complaints from the villagers so she supposed he stayed within the law, although she never did find out how Master Pickless came to have two broken legs. The story he had told her was unconvincing. As for Ridley, a man of appalling habits, she could not understand why the steward had not interceded. Having appealed to him on a number of occasions, as she was the one delivering the babies or mopping up after the miscarriages, he always had some reason why he should do nothing. His reasoning usually came back to the young women being more than willing to play. She knew her neighbours and some of their secrets but something was eating away at them. She could smell the fear.

Her plan to bring Annie here was working. Already her niece and the two young soldiers were beginning to dig deep, searching for the corrosion: for the blight affecting her community.

An immediate problem was the animosity between the two looka-like cats. Both smart familiars with powerful telepathic skills, they sat glaring at each other, neither eating nor drinking. As though they read her thoughts Rosamund yawned, stood and treated herself to a big stretch. Meg's cat, Bea, followed suit. They approached one another, circled around three times with tails pointing to the roof, and walked to the door. Meg smiled, shook her head, and opened the door for the feline familiars.

38

Jenet threw her arms around Annie. 'It's luvly to see thee!" she cried. They settled down for a chat. Jenet told her that the baby was fussing more than usual and seemed hungry, even after a feed.

"Have you decided what his name is," asked Annie.

"Thomas, after me dad," said Jenet firmly, and then burst into tears. "We've got to get 'im out of prison; everybody knows 'e didn't do it. T'trouble is 'e were off wi' fleeces t'coast when it 'appened, so who's goin' to tell?"

Annie realized she'd found her reason to visit Father John. She did not say anything to Jenet, but to calm her down, changed the subject and asked her if she had seen Jack or Will lately. Jenet sniffed a few times and then told Annie that Jack had called in to see her.

"Well, not me really, it were Mistress Davey, I suppose, but we 'ad a chat an' 'e coo'd wi' babby which were reight luvly t'see."

As Jenet was telling her story, a fetching blush bloomed on her face. Annie reckoned the attraction went both ways. However, it sounded as though Jenet's fretting was affecting her ability to produce breastmilk. Blessed Thistle and Goat's Rue infusions would help. Annie reminded the young mother to boil the water first. She said her goodbyes and moved on to her next visit.

Annie eventually completed her calls, having given out a variety of herbs and instructions on their use. The November day was drawing in. She breathed in a mingled aroma of wood smoke and autumn decay, as familiar to her here as at home in her century and for a moment she felt such a pang of homesickness it caught her breath.

Now she stood outside of Father John's cottage. Belatedly realizing it might be better if Meg had accompanied her, she stood there dithering when the door opened and a woman stared at her.

"Did tha want summat?" the woman asked.

Annie blushed. "I'm sorry, I couldn't decide whether to knock or not."

"If tha wants to see t'Father, you'll find 'im in t'church." After offering that abrupt comment, the woman firmly closed the door.

Annie made her way next door and stared at the big church door. Should she walk straight in or knock? Feeling awkward, not knowing the protocol for entering a church when there was no service, she knocked. Nothing happened. Tentatively pushing the heavy door open, she tiptoed through the porch and peered inside the nave. Light filtering in through the shutters allowed her to see all the way to the chancel. Staying close to the protection of the pillars, and moving slowly down the nave, she saw the figure of the priest prostrate on the floor before the stone altar, his arms held out to the sides forming a cross. Annie stopped: she had better wait until he had finished praying—or was he paying penance? She sank to the ground, making as little noise as possible.

The stone slabs offered no comfort against the cold. After what seemed like an eternity, she began to shiver. The priest rose from the floor with effort; he may have been disturbed by her chattering teeth, or perhaps he had finished.

He turned around and saw Annie crouched there.

"I know you! You are the cousin of the new innkeeper who came to see me. What do you want?"

Annie could hear no friendliness in his voice, and he showed no embarrassment at her seeing him prostrate before his God.

"I c-came t-to s-see you about the B-Bagsworth family. I have b-been looking after Jenet for my Aunt M-meg, Mistress Wistowe."

Father John's features softened. "You are freezing, child. Come with me into the house and sit before the hearth. I'll ask my housekeeper to make you a warm drink."

They sat by the fire. The same woman who had answered the door previously, placed a bowl of mulled wine into Annie's cold hands. Annie smiled her thanks but the woman's face remained blank. She left without speaking.

Father John asked what he could do to help. Annie explained how she had taken Mistress Bagsworth and her young son into York so she could visit her husband in jail and take him food. Jenet and her baby were staying with Mistress Davey and her son had promised to keep an eye on the house and the animals.

"It is so unnecessary. Jenet is worried sick about her dad, and missing her mam and brother. I am concerned her fretting is affecting her milk supply. A new mother needs to focus on her baby during the lying-in period to give the baby every chance to survive."

"I know of all that has happened," Father John sighed. "What do you expect of me?"

"Then you know Tom could not have killed the innkeeper," Annie paused and took a deep breath, "because he wasn't in the village during the time the innkeeper disappeared. He'd gone on the trip to the coast and I believe most of the villagers know that, so I am sure you know too." She stopped talking abruptly.

Father John ignored the reference to the smuggling. "Then who do you think killed Master Ridley?"

"I don't know. We have heard so many stories. Two men dragged him out waving swords. Three men dragged him out waving daggers. The attackers killed him in the kitchen. The devil was responsible. An angry father or son bashed his head in. Steward Sneed seems to be involved in this, maybe he did it."

"Child, you could get into serious trouble saying those things," admonished the Father. "Best you stay out of it."

Annie's stubborn Yorkshire temperament came to the fore.

"I need your help to get Tom released from jail. He is innocent; whoever else is guilty. Please help me. If you know of all the goings on in the village, you must know about the smuggling."

Silence met that remark. Annie heard a gasp from the next room; the housekeeper must be eavesdropping.

"My dear child," the priest began, "if I agree to keep this conversation within the sanctity of the confessional, I strongly suggest you repeat not one word of it outside this room, for your own safety."

Annie opened her mouth to protest. Father John raised his hands. "I will; however, promise to do what I can for Tom. I shall have to find someone who will vouch for him by saying he was with him during the time in question. I realize that may be an untruth but sometimes God works in mysterious ways. I promise to get a message to Prior Gilbert who might intercede for Tom in York.'

Annie left the church house feeling exhausted but triumphant. It was not until she reached home that she realized Father John had completely avoided the subject of smuggling.

39

Jack's head ached and his eye throbbed. He had remained shuttered in his room studying the cramped script in Ridley's wool records for more than an hour. He expected Will to have come bursting into the room asking if he had nothing better to do, but no, peace still reigned. Jack felt elated: he figured he had cracked the wool code.

Whoever recorded the information had been meticulous, and he presumed it to be the late innkeeper as the handwriting compared favourably to the other recent financial records belonging to the inn. Interestingly, three long columns flowed down the pages: one registered the number of smuggled sacks coming in from the various farms each time, with an equal number going out. The second column recorded the number of woolsacks pilfered by Ridley from the main tally. The amounts of money beside these numbers had grown impressively over the years and the second column accounted for money going straight into Ridley's coffers. The third column documented small amounts of coins debited from the filched woolsack column. It did not record who received these coins.

Ridley must have been paid twice; once for his role in the smuggling as organizer of the packing and transport of the fleeces, and once for appropriating a number of woolsacks for himself each time. Jack suspected Steward Sneed's fleece tallies would not match. If Sneed didn't take it upon himself to count each shipment of woolsacks, Ridley could give him any number he so desired and Sneed would be no wiser; an open invitation for knavery. These lists did not tell who was boss or where the rest of the money went. He hoped to find out more on his trip to the coast.

He went to the kitchen after changing his wet clothes and hiding the roles under the slab again. 'Call me Aggie' threw up her arms when she saw his face. He could see she already knew of the fight. The whole village probably knew by now, nothing could beat the speed of local gossip. To her credit, she asked no questions and made up a vinegar poultice for his eye as she told him that the gaffer had gone for a walk to the village.

40

Will had decided to take a break and visit Annie, maybe break the news gently that Jack had been in a fight with one of Bailiff Crompton's bullyboys. It wasn't the best excuse—truth to tell, he just wanted to see her. She was going to see Jack's black eye anyway, so better to be forewarned.

Knocking on the door of the cottage, his mind focused on his mission, Will did not notice *two* black cats watching him curiously from each side of the door. His jaw dropped when a strange woman came to the door. Will asked to speak to Annie, his mouth suddenly dry.

"You must be Will, please come in. I'm your Aunt Meg, don't you remember me?" Meg asked teasingly.

Will's mouth fell open, he knew he had invented their relationship impulsively, and now here she was, in the flesh. He gulped and offered a weak good morrow.

"Annie is out on her rounds, I don't know when she will be back. Ale?"

Will settled down with a mug of ale, Meg with something hot and fragrant. He looked with curiosity at this very real relative of Annie: Mistress Wistowe, the villagers had called her. He saw an older woman, still beautiful; clear grey eyes remarkably like Annie's with her hair covered under a swath of soft wool and a face reflecting calmness and intelligence.

"What worries you, Will?"

The question took Will by surprise; was this woman a witch that she could read him so easily?

"Why, nothing, well, almost nothing, well…" Then to his own surprise, Will surrendered his guard and revealed his dream of owning an inn, his gift of gold from King Henry, the challenges of running 'The King's Head', his attempts to find the murderer of Master Ridley, his growing attraction to her niece, Annie; the serious threats made against Annie by Steward Sneed and…

"…People think I do not know the inn is a centre for smuggling wool abroad. Of course, I do, I am not blind, nor am I deaf, but I have to stay loyal to my king; after all, he gave me the money to make a new life. I cannot cheat him."

Will hung his head in exhaustion. He had no idea why he had babbled on to this woman whom he had never seen before. He felt Mistress Wistowe's fingers under his chin as she gently lifted his head up to look into his eyes.

"No wonder you are anxious, you carry a lot of weight on your shoulders. As far as the smuggling is concerned, do not make it *your* concern. Although you say you are neither blind nor deaf, it may be to the good to be so. Smuggling will continue with or without you. I am pleased you are interested in finding out about what happened to Master Ridley. I suggest you treat your dealings with Steward Sneed cautiously. He holds much power and is not afraid to use it. I wonder why he has singled out my niece. She has done nothing that I am aware of to warrant such threats."

"I do believe the steward is intent on using the threats to Mistress Thornton to keep us in line. I mean, the accusation that she is a witch is ridiculous. There is no way he can prove it but he is a devious man."

Meg carefully placed her bowl on the table. "Now, your attraction to Annie *may* be a matter of some worry."

Will startled and felt even more apprehensive.

"You and my niece have just met. You don't really know each other yet. Annie came here from a different place and her stay here is only temporary; once her business is completed, she will be going back. In addition, I understand the villagers believe you to be cousins, so marriage is impossible. I see too many obstacles in your path. You'll do better to find yourself a local lass."

Will agreed he and Annie had just met but he couldn't get her out of his mind. He believed they were meant for each other. Of course, he had no idea how Annie felt about him…

At that moment Annie came through the door, removing her shawl and saying, "I need a chamomile infusion so badl—" She stopped abruptly when she saw Will. "—Will, what brings you here? Is something wrong? I swear I couldn't bear it if there is."

Will jumped up and held out his arms. Annie fell into them as though she belonged there. He guided her to his stool. She held his hand tightly as she shared the story of her visit with Father John.

"You took a huge risk," Will protested. "What if he's in league with the steward? Sneed will be after you with his charges of witchcraft!"

"Oh, so Sneed started that? I realize I took a risk, but my main concern is for the Bagsworth family. All of these men planning and plotting and poor Tom is rotting in jail and Jenet is fretting so much it is affecting her ability to feed her baby."

This young woman was made of more spirited stuff than the other young women he had known. The girls he knew in York had been softly spoken, biddable females.

"By the way," Will took a deep breath, "I thought you should know; Jack got into a bit of a scrap with one of the bailiff's bully-boys—"

"—Oh my God, is he alright," Annie leapt up.

"Jack's tough, but he will have a magnificent black eye."

"Tell your friend Jack I'll come and see him," said Meg. "I want to make his acquaintance anyway. I'll make a chamomile infusion for us and you can tell me all about your adventures in France."

When Meg bent toward the hearth to heat the water, Will and Annie turned and gazed into each other's eyes.

Will heard Mistress Wistowe's voice from a long way off.

"It *is* good news that Father John is going to do something, so maybe we will see Tom back here soon."
Her voice faded away.

41

Late November, Hallamby, Yorkshire, 2015

Mary heard the front door slam as she was halfway up the stairs. She and Jonathon had just had another big row. Well, not her really, just Jonathon. Same old stuff. She could still see his red, angry face.

"God damn it, Mary: I'm your husband but I never see you. You come home from work and disappear upstairs for hours. When's the last time we sat down to a meal together? If I have to live on any more of Sainsbury's warmed up dinners, I might as well be single. And as for sex—well, forget it—I have!"

She heard his words but they meant nothing.

"Jonathon, I can see that you are upset but I have to write this novel. It's more important than anything."

"More important than us? More important than our marriage? I get the message. Don't bother about dinner, not that you do anyway. I'm off to the pub."

Mary checked her reflection in the bathroom on her way to her little office. Her blond hair, which she meticulously kept styled in a short bob, looked more shaggy than chic. She traced the black rings under her eyes with a shaking finger. She stroked her cheekbones. She'd never noticed she had cheekbones before. Who was this woman in the mirror? Was this how writers were supposed to look? Striking a pose, Mary spoke to this new image; *can't be helped—a writer's gotta do what a writer's gotta do.* She laughed at her terrible attempt at an American accent and sat down at the laptop.

42

Late November, Hallamby, Yorkshire, 1415

Following Annie's visit, Father John asked Florrie to sit with him. Florrie put down her besom and carefully removed her pinny. She was a small woman with sharp, tired-looking features. Her thin, bowed shoulders carried the world's burdens. The lines carved into her face painted a picture of resignation. Florrie Ridley always expected the worst.

Florrie sat down, rubbing her dry, work-worn hands together. The sound grated on the ears of Father John who immediately felt a pang of remorse for his irritation. His hearth-mate had heard the conversation between John and Annie so did not require updating.

"Why did tha tell 'er tha would do somethin' for Tom Bagsworth; tha's puttin' us at risk?"

"It seems to me we are compounding one sin with another if we allow Tom and his family to be punished for something we know the man didn't do." John kept his voice gentle, well aware that Florrie's nervous disposition could quickly cause her to unravel. "Perhaps if I am able to get Tom released it will ease the burden we carry. I shall not involve the steward, but, as I told Annie, I will intercede with Prior Gilbert."

"T'Prior knows nowt about this mess wi' t'innkeeper, dus 'e? As far as every Tom, Dick, and 'Arry round 'ere know's, 'e's just disappeared."

"I did hear a rumour, quietly spoken, that some men found the body and took it to the Manor House."

"Load o' rubbish, "Florrie shook her head. "T'body's vanished."

"Where is the body, Florrie? Why are you so sure it has vanished?" Sometimes Florrie surprised him with her ability to know of events in the village even though she did not join in village activities; perhaps she had a point.

"It just meks sense, dunt it. We 'ad a body then we dint. Its niver bin seen since."

"We could say he has run away," Father John mused. "He didn't come from this village in the first place. He got himself into all sorts of trouble here and decided to leave. Steward Sneed presumed that Tom Bagsworth had something to do with his disappearance because of his daughter's pregnancy, but it is beyond doubt an error.

"Prior Gilbert does not know of you, Florrie, so you are not a factor and Ridley never did tell him you live with me because I continued to pay him for his silence. I would have had to go before the Church Court and maybe lose my living had he done so."

"We can move on, can't we, John, and put this be'ind us?"

He reached out and enclosed her hands in his two big ones, his earlier irritation forgotten.

"Oh yes, my dear, we promised to take care of each other, and we will continue to do so."

43

The days grew colder as winter nibbled at the edge of soggy November. Annie and her Aunt Meg had much to keep them busy. When nursing duties did not take their time, Meg schooled her niece on invocations, spellmaking, and chants as well as the use of herbs in both magic and medicine.

Annie had laughed when she first saw her neighbours wrapped in sheepskins but soon appreciated the warmth a sheepskin supplied. More and more she tended to chilblains created by the cold, along with chesty coughs and achy joints. A balm made from Adder's Tongue Fern cured chilblains and a concoction made from cowslips worked well as an expectorant. Annie shook her head in amazement comparing remedies from the different centuries.

The villagers still had to work outside in the frosty air, repairing the holes in the London to York road and cutting back the trees to prevent surprise attacks by robbers. Men who worked with blunt axes in cold weather regularly turned up on Mistress Wistowe's doorstep with gashes to arms and legs. Common Plantain, crushed and placed directly into the wounds, helped with healing.

As the village women toiled to preserve the harvest by pickling and drying, Mistress Wistowe's pantry filled up with the results of her and her niece's labour: payment for their nursing efforts.

Annie came home one day full of chatter about 'pig killing day'.

"Everybody is talking about it, Aunt Meg. It sounds as though this is a big event."

"Oh, it is. Pig killing happens at the end of every year and the villagers really look forward to it."

"It's a bit hard on the pigs, isn't it?"

"The pigs have had a good life rolling in mud and foraging for food on the waste ground and they spend the autumn fattening up on fallen acorns in the forest. It's too difficult to feed them all winter so they have to go. The meat they provide will keep bellies full 'till spring."

"Old Josiah told me he'd heard the pig slaughterer has reached Sutton, just south of us, so it won't be long before he comes here."

Meg paused; she was in the process of pouring ale into a barrel, about to make her year's supply of vinegar. "It's what comes after the pig killing that everyone enjoys even more."

"What's that?"

"The Great Pig Feast!"

* * *

Up at the inn, Jack was on tenterhooks waiting for word about the next trip. He and Will had settled into an uneventful routine. 'Call me Aggie' was busy preparing her pickles, vegetables soaked in brine and herbs. Will had butchered the old sheep he had bought and it lay salted in a barrel. Kegs of ale were satisfactorily full and brewing continued unabated by the silent brewster. The number of guests had slowed a little as the weather grew colder, but there were still enough hardy travelers to keep the innkeepers busy.

He anticipated the inevitable repercussions from his fight with Asne. Strangely, it was as though it had never happened, except for his colourful eye: more blues and purples than black. The inn staff must have known of the fight, as each of them would look quickly at his face then slide their gaze away. He kept the secrets of the wool smuggling records to himself and felt guilty about not sharing his discovery, as he suspected Ridley's account rolls might hold the answer to the dishonest innkeeper's death. He did not know how Will would react to absolute proof of the smuggling business happening under their noses. It was curious how quiet all that business with the innkeeper had become, and, where had the body gone? Perhaps someone buried it a little deeper this time, but why wouldn't they have buried it in the village graveyard? There were too many questions and no one appeared to be looking for the answers.

Poor Tom Bagsworth remained in jail in York for a murder lacking a body for evidence. How cold it must be in prison at this time of the year; a man could succumb to lung fever or the flux. Jack gave up thinking; it had begun to hurt his brain, unless he happened to be thinking about Jenet.

Will interrupted his musings when he came into their quarters. "Here's a visitor for you, Jack." He went back to the door and brought in Mistress Wistowe. "Meet my comrade-in-arms, Jack Fletcher. Jack, this is Annie's aunt, Mistress Wistowe. She's heard about your war wound and wishes to look at your eye."

Jack jumped up from his bed. He had heard about the newly arrived and existing—not imagined—aunt, from Will. His first impression was how much she resembled Annie: the same grey eyes.

"Good day, Jack. I am pleased to meet you. I have heard so much about you from Annie I feel I have known you for a while."

Mistress Wistowe took his face into her warm hands and looked closely at his colourful eye, gently lifting his eyelid.

"I've brought you some dried Eyebright. Have your cook make up an infusion using boiled water and put two drops into your eye at breakfast, dinner, and suppertime. Use a clean rag. Ask Will for help if needed. The whites of your eye are inflamed. This will soothe the tissues and aid healing."

Jack stared at her. She seemed so calm and organized. She might be a good person to have on their team.

"I am grateful, Mistress. We have a great affection for your niece. It behooves us to watch out for her, and to keep her safe in these times."

He saw a small smile appear on Mistress Wistowe's face. He could not discern its meaning. He shrugged. "Shall we go to the kitchen and take advantage of the quietness to enjoy some of our cook's cakes. She can perform wonders with honey and raisins. We will tell you of our adventures since arriving here—all so unexpected."

44

Father John kept his promise to Annie. He informed Steward Sneed that he intended to spend a few days in York on parish business and rode out on a horse borrowed from Hallamby Manor. He had ensured Florrie was feeling less anxious and could occupy herself with plenty of chores.

His first task was to discover where Prior Gilbert might be. He might be visiting any one of a number of manors, his family holding lands for both the King and the Church. When the founder of Kirkham Priory, Walter l'Espee, gave lands to the Augustinian Order in 1130 to build three monasteries, he included manors located in Yorkshire, Northumberland, and Lincolnshire. Father John reasoned Prior Gilbert was more likely to be in residence at Kirkham Priory, the head of the community. Once he arrived in York, he would enquire of the Minster clergy.

As his horse ambled along the hard-packed road, Father John ruminated on his village; it did not feel like it used to. Life was onerous for the peasants, living under the yoke of a powerful aristocracy. He did his best to ease their journey through life, not just with prayers but also with practical help: coins to pay for medicines from Mistress Wistowe, extra food bought from villagers with excess produce, warm wool cloth from York for villagers no longer able to spin and weave. It was becoming more difficult to offer aid to his parishioners latterly. When did it all start going wrong?

He remembered meeting Francis Sneed for the first time. The man came into his church for Vespers and lingered after the service. He approached the priest, asking if he knew of any employment in the area for an educated man. John wondered at the time why the man would not have gone to York; his chances would be better there. Prior Gilbert was desperately searching for a steward so he arranged for Sneed to see him. Sneed secured the position and had been there for—what—five years now. Ridley and Crompton appeared on the scene shortly after. Ridley had been a thorn in his side ever since. It seemed to him the atmosphere in the village had changed since their arrival.

Leaving these depressing thoughts behind, the priest enjoyed his ride to the great city. He rarely left the village, so it felt like an adventure. He enjoyed observing all the travellers and vendors, both coming and going. Different dialects and some foreign languages surrounded him: Italian definitely, and maybe Dutch. Cloth merchants from Europe often came to York on business. No sun broke through the heavy, grey clouds, but it was not raining, a blessing for which he thanked God.

Entering York through Micklegate Bar, Father John thrilled at the beauty and majesty of the entrance, although he averted his eyes from the head of Baron Scrope and muttered a prayer for the poor man's soul. The crowded streets of Micklegate and Lower Petergate slowed his progress but he was content to let his placid horse take him ever closer to York Minster, an easy route to follow, as the soaring spires were visible at each turn.

Father John had spent time in York when he was receiving his church schooling but had forgotten how noisy and busy York could be. The cries of the vendors competed with each other in the marketplace, their voices carrying over the rooftops. Children in rags and with dirty faces darted here and there, holding out their hands for coins, and risking injury under his horse's hooves. Dogs slunk along the edges of the buildings looking for scraps or fighting over a rotting morsel. Wagons loaded with produce rumbled past him, either bringing goods into the city or taking them out.

The priest sought the city within the city, the Liberty of Saint Peter. The walls around the Liberty were twelve feet high. Entering by one of the four guarded gates his immediate sensation was of relief. The sense of harmony and orderliness almost overwhelmed him after the noise and chaos outside of the walls. A grassed and cobbled precinct lay inside. This walled city belonged to the Church and had its own laws, court and prison. The area contained the Archbishop of York's sprawling palace with its cloisters, hall and chapel.

As a village priest, John was far too low in the ranks to deal with the princes of Holy Mother Church; he looked for the general office where he might find another lowly cleric. Eventually, he succeeded in finding the building, after asking directions from some tonsured monks.

A scribe, busily writing in a small alcove, ignored his question as to where he might find Prior Gilbert. After repeating his question in a firmer and louder voice, the scribe tutted at being disturbed, saying he had better things to do than chase around for any Tom, Dick or... A steely glare from Father John dried up his muttering and he departed to make enquiries. He returned after a few minutes.

"E's at 'is Priory at Kirkham."

Curfew loomed so John asked the cleric where he might rest for the night. The cleric, more amiably this time, directed him to a dormitory for transient clerics, with adjacent stabling for his tired horse. He ate bread and cheese in the empty refectory, washed down with a watery red wine, and returned to the long dormitory with beds situated down both sides. Surprisingly, most were occupied by snoring bodies; it seemed people were always on the move. Despite the chorus of snores, the Father slept well and retained no memory of the calls for prayer at Matins and Lauds.

Dawn had not arrived when Father John left York via Monk Bar: newly-built and the largest and most ornate defensive entrance to York. As he passed through the raised portcullis, he called a greeting to the guards standing there.

One guard responded with a cheerful wave. "Watch tha back goin' through t'forest, Father; there's sum bloody big wolves in there."

The road led northeast to Kirkham Priory, half a day's ride away. Mother Nature treated the traveller to a beautiful sunrise of reds and golds as the sun rose over the horizon, but before long, the usual grey clouds moved in and darkened the day. He prayed the colourful sunrise didn't warn of poor weather ahead. An oft-proved saying: 'Red sky at night; shepherd's delight. Red sky at morning: shepherd's warning' came to mind.

The ride through the Royal Forest of Galtres proved uneventful: he ran into neither wolves nor hunting parties. No pigs crossed his path feeding on acorns, their owners having been granted the right of pannage—the practise of releasing pigs into the forest to eat fallen nuts.

Whenever the priest reflected back on that trip, he remembered the moment the sun reappeared. The heavy bank of clouds moved on just as he neared the Priory. The site of Kirkham Priory was stunning: the planners had chosen well. The buildings rose on a sloping plateau next to the River Derwent, surrounded by orchards, gardens, and, down by the river, mills. On both sides of the river, the wooded green hills created a natural amphitheatre for the Priory. The sun's suddenly emerging rays bathed the mellow stone buildings with a golden glow. The heavens were gracing the Priory with a benediction.

When traversing an impressively three-arched stone bridge across the Derwent, his horse's hooves clattered on the wooden planks, disturbing the tranquillity of the setting. A small stone cross was located on the other side of the bridge, left of an imposing stone gateway. Father John dismounted stiffly, standing before the cross and offering grateful thanks for his safe arrival.

The arching gateway to Kirkham Priory stood two stories high, its façade covered with intricate carvings and sculptures. Sculptures of Saint George and the Dragon were carved on the left and David and Goliath on the right. Above the sculptures, he recognized the Arms of previous benefactors, amongst them the founder of the Priory, Walter L'Espee and, later, the de Ros family. Both families had strong links with Helmsley Castle, a few miles away. Father John scratched his almost bald pate; Prior Gilbert had connections to the de Ros family, a source of power and influence that might facilitate the release of Tom Bagsworth from gaol.

Rumours floated around the corridors of Mother Church of Kirkham Priory being in debt and having to struggle to maintain its full number of canons but Father John could see no signs of poverty, on the contrary; a sense of lushness, of completeness, surrounded the whole area.

A monk laboured just inside the gateway, scraping lichens off the north side, his black scapular protecting his undyed wool tunic, hitched up to allow freedom of movement. The monk's muscular legs boasted skin the colour of chestnuts from a summer spent outdoors. John asked to see Prior Gilbert. The man unhitched his robe and, without speaking, led him through a vaulted archway into the cloisters. When John opened his mouth to comment on the architecture, the monk placed his forefinger against his mouth and shook his head—no talking in the cloisters.

The walls of the rectangular covered walkway consisted of a series of graceful arches looking out onto a central garden. To the west of the cloisters, the walls of the church acted as a link to both the church and other buildings, such as the library, the refectory and kitchens, and the domiciliary areas for the monks. John looked with interest at the formal layout of the garden, sheltered and on the south side of the building. Plants were still flourishing and the well-ordered beds displayed a variety of vegetables and herbs, each raised bed bordered with low hedges of Box. Two monks worked there on their knees, their hands deep in the soil. Another archway led them into a beautifully decorated Chapter House where they found Prior Gilbert examining the impressive tiled floor with another man, bearded and dressed in black: one of the canons, he presumed. Prior Gilbert immediately recognized Father John and held out his ringed hand for a reverential kiss.

Prior Gilbert turned to the man in black robes, "Canon Hugh, this is Father John, priest of the village of Hallamby: as you know, one of our endowment manors. Why have you come all this way, Father?" He then gestured to the monk who brought the Father. "Brother Simon, be so good as to fetch the Father some ale to refresh him. Please, Father, do sit with me. Is there something amiss in Hallamby that has caused you to travel so far?"

Father John relaxed at the warm welcome and the perceptive question, although he knew of Prior Gilbert's reputation as a fair and considerate prelate. He had not seen Prior Gilbert for a long time and felt sad to see new signs of aging: his hair now fully white, although, unlike his own sparse locks, the Prior still had a thick, wiry crop ringing his shaved head and matching his bushy eyebrows. His bearing remained upright and his eyes sharp. He resembled a humble monk in his undyed wool tunic, unreflective of his high status.

"You are correct, my lord. A ticklish situation has developed. I trust you remember a Master Ridley, innkeeper at 'The King's Head.'"

"I do, vaguely. I believe he attended a supper one time at the Manor House. He seemed a surly man for an innkeeper, perhaps more suited to be a gatekeeper." The Prior smiled at his own joke.

"Well, he has disappeared. He was not a good man, my Lord, I hate to speak ill of the d—, anyone, but he did not treat his servants well and over time became responsible for some of the young girls' pregnancies. When he disappeared, Steward Sneed found a witness who stated one of the villagers had killed him, a man called Tom Bagsworth. He came under suspicion as his only daughter was one of the young women with child."

Prior Gilbert shook his head sadly.

Father John continued, "Tom has been confined and taken to jail in York where he has since languished. It is now thought that Master Ridley has left the village, the villagers being disturbed by his behaviour."

"Has there been any sign of him?"

"None, my Lord, and a villager swore to me that he and Tom were working together outside of the village during the time the innkeeper disappeared. I know this villager and I know Tom. I believe them both to be good and honest men. I am here to ask if you can use your influence to have Tom released and returned home. His family is completely disrupted by this and his daughter, having had her baby, is distraught, to the point where she is having difficulty nourishing her child."

"I am perplexed as to how such a situation could have continued with no recourse to the law. Did Steward Sneed not know of this man's reprehensible behaviour?"

Father John considered his answer most carefully.

"Steward Sneed has many responsibilities and relies on his bailiff to keep the peace. I, too, found myself frustrated with the lack of action on the part of the bailiff."

"I will make enquiries and see what I can do. Thank you for bringing this matter to my attention. I trust your judgement in this. You do realize that this is not a Church matter, but is business for the Assize Courts; however, I may have some influence."

Prior Gilbert called to Father John's monk guide and asked him to give Father John a pot of honey and a round of cheese for Steward Sneed with his compliments. He invited Father John to seek repast in the monks' refectory and bid the Father good day.

Father John followed his silent guide to the refectory. His heart swelled at the kind reception from the august Prior. He would have liked to spend time in the Priory church thanking God for his blessings on this undertaking but the day was rapidly moving on and he was a long way from home.

Through gestures, the monk invited him to wash his hands at the decorative yet functional lavatorium outside of the refectory before eating. The basins sat beneath a graceful stone arcade. Running water from the River Derwent arrived at the lavatorium through lead pipes and elegant bronze taps.

They returned to the cloister and entered the dining area under a finely sculptured Romanesque arch, the stone carved with geometric shapes and ferocious heads. Father John blinked reflexively at the light reflecting from the whitewashed walls of the refectory; a contrast from the previous grey stone walls. The monk indicated he should sit at the long, rough-hewn oak table occupying the centre, and, leaving the Father to gaze around the room, went out to the kitchen, bringing back a platter of bread still warm from the oven and a wedge of ewe's milk cheese. A wooden bowl of apples sat between the two men.

"They're Pearmain and Costard, from our own trees." The previously silent monk, taking advantage of his escape from his physical work, proved himself as talkative as the women in Hallamby village.

"The pear shaped one is the Pearmain and the ribbed one is the Costard. Both are sweet varieties. I am Brother Simon. I prune the trees. Enjoy. You asked me earlier about this building but we obey the silence rule when in the cloisters. Are you aware of the history of Kirkham?"

Having found a receptive audience, Brother Simon proceeded to share three hundred years of history and Father John found his eyes glazing over as his early start that morning caught up with him. He finally had to interrupt the verbal flow in order to be able to return home before dark. He did find out that Kirkham had strong ties with the larger Rievaulx Abbey, albeit a Cistercian Order, not Augustinian.

After thanking Brother Simon for his hospitality, the priest found his way to the stable and saddled his rested and fed horse; feeling rested and well fed himself. Placing the gifted cheese and honey in his saddlebag, he climbed into the saddle, and turned the horse's head toward Hallamby by way of the River Derwent. As the weak November sun continued its passage westward across the sky, the birds began their evensong. The waters of the Derwent gurgled and burbled their way south to join the imposing River Ouse, and Father John joined in the chorus humming pieces of 'Agnus Dei', feeling more optimistic about the future.

45

Jack's mind teased him constantly about Ridley's moneymaking schemes. If Ridley's lists were to be believed, he had been accumulating an impressive amount of money over the years. So, where was it? Where had he hidden it? Again, he examined their private quarters; surely, it was hiding under another flagstone, but he could see no irregularities; he had gone on his hands and knees and tapped every one. He wracked his brain for other sites but none came to mind. The wily innkeeper would be reluctant to have the cache too far from his person. He resolved to keep his eyes peeled.

Other matters teased his brain.

Not telling Will about finding the smuggling accounts worried him, yet he knew Will chose to ignore the glaring fact that the inn was a centre for wool smuggling. He had been thinking deeply about what Will had said about Jenet—her not being at fault for being left with a bairn to raise on her own. He realized he had not known the young woman long but he was attracted to her, and deep down, he wanted a home and a family to replace the one he had lost.

After mulling things over, he decided to go find Will and talk to him about Jenet, information about the smuggling account could wait.

Jack found his friend in the stables, inspecting the stalls. Having passed young Jed out in the courtyard, he had Will to himself.

"What would you say if I said I was going to ask Jenet to become betrothed to me?" Jack looked earnestly at Will. "Would you think me rash—or worse—stupid?"

Will wrapped his arm around his friend's shoulder. "I honestly can't think of a better thing for you to do. As I said before, she seems a good lass and I know you miss your family. Looks like you might have a ready-made one there."

With a light heart, Jack planned to make a trip into the village once he had completed his morning chores and ask Jenet to be his betrothed. First, he wanted to go into the kitchen to entice some dried fruits out of 'call me Aggie' as a gift for his soon-to-be sweetheart—or so he hoped.

Jenet greeted him at Mistress Davies' cottage with a cry of alarm. Jack was startled—he had forgotten about his black eye. Despite his explanation of walking into a door, Jenet's look told him the story of the fight had reached her. She insisted on heating some water and tenderly bathing his eye. Even though Mistress Davey stood behind them, fussing and making sympathetic noises, it seemed only natural that the young couple's heads came closer and closer together, until their noses were almost touching.

A cough from Mistress Davies shot them apart.

Jack cleared his throat. "Mistress Davies, I am asking you to stand in for Master and Mistress Bagshaw today. I have a question to ask Mistress Jenet."

Woman and girl stared at Jack with big eyes.

Jack cleared his throat, grasped Jenet's hand, and in a firm voice said, "Mistress Jenet, will you become my betrothed?"

Jenet burst into tears. Mistress Davies burst into tears, and right on cue, baby Thomas woke up and called imperiously for his dinner.

When all the crying ceased and baby Thomas was in his rightful place at his mother's breast, Jenet shyly said yes.

When Jack eventually said his goodbyes, Mistress Davey told him he had become a hero in the village, having stood up to the village bully. The newly betrothed Jack floated home: he swore his feet never touched the ground.

As soon as Jack returned he looked for Will to share his good fortune. Will appeared delighted for his friend and shared *his* good news about Annie.

"I didn't tell you this before but Annie and I are in love and plan to marry but there is a problem. I know our love is sudden too. Maybe all this is happening because you and I are sick of roaming and want to settle down. There are a few difficulties for Annie and me, though. Mistress Wistowe has warned that Annie will be going back from whence she came. I do not know where that is unless it is York. Either way, I *will* be with her. Do not share this with anyone, even Jenet. The whole village thinks we're cousins and it's too complicated to change that story."

"What shall we do about the inn if you go away?" Jack looked worried. "I was hoping running the inn with you would provide the means of supporting my new family."

"We'll work something out. Whatever happens, I'll make sure my mate Jack is taken care of."

Jack felt a twinge of guilt about not sharing the information about the smuggling records. Then he decided once again that Will was better off not knowing. They both headed to the kitchen to celebrate with tankards of ale. They would use the pewter as benefiting a celebration of love.

"So what do you know about pig killing and the Pig Feast, Aggie?"

Jack perched on the corner of the boards, drinking his ale from his fancy pewter tankard. 'Call me Aggie' swatted him off.

"A pig slaughterer travels around t'villages and does t'job for pay. Most of t'village turns out to 'elp, men doin' cuttin', women cleanin' up an' keepin' 'em all fed. Pigs are 'ung and drained, an' blood's used in blood pudding and sausages. Most of meat is packed in salt. Sum fresh meat is saved for t'Great Pig Feast. That's 'eld at Manor House, usually, and we all go. It's a reight dress up time, Sunday Best, and all that. Owt else tha wants to know?"

"I think you covered everything," Jack replied, laughing. "Do you think it might be a good time to have a wedding?"

"Call me Aggie" gave a whoop of delight. "Thy weddin'?"

"Aye, Jenet Bagsworth and me."

"A bit sudden, but not a bad idea; that baby needs a dad. T'would be good if Tom Bagsworth and 'is wife are there to see their lass wed." Jack sobered. "Aye, we have to hope that Tom will be released."

46

Father John returned home, weary, but content. He had done his best in difficult circumstances, even though he may have put himself at risk. The following day would do to take Prior Gilbert's gifts to the Manor House. He had returned the horse to the Manor stables and now he could sit back and enjoy Florrie's pottage and a goblet of good French wine.

The next morning, just before Sext, Father John made his way to the Manor House bearing the cheese and honey. Matilda let him in and went to find Steward Sneed.

"Did you complete your business in York?" asked Sneed as he came toward Father John.

"I did, Steward."

"Does the business concern Hallamby Manor?"

"I petitioned Prior Gilbert regarding the release of Tom Bagsworth. He sent you these gifts, with his blessing, by the way."

A heavy silence descended. Steward Sneed ignored the gifts and stared at the Father.

"You did what?"

"I believe Tom Bagsworth is suffering in jail for no reason. I know, unequivocally, that he was away from the village the night that Ridley disappeared." He did not add—*and so do you.*

"But we have witnesses who swore they saw him coming from the inn dragging Ridley to his death. Besides, what right do you have to interfere? You should have checked with me first. What did the Prior have to say? I hoped we could spare him the anguish of knowing there had been a murder."

Steward Sneed's face resembled an overripe, purple plum threatening to burst its skin.

"Please calm yourself, Steward. How can there have been a murder, I know of no body, do you? We heard many different versions of what had happened. I informed Prior Gilbert that Ridley has disappeared and he has probably gone back to his old haunts knowing how upset and angry people are with him. I am sure you and I wish to save the Prior the trouble investigating the matter when he may find other things to be concerned about."

Father John looked meaningfully at the steward. Sneed calmed a little and his complexion became less plum-like.

"I reiterate there is no body: ergo, there is no murder. So I imagine your witnesses were in their cups and invented the whole story for attention or excitement, or," the priest paused, "a reward; and Ridley did, in fact, leave the area."

"I do insist that you should have consulted me first; however, it appears there is no damage done and you may have done well for the village, after all. How did the Prior respond?"

"He has agreed to make enquiries about a possible release."

"Excellent!" Sneed rubbed his hands together. "Now let us enjoy a robust burgundy and a piece of this excellent cheese. We will take this opportunity to discuss the arrangements for the upcoming pig feast. I understand the pig slaughterer will arrive soon."

47

The word came to Jack via young Cissie.

"Tonight!"

Jack needed to concoct a story for Will about having to go away for a few days, but right now he could not think of one. He could say he had to go to York, but Will would expect him to go and see his parents, Master and Mistress Boucher. As soon as he had that thought a sense of loss over his parents' deaths hit him—the pain never eased. His parents and younger sister had died when a wave of Cholera swept through York. He and Will had left for France shortly thereafter.

Where else would he want or need to go? Nothing came to mind. He would have to tell the truth. He asked Will to meet him in their room before Sext, the quietest time of day as the previous night's guests had departed and the new ones had not yet arrived. Will entered the room with a concerned look on his face.

"What's wrong?"

"I have to go away for a few days on business."

"What sort of business?"

"Wool business."

"Stay safe," was the terse response. No further questions were proffered and Will turned and left the room. Jack sat on his mattress, baffled. Then the answer came to him. Will continued to be deaf and blind regarding the wool business. So be it.

He leaped off the mattress and began to make preparations. His gear soon piled up: wool shirts, his leather jerkin, a waxed cape for wet weather, a hood, and his best strong leather boots. The Yorkshire

Moors could be bitterly cold as there were no obstacles to stop the wind from howling across the whole expanse; only stunted trees and gorse bushes grew above the ground.

The rest of the day passed agonizingly slowly. The first sign of activity would be the arrival of Dick with his cart piled high with bags of wool, so he was on high alert for the sound of horses' hooves and cartwheels. Meanwhile, he completed his usual duties at the inn and managed a sprint into the village to see Jenet and tell her he would be away for a few days. Jack then spent time in the kitchen, surreptitiously gathering food for his journey, but observed by 'call me Aggie' with a knowing smile on her face. Will stayed out of his way so no further conversation ensued, which suited Jack.

At last, the clip-clop of hooves on the cobblestones and the rumble of iron cartwheels. The guests were in the hall having their evening meal. The about-to-be-smuggler picked up his belongings and made his way to the back of the inn where he found Dick leaning against his cart, talking to his hard working horse, Harry. Sam and Red Rob were already unloading the large rolled bags and transporting them into the small room.

"How's tha doin'?" Dick looked at Jack's face. 'Nice eye, by t'way. Walk into a door, did tha? I 'ear tha's goin' t'coast with this lot. Won't be easy."

"I'm not used to easy. I was a soldier, remember."

Jack gave Harry a good scratch on his nose and went into the packing room. Three different women were there from the previous time and had already started on the stuffing and sewing up of the woolsacks. The woman sewing the sacks closed looked up at Jack as he came in.

"Does tha want t'same number of sacks as Master Ridley 'ad?" Jack tensed. She must mean Ridley's filched sacks.

"How do you tell them apart?"

"Ee lad, it's easy, I just use a different coloured twine for 'is sacks."

"Clever," Jack acknowledged. "However, I won't be following the same system as Master Ridley, so you don't need to use a different thread."

The women looked at one another with raised eyebrows; whether his decision met with their approval or not, he couldn't tell.

Jack watched in fascination as the bags came in, the women quickly removing the rolled fleeces from their original wrappings and repacking them into woolsacks. One of the women explained to the novice that they did this so the woolsacks met the standard required by the continental market.

"They pay what's due accordin' to size: a woolsack's a woolsack anywhere."

After what seemed to be an interminable length of time during which he had nothing to do and no one volunteered any more information, Jack once again heard the sound of hooves clattering outside. He eagerly went out to see. A line of eight horses, all bays, with sturdy short legs and muscular bodies stood next to Dick's cart. He had seen them previously in the Manor House pasture. Dick was still outside keeping an eye on them and told Jack they were known as Chapman horses because travelling merchants known as 'chapmen' preferred them to other packhorses. The monasteries and abbeys in Yorkshire had bred them. They were valued for their hardiness and calm temperament.

Sam and Rob came over to the cart and Sam slapped Jack on the back.

"This is it then, tha first job. Is tha up for it?"

Jack took a moment to study both men. He wanted to get the measure of them as he may well be putting his life into their hands. Uncommonly, Sam looked almost as tall as he did: Yorkshire men tended to be short and stocky rather than tall. Sharp blue eyes gazed back at him. A light brown straggly beard and mustache adorned his lower features and his hair hung to the collar of his leather jerkin. His shoulders were broad enough: he would handle the horses and the contraband easily, but he would be a tough man to cross. Jack shifted his gaze to Rob, the younger of the two smugglers. The nickname 'Red Rob' described him perfectly. Here stood a man made for laughing and joking. Freckles covered his open countenance. A shock of wiry red hair topped red bushy eyebrows and his bright green eyes sparkled with mischief. Rob was a head shorter than his mate was but still had the look of a man who could carry his share of the load.

"I believe I am, and looking forward to it too," Jack answered.

Sam looked derisively at Jack's face. "Next time tha picks a fight, mek sure tha's got back up." He snorted and turned to talk to Dick.

The horses were evenly loaded with woolsacks and supplies for the journey and the three men hoisted their backpacks and waved goodbye to Dick. They were off. The Compline bell chimed as they left the village heading north with Sam in front, Jack in the middle of the horses and Rob bringing up the rear. Rob had explained to Jack that they would follow the River Derwent all the way to a village called Pickering: the entryway to the moors. By using that route, they would avoid passing near York, with much less chance of detection.

"Tha'll be used to long marches then, 'avin' been a soldier?" Sam called from the front.

"Aye, and on an empty belly," Jack responded. "Sometimes we'd be a long way ahead of the supply wagons. I've eaten many a raw turnip. They don't settle well."

"We'll be alreight for grub on this trip," Red Rob called from the back of the line. "An' they treat us reight well at t'coast—if tha likes fish, that is."

Silence reigned. Jack's earlier sense of excitement lessened as he settled into the rhythm of the march. He was thoroughly enjoying himself and reminded himself of the reason he'd volunteered to do this—for information—not just to have fun.

48

While Jack embarked on his new adventure, Annie planned for the next day. She wanted to visit Father John to find out if he thought the release of Tom Bagsworth might be imminent. She had to see Jenet as she still had concerns about her breastmilk supply. She would visit Father John and then Jenet, just in case she could take good news for the new mother.

That same evening Annie and Meg sat by the hearth fire in the gathering gloom and had a serious talk about what the future might hold for her and Will. Meg listed the three obvious options: the romance did not progress and Annie would go home alone; Annie stayed in the fifteenth century and married Will; Annie went home and Will accompanied her.

"Well, the first is out of the question, and are the second and third viable options?" asked Annie.

"I don't see why not. Many people are living in different times from their own. We live in parallel universes. Consider how much the world around you matters. You often mention the lack of, what do you call it—'running water', and a strange word—antibotix."

"It's 'antibiotics' Aunt Meg, and you wouldn't believe what they can do for some of the severe infections we see around here. I agree; it is frustrating when I know there are cures in the future for some of the problems we encounter here. I *can* see into the future because I am from the future. If I didn't know these things then it wouldn't be a concern.

"By the way, I keep meaning to ask you. When I was at the Bagshaws for Jenet's birth, her mother asked me to hear her daughter's confession. I had no idea what she meant. I'm a midwife, not a priest."

"Ah," Meg nodded. "So many women die in childbirth, we midwives have the right to hear their confession before they go into heavy labour. And, sadly, because so many babies die at birth we have the right to baptise them so they do not enter limbo, according to the doctrine of the Church."

Annie stared at her aunt in dismay. "I'll show you some of the techniques we use in my world; maybe you will save a few more lives."

"Time travel provides some interesting dilemmas," her aunt sighed. "It's like having an extra skill similar to our ability as witches: some of your knowledge brought from the future can be used here and some is inappropriate or just not possible."

"Have you travelled through time, Aunt Meg?"

"Many times, my sweet. I would never have risked bringing you here if I hadn't tried myself."

"So tell me where you've been." Annie leaned forward, her eyes sparkling with interest and her preoccupation with her future momentarily forgotten. Rosamund jumped on her knee, as though, she too wanted to hear. Her friend, Bea lay curled up at the feet of her mistress, the smug look on her face saying, "I was there too."

"I have a dear friend living in York—I should say Jorvik—during the time of the Danelaw: that's in the year of our Lord nine hundred and something. She married a Viking who became a fisherman when his pirating days ended."

"I know of Jorvik," Annie exclaimed. "Excavations were being done in York a few years ago, around Coppergate, for a new shopping centre or something. They found all sorts of remains of a Viking settlement. It's a popular tourist place now. Where else have you been?"

"I've travelled as far back as the time of the Roman occupation of Britain—I have friends there— and to ancient Greece—and that's enough of all that for now." Meg rose and stretched her back. "I'll heat some water. The curfew is almost upon us, we'll enjoy a chamomile infusion before bed."

The two women stared into the charcoal embers of the fire as they sipped their drinks.

"I still don't know what to do," Annie murmured, breathing in the aroma of chamomile. "And I do still feel anxious about how and when

I go home. I can't imagine being away from Will—and what about my parents and my job. They must be missing me by now."

"When we tangle with time a remarkable transpiration takes place. You'll find, on returning to your century, time has shrunk: a week is as a day, a month is as a week. Time is always illusory, fleeting as a starburst or dragging as though anchored to a rock. You won't have been away as long as you think."

As Annie lay on the straw mattress beside an already sleeping Meg, Rosamund came and sat beside her. The cat stared into Annie's sleepy eyes and began to purr. Rosamund's rhythmic purring sent Annie into a deep theta state; her eyes closed and her breathing deepened. An image of her friend, Mary, in the twenty-first century, appeared in front of her. Mary looked pale with deep, black shadows under her eyes. Her face, normally round, looked full of sharp edges. She was muttering to herself.

"... *I have to bring Annie back. She belongs here. She is my friend. She has no business being with Will. I have to make this happen. I have the power. I'll write it down and it will happen...I have no time to waste on them falling in love. I have too many people in the village to care for...*

Annie sat up abruptly, dislodging Rosamund. Her aunt rolled over, muttering and pulling the shared blanket over her head.

"Oh, Rosamund, what have I done. I feel terrible. Here I am absorbed in this village and its people and I forgot about Mary. That spell I was attempting must have affected her. She looks awful; she's lost weight and she's rambling. I have to do something. First thing in the morning I'll talk to my aunt.'

It took a long time to fall asleep again; Mary's face haunted her. Then she dreamed she and her friend were wrestling. Will was there and tried to pull the two women apart but they rolled away from him and went over a cliff!

She awoke yelling, soaked in sweat and exhausted. Her eyes were grainy black holes.

When Annie shared her vision of the previous evening with her concerned aunt, Aunt Meg shook her head. "I was worried when you told me you were in the process of casting a creativity spell before you arrived here. You see, I had done the same."

Annie stared at her aunt. "What, you had also cast a creativity spell for Mary?"

"That's what I'm telling you. It was all part of my plan of bringing you here to solve the village problems and I thought your friend could write the story. It would give her some practice: help her to get started. She wouldn't need her imagination because the story would be fed to her. Unfortunately, I didn't know you were planning something similar. I believe she has received a twofold measure if you see what I mean. No wonder she is falling apart. She has become obsessed. She believes she is controlling events here. We must help the poor girl."

Meg heated some water so Annie could wash the sweat off her body and steeped some mint for an infusion.

When they were feeling refreshed, Aunt Meg suggested they communicate with Mary immediately.

"I know what to do. Follow my lead and note how gentle the vibrations will be. We don't have to rattle the walls." Meg smiled to soften the comment.

Meg called Bea to her and the four of them sat in a circle: cat, woman, cat, and woman. Each woman placed her right hand gently on the head of her familiar and her left hand on the other familiar so their hands touched, closing the circle. The cats began purring and Meg and Annie hummed in harmony. The sound became louder, filling all corners of the room, creating gentle vibrations. Air in the centre of the circle shimmered with light and moved like the ripples on a pond when caressed by a gentle wind. Filaments formed, glowing and waving in the energy field. The threads merged, then separated. Mary's face appeared and then fragmented. The image slowly strengthened and became solid.

Annie spoke. "Mary, this is Annie, can you hear my voice? Can you see my face?"

Mary looked startled and then frightened.

"Please don't be afraid, Mary, you know I'm your friend and I want to help you."

Mary's eyes widened, her breathing became rapid, and she swallowed convulsively. Annie needed to calm her. How could she explain this strange method of communication?

"Think of this as being like skyping, even though we live in different worlds we can see and speak to one another."

On hearing these words, Mary took a deep breath and nodded her head. "Annie, where are you? What's happening? I don't understand anything. I thought you might have gone off to the coast for a few days and anticipated a postcard at some point but seeing you in such a weird way proves there is some hocus pocus going on. Even as I write about you, I have no way of knowing if any of it is true or something I've dreamed. Have you put a spell on me? I don't understand this witchy stuff, but I am going crazy here. Jonathon is threatening to leave me. I can't sleep or eat. All I know is I'm compelled to write this story and keep everyone safe, especially you and the little baby, and, of course, Will."

Mary began to sob, making a keening sound, tears rolling down her face. On witnessing her friend's pain Annie thought her own heart would break. What had she generated through her meddling? How could she make things better?

"I decided to help you with your writing career by trying a creativity spell. I hoped to kick-start your imagination but I didn't plan to be in your story, nor did I anticipate such a powerful spell. I have a problem with overdoing spells. I haven't told you I'm a witch because I'm not sure what I'm doing most of the time. I didn't think you would understand.

"When Rosamund and I travelled back in time so abruptly, I thought I had messed up the spell but it turns out my aunt who lives in the fifteenth century sent for me. She is also a midwife and healer and is teaching me witchcraft—but you know all of this because you are writing it down—I can see it gets confusing. You don't have to take on the burden of responsibility for the actions of the people in your story. This is real life; it's not fiction. Your task is to write it down and the result will be a novel for you."

Mary became calmer but looked mystified. "So you're saying Will, Jack, and Sneed live in a real world in the fifteenth century and I didn't create them and I can't decide what they say and do? I thought I had become a writer. Do you mean you're putting the words into my head by some weird magic means and I'm just writing them down—like a secretary?"

"Well, not quite as you describe—"

"But I want to be a writer, not a secretary. I'm not happy about this at all."

Meg joined in the conversation.

"Hello, Mary. I am Annie's Aunt Meg. Annie is correct in what she is telling you. Your story is taking place right now in my century. We have created a way for you to record Annie's adventures: look at it as a great opportunity to develop your writing skills. Annie and I had a communication problem (Annie raised her eyebrows at her aunt); as a result, you are under the influence of some powerful magic which is making you feel compelled to write *and* to control events. I realize how crazy this all sounds but it is fixable. Can you see my face?"

Mary nodded but did not appear convinced nor appeased by what she had heard.

"Look into my eyes and listen carefully. I suggest you make an infusion of chamomile, drink it slowly, and then have a long sleep. When you wake up you will feel much better. Give your husband a hug and do not write anything for two days. You will know what to write when the time comes. The story will continue to unfold."

Mary's face faded from view along with the light. Meg explained she had added a little spell to help the chamomile infusion work most effectively. "All will be well," she reassured her niece with a smile.

49

A half-moon provided enough illumination for the men and horses to make their way along a well-used path beside the Derwent River in the Vale of York, an area of flat, fertile farmland.

Although Rob had started the journey with a constant chatter, pointing out different landmarks, silence now prevailed; only the muted sounds of the horses' hooves moving along the hard-packed trail provided a soothing rhythm.

Jack relished the quiet. He was contemplating how to ask the questions to get the answers he wanted. Who in the village gave the orders regarding the smuggling? Someone had to organize the movement of the fleeces from the surrounding area. How did they connect with the ship that took the goods to France and brought the wine back? Where did the profits go? Who was getting rich?

When the smugglers came to a stone bridge across the Derwent, Rob called out the name of the small village on the other side.

"This is Stanford Bridge. Lots of stories passed down about a big battle 'ere wi' Vikings an' King Harold years ago."

"I learned about it in school," responded Jack. "I even remember the date, the most famous date in our history: 1066. We were always tested on that date. King Harold of England marched all the way from London to defeat King Harald Hadrada of Norway, but then he had to march back down south to fight William of Normandy. He lost that battle and the Norman French conquered England."

"Ay, an' we've been slaves t'bastards ever since," called Sam from the front. "Now shut tha gobs less t'ole village wakes up."

Sam called a halt after they passed through the small village and led them to an access spot on the river, leading the horses down the shallow bank to drink. The three men shared a cup of ale poured from a leather sack.

Jack chanced a question. "Did Master Ridley ever travel with you?"

"Nay, that man liked the softer life." Sam snorted at the thought. "Let's get goin'."

Sam would be a hard nut to crack.

Owls hooted several times, and once one flew low over their heads as it bore down upon its prey. As it disappeared into the darkness Rob called from the back, "They call us wool smugglers 'owlers'. A suppose it's 'cos we're out at night, like owls."

Frequent soft splashes in the river demonstrated its occupants remained industrious at night. Jack had completed many night marches but none felt as peaceful, or as serene, as this one.

The pace continued, easily and evenly, the long night offering full cover of darkness. Just as his legs began to feel weary, Jack saw the outline of a large abbey ahead. After crossing another impressive stone bridge over the Derwent, Sam halted the lead horse.

"That's Kirkham Priory. We're mekkin' good time. We'll stop back here for a little bit, an' give t'orses a break."

They broke out the bread, cheese and ale and sat in companionable silence as the horses took advantage of the halt and grazed on the side of the river. The gentle sound of water tumbling down a weir further along the river accompanied their meal.

"Tell us about France an' our King 'Enry," said Rob. "Is 'e as brave as everybody says? An' what are French lasses like? Did tha get to kiss any of 'em?"

Jack laughed. "There was no time for kissing girls and they wouldn't want to kiss the enemy. As for King Henry, he's a courageous soldier and I think he cares about his men. But it was hard going in France most of the time: we had to forage for food in the countryside and there was never enough."

"What's it like, knowin' tha's goin' into battle an' tha might die?"

"It's scary. Every man faced it in his own way. Some prayed, some drank the fear away, some puked their guts out, and some laughed and told jokes."

"What about thee?" Sam suddenly entered the conversation. "What did tha do?"

"I stayed close to my mates, mainly Will. We longbowmen were a close bunch and knew we had one another's back. It meant something, that brotherhood of archers. The French looked down on us. We didn't play by their fancy rules: war was a game to them. They thought we were common—not knightly enough. That's how we won at Agincourt."

By now, both Sam and Rob were leaning forward, eager to hear first-hand about the now-famous battle.

"The French Army was much bigger than ours and lots of our men were weak from hunger and dysentery so we didn't really stand a chance but King Henry made a powerful speech to put heart into us. The French knights wore heavy armour and both the knights and the horses became trapped in the mud on the battlefield. We archers rained arrows down on them. We won the battle and the French lost thousands of men. But war isn't glorious; it's bloody chaos most of the time."

Jack realized all this talk was not getting him closer to the identity of the organizers of the wool smuggling operation, but he sensed that the tales of army life and battles, helped Sam and Rob view him with less suspicion. The men regrouped the horses and continued on their way.

At a village called Malton the smugglers left the Derwent behind and followed a small beck leading the way to Pickering. Eventually, the outline of a settlement loomed before them.

"We'll stop 'ere for a bit." Sam explained that Pickering provided a favourable place to have a break before making the long march across the moors to the coast.

After a rest, appreciated by both men and horses, they moved quietly through the small market town, past a stone cross in the centre of the marketplace, and the dark outline of a large stone church with a tall steeple. The town lay in total darkness; the only sounds were those of the muffled hooves of the horses and the burbling of the beck. At the far side of the town, a large castle silhouetted against the sky came into view. Jack recognized the shape as being similar to the two castles in York. The men left the castle behind, moving as quietly as possible, and climbed a long, steep rise onto the Yorkshire Moors.

The change in the landscape was dramatic, even in the dark. No sense of gentle rolling scenery now as the landscape opened wide before them. The strengthening wind caused a dramatic drop in temperature. A solitary, stunted, windswept tree lay ahead. Sam stopped the tiny column.

"We're moving nor'-east now and following an old road called Wade's Causeway t'coast. It were built a long time since. It's called 'Old Wife's Trod' by t'locals. Seems a giant built it so's t'wife could tek cow t'market. More likely, t'Romans built it hundreds of years back. T'causeway meks it easier for us as there's boggy patches up 'ere and hard to see in t'dark. Only trouble is, it's not wide in parts, so don't wander off t'side."

The sky had darkened and the cloud layer was building, hiding the moon. Decreased visibility forced them to move cautiously even though the terrain was not difficult. Then the wind became even stronger with sudden gusts, followed by driving rain. They stopped to don their wet weather clothing and secure the skins protecting the woolsacks. The serene and easy walk was now a memory: they were battling the elements. Sam could not use the lanterns due to the driving rain, so they put their heads down and moved forward as best they could. Even the horses kept their heads down as they walked stoically into the wind and rain on the ancient, narrow causeway.

Jack lost any awareness of passing time. He focused on putting one foot in front of the other. This was like a forced march in France. They ate and drank as they walked. The poor horses would have to wait. He had no idea how Tom Bagshaw had managed to endure: he must be stronger than he looked.

After what seemed an eternity the rain stopped as suddenly as it had begun and the cloud cover rolled away. The sky was much lighter than Jack had expected and he could smell the sea. Another magnificent abbey dominated the horizon, beautifully framed by the sky. The clear, stirring sound of bells ringing broke the silence as they came closer.

"That's Whitby Abbey," called Sam over his shoulder. "We're just goin' to follow t'coast down to Robin Hood's Bay an' we're done. Believe it or not, them bells are ringing Sext. It's dinnertime."

Jack could not believe it: they had been walking since yesterday evening and, if the sun had been shining, it would be directly overhead.

A great view of the sea lay before the weary smugglers along the top of the high limestone cliffs. No fishing boats occupied the tiny harbour of Whitby: the fishermen must have gone out at dawn. They didn't linger though as they left Whitby behind; their destination was five more miles down the coast. Jack ignored his fatigue and enjoyed the last few miles: the smell of the salt air; the sight and sound of the waves breaking on the shore (as long as his feet were on land), and the horizon stretching as far as his tired eyes could see.

"Here we are, Robin 'ood's Bay," called Sam. "Known t'locals as Baytown. Praise the Lord we're 'ere."

"Can't wait for an ale and a pie," Rob muttered.

They descended a steep, narrow path. Only a few dozen wattle and daub cottages clung to the cliff face, looking like limpets on the side of a rock pool. Surely, a sea gale would blow these fragile homes out to sea. Jack wondered desperately where Rob's ale and pie were coming from as his stomach rumbled.

Sam, Rob and the horses demonstrated their familiarity with the route. The tired horses were sure-footed on the steep path. They stopped without orders from Sam at a cottage halfway down. A man came out immediately and led them behind the small cottage where an opening like a cave had been carved out of the limestone itself. The Baytown native was small and muscular; his weather-beaten face looked like old, well-cured leather, from years of being at sea. The cleverly carved space provided shelter for the animals and water; hay and a treat of oats were waiting for them. The men removed the woolsacks and piled them in front of the cave opening. They gave the tired horses a rubdown with bunches of hay and thankfully turned toward the cottage door.

"No special sacks this time?" The fisherman bent to examine the sacks.

Jack realized he may have made an error in not following the usual routine.

"Sum changes back 'ome, we'll 'ave to see 'ow it goes," Sam turned back.

"Aye, nowt niver stays same. We just 'ave to wait for 'igh tide now. Go get summat to eat and 'ave a kip, T'wife's got a pie frum Whitby."

The three men ducked their heads as they went through a small, low door into a tiny, dark living area. A window, with wooden shutters not more than two hands square, allowed in a pallid light. Once Jack's eyes had adjusted to the gloom, he looked around the cramped space. As in the Hallamby cottages, a central hearth provided the means to heat and cook, although only ashes were present. Two rudimentary benches sat against the sloping wall, next to an uneven table. An alcove at the back of the room held a mattress. A tiny woman came toward them, dressed in a coarse undyed wool dress with a cloth tied at her waist. Jack guessed her to be the fisherman's wife. Had he arrived in the land of pixies? His own height meant his head brushed against the roof beams in the low room. The diminutive hostess welcomed them, greeting Sam and Rob by name and nodding at Jack.

"We 'ad a fish pie brought frum Whitby for thee. A know 'ow much tha enjoys it, Robbie. Get this down thee."

She brought each man a trencher of stale black bread piled with boiled onions. A tankard of ale accompanied the fish pie, juicy with chunks of firm, white fish and topped with a crisp golden pastry.

As they were eating, Sam explained the locals of Baytown would take care of the rest of the business. Jack presumed that 'the rest' meant getting the woolsacks to the boats and the wine back to the cottage. They finished their meal and lay down to sleep on the mattress, lying on their sides so they could all fit. Each man was asleep as soon as his head hit the sack.

50

Hallamby buzzed with the news. Work could wait: people deserted the sheep in the fields; left the threshing flails in the barns; let go of the shuttle by their looms, and dropped their water buckets by the river.

Tom Bagsworth was free. Dick Radcliffe returned from York that afternoon, bringing the Bagsworth family on the back of his cart in a triumphant procession down the main street. As the news spread and people gathered, they followed the cart, cheering and waving. Children skipped and danced at the side of the cart as it rumbled along the dusty road. 'Arry, ears twitching and head held high, ignored the rabble, maintaining his dignity. The scene had all the markings of a royal visit from young King Henry.

The villagers gathered in front of the Bosworth's cottage; they had not come empty handed either. Arms were full of bread, milk, and ale; pots of pottage and eggs still warm; firewood and buckets of water. The church bell rang and kept on ringing.

Tom looked pale and thin following his incarceration. Mistress Bagsworth also looked pale and thin, no doubt from worry, but they both had tears of happiness rolling down their faces. Their son hopped off the cart and dashed to find his mates. The people lined up outside the cottage and filed through the Bagsworth's humble home leaving their gifts of food, along with smiles and hugs.

When Annie and Meg heard the news they dropped what they were doing, gathered up bunches of dried nettles—to restore general well being, and Vervain and Mugwort—for the nervous system.

"By the way, what is the name of their son, I never did find out?"

"Tinnicotes," Meg grinned. "Named after his great grandfather, and otherwise known as 'Tinny.'"

* * *

Father John heard the news as he went into the church to ring the bell for Nones. He took it as a sign from God that right had prevailed so he rang the bell with gusto and kept on ringing it, his heart swelling in his chest.

* * *

Steward Sneed heard the Nones bell ringing, the sound drifting over the fields. When he realized the carillon continued, he sent Matilda into the village to discover the cause. Matilda met Reeve Brighouse coming the other way, bursting with the news. They both hurried back to the Manor House to bring the information to the steward. "All's well that ends well," Steward Sneed rubbed his hands. "Mayhap we'll hear no more of this matter. Reeve, take some pence into the village, and purchase a cask of ale for the villagers. Ensure they learn it is a gift from me, and it won't hurt to let everyone know I had some influence in arranging Bagsworth's return."

* * *

When Annie and Meg arrived at the Bagsworth's cottage and saw the gathering of people there, they decided to return later; instead, they went on to the church. They guessed Father John would be there as the bell continued to ring and that is where they found him. Annie and Meg waited patiently until he stopped ringing the bell. He came towards them smiling and sweating, his few tonsured grey hairs standing straight up. Annie ran up to him and gave him a big hug. Father John disentangled himself with an embarrassed laugh and the three of them stood beaming at each other.

"Thank you so much for what you did, Father," Annie had tears in her eyes. The priest looked at Meg and nodded at her.

"Good morrow, Mistress Wistowe. It is good to see that you have returned." He turned to Annie. "Really, Mistress Thornton, this is Prior Gilbert's achievement. I just made him aware of the circumstances."

"You are too humble Father; please take some of the credit. The whole village is rejoicing."

"All's well that ends well," the priest smiled. "Thanks be to God; we can all put this behind us."

* * *

Jenet, carrying baby Thomas, raced up the street and the crowd cleared a path for her.

"Cum on, luv, cum on; get inside. Show 'em babby." Friendly arms pushed Jenet through the door. As soon as Jenet saw her parents sitting on either side of the table, piled high with food, she burst into tears.

"I've missed thee both so much. And look, look at tha grandson." She held out baby Thomas, thrusting him into her dad's arms. Tom clutched the baby, holding him as if he was made of glass.

"We called 'im Thomas, Dad, after you."

On hearing this, Tom Bagshaw burst into tears too. "A thought a'd nivver see me grandsun grow up," he stuttered through his tears. "Nay, a nivver thought a'd see me 'ome again."

More tears flowed. When Jenet looked around at the people crowded into the room, she could see they were crying too.

"There's more news, Mam, Dad. Am getting' wed. Jack Fletcher up at t'inn as asked me to be 'is betrothed."

That evening in Hallamby everyone ignored the curfew. All went into the church for a service of thanksgiving. As soon as they had thanked God, the villagers poured onto the village green, now illuminated by torches. Tom and Elsie Bagsworth were, with great ceremony, settled on a bench and wrapped in a wool blanket. Much supping of ale, dancing, and general rejoicing took place on the village green to celebrate the return of one of their lambs. Reeve Brighouse joined in, and made sure all knew their powerful steward had rescued Tom Bagsworth and had bought the ale, of which he imbibed a goodly share. Of Cartwright and Butts, there was no sign.

Jenet watched the festivities with Thomas in her arms and, as happy as she felt at the return of her parents, wondered where her sweetheart was right now.

51

Jack awoke from a deep and refreshing sleep. His two companions still snored away. He had no sense of how long he had slept but daylight still peeped through the slats covering the rude window openings. He went outside, remembering to duck his head, and looked in wonder at the scene below him.

Standing almost atop the towering cliffs, Jack had a bird's eye view of Robin Hood's Bay. The bay's beautifully curved line enclosed a vivid blue sea, sparkling in the sunlight. A small sandy beach lay between the water and the base of the limestone cliffs. It was difficult to tell where the sea ended and the sky began. White, streaky clouds were moving fast high above. It could have been a summer's day except for the brisk wind, which had a cold bite to it. The seagulls spiralled above and below the cliffs, exploiting the wind to perform their acrobatics, their piecing cries of *keow, keow* echoing off the cliff face.

A small ship lay out to sea with its sails neatly furled. It rode at anchor, tossed up and down by the white-capped waves. Jack shuddered, remembering the boat ride from Calais to Dover. Why was it always him delivering tributes to the sea—never Will? He shook his head to dislodge the humiliating memory of seasickness. Men, looking quite small from Jack's view high on the cliff, were moving about on the beach.

The fisherman's wife came outside and joined Jack.

"It's a fine-looking day," Jack turned to greet her.

"Aye, enjoy it while tha can. We've got an east wind blowin'. That alus sends in a sea fret, good for us, though, less chance of nosy duty men seein' anythin.'"

"What's a sea fret?"

"You inlanders call it a fog, but it's just 'ere by t'sea. Go inland an' there's nowt."

"Have you had trouble in the past from the duty men?"

"Nay, they're usually in Whitby or Scarbro' watchin' boats there. They dunt seem to bother wi' us. But there's alus a first time."

"So what's happening down there now?"

"They're waitin' for tide to turn, t'bring ship further in."

"How will they get the woolsacks down to the beach?" Jack marvelled at the steep and narrow path.

"Ee, lad, they're already down there. There's so many tunnels in these cliffs, it's like a giant rabbit warren. Woolsacks'll be sittin' in a cave at bottom, an' as soon as ship comes in closer wi' tide they'll be tekken out in t'row boats, quick as ye like. Then t'row boats'll bring wine kegs back. Our men'll carry 'em up 'ere, and you lot will load t'orses and off tha'll go."

"I suppose it's been done many times and every man jack knows his job?"

"Aye, tha's got that reight. Is tha ready for a drink an' summat to eat?"

They went back inside. It took a while again for Jack's eyes to adjust to the darkness. Sam and Rob were awake and sitting on the rush-covered floor, looking at ease. The mistress of the house brought ale in a large jug and three trenchers of black bread, piled up with more boiled onions, mixed with dried fish. The men attacked the food with gusto and the ale went down quickly. Their hostess refilled the jug and it just as quickly emptied. Sam and Rob seemed to have quite a thirst on.

"What's up, Jack, can't tek tha drink? We'll be 'ere for a while. Relax. Sup up." Sam grinned and lifted his own mug to his mouth, drinking noisily.

Jack raised his tankard and supped. There might be an opportunity here to get some answers. The tongues of the smugglers were becoming increasingly looser.

"I'm really enjoying this trip," he offered. "Thanks for the lessons. I hope I can take more trips with you."

"Aye, well, tha's not a bad lad, even if tha talksh funny," Sam showed the beginning of a slur. He dug his elbow into his mate's ribs and guffawed.

"How do we sort out the money?" Jack risked asking.

"We dunt. Them buggars dunt trust us to 'andle that. It's all done 'igher up. I'll be 'anded a sealed package by t'captin. It's more than me life's worth if that seal's broke. We'll get paid when we get back an' deliver wine an' t'package t'Manor 'ouse. 'Ey up, a just 'ad a thought! Captin'll give us a package for t'innkeeper frum last trip as well. What's to do about that?"

"Who looks after the packages, is it the steward?"

"Nay, not package for t'innkeeper, we keep that one separate. An' shteward won't dirty them lily white 'ands. Bailiff teks package an' pays us out. Mind you, shteward sees t' wine and 'as a list of number of woolsacks goin' out, he keeps a closhe eye on evrythin'. Then all t'farms that sent their fleeces 'ave to be paid, but that's nowt t'do wi' us."

"I'll take the innkeeper's package. It belongs to the inn, anyway."

Neither of the men challenged him.

Sam began slurring his words more and more. Rob matched the drinking, mug for mug. Jack figured this might be his best opportunity to get some answers.

"Where did the innkeeper fit into all of this; you told me earlier that he played a role?"

"He did nowt except gather in t'money. He were an idle sod, as t'Lord ish my witnesh." Sam raised his eyes to heaven, apparently appealing to God to support him.

"I have to say it was a clever scheme he had going, just taking a few extra packs for himself. How did that work?"

"Ridley an' captin worked it between "em. T'captin sold extra wool off in Calais. Captin took biggest risk, 'cos he only got whatever price were in Frenchie land, but am guessing Ridley did well out of it or 'e wouldn't have bothered. We got a few extra pennies to keep our mouths shut."

"Aye, nowt to do with us what big nobs get up to," piped up Rob.

"It seems to me you lot lost out of some extra income when the innkeeper went missing. By the way, do you know where he went?" He let that comment hang in the air. *Let the bait bring in the fish.*

Sam sniggered. "It were all a joke. T'ole village were paid, just about, to tell a different tale on what 'appened to 'im." He hiccupped. "An' inn were set up t'look like it did after travellers 'ad gone. Worked well, din't it, fooled anybody stickin' their nose in." He looked at Jack from under his eyebrows when he said that.

"I am impressed. Who thought that up?" He held his breath.

"We dunt know," Rob shook his head from side to side drunkenly. "It were smithy, Big John, who told ev'rybody what to do."

"But what did happen to Ridley, does anybody know?"

Sam fell over abruptly and began snoring.

"Good idea," said Rob and did the same.

Jack pondered the new information. He was still no wiser on who did Ridley in. He still didn't know how this smuggling benefited the whole village, and it must, because they all protected it. Maybe the steward was a good man, running the smuggling game for the benefit of all.

With that profound thought, he joined Sam and Rob for another snooze.

The diminutive mistress of the house predicted correctly. When the three men woke up again, the sea fret had moved in. They went outside. The bay had vanished. The air they breathed was heavy with moisture. It beaded on their eyebrows and hair. It floated around them in fragments, offering a beguiling glimpse of sea, and of limestone cliffs and cottages before it thickened and blotted out the view. Voices floated up toward Jack and his bleary-eyed mates. Men were still working down there, even though they couldn't be seen. The three men asked for a bucket of water and gave themselves a good scrub down, then went out back to see to the horses and prepare them for the return trip. Sam remained quiet, grunting out his orders to the other two. He would offer a sideways look at Jack now and again. Jack figured he was wondering what he had said while in his cups.

They heard voices, faintly at first, then growing louder; the words sounded hollow, echoing, as though bouncing off the rock walls. Their host materialised out of a crevice in the rock, carrying a wooden keg on his shoulder. Three more men followed, each with the same load, all of small stature, and the same leathery looking skin. They unloaded the kegs, stretched out their backs, and turned around to go back.

"'Ey, lads, tha can 'elp us. Follow us back down."

Sam groaned. "I 'ope it'll only be one trip."

They followed the fishermen into the inside of the pitch-dark cliff. A narrow tunnel sloped steeply downwards. Soon a glow appeared and became brighter. The glow came from rushes dipped in, what smelled like rancid fish oil. Iron brackets set in the rock supported the torches. The rank odour and the smoke were aggravating. Jack tried holding his breath but soon found there was a limit to that remedy. As they descended, Jack realized the rushes were positioned at equal distances so they went from almost dark to light and back to dark. He tried to breathe only in the dark space. The smoke and smell didn't appear to bother the fishermen who continued chatting in an almost incomprehensible Yorkshire dialect.

The tunnel opened out into a narrow cave that grew wider closer to the beach. The men drew in deep breaths of heavy, moist, and salty air; the soft, wet fog was blurring the edges of everything. Jack could see shadowy shapes ahead of them, the forms materializing into the seamen from the ship, carrying more kegs.

The fishermen handed the landlubbers a keg each to hoist onto their shoulders and off they went, back into the cliff tunnel. Jack would never forget that climb to the top. His thighs and calves screamed with the effort and his breath was harsh in his throat. The hardy seamen soon left the threesome behind and, judging by the groans he heard from Sam and Rob, they were suffering more than he was.

"The Lord have mercy!" Sam's plea for help as they emerged out of the tunnel made the locals laugh as he collapsed on the rock floor, sending his barrel rolling.

"They dunt breed 'em tough enough inland," one of them cackled.

"That'll be eleven kegs. We've got four more to pick up; we'll get 'em; you softies rest."

They chortled again at the inlanders' pitiful performance and went back down the tunnel.

When the three softies had recovered sufficiently, they staggered inside to bowls of dried fish stew.

"That'll stick to tha ribs and get thee 'ome," said the tiny mistress. Sam didn't look too keen but manfully swallowed down the contents of his bowl.

The horses were ready to go, each carrying two kegs to balance their loads. One horse carried supplies for the journey. Jack did the math. Fifteen medium-sized kegs came up the cliff and fourteen were leaving. Just as the fish stew had stuck to their ribs, each participant in these endeavors managed to get something stuck to his fingers. Sam thrust a small package sealed with wax at Jack. He neither spoke nor offered eye contact.

They said their goodbyes to their hosts and partners in crime and began their journey back.

The sea fret still protected them as they passed by Whitby and turned west on to Wade's Causeway.

"We'll soon be out of this stuff," volunteered Rob from the back.

Sam remained silent.

Rob prophesied well. A short way onto the moors the fret became thinner and patchy and then vanished. The tail end of daylight showed them the way. At last, Jack could see the moor in all of its splendour, even in November. The rolling, heather-covered moorland stretched away as far as the eye could see. Wade's Causeway cut a swathe through the heather and grasses. Birds were busy in the twilight. Rabbits bounded away at their approach.

"Pity we dunt 'ave time to set sum traps," called Rob. "Be nice to 'ave a roast coney for tea."

A rarely seen red and gold sunset led the way westward, giving a deep red colour to the now dried heather and lifting Jack's spirits as his thoughts turned to Jenet and their future together. Inevitably, darkness set in and the men plodded onward. They eventually left the rolling plateau that formed the moors and came down into the flatter, gentle farmland of the Vale of Pickering, then onto Malton where they joined up with the River Derwent.

Other than a few short breaks for both horses and men, the pace had been steady, conversation had been nil and the men had stayed with their own thoughts.

"Not far now," Rob encouraged from his rear position. "Soon be home."

Jack realized with a start that Hallamby *was* home. He had found a home.

52

Will missed his mate, Jack. He had forgotten how well they worked as a team during their army days. Without Jack, he seemed to chase his tail round in circles, never quite catching it. He could not take his mind off the problem he had created by telling everyone that he and Annie shared the same blood. Somehow, he had to alter their relationship in the eyes of the villagers or he and Annie would need to leave Hallamby in order to be together.

Will brooded on the mystery of the dead innkeeper. He had not attended the celebration of the return of the Bagsworths as he remained at the inn; however, the staff told him all about it. Annie shared with him the excitement and happiness she felt upon the return of the family. Although he was thankful for Tom's release, the mystery of who had done the deed in the first place remained unsolved. Will remembered Sneed's warning, but he liked his quiver full of arrows when taking aim, and if knowledge equaled arrows, he lacked some.

He decided to visit Father John at the first opportunity. He was the man who might solve both puzzles: the cousin challenge and the riddle of Ridley. When a break came in his routine after Nones, he left word with 'call me Aggie' and headed to the church house.

Father John greeted Will cordially enough and invited him into his home. The walk from the inn in the crisp December air had made Will's skin tingle. He was thankful to see a respectable fire burning in the hearth.

"Ale or wine?"

"Ale, thank you."

Once they had settled by the fire with their drinks, a pause descended on the pair. As the silence deepened, Will shifted uncomfortably on his bench. He began to tell his story haltingly of how he met Annie, with the smoke pouring out of the cottage and finding her unconscious. Better not to mention seeing the words swirling in the smoke. Anyway, it could have been an illusion brought on by his tiredness.

"How strange. What had caused Mistress Thornton to be unconscious and what caused the fire?" Father John leaned forward, looking intently into Will's eyes.

"I don't know. That's how we found her. I thought she might have fallen asleep, being tired from her journey. It turned out not to be smoke but steam coming from a pot by the hearth. Her cat slept too. I agree the circumstances are unusual but both she and the cat woke up with no problems."

Will smiled as he remembered Jack cursing Rosamund.

"Annie, I mean Mistress Thornton, made us something to eat and we slept in her out-house. When Mistress Davey arrived the next morning and I introduced myself as Mistress Thornton's cousin, my intent was to protect her reputation. The story would have travelled around the village like wildfire had the neighbour thought she sheltered two unknown men for the night. I was not aware that she, like us, had just arrived in the village. Now we, well, we have fallen in love," Will paused, his cheeks reddening, "and want to wed, but we can't because everyone thinks of us as cousins and Mistress Wistowe as my aunt. What a mess."

"My understanding is that you have spent quite an amount of time alone with Mistress Thornton, allowed only because of your kinship. I ask you, under oath, to tell me you did not take advantage of the lack of a chaperone?"

Father John looked even more intensely at Will. Sweat trickle down his spine at this unexpected interrogation. He jumped up from his bench.

"By the Blood of Christ, I swear I have not put Annie in jeopardy. Besides, I most often had Jack with me, and later, Mistress Wistowe. Our love is so new, we're still getting used to it."

"Sit down and calm yourself. I must ask these questions. Do you know how Mistress Thornton arrived here? It seems she just appeared. How came *you* to Hallamby? It is a tiny village, almost off the beaten track."

"I don't know how she travelled here. I do know the village expected her. Mistress Davey arrived with food the following morning and explained how Mistress Thornton's aunt told her to watch for her. As to how we came here—we travelled from Dover, our destination York. We planned to stay at the inn on the York road. When we found it empty and in darkness, we decided to chance our luck in the nearest village. You know it is not safe to remain on the highway at night. We hoped to bed down in an outbuilding or barn." Will chose not to mention the extraordinary comment from Mistress Davies that she had anticipated their arrival.

"What is it you expect me to do? I cannot say you lied, it discredits both of you."

"Can you prove we are not cousins through records? We both are York born. The Church must have registered our births. The records will show I made a mistake. A mistake is preferable to a lie."

"The Papal registers in York contain many records related to consanguinity, meaning cousinhood, as well as a birth registry. When I next have to go to the city I will check for you."

Will's mind started racing and sweat broke out on his forehead. He leapt up again and began pacing in the long, narrow room. "That is too long to wait. Look, Father, I will accompany you to York and pay for any expenses. We will stay at a superior inn as a treat; enjoy each other's company and a diversity of food. What do you say?"

"Sit, Will, calm yourself. Sounds like bribery to me; however, I'm agreeable." A shadow fell across the Father's face as he spoke, but then he smiled.

"Good, then that is settled. As soon as Jack comes back I'll return and we'll make a plan."

Father John stood. "Where has Jack gone?"

"Er, he just went to sort out some business, York way, for a couple of days. He should be back today or tomorrow."

"I pray his business will be successful for all our sakes. I shall await your word."

Will looked curiously at the Father following these enigmatic comments but as no more followed, he took his leave.

53

The weary smugglers arrived back at the inn.

"Tha's not dun yet," grunted Sam. "We 'ave to tek 'orses back t'Manor 'Ouse."

These were the first words he had spoken for a long time. Did Sam's silence come from the after effects of his drinking or from concern that he may have revealed too much.

It occurred to Jack that he might take the blame for leaking the details, creating repercussions for Annie. Steward Sneed made it clear he would punish her for any mishaps. A worm of worry crawled in his gut. He had no choice but to tell Will. He did not want to cause problems for any of them.

They unloaded half of the wine kegs and placed them in the wool packing room after following Sam's gruff instructions.

"Last stop, Manor 'Ouse," Rob's voice sounded as though he had dragged it up from his boots.

The horses looked tired: their heads lowered and legs heavy. They needed much encouragement to keep moving forward. The long night had passed and the sky was lighter.

"When we land at t'Manor, stay wi' t'orses. I'll go find t'bailiff."

Sam trundled off to knock on the big door of the Manor House, leaving Rob and Jack to stroke the horses and talk to them, promising they would be in their stable soon.

Sam returned. He led them to the back of the Manor where they deposited the remaining wine kegs inside of the back door.

Not a bad haul for the steward.

The exhausted men led the horses into the stables and released them from their tackle. They filled the water buckets and hayracks, gave them all quick rub down and a friendly pat, and staggered out.

Sam turned to Rob and Jack once they had left the shadow of the Manor House and gave each of them five silver groats.

"That's it," he said. "Bugger off and keep tha gob shut."

… And thank you, retorted Jack mentally as he made his weary way back to the inn.

Will was in the hall, moving amongst the guests, chatting and pouring ale to wash down the oatmeal. He looked the image of the perfect innkeeper. Jack pointed to the kitchen door and made his way there. By the time Will arrived, he was pouring himself an ale.

"How are you?" Will asked, filling a tankard for himself.

"Exhausted, and happy to be home; it really feels like home."

"Well, enjoy your drink, get some food and I'll see you in our room. "It's good to have you back."

Jack blinked. These were strong words coming from Will, not known for expressing emotion. Maybe it had something to do with having fallen in love. He reminded himself to warn Will about Sam, and their concern for Annie.

Jack dished up a big bowl of oatmeal, thankful it wouldn't taste of fish. He had no desire to see another meal of dried fish for some time.

When Will entered their private quarters, Jack lay on his mattress, his belly full of oatmeal, his ale finished.

"Before you tell me about your trip, Jack, I should tell you that Jenet's father has been freed from jail and he and his wife are back home. Jenet is with them."

"The Lord be praised. That's good news indeed." Jack sat up. "I've learned so much on my trip. I need to know how much you wish to know."

Will smiled. "Tell me all."

"Yorkshire is the most beautiful place in the world, even in the dark. The River Derwent sings as it travels. The moors are magnificent and the coast is glorious…"

Will laughed. "I think the ale might be going to your head; leave out the scenery and tell me the rest."

Jack recounted his adventures, being careful to leave out the word 'smuggling' as well as descriptions of the scenery.

"Sam's the leader. I walked in the middle of the packhorses, and Rob was at the back—do remind me to clean my boots tomorrow—I left them in the stables. When we arrived at Robin Hood's Bay—or 'Baytown'—as the locals call it; we were treated really well and ate lots of dried fish, which I could happily leave alone for a while."

Will shifted impatiently. "Get to the facts."

"Well, Sam got into the ale which really loosened his tongue. He told me in so many words that Sneed runs the smu—organization and the bailiff handles the money. All the people involved seem to get something stuck to their fingers. For example, our late innkeeper had a little ongoing arrangement that included buying the silence of quite a few participants."

Jack explained to Will about the extra woolsacks, colour coded by the village women, passed on to the fishermen, then to the captain of the ship.

"They all gained a few coins from the underhand deal within an underhand deal. I expect that's why the villagers kept that particular secret. I imagine the innkeeper and the captain made the most profit. In fact, I have the innkeeper's payment for the last coast run. I received five groats for my work—that's good pay—if you remember, we got a groat a day from King Henry for fighting for him."

He pulled the now soiled and creased package meant for Ridley out from his belt pouch. It held ten groats. "That's not a bad profit for somebody else's work."

Will shook his head at the cleverness of it all. "So Sneed is the leader, is he?"

"In it up to his floppy little hat. But I don't believe he knows about Ridley's side transactions."

"That's why he didn't want the Prior's men sniffing around here looking for the missing innkeeper. He deliberately hushed it all up and, somehow, got rid of the body." Will shook his head.

"And that's another thing I found out. That whole scene at the inn: remember when we came up here with Annie and found the place in such a mess? It was all a setup, a performance put on for anyone to see. Rob said Big John, the Smithy, told them what to do."

Sensitive to Will's obsession with the missing innkeeper, Jack quickly changed the subject. "I noticed that Sam, once he had sobered up, wouldn't look at me, or talk to me, for that matter. I think he may regret his confidences. I'm worried that he may try to protect himself by setting me up."

"What do you mean?"

"What if he's afraid I'll leak the information about the smuggling and implicate him? If he comes up with a story that makes me look like the guilty one, it could affect Annie. Do you remember Sneed's threat about us keeping things running smoothly at the inn or they would look closer at Annie and her so-called 'suspicious behaviour'?"

The colour drained from Will's face.

"God's Teeth and Blood! This is not good. Sneed will be on it like a hawk after a mouse. What can we do to protect her?"

"I could try talking to Sam and Rob and reassure them that I am with them all the way and will not be opening my mouth."

"Do you think that will be enough to protect Annie?"

"We'll see how they react. I imagine they are wary of Sneed and Bailiff Crompton. They're all warning me to 'keep my gob shut', as they're fond of saying. Don't let us forget those two lovelies, Cartwright and Butts. They're the heavies for Sneed."

"It is all so complicated. A soldier's life is much simpler. I'm hoping to take a couple of days off and go into York with Father John, but now I daren't risk leaving Annie."

Will explained the plan to consult the birth records in York. He intended to use the journey to find out the role of the priest in all of the dealings and intrigues going on around them.

"Let me calm Sam and Rob down and then you can go," said Jack. I will keep my eye on Annie while you are away. You can't say life is boring around here," he gave a huge yawn. "Well, I'm for sleep, before I go and see Jenet. Good day."

54

Events happened quickly the following day. Once free of obligations at the inn, Jack sought out Sam and Rob in the village where he found them chopping up logs dragged in from the forest.

"I just wanted to say thanks for taking me on the trip the other day. I really enjoy your company and admire your guts. That's not an easy job you are both doing."

Sam leaned on his axe and stared at Jack, his face expressionless. Rob, however, grinned and slapped Jack's back. "Aye, it were a bit o' fun, weren't it. Tha dint do too bad, thisen."

Jack looked steadfastly into Sam's eyes. "It's important to me that you believe I know how to keep my mouth shut about anything that occurred when we were together, either by word or deed. I value your comradeship and will do nothing to jeopardise it."

Sam responded with his usual grunt, but he looked relieved and went back to his chopping. Rob winked.

Feeling better, Jack called in on Mistress Davey. He was looking forward to seeing Jenet, forgetting Will had told him she had returned home to her parents. Mistress Davey welcomed him as usual.

"'Ave an ale," she fussed. "I really miss Jenet an' t'babby. They were good company for me. It's a pity tha missed Tom's cummin' 'ome party t'uther evenin'. It were funny watchin' all me neighbours actin' daft, especially Reeve Brig'ouse. "'E 'ad way too much ale. Daft bugger kept callin' Mistress Thornton a witch an' that 'e would 'ave 'er burned. 'E were still mithered about thee an' Will sendin' 'im off with 'is tail between 'is legs."

Jack stiffened. How could it be, each time he turned around, someone threatened Annie? She worked hard in the village helping the people with their illnesses and babies. He couldn't understand it. As he was leaving he asked Mistress Davey to inform him if she heard of any more threats against Annie.

The Bagsworths were his next stop. Jenet was spinning wool and her mother worked at the loom. Tom lay on the mattress with baby Thomas curled in his arms. Jack felt awkward and shy: an unusual feeling for him. He realiszd this was the first opportunity he'd had to meet his new parents to be.

After acknowledging Jenet's mother and his betrothed, Jack sat on the floor beside Tom. "How are you, Master Bagsworth?"

"Fair t'middlin'," Tom Bagsworth sat up, still cradling the baby. "Am tryin' t'do more every day an' Mistress Wistowe 'as made up packages of green twiggy stuff for me to tek; tastes bad but a suppose it dus me good."

Jack took a good look at his fellow smuggler and marvelled that this pale, slight man had been able to make the journey to the coast, not once but repeatedly. He looked as though a stiff breeze would blow him over, never mind the howling gales on the moors, yet Sam and Red Rob had praised his determination and staying power.

After they talked about his and Jenet's betrothal and plans for the wedding itself, which was to take place on the day of the Great Pig Feast, Jack brought up his recent trip to the coast.

"I just thought you might like to know that your job will be waiting for you when you are stronger," he lifted his hands at the look of distress displayed on both Tom and his wife's faces. "Don't worry; I won't share this with anyone." Jack gave a slight shake of his head. He seemed to be saying that constantly.

"How did tha get on wi' Sam an' Red Rob?" asked Tom. "They're grand lads, an' they'll watch tha back for thee."

"Really well, I enjoyed their company a lot. They told me how much they missed having you along too. Steward Sneed has done a good job of organizing this business, hasn't he?"

Tom was slow to answer. He looked down at his sleeping grandson and stroked his head.

Then, "Oh, aye, 'e does as 'e's told, well enough."

Jack dare not speak. He sensed he was about to learn something important.

"'E's not t'gaffer. Father John 'olds reins. "'E's big boss. Not too many folk know that though; keep that one under thy 'at. Am only tellin' thee cos tha's family now."

Now Jack was speechless.

When he had recovered, and was able to reconnect his voice to his brain, he asked why the Father would involve himself in such a risky business.

"Well, a suppose everybody in England dus smugglin'; it's a way o' life, i'n't it? Anyhow, he does it for t'village. Owt 'e gets goes t'people, poor uns, old uns, 'ungry uns. Who does tha think kept us frum starvin' when I 'urt me back?"

Jack kept his silence, his mind still reeling at this disclosure.

"That's one o' reasons he were so mad wi' t'innkeeper. Father John knew Ridley were skimmin' top off income with 'is different colored woolsacks. He were stealin' food out o' folk's mouths really. An' us lads daren't say nowt. A know we made a few pennies out of it but we were in a spot. If we'd a said owt, bullyboys would 'ave shut us up wi' their clubs."

Mistress Bagsworth jumped into the conversation.

"I 'eard Father John tried to get t'steward to do summat about him, but he never would, a dunt know why."

"It amazes me that Master Ridley was able to get away with so much for so long. You'd almost think he knew some secret thing about the steward or Father John that meant they were afraid to censor him."

"Aye, well, we wouldn't know owt about that." Tom shrugged his shoulders. "We leave that sort o' stuff t'higher ups."

"I must be off." Jack stood up and stretched his long legs. "Mistress Bagsworth, here is the money I received from my trip to the coast. It belongs to Tom really. There is a bit more than usual. Please use it for any wedding costs. I am sure Dick Radcliffe will bring you cloth back from York for new clothes if you ask him. Jenet, do you want to see me out?"

He and Jenet spent a satisfactory few minutes at the doorway, murmuring sweet nothings in each other's ear. Their canoodling ended when baby Thomas woke up and decided to call his mother back with a vigorous demand for food.

Before Jack went back to the inn, he called in on Annie to bring her up to date on the latest information. She showed keen interest in the news that Father John was in charge of the smuggling operation and that he was the one who gave the orders to Sneed and Bailiff Crompton. She marveled at Ridley's double-dealings with the woolsacks. Jack had told her previously about the late innkeeper skimming the inn's wine account.

It had been a long day and Jack was ready for home. The weather surprised him when he left Annie's cottage. A thick, grey, wet fog had crept in, creating blurred edges to the buildings and muffling any sound. The poor visibility caused Jack to walk slowly up the deserted village street; even the village dogs had gone to ground. His thoughts turned to the cheery hall of the inn and the comforts he would find therein. Leaving the church and the village behind, he headed on the path toward the main road. The inhabitants of the rookery were quiet, the creeping fog having subdued the birds. The fog grew denser and wetter. Jack kept his head down and followed his feet on the dirt trail. He came to an abrupt stop as two figures materialized out of the murkiness.

"'Ello, Jack," the larger of the two figures spoke. "Out 'ere on thy own? That's not good for thy 'ealth."

The other shape laughed. "Tha'll catch tha death o' cold, or summat worse."

Jack's mouth dried up instantly. He felt just like he did before going into battle: heart thumping, a metallic taste in his mouth. The odds were not good and with a sinking feeling in his gut he saw Butts and Cartwright had stout staves in their hands. He pulled his dagger from his sheath. "Come on then lads; do your worst, but you'll pay too." That was pure bravado but he prepared for battle.

"Not so fast, me brave bucks. Dus tha think tha can tek on three of us?"

From behind Jack two shapes lumbered out of the fog to stand on either side of him. They, too, had solid looking clubs which they tapped the rhythmically into the palms of their hands.

"An' there's more where we've cum frum, it'll just tek a whistle. A think tha's outnumbered."

Sam and Rob laughed as the two men melted away into the fog. Jack turned to them, shaking with relief. "I would have given it my best shot, but I've never been so glad to see anyone in my life. Tom told me you two would watch my back."

"We've bin watchin' it since thy 'ad tha fight wi' Asne. T'ole village 'as been watchin'. We knew they'd cum back; it's their nature." Sam reached out his hand to pat Jack's arm. "Cum on then; tha can buy us an ale at thy place."

55

After Jack left, Meg went to the bakery for bread, exclaiming about the thickness of the fog as she went out of the door. Annie had planned to make up some herb packages, so spent a few moments gathering up her ingredients. She wanted to follow a recipe for salve her aunt had given her for her elderly patients with aching joints. Raiding the herbal supply chest, she took out dried radish, bishopwort, wormwood, and cropleek. As she pounded the dried plants into a powder, she pondered the news Jack had brought earlier.

She needed to get all the facts straight in her head; so much had happened in a short period. Ridley's death was no nearer to being solved.

As she did so often, she talked to Rosamund. "It's time for action, Rosamund, or we'll never get home. I need to get all of the facts straight in my head, given what I know and what Will and Jack have shared with me; I wish I had access to my laptop, but I'll have to make do with my fingers."

With each pound of the pestle into the bowl, Annie listed aloud what she knew.

"One. Just before I arrived here, a big storm hit, used by my aunt to raise the energy to bring me here. During the storm, Ridley disappeared, not seen alive again.

"Two. People are telling different stories in the village about what happened to him. Who organized that and why?

"Three. The scene at the inn following his disappearance was apparently staged, to add to the confusion. Who ordered that and why?

"Four. The pigs found Ridley's body, buried—but not well

buried—in the forest. A burial done in haste?

"Five. The villagers took the body to the Manor House barn and it disappeared. Sneed and the bailiff were definitely involved in that vanishing act. It's strange that none of the men who brought the body back from the forest remember doing that. Had they been threatened or bribed to keep quiet?

"Six. Immediately after the body appeared then disappeared, Sneed arrested Tom Bagsworth and had him delivered to a jail in York. Tom had been away at the time of Ridley's disappearance on the coastal run, which Sneed would have known about, as he is involved with the smuggling. Why did he make Tom a scapegoat? Was he setting up a smokescreen, and if so, why?

"Seven. Father John gave refuge to Ridley's wife. They are, according to village gossip, living as husband and wife. The priest knew of Ridley's other activities too, such as expropriating money from the sale of woolsacks and wine, and forcing himself on the young women at the inn. Where did that leave him in his relationship with Ridley?

"Eight. I saw Father John, prostrate before the altar, seemingly doing penance. Why? Yet he had helped to rescue Tom from jail and he used the money from smuggling to help the villagers. Could such a good man be a murderer?"

Still mulling over the events, Annie began to boil the powdered herbs in tallow, adding celandine, and red nettle. The stink of the tallow made her nose wrinkle. She stirred the glutinous mess with a wooden spoon.

Where was she…?

"Nine. Will let slip that the accusations of witchcraft against me had been instigated by Sneed. Was his purpose just to make us do his bidding? On the other hand, is he hiding something and afraid we'll find out?

"Ten. Where does Prior Gilbert fit in to all of these machinations? He doesn't appear to visit this manor often, even though his Order owns it, leaving Sneed with a free hand.

"Oh, Rosamund, my head aches and I've run out of fingers. Maybe Florrie, who lives with Father John, might have some answers for me. I'll have to be careful; it will require all of my skill, but maybe she can shed some light on the relationship between the innkeeper and the priest.

"The whole village seems to love the Father. Maybe all of this planned confusion is to protect him because he committed the murder. He definitely has motive, although we're a bit short on opportunity. I suppose a thump on the head is as easy a method as any other. He and Will are heading into York on business tomorrow so I'll visit Florrie then."

As Annie spooned the newly made salve into little clay pots, she felt a sense of satisfaction. "Time well spent, Rosamund. We have a plan."

56

Will and Father John left for York at sunrise on borrowed horses from the Manor House stables. Will anticipated sorting out the Gordian knot of cousinhood he had created and finally seeing his parents. In addition, Meg and Annie had given him specific instruction to buy cloth for the women to sew wedding clothes for Jack.

The two men chatted companionably along the London to York road, now less busy so late in the season. Father John expressed curiosity about Will's war experience.

"How close did you feel to God before a battle? Were you able to feel his protection?"

Will thought about his response with care. "I always find it interesting that both sides pray to the same God for his protection and the winning side claims God is with them. I'm not sure how God sorts it out. I can tell you, though; every soldier hopes God is looking out for him the night before a battle."

"Did you fear death, or is that a silly question?"

"I think we all fear death, Father, no matter what the Church tells us; it is still the great unknown and who knows what sins we have committed in the past that might come back to send us into eternal damnation."

Father John didn't speak for a while. The horses walked on with an easy rhythm, their ears pricked for the sounds around them.

Then, "My son, do you believe in the power of the sacrament of confession? I would hope you had priests available in your camp so you could be shriven prior to battle."

"We did and most men sought them out. What about you Father, who do you go to in order to be shriven, or—" Will laughed—"perhaps you don't commit sins."

Silence reigned.

There were no delays at the ferry. The horses walked onto the barge placidly, their easy-going temperament on display, but the relaxed companionship of the earlier journey enjoyed by the two men had ended: Father John seemed sunk in his own thoughts. Just like the city of York, Will sensed the priest had built a defensive wall around himself.

Church bells proclaiming Sext were ringing throughout York, the Minster bells resonating above all the others as the two men rode through Micklegate Bar. As they made their way along busy Micklegate, Father John cheered up and began chatting about his memories of the city.

"Long ago I came here as a student. I had to work hard to learn my Latin and the Rites of the Holy Mother Church. Nevertheless, we young students had fun too. There are many taverns in York and I knew most of them well. Living here made such a change from village life; there was a sense of freedom, of not being watched and judged all the time."

"Do you enjoy what you do, Father, being responsible for all of those souls?"

"It is my life's work: enjoyment is not a factor."

Upon that austere comment, the horses clattered into the yard of the 'The Black Sheep', a substantial inn on Lower Petergate and not far from York Minster.

The inn sprawled in an untidy fashion along the street as an assortment of rooms had been added on higgledy-piggledy over the years. Its timber-framed exterior displayed a pleasing contrast between the blackened beams and the white plaster. Many small windows had the luxury of glass panes through which cheerful lighting glowed.

An ostler took control of the horses, leading them off to the stables. Will and Father John stretched thankfully and made their way into the main hall to find their host. Will was curious to see how a hostelry in a city compared to his country inn.

As they stood inside the hall, Will raised his eyes to canopied oak rafters and felt the welcoming heat from a blazing log fire set in a great open stone built hearth with its own chimney. Walls with lustrous oak panels at the base and white plaster above framed the great room. Paintings and sketches of York landmarks and softly glowing horse brasses decorated the plaster. Customers ate and drank at highly polished, long trestle tables and benches; a low murmur of conversation added to the sense of a well-run establishment.

Their host, a large man with an equally large belly, greeted them cordially and offered a private chamber but Father John demurred—too costly—so he showed them the cheaper sleeping area, a long room with communal beds laid out in a straight line.

After enjoying a mutton pie and an excellent ale, Will and Father John walked to the walled city, the Liberty of Saint Peter, situated behind the Minster. Curfew was still a way off so they had plenty of time for their investigations. It took a while to find the building holding the papal registers: a small building, dwarfed by the Archbishop's Palace. These papal registers contained entries referring to consanguinity between couples. The Church forbade marriage between fourth cousins and those more closely related. Father John requested birth registration records for the period when Annie might have been born, as her age was a mystery to the pair.

The helpful cleric on duty guided them through the crowded and elegant Latin script but Annie Thornton's name was not there. Older documents revealed Meg (Margaret) Wistowe, and her sister Berta.

According to the Papal registers, Annie did not exist.

"We can look at it in a positive way," Father John calmed a frustrated Will. "We have not been able to show a cousinly relationship between the two of you, so I can share that fact with the community."

Will blew out his breath; this had been the purpose of the visit after all. Weight lifted from his shoulders. Thanking the cleric for his help, they turned toward one of the gates leading them out of the walled city. A group of boisterous and inebriated young men rushed through the gate, almost knocking Father John over. Two of them stopped to apologize and dust him off, and then ran on to join their companions.

Father John shook his head and laughed. "They'll be the chantry priests. They live inside the Liberty of Saint Peter but go out into the town to drink and carouse. I'll bet the authorities were chasing them."

As he predicted, on the other side of the gate stood two burly men with staffs, looking exasperated.

Will put his arm around the shoulders of the shorter man, "If you are recovered from your brush with drunken priests we'll call in and surprise my parents. They can sup with us at the inn."

The butcher shops in the Shambles were getting ready to close as the pair navigated the cobbles between the overhanging buildings and avoided the central channel used for draining blood and offal.

Will strode into his father's shop with a big grin on his face. His father, busily scrubbing down the heavy chopping block, gave a shout of surprise and came around to the front, crushing Will in his burly arms. Hearing the raised voice of her husband, Mistress Boucher hurried out from the back of the shop. She burst into tears at the sight of her tall, broad-shouldered, handsome, grown-up son.

Will tried to conceal his surprise at his parents' grey hair and heavier build. In his mind, they had remained the same as when he left home. He had not considered they would age while he was away.

Once the greetings were over Will invited his parents back to the inn. "We'll join thee there as soon as we've cleaned up, both t'shop and ourselves," an excited Mistress Boucher exclaimed.

A short while later they were all seated at the boards of 'The Black Sheep' with trenchers groaning under the weight of food. Will's parents ordered pork trotters.

"Good plain English food," his dad commented after hearing the selection of dishes.

Father John and Will, being more adventurous, had ordered Mawmenny, a spicy chicken stew, of Eastern origin. A selection of roast vegetables accompanied the dishes served on pewter trenchers: no stale bread trenchers in this establishment. A huge log fire crackled, generating both cheer and warmth. Candles and rushlights created a flattering glow around the elegant room. The low sound of conversation surrounded them.

Will took note of everything: the quality of the tapestries on the walls, the solid looking furniture, and the quiet courtesy of the servers. He promised himself that his inn would offer the same quality of service.

He raised his goblet of red wine. "I offer a toast to my parents; to

York and to my future bride."

His mother's eyes sparkled. "You are to marry? Who is she? Is she a Frenchie or Yorkshire lass?"

"She is definitely a Yorkshire lass, born in York. Do you have a memory of a family called Thornton? They would have had children near my age."

Mistress Boucher added more wrinkles to her forehead with the effort of remembering. "I don't know of one, does tha, Walt?"

Walter Boucher shook his head. "Nay, none come t'mind. Does this mean tha's going to join us in t'business, son?' His hope-filled look gave Will a twinge of guilt.

"No, Dad. I'm planning to have my own inn. I've got enough funds to buy one." He then shared his story of King Henry and himself and the gift of the royal glove filled with coins. His three listeners were quiet and looked at him with awe.

The level of conversation rose around them. Will looked around at his eating companions. He had noticed the surge of voices after a new group of travellers entered the hall and sat at the long table. The men were talking excitedly to other diners. He listened in on the conversation…

…King Henry had returned from France to London. He stood down the remains of his army in Calais and had only a small retinue with him, plus his important French prisoners. The Corporation of London put on extravagant displays of pageantry to celebrate the king's victory. Henry was welcomed outside the city at Blackheath by twenty thousand citizens wearing red clothes together with red and white hoods. The king came into their midst wearing a gown of purple, not his customary armour. The Londoners shouted and cheered him. Massive choirs sang hymns of…

…Will turned back to his guests after silently raising his goblet and blessing his king for giving him a choice between being an innkeeper or a butcher.

Following a relaxing evening of good food and wine, Master and Mistress Boucher took their leave with promises from Will of more frequent visits. Will's mother entreated her son to introduce his sweetheart soon.

Will and Father John settled back for a brandy.

"Solid parents you have there, Will. I can see why your father is disappointed you are not to join him."

"It's an old argument: we've been over it many times. I will try to see more of them now I'm back. After this evening, I realize that family is important. Do you have family, Father?"

"No, nobody left I'm afraid. Between the pestilence and the hard life our people lead, all my lot are dead."

"It's fortunate that you have Mistress Ridley, otherwise, your life could be lonely."

Father John, now mellowed by the relaxing evening, responded. "Florrie and I are good for each other. I require looking after and she needs loving care. She suffered greatly when she lived with Ridley."

"I gather your relationship with the innkeeper was strained?"

"As I have told you before, I will not speak ill of the man. I do admit that life is sweeter without his presence."

"Do you have any ideas on who or what may have caused him to be no longer with us, Father?"

Father John stood and carefully placed his now empty brandy goblet on the boards. "Let us part as colleagues, if not as confidants, Will. I thank you for a pleasant evening; however, I am to bed. Good night."

Will sat alone, sipping his brandy. Not much meat on that bone; he might as well go to bed too, but something was tugging at the back of his mind. He had lost the thought in the intensity of searching the Church documents and then the excitement of seeing his parents again. It was back now, like an itch. Something struck him earlier today and he had put it out of his mind. There would be no sleep until he teased it out.

It was something to do with the journey. Father John had retreated within himself at one point. What caused that? Will swirled the brandy dregs around looking into the spinning liquid for an answer. It was when Will had noted that it was as though the priest had built a defensive wall around himself.

Eureka! He had it! When Will had made the joking comment about 'perhaps you don't commit sins', that was when Father John built the wall. Now what was that about, guilty conscience, perhaps? Now he wouldn't be able to sleep for wondering what sin the priest was guilty of having committed.

57

Annie resolved the following day to follow her plan of talking to Father John's housekeeper. She found it hard to focus on her patients' care as she and her aunt made their rounds. At one point, her aunt asked if she was feeling unwell.

"Annie, I can feel your agitation. It flows from you in waves. Is something bothering you?"

Annie shook her head. "I'm just tired, Aunt Meg. It will pass."

The two elderly patients with arthritis were thrilled to receive the salve that Annie had made, despite its stinky aroma, and her aunt complemented her niece on her herbal skills. A horehound syrup soothed the persistent cough of a young child, and Annie completed a pre-natal examination on a six-month pregnant woman, showing her fascinated aunt twenty-first century methods. Eventually, the two women completed their visits and returned to the cottage.

Meg put away unused supplies, and keeping her shawl wrapped around her shoulders, informed her niece she was going to visit a friend for an hour.

"Mistress Browning will show me how to dye my yarn using gall-nuts. Do you want to accompany me, Annie? You told me before you had an interest in using nature's materials to make dyes. It may provide a distraction for you."

"No, thank you, Aunt Meg, I think I will meditate. Meditation always calms me. I've neglected my practice since coming here." Annie crossed her fingers behind her back as she spoke the untruth. Her aunt would not approve of what she was about to do, but the urge to solve the mystery of the death of the innkeeper was like an itch she was not able to scratch.

Annie saw her aunt out of the door and then began pacing around the room, watched by two curious cats.

"Rosamund, I am determined to visit Florrie Ridley. She has the strongest connection to both the innkeeper and the priest. That link cannot be a coincidence. In all of the detective stories I have ever read, the detective never believes in coincidences. It seems to me the key people in this whole jumble are the priest, the late innkeeper, the steward, and right in the middle is Florrie Ridley. I *am* going to find out more about the relationship between the priest and the innkeeper. Somehow, that's key to the whole puzzle."

Rosamund meowed her disapproval but Annie ignored her.

"I don't care what you think; I know this is the only way I can obtain the information I need."

Rosamund meowed even louder, swinging her tail and reaching out with her front paws to stop Annie as she walked toward the cottage door.

"Stop it, Rosamund. Now you've clawed my gown and pulled the threads. I am going."

Annie lifted her shawl from its hook by the door and left the cottage, leaving behind an agitated, tail-twitching cat.

Walking hurriedly down the village street, Annie kept a lookout for her aunt. She was nowhere in sight. The day was drawing in and the air was cool, the street empty of people. Annie mentally thanked Mistress Bagshaw for her lovely warm shawl as she wrapped it snugly around her shoulders. She stood for a few minutes by the village pond, watching a family of ducks feeding and took some deep breaths. Tact and diplomacy were of the essence, not her strongest attributes, she reminded herself.

Florrie answered the knock at her door. "T'Father's away, 'e'll be back in a couple of days." She started to close the door.

"I know," Annie reached out her arm to hold the door open. "He's gone with my Will. You and I met before when I visited Father John. I'm Annie Thornton, niece to Mistress Wistowe. I thought you and I could get to know each other, seeing as our men are away together. I've brought some herbs we can brew up for a pleasant drink."

"A don't usually bother wi' small talk. Nivver did me no good."

"I'm sure Father John would be pleased about us being neigh-bourly and my aunt, Mistress Wistowe sends her regards." Annie crossed her fingers behind her back again at another white lie.

Florrie reluctantly opened the door wider and let Annie in. She led her to the same room Annie had sat in on her previous visit. A fire burned on the hearthstone.

"If you would be so kind as to boil some water I'll make an infu-sion for us. I brought some chamomile; it is pleasant and calming to drink."

Florrie hooked a small pot of water over the fire. Her lowered eyes, hunched shoulders, and back turned to Annie made it plain: she didn't want Annie there.

Annie stared at Florrie's rigid back, frantically trying to think of something to say that would relax the housekeeper.

"I know Will and I have only known each other for a short time but we were attracted to each other from the beginning. Do you be-lieve in love at first sight, Mistress Ridley?"

Florrie slowly turned around to face her visitor. Annie sighed with relief; at least that was a start.

"A nivver 'eard of owt so daft. Any'ow, it's nowt t'do wi' me if tha plans t'marry or not."

Annie gave the dried chamomile leaves to Florrie, continuing her chatter about herself and Will. Florrie poured the chamomile infu-sion into two bowls, seemingly not liking the smell as she wrinkled her nose.

She handed a bowl to Annie. "Aye, that's why they've gone t'York, to check t'church register, births, an' such, mek sure tha's not cousins, as everybody thinks. So t'Father were tellin' me."

Annie nearly choked. Oh, my God, they could search all day. Her name wouldn't be there. She hadn't been born.

"Is tha all reight, mistress? Tha drink's not calmin' thee too much. Mebby tha needs a sip of wine instead?"

Annie recovered, her face flushed from coughing. "I'm fine, thank you. I'll enjoy the chamomile."

Florrie didn't offer any further conversation, but she appeared to relax a little. They sat in reasonable companionship, sipping their drinks.

"I like Father John," Annie took advantage of the moment. "He cares for all the villagers, young and old, and the villagers really like him too. I understand he was born here. Were you?"

"Nay, I were born a few miles frum 'ere. Came t'village sum years ago now. Am still seen as an incomer though, not one o' them."

"I suppose you came here with Master Ridley when he became the innkeeper at the 'King's Head'?"

"Aye."

Tentatively now, Annie leaned forward, "I did hear that Master Ridley was not kind to you. How wonderful that Father John was able to take you in and give you work."

The look Florrie gave her visitor would have soured milk. "Sounds like tha's been listenin' to old biddies' tales in t'village. I'd do owt for t'Father, he's been good to me, unlike t'uther un."

"I get the feeling the whole village would do anything for Father John."

"Aye, that's true. 'E's good to 'em."

The two women sat in silence, each contemplating their drinks.

Annie cleared her throat. "I can imagine how awkward it must have been, Father John and Master Ridley living and working in the same small village. How did you all cope?"

"We just did, an' what's that to thee?"

"I was just thinking about you and how you had to manage. You were caught in the middle, it seems to me. I'm sure your former husband resented the fact that you left him and I'd heard Father John was unhappy with the innkeeper because of his behaviour toward the young girls at the inn, and," diplomacy now forgotten, Annie leaned forward eagerly, "apparently, he knew Ridley was skimming profits from the wool smugg—"

"—'Ow dare tha push tha way into this 'ouse and stick tha nose in our lives. Tha's only just cum t'village. It's none of thy business. Get out! Get out now an' tek tha poison with thee!"

With this outburst, Florrie jumped up and pushed Annie off her seat and toward the door, sending her bowl of hot liquid flying.

"Keep talkin' like that an' tha'll find thissen in trouble!" she screamed at Annie's back.

On hearing the threat, Annie had had enough. She turned back toward Florrie.

"Don't threat—"

Annie saw a blurred movement in her peripheral vision. A sharp pain pierced the left side of her head. Reaching out to grasp something to stop her descent, she found only empty air. Darkness fell.

58

Jack moved around the hall, chatting with his guests as they ate their evening meal. He was relishing his solo role as host and still felt relieved to be uninjured and alive, thanks to Sam and Rob, who took full advantage of their friend and enjoyed a couple of ales before going back to the village.

The ambiance of the evening shattered as the door to the Inn flew open and in rushed a dishevelled figure.

"Master Hall, Jack, Annie is missing!"

It was Meg, looking wildly around the room, as though she might find Annie there. The startled guests stopped eating. Jack caught Meg by the shoulders and quickly maneuvered her into his private quarters.

"What's happened, Mistress Wistowe, to alarm you so much?"

"I told you; Annie is missing. I left her at home after we had finished work. She'd been behaving oddly all day. I could sense her energy: restless, almost feverish. When I came home—I was only gone a short time—she wasn't there. Apparently, she went to see Florrie Ridley at the church house. She planned to ask her questions about Father John and his connection to the innkeeper. She knew I wouldn't approve. I went to the church house and spoke with Mistress Ridley. She said Annie hadn't been there. The cats have disappeared too. They always come home at this time to eat. I've been all over the village looking for her. No-one's seen her." The usually calm Mistress Wistowe burst into tears. "I know something has happened to her. I can feel it."

Jack tried to hide his concern. There had been enough threats against Annie that this could be serious, and Will away too. God's Teeth, what a mess.

"We'll find her, Mistress Wistowe. You go home in case she returns, all repentant from worrying you. In fact, I'll take you back myself and look for some help to search for her."

Meg wiped her teary face with her hand and wrapped her shawl back around her shoulders. After telling Aggie he intended to go out and the reason why, Jack accompanied Annie's aunt home. The moon being on the wane, the night offered little light and he had left in haste without a lighted torch to guide them; nevertheless, they knew the way well enough. Jack kept Mistress Wistowe close to him and watched out for the two bullyboys with his hand on his dagger. He figured they must have been sulking somewhere else, as there was no sign of them. He saw Mistress Wistowe home without incident. Neither Annie nor the cats had returned.

"Do make yourself a warm drink and relax. I'm sure all will be well." Jack threw some sticks on the hearth fire embers.

Meg shook her head. "I will never forgive myself if anything happens to Annie. It's my fault she's here at all. I must go with you; it is the least I can do."

Jack managed to persuade the distraught woman to stay at home in case Annie returned. He needed to recruit Sam and Rob to help and reckoned the most likely place to find them would be at the latest alehouse. He walked rapidly down the main street until he spotted the ale-stake and knocked on the door. The ale seller opened the door, no doubt expecting another customer. She bid him enter. It took a few seconds for his eyes to become accustomed to the gloom. He could make out quite a few figures illuminated in the firelight as they sat grouped around the hearth.

"Hey, it's our mate, Jack." Sam called from the group, sounding as though a few more ales had slipped down his throat. "'Ave a drink wi' us, Jack."

"Sam, Rob, I need your help. Mistress Thornton, the one who has been looking after the babies and the sick in the village, is missing. We have to mount a search."

To Jack's surprise a different voice called out, "Nay, lad, we'll all 'elp."

The whole group stood and trooped out of the cottage. The look of dismay on the face of the ale seller would have been amusing on a different occasion.

Jack surveyed his search party, all swaying, but willing.

Rob called out, "me an' Sam'll go get sum faggots for torches. Can't see me 'and in frunt o' me face."

They were back shortly with faggots lit from the ale seller's hearth and the search party went up and down the village street, knocking on each door, Jack asking the same question, "had anyone seen Mistress Thornton?" After repeatedly clarifying that Jack was talking about *after* her usual visits to help the sick, the answers were always the same: no one had set eyes upon the young woman. They finally arrived at the church house. Mistress Wistowe had mentioned that Annie had been to see the housekeeper.

Jack knocked at the door. He knocked again, louder this time. Finally, the door opened and Florrie stood there—swaying.

"Whast tha want?" The housekeeper slurred her words, and looked unkempt with her hair straggling out from under her coif.

"We're looking for Mistress Thornton, Mistress Ridley. Have you seen her this evening?"

"Why would tha bother me? What would I have to do wi' 'ere? Yon biddy, 'ere aunt, were 'ere earlier an' a told 'er t'same thing: She. 'Asn't. Been. 'Ere." She stepped back and slammed the door.

"She were drunk!" a voice from the group called. "Eeh by gum, in t'church 'ouse an' all."

Another voice piped up. "Where now, gaffer, mebbe we should look in t'forest?"

Jack groaned. "A good idea." God forbid they find her there, dead.

They all trooped off and began crashing around in the same area where the pigs found the innkeeper, to no avail. The search party regrouped at the village green. They had not lingered in the forest. The only sights they saw were yellow eyes watching them from the trees. Wolves might fancy an evening meal of ale-soaked villagers.

"Thanks for your help," he addressed his troops. "I'm going over to the Manor House to see if they have seen Mistress Thornton. You're all welcome to come with me."

Much shuffling of feet from the search party greeted this invitation. Enthusiasm had dissipated along with the alcohol. The group spokesman raised his hand.

"I think we're dun for t'night, gaffer. We'll 'elp out t'morra if tha needs us."

They moved on to their homes, leaving Sam and Rob behind.

"We'll go over there wi' thee," Sam volunteered, "but we'll stay back frum t'door, if tha sees what I mean."

Jack understood they didn't want the inhabitants of the Manor House to recognize them.

"Fine with me."

The two men stayed back in the shadows and Jack marched up to the big oak door and rapped hard. Matilda appeared. "What's tha want?"

"I need to speak to Steward Sneed on urgent business."

"Well, tha can't. 'E's not 'ere."

"What's t'problem, Matilda, at this time o' night? It's long past curfew." Bailiff Crompton's bulk filled the doorway, the flickering light from the great hall backlighting him, making it hard for Jack to make out his features.

"It's me, Jack Fletcher. Can I come in? I have urgent business."

"Nay, Master Fletcher, it's too late of an evenin'. What is thy urgent business?"

"Mistress Thornton is missing. I hoped someone at the Manor House had seen her."

The bailiff started to close the door. "No-one's seen 'ide nor 'air of 'er. Good night to thee."

Frustrated and disconsolate, Jack walked back to his mates. Guilt overwhelmed him; his heart weighed as heavy as a stone sitting in his chest. So much for his previous statement to Mistress Wistowe that he and Will were committed to protecting her niece.

"I don't know what else to do right now. Perhaps we should start again at first light. I have to go back to the village to see Annie's aunt and let her know we've had no success."

"We'll walk back wi' thee, Jack. We'll get goin' again in t'mornin'."

59

Rosamund and Bea watched the bailiff dismiss Jack. They had been mounting a surveillance on the Manor House for a while. Their adventure started when Meg came back to the cottage after visiting her friend. Rosamund wound herself around Meg's skirts until she had her attention.

"What do you want, Rosie? Are you hungry? No. What is it? Are you trying to tell me something?"

Yes I am, and do not call me Rosie.

Meg finally sat Rosamund on her knee and the cat stared into her eyes, sending the message that Annie had gone to see Florrie Ridley and planned to question her about the innkeeper and Father John. Rosamund shared her anxiety about the rashness of the act.

"I agree, I believe that was a foolish thing to do but she hasn't been gone long. I'm sure she'll be back shortly bursting with new information."

Meg's response did not suit Rosamund who leapt to the ground, signalling Bea to follow her. The two cats set off to the church house. Rosamund believed Bea's helpmate was just a little too casual about Annie's mission. She intended to check for herself.

The two cats hid behind a bush still bearing some late autumn leaves and became watchful statues. They did not have long to wait. Two men, leading a horse, came along the street. They were hard to see in the gathering gloom but cats' eyes are made for such a task. A woman accompanied them. She moved ahead and opened the door to the church house. They tethered the horse to the fence and went inside. The men soon came out carrying a rolled bundle, which they placed over the back of the horse and secured with rope.

"Get in t'ouse and keep tha trap shut," one of the men growled. The woman scurried in and closed the door. The men walked the horse slowly across the fields. The cats followed from a safe distance and found themselves at the back door of the Manor House.

"Open t'door, Jobe, then get back 'ere an' 'elp me."

Jobe followed his orders and the two men carried the bundle through the doorway, kicking the door closed behind them.

The cats settled down for an all-night vigil. Rosamund needed to get into the Manor House to confirm the bundle contained *she who shared her life,* and then pass the information to Jack using her telepathic skills.

The cats took turns at sleeping and watching, keeping close together to conserve their warmth. The long, cold, and dark December night eventually ended. The dawn arrived agonizingly slowly and, at last, the back door opened.

A young woman came out of the door, carrying a pot brimming with liquid in her arms. Rosamund had seen her in the village a few times, usually on the arm of a young man. The woman, a girl really, put the pot on the ground and propped open the door with a stone. She disappeared around the corner with the pot. Rosamund wasted no time and shot through the open door, leaving Bea to keep watch.

* * *

Steward Sneed sat close to the blazing log fire. He had no fat on his long bony frame so felt perpetually chilled. The North of England was such a godforsaken place in contrast to his home county of Kent. It had terrible weather and idiots for people, and they all talked as though they had nails in their mouths. The food did not suffice either: the main ingredient of most dishes seemed to be turnips. Only his lucrative business dealings kept him here, otherwise he'd go south in a flash where the people were civilized, the food was of a varied and high quality, and the women refined and amenable. He sipped his mulled wine appreciatively (thank the Lord for France). His bailiff was recounting Jack Fletcher's visit.

"Remind me again, Bailiff Crompton, why we are protecting Florrie?"

"Because she's me sister, sir. She came with Ridley an' me when we arrived 'ere. And she's been a faithful 'elp to you over t'years. Even after she left Ridley an' ran to t'priest—silly bugger she were for doin' that—it worked for thee. Tha knows every step Father John teks, an' many uthers in t'village besides. She keeps 'er mouth shut, as well, about what 'appens 'ere wi' thy business, just like me, *sir*."

Sneed was not slow to hear the emphasis on the 'sir'.

"I know, I know," he said, waving his long arms in the air. "I just wish she would control her temper. I don't want to have to hide another body. The pigs will get too fat." He chuckled at his little joke. "Nevertheless, we must make sure Mistress Thornton recovers. We can't burn a dead witch." He turned to Matilda. "How is she?"

"She's still unconscious and 'as a nasty bruise on 'er 'ead, but she's moaning a bit an' movin' more."

"Excellent. Keep a close eye on her. Ensure the storage room remains locked. Spread the word we have evidence she is a witch and we are transporting her to York to stand trial for witchcraft. That should keep her out of people's way. Let me know the minute she regains consciousness. Arrange for Butts and Cartwright take her to York. If she doesn't gain consciousness I'll have to think of something else."

* * *

Rosamund, positioned just outside the entrance to the great hall, found the conversation to be illuminating and tucked it away to share later. In the meantime, she had to find the locked door. Most of the rooms lacked doors, but she eventually came to one and sat, listening. Her highly tuned hearing picked up soft moaning from inside. Hiding behind a wooden chest placed against the wall, the cat waited. A woman came down the hall carrying a bowl and talking to herself. "Men. They 'ave no idea 'ow much work this is. Aven't a got enough t'do without 'avin' to tek on nursin' duties?"

Rosamund recognized the voice; it belonged to the same woman who had been part of the conversation she had heard earlier. Placing the bowl on the floor, the woman unhooked a bunch of keys from the belt around her waist. As she opened the door, Rosamund crept in behind her, hiding behind her skirts—to no avail—the woman spotted her.

"'Ow did tha get in 'ere, damned cat? Out! Out! A well-aimed kick sent Rosamund back out of the door, but not before she saw a familiar shape on a mattress. *She who shares my life* was in the room.

Rosamund streaked back down the hallway to the door that gained her entry. She hid behind a large barrel. The room offered many enticing smells, including mice. She determined to ignore the gurgling of her empty stomach; soon, someone would open the door again.

The young woman who had propped open the door before, did so again with her arms full of bed covers, granting Rosamund her freedom. Re-united with Bea, the little black cat and her faithful accomplice set off to find Jack.

60

Jack rose before dawn. He paced around the kitchen wearing out Aggie's ears as he filled her in on last evening's activities and failures.

"I don't know which way to turn and Will should be home this afternoon. How can I tell him Annie is missing? Aggie, what am I to do?"

"First things first." Ever the pragmatist, Aggie continued, "Get sum porridge down tha throat, tha needs the energy to do what thy 'as to do."

"And *what* is it I have to do?"

"Facts, lad, tha needs facts. She won't 'ave run off by 'erself. So, who'll gain from Mistress Thornton's disappearance? What dus she know? Where could they 'ave put 'er? We live in a small village. There aren't too many places tha can 'ide sumbody. Tha knows when she went missin'. Who were last person she talked to? Work from there."

Jack looked at Aggie in astonishment. "How do you know all that?"

"Me dad were a thinker. 'E taught me to look at stuff sensibly. Just because I turned into a cook dunt mean I can't think."

The kitchen door opened and Rosamund and Bea padded in.

"I 'ope its alright to let 'em in," called the perky voice of Cissie, the serving girl. "They were scratchin' at front door."

The two black cats began winding themselves around the cook.

"Poor lambs, you look 'ungry, get this down thee both." Aggie put down milk and pork bits. The two felines attacked the food as though they were starving.

When they had finished eating Jack went over to Rosamund and picked her up.

"Where have you two been? It's bad enough we've lost Annie, but we were worried about you two as well." He stroked Rosemond's thick fur. She flinched as his hand passed over her ribs. "What's this? Are you injured? You've been having an adventure."

Jack sat down on a bench and looked into Rosemond's eyes as he stroked her ears. Rosamund stared back—hard. A voice came into his head, a feminine voice, highly pitched, and remarkably catlike. *She who shares my life is at the Manor... She is lying in a locked room... The men plan to send her to York as a witch... She who shares my life is at the Manor... She is lying in a...*

"Oh, by the Lord, I hear you!" cried Jack. "Aggie, the cat is talking to me. She who shares my life? Rosamund must mean Annie. Annie is a prisoner in the Manor House. She's sleeping, maybe drugged, or unconscious. The men—I guess that's the steward and his bailiff—think she's a witch. Am I going crazy, listening to a cat? I didn't sleep well, perhaps that's it!"

He saw the look of disgust on Rosamund's face.

"Sorry, Rosie, I believe you."

He heard the voice in his head say *do not call me Rosie* as she leapt off his knee with a mew of pain.

Aggie shook her head. "This is a fine muddle. We've got talking cats and a kidnapped witch. Even me dad couldn't sort this lot out."

"Aggie, help me. What do I do? It's no good going to the steward. I know he won't see me, and it looks like the bailiff is in it with him. He was determined to get rid of me last night. Now we know why—Annie was in the Manor House all the time."

"Well, tha can't let 'er get sent off to York. Tha'll never get 'er back. Mebbe thy 'as to start at beginnin'. It seems to me this all goes back to t'disappearin' innkeeper. Did tha say Annie 'ad gone to see Florrie at church 'ouse?"

"Mistress Wistowe told me so, but Florrie said she hadn't. Mind you, she looked drunk when I saw her."

"That's peculiar in itself, 'cos I've niver 'eard nowt about Florrie Ridley drinkin'."

Jack stood. "I'm going to take the cats back and have a word with Mistress Wistowe. She needs to know what's happening anyway. Will you look after things again, Aggie?"

Aggie agreed to be the gaffer and Jack marched out with a cat under each arm. He ignored Jobe, standing guard outside the door. As he walked away he realized neither of the two henchmen had been on guard yesterday evening when he left with Mistress Wistowe. Odd, one of them always stood on duty, resembling a truculent gargoyle.

61

After a robust breakfast of frumenty made rich with the flavour of eggs, Will and Father John prepared to leave. Will thoroughly enjoyed his stay in the well-established city inn and made mental notes on how he might improve his own establishment, as and when he acquired one. He made a pledge that he would investigate having a carpenter build him oak tables and benches; perhaps Mistress Davey's son would be interested. In the meantime, at least he could encourage 'call me Aggie' to experiment with a wider variety of foods.

Their host offered them advice on where to go to get the best cloth for the most reasonable price and they set off to buy Jack's wedding finery. Meg and Annie had wisely given them precise instructions so the task of choosing the fine wool cloth was easy. Packing the purchases in their saddlebags, the two men set off to Hallamby. Neither renewed the previous evening's discussion and stayed with safer topics once again. Both talked about looking forward to being back in the village: Will, because he could now make plans for his betrothal to Annie and Father John because the pig-killing was almost upon them. He always enjoyed the feast that followed. Fortunately, they did not know what awaited them at home.

62

Meg had not slept, nor did she plan to sleep. It was time for some serious divination. Bea's help was invaluable for Meg's practise but she would have to manage without her familiar. Filling the largest bowl with water brought from the river yesterday, Meg placed it in the centre of the table. Two beeswax candles illuminated the dark room, casting a warm, flickering light over Meg as she crouched over the bowl and filling the cottage with the sweet smell of honey.

Meg began to hum. Missing Bea to assist with her purring, Meg hummed louder and longer. She had reached the point of trembling exhaustion when the vibrations increased and energy quickened in the room. Flames from the candles brightened and small ripples appeared on the surface of the water. Meg gazed at the water. External sounds disappeared.

The ripples calmed and Meg gasped as the image of a small body appeared, curled into a ball. A red glow emanated from the form but frustratingly, she was unable to sense the surroundings.

Annie! Her niece was still alive.

When Jack arrived with Rosamund and Bea in tow, he looked as drained as Meg felt; pale faced and red-rimmed eyes with dark shadows underneath.

Meg picked up both cats and buried her face in Bea's thick, black fur. "Where have you been? I have been out of my mind with worry. It's awful enough with Annie missing, but you two disappeared at the same time."

When Jack told her about Annie's location, Meg was both horrified and relieved. "How did you find out?"

"I know you'll think I'm crazy, but Rosamund told me. I don't know how she knows, but she does and somehow, she told me. I pray to God Annie is still alive."

"No, you're not crazy. Both Bea and Rosamund are exceptional cats. Cats are intuitive anyway and these two are especially so. Bea shares her thoughts with me and you are lucky that Rosamund likes you so much she does the same with you—and yes, Annie is still alive."

"Thank the Lord, I thought I was imagining things," Jack gave a heartfelt sigh. He looked at Meg with curiosity. "How do you know she's still alive?"

"Oh, I just sense it. I would know."

He threw her a quizzical look. "By the way, Rosamund is injured; it must be a result of last night's adventure." He showed Meg the painful area on Rosemond's ribs.

"A comfrey poultice will fix that. I'll bind it to her and she can rest."

While Meg tended to Rosamund and Bea watched anxiously, Jack started pacing again.

"What to do, Mistress Wistowe? What to do?"

"I am thinking, Jack. This situation requires cunning rather than strength. I wish to sit quietly while the cats are resting. Why don't you visit Jenet for a while?"

Jack never needed an excuse to see Jenet. He left in a trice.

Meg settled with the cats by her side, Bea, her familiar, closer to her. "How interesting that Steward Sneed appears to be at the centre of this web of malevolence affecting our village. Annie must have triggered this reaction through her probing. It is my fault; I brought her here and encouraged her to do exactly what she was doing. Help me, my furry friends; help me to steer the right course, the safest course, to bring Annie back to us."

Jack arrived back at Meg's home.

"Are you finished thinking?"

"I am," replied Meg with a gentle smile. "I believe Annie has to get herself out of her predicament. If we try to interfere in any public way, we risk having the power of the law brought against us by the steward and his bailiff. Who knows what new allegations they can choose to throw at us?

"We can work better behind the scenes. Annie will have to go deep inside herself and discover skills she is not yet aware she possesses. She has to be safe once she is free, so we have to find something we can use against the steward and his henchmen so they cannot retaliate."

"I do believe we might have something," Jack's facial expression brightened. "I shared with Annie that the innkeeper had kept a meticulous account of his fraudulent dealings. I'm guessing he may not be the only one. Surely, the steward, who keeps records of all the activity in the manor, knew what Ridley was up to, yet he didn't stop him. What if—and I realize we have no evidence yet—what if Sneed is up to no good? He seems to have a free hand in managing the affairs of Hallamby Manor. Ridley may have known of his crimes and threatened to tell Prior Gilbert, which protected him from any action on the steward's part. The manorial account rolls the steward keeps for Prior Gilbert may prove it; he goes to great lengths to keep the Prior from visiting. Talk about a nest of vipers."

"To prove Steward Sneed is dishonest we would have to examine the rolls ourselves." Meg shook her head. "I believe all things are possible, I hope we can find a way to do so."

"I'm sure Father John could tell us what duties are the responsibilities of the steward." Jack groaned. "They'll be back this afternoon. I don't know how I can face Will and tell him about Annie. I promised him I would keep an eye on her. I've let all my friends down."

Meg attempted to comfort him before he left, but she could see he was deeply distressed and would not be consoled.

"We have a problem to solve," she murmured to Bea and Rosamund, stroking the fur of both. "We have to help Annie to help herself. She is a witch but just at the beginning of her practice. This is an opportunity for her to gain confidence in her abilities, yet we must ensure she remains safe. Focus your energies on Annie. We will send her guile, send her wisdom and send her our love."

63

Annie tried to open her eyes. The effort proved too great and she spiralled dizzily down a long black tunnel. Later, she heard voices coming from a great distance. Attempting to lift her head created a disastrous return to the tunnel. She wouldn't try that again.

Floating in a world of darkness, Annie occasionally heard a voice, felt someone wipe her face, became aware of liquid being trickled into her mouth and noted the constant pain at the side of her head. It seemed easier to stay in the darkness and not make the effort to move. She would remain sleeping, dream her dreams, and not disturb the tranquility...

...she was driving her car but couldn't see the road, freezing with terror when she realized the reason for her poor visibility—her eyes were closed. Nebulous shapes loomed up but not clearly enough to avoid hitting them. After frantically careening all over the road like the ball in a pinball machine, she managed to pull the car over beside a high green hedge and turned off the engine with a shaking hand. Trembling fingers reached up to her eyes but were unable to force her eyelids open. The phone lay on the passenger seat. If she could reach it, she would call Mary to rescue her.

64

December 2015, Hallamby, Yorkshire

"Okay, It's time to end this. Listen to me, Annie. ANNIE, this is Mary. You have to fettle yourself. That's an old Yorkshire word, 'fettle'. You MUST sort yourself out. You have to get up from that god-awful mattress and MOVE! If you are a witch, and I do believe you are, then do something witchy. I'm not supposed to be able to control anything, right? I just write stuff down. I'm changing the rules. OPEN YOUR EYES AND GET UP!

65

December 1415, Hallamby, Yorkshire

Annie's eyes shot open. She was awake and in freefall, landing softly onto something that rustled. Relief flooded throughout her body; she was safe. Feeling the mattress with her hands, Annie realized she was not in the car, but home in bed. Rolling into a ball, she sank gratefully back into sleep, but not for long. Mary's voice persisted in calling her to get up.

It's okay Mary. You saved me. Now go away. I'm sleeping. It's not time for work. Now what? Rosamund, is that you? Curl up beside me and keep me warm. Ah, I can hear you purring. Who is shouting at me?

"Will you all be QUIET?" Annie sat up, irritated. The room spun around her making her nauseated. Her head hurt. Had she been to the pub? She had no memory of going out for a drink. Why would Mary leave her if she were drunk? But none of that that made sense; she never got drunk.

The world eventually stopped spinning. Annie ran her tongue over dry, cracked lips. Risking opening one eye, she thanked the Goddess that she could. What a frightening dream that had been. A bowl of liquid sat beside her. Where was she? Slowly, Annie looked around, not recognizing her surroundings. The room was in shadow. A shuttered opening high on a wall allowed in a dim light. Sacks bulging with their contents were stacked around the walls. A pile of trestles leaned precariously in one corner. Wooden casks formed a pyramid in another. Excruciatingly slowly, she crawled to the door. It was locked! Crawling back to her straw pallet at the same pace, she lay down, exhausted by the effort.

A key turned in the lock. Annie instinctively closed her eyes.

"Still sleeping, is tha? Me mam said I should try to get thee up, but I don't see t'point if tha's not awake. Steward's gettin' a bit mithered. Wants thee out of 'ere and in t'jail in York. Bailiff says tha's a witch and tha's goin' to burn at t'stake. Them two bullies o' bailiff's are waitin' to tek thee as soon as tha's awake. Tha dunt look too witchy reight now. 'Ey up, tha's not dead, is tha?"

A bony finger poked Annie's ribs making her grunt.

"Thanks be to God for that."

The door closed. The key turned in the lock. Annie sat up again, slowly, and waited for the room to stop whirling around.

She was a prisoner in the Manor House. The steward had finally made good on his promise to have her branded a witch. How did she get here? She remembered talking to Rosamund about going to visit Father John's housekeeper but try as she might, a fog clouded her mind; the rest was blank.

Where were Will and Jack? Why were they not breaking down the door to rescue her? Perhaps they didn't know. Aunt Meg should know, she's a witch, for goodness sake! Annie panicked, her body shaking uncontrollably, tears coursing down her cheeks. She didn't belong here. She should be back home in the twenty-first century where all these bad people were dead. All of the stories she had ever read about witches burning at the stake came flooding into her head. Joan of Arc—how terrible that had been—the crowds cheering and willing the flames to move higher—STOP!

Annie drew a shaky breath. That kind of thinking would not help. Mentally straightening her spine, she took a few more deep breaths. Surely, Aunt Meg would be missing her by now. Could she use her magic to rescue Annie? Wait a minute; Annie reminded herself that she, too, had witchy powers; just a newbie, but still… It looked as though she must save herself. Time was running out. As soon as Sneed found out she had regained consciousness she would be off to York with those two horrible men. She needed Rosamund to help her. Did she hear Rosamund purring earlier, or was that a dream too, like Mary's voice?

Rosamund, I need you, come to me. I must think of a plan, a clever and devious plan. Meg is always appealing to the Divine Goddess. I'll do the same and ask the Goddess for help. It can't hurt. Maybe she can get me out of here and stop Sneed. I will worry about everything else once I am free and safe.

Annie lay down again and, trying to ignore the mouldy smell floating up from the pallet, eventually fell into a deep sleep.

She was floating on a white cushion of light amongst cottony, cumulus clouds. Her body felt light, ethereal, one with the cloud. She lifted her arm, so weightless it floated. Gazing in awe at her hand, she saw right through the flesh to the delicate red and blue pathways, the white intricate bones (so many of them). She raised herself dreamily on her cushion and called for the Goddess. Her voice carried across the clouds sounding like chords played on a harp. Nothing happened. She called again.

I hear you, Annie; I am coming.

This voice reminded her of spring water bubbling out of the ground. She scanned the blue horizon and saw a tiny moving spot emerging from infinity. It grew closer and larger until it became visible as a glorious, galloping white horse with his long tail flowing impossibly long, like a waterfall. The Goddess rode the horse and held his abundant mane in her hands. The horse stopped in front of Annie and bending his front legs, bowed his head. The Goddess floated off his back and held out her arms as she walked towards Annie, her white robes swirling around her, her golden hair billowing around her head. Annie thought she looked a little like Meg. She spoke: once again, Annie heard the gentle murmur of water flowing.

"Child, you called me and asked for my help. Here I am. Think of what these men who have trapped you fear the most—discovery! They are dishonest men. They have no shame about stealing from others. Know this: the steward is a vainglorious man. He likes to keep a record of his triumphs; therein lies the proof of his treachery. You cannot overcome him using strength but you can out-think him by using cunning and

perspicacity."

The Goddess floated back onto her steed and rode away. Annie watched until they became a tiny speck in the cosmos.

She continued to float on her bed of light, contemplating the words of the Divine Goddess. Rosamund emerged out of the clouds and flew towards her.

"She who shares my life, I know you need my help. I will come to you. Think in the twenty-first century."

Annie awoke. She took a few minutes to gather her thoughts, realizing her circumstances were dire. As reality flooded in and her heart started to race she forced herself to breathe deeply. She shook her head—gently. What a bizarre dream. She tried to remember all of it. Did the mysterious Goddess and Rosamund visit her? The Goddess talked about keeping records—she mentioned the steward. What word did the Goddess use—perspicacity—what did it mean? Impractical advice to give her if she couldn't understand it. In addition, Rosamund told her to think in the twenty-first century. Perhaps it meant having the advantage of knowing things these people did not. She absentmindedly fondled the fine gold chain around her neck.

It would be wise to cultivate an ally from the Manor House camp. Who belonged to the young voice she heard earlier? The child sounded malleable. Annie must convince her to help and let Sneed believe she was still unconscious.

Annie made her decision. She would work on the person with the young voice and hope to find a way to buy her silence.

66

Father John and Will expressed relief at arriving at the Manor House stables. The light was fading from the day and a fine rain fell. They dismounted and stretched their aching backs and stiff muscles. The stableboy came out and took hold of the tired horses.

Father John patted the flank of his horse. "We must pay our respects to Steward Sneed, and thank him for the use of the horses."

The two weary men made their way over to the entrance. Father John raised his hand and rapped hard. Matilda opened the door and her eyes widened when she saw Father John and Will standing there.

"I'll 'ave t'see if master's 'ome," she mumbled as she closed the door quickly.

"Odd," commented Father John.

It seemed a while before the door opened again. "Steward says to enter."

"Welcome, welcome." A jovial sounding Sneed stood in his usual spot next to the fireplace. "Come by the fire and warm yourselves. A successful journey to York, I trust. Church business, I imagine."

"It was, Steward. We just called to say thank you for the loan of the horses."

"Anytime, sir, anytime. And you, Will, did you complete your business and did you get to see your parents? I understand you to have said they lived in York."

"I did, Steward. My business was successful and we enjoyed a pleasant dinner with my parents. I'm pleased to be back and looking forward to getting back to work at the inn and to seeing my betrothed again."

"Your betrothed! Oh, this is news indeed," said Sneed. "You young men do not waste any time these days with the affairs of the heart. Who is the fortunate young woman?"

"Mistress Thornton has agreed to be my wife," Will proudly announced.

A log split in the hearth: the sound fell heavily into the silent room.

* * *

Annie's eyes flew open. She had heard Will's voice.

"Ee, tha's awake," squealed the young woman, sent in to guard Annie when the unexpected guests arrived. Annie observed the owner of the voice for the first time. It was vital that she get this young person to work with her. She saw a young girl—she couldn't be more than Jenet's age, fourteen or fifteen—freckled face, long blond plaits tied with blue ribbons.

"I 'ave to go tell t'steward tha's woken up. Jobe an' Asne are waitin' to tek thee t'York. Steward says they're goin' to burn thee 'cos tha's a witch. Seems a shame really. A know tha's bin lookin' after babbies in village an' me aunty likes thee." The girl started toward the door.

"Please," Annie whispered. "You know I'm a witch, don't you. If you keep quiet about me being awake, I'll make a spell for you to achieve your greatest wish."

"Me greatest wish!" squealed the girl again walking back to her prisoner. Then she stopped and held up her hand, crossing her forefinger over her thumb. "Tha won't 'ex me, will tha? A 'eard as 'ow witches can shrivel thee up t'nuthin'."

"Shshsh. I would never hurt you. I work only for good. I will give you a spell that will work on anything you choose; however, you have to keep the secret that I am awake and help me in other ways. This is the only way the spell will work. What is your name?"

"Am called Ada. Can thy 'elp me sweet'eart to ask me to wed 'im? A know 'e luvs me. 'E just can't seem t'tek next step an' am not gettin' any younger."

Annie smiled at this ridiculous statement. "That's an easy spell as long as you truly love each other."

Ada squealed again.

"Please be quiet, they'll hear you. That voice I heard, it sounded like my betrothed, Master Boucher, from the inn?"

"Aye, it is. 'Im an' t'Father are 'ere. Is 'e your sweet'eart then? That's reight luvly."

"Will you take a message to him for me?"

"Nay, I can't do that, 'appen they'll see me. More than me life's worth. Me mam'd kill me."

"Who's your mam?"

"Why, it's Matilda who works 'ere. She looks after t'steward. Tha knows 'er sister, Mistress Davey, in t'village. She's me Aunty Saby. She's t'one who likes thee."

"Do you ever go to the village?"

"Aye, lots o' times, if I've dun me work, am free. That's when a see me sweet'eart, Nate. It's t'pig-killing day tomorrow, as well. A'll be there all day."

"I'll give you a spell I promise will work if you'll take a message to Master Fletcher at the inn on the big road, 'The King's Head', and, if you see a small black cat who answers to the name Rosamund hanging around, bring her to me. Will you try and go tonight?"

Ada wriggled with excitement. "A'll do it. What's t'spell?"

Annie heard Rosamund's voice, a repeat of how she had spoken to Annie in her dream. *Remember the twenty-first century.* Reaching behind her neck, she unfastened a gold chain with a small golden locket attached, hidden from view by her gown. She removed the locket from the chain.

"This is strong magic," Annie murmured to the quivering girl. "Look." Opening the locket, she showed Ada the miniature photos. "These are two great witches: my mother and father."

"How did they get in there? Did tha shrink 'em wi' magic?"

Annie realized that Ada had never seen a photograph. "No. This is how they look, as in a painting or drawing."

Ada nodded. She was familiar with the wall paintings on the Manor House walls and in the church.

Annie continued. "This is a golden heart; it represents love. You must place it next to your heart and before you go to sleep say quietly to yourself:

"Thou hast my heart and I have thine,
Together, 'til the end of time."

Ada repeated the spell three times until she had memorized it. She was still shaking. Annie wasn't sure whether the girl was excited, frightened or a mixture of both. She placed the locket in the palm of Ada's trembling hand and closed her fingers over it.

"Remember, don't tell anyone, and keep the golden heart secret or the spell won't work. Please bring me some parchment and the tools to write. An important person like Steward Sneed must keep records, so I am sure you will find writing materials in his work area. And keep an eye out for a black cat."

When the girl had gone Annie lay down, mentally apologizing to Ada for using her, although she hoped the spell was a sound one. She was the one shaking now, but with exhaustion. If she had interpreted her dream correctly, it seemed the mysterious Goddess was telling her to search for Sneed's records and that the contents would incriminate him. As Annie had no head for figures, she would have to come up with a plan to locate the records and make them accessible to Jack. She knew Jack enjoyed pouring over rows of figures, just as he had done with the innkeeper's records.

Young Ada was Annie's best chance to succeed; she had put her plan into action. Now for the hardest part: she had to wait.

67

After leaving the Manor House, Will and Father John walked to the village in easy companionship. The Father turned toward his house and Will continued down the main street. His heartbeat quickened as he anticipated seeing Annie and sharing the good news with her. Meg opened the door to his knock.

"Will, do come in." She held both his hands, pulled him in to the room and sat him down on the bench. In a calm and gentle voice, she explained what had happened. Will jumped up with a cry of anguish.

"I'm going to see the steward now and demand that he release Annie."

Meg guided him back to the bench.

"I advise you not to go and see the steward. He could choose to arrest you too. What will that achieve? Annie is not helpless; she has many skills at her disposal. She may require a little help from her friends."

Meg talked about Jack's theory of the steward's possibly corrupt practices, which an examination of the manorial accounts might reveal. If the records showed Sneed to be dishonest, they could appeal to Prior Gilbert for help.

"We have to prevent Sneed and his cronies from causing more damage."

"I'm going to see Father John right now," a still agitated Will moved toward the door. "I must do something."

"Yes, of course, but please stay away from the Manor House, if we alarm Sneed he may act rashly."

The light was fading from the day as Will ran up the road and knocked hard on the church house door. An ashen-faced Father appeared.

"It is not a good time right now, Will. I'll talk with you later."

"Sorry, Father. It has to be now." He pushed by the priest and went inside the house to the main living area. Something momentous had occurred. The room reflected chaos. Furniture lay overturned with one bench smashed. One of the walls had a new dent, probably caused by a cracked wooden goblet lying close by. Red splashes radiated up the wall. A wine flagon sat on the table. Grey ash coated the hearth and an iron poker leaned crookedly against the wall. A familiar looking shawl lay in a crumpled heap on the floor. Will picked it up.

"This is Mistress Thornton's shawl. What happened here, Father?"

Father John sank to his knees. "I don't know. I cannot find her. This is not good, not good at all."

"Do you mean Mistress Ridley? It gets worse, Father. Apparently, Mistress Thornton came here yesterday. She planned to talk to your housekeeper about the death of the innkeeper. No one has seen her since but as outlandish as it sounds, we now know she is a prisoner in the Manor House. She was there when you and I returned the horses this evening; I believe that explains the odd behaviour of Matilda and Sneed. Sneed is saying she is a witch and is threatening to send her to York for trial. Father John, would you have any idea what might have happened when Annie called here?"

"As God is my Judge, I do not know. We have to go and find Florrie. She is not well, her condition is delic—."

A loud knock at the door interrupted him. The priest rose and ran to the door with Will right behind him. A group of men stood there in the dark. They carried a dripping wet bundle on a stretcher of wattle fencing.

"So sorry, Father. It's Mistress Ridley. We were fishing in t'river. She were caught up on t'fish weir.

Father John collapsed. Will caught him before he hit the floor. He asked the men to come inside and they lay their burden down onto the rushes.

"Thank you. I will look after the Father now. Please be so good as to fetch Jack Fletcher from the inn and Mistress Wistowe from her home. Tell her to bring her herbs."

Meg arrived at the church house, breathless from rushing, and examined the housekeeper. She shook her head after a quick look at the waxy face and checking for breath emerging from the blue-tinged lips. Florrie Ridley had departed this life. Meg then tended to a shocked Father John, his teeth chattering, his body shaking. Jack arrived shortly after, also breathless from running the whole way.

Will and Jack both began speaking at the same time. They stopped and started again.

"You first," said Will.

Jack told him everything, adding his apologies for not protecting Annie and preventing her abduction. Will was desperate to believe Annie was alive and uninjured, but how did Jack know? He looked at his friend in disbelief when Jack cautiously told him a cat revealed Annie's location. Meg came to Jack's rescue, explaining, as best she could, the cats were unique. Will shook his head. Were Meg and Jack losing their minds?

Father John had recovered sufficiently to listen to the conversation. He turned to Meg. "Mistress Wistowe, did you tell Will that Mistress Thornton came here to see Florrie about the death of her husband?"

"So I believe," Meg replied. "We don't know what happened later except a witness reported seeing a woman let two men into your house. They came out carrying a rolled bundle, placed it on a horse, and took it to the Manor House."

Father John groaned and held his head in his hands.

"I knew all of this would lead to more trouble. A sin is a sin. Mea culpa. Mea culpa." He rocked in great distress.

Meg knelt down to comfort the poor man. "You are not a sinful man, Father. You are an honourable person, a man of God. We all know that. Calm yourself."

"Is this to do with the death of the innkeeper, Father John?" Will moved to Father John's other side and kneeled beside him.

"A short time after he arrived here, Ridley found out I was in charge of the wool smuggling operation. That wasn't a problem, as he became part of it, but he was aware of my share of the proceeds.

He threatened to tell Prior Gilbert about Florrie and me. As a result, he has extorted money from me for years. In the eyes of the Church, Florrie and I had committed adultery. I could be brought before the Church Courts and lose my living. He came to the house for his money the night of the storm. I pleaded with him to stop his demands. I started the smuggling as a way of supporting the people in this village. They have so little and work so hard. This last time he demanded more money than usual. He laughed at me when I tried to appeal to his better nature. Florrie must have heard him. She came up behind him and struck him over the head with the poker before I could stop her. He fell backwards and caught his head on the edge of the hearthstone. He died there and then, whether from the blow from the poker or from the hearth I do not know." The priest paused and made the sign of the cross.

"The noise from the storm covered my tracks as I made my way to the manor stables unnoticed and brought back a horse. Florrie and I took the body into the forest and buried it, but not very well, as it turned out. I arranged for Big John to pay the villagers to tell different stories and to set up the inn to look as though a disaster had occurred. The villagers hated Ridley so were pleased to help. They assumed I was the one responsible for the innkeeper's disappearance. They protected me."

He stopped talking abruptly and began rocking backwards and forwards again. When he had calmed himself sufficiently he spoke again.

"I think the same thing may have happened here with Mistress Thornton. It is possible, if she started asking Florrie questions about the innkeeper, Florrie may have panicked."

"But she didn't kill her, did she?" Will leapt to his feet in distress.

"No," said Meg quickly. "They wouldn't have taken her to the Manor House if she were dead. They would have disposed of the body as soon as possible. Father, I am so sorry about Florrie but we still have a crisis on our hands. What can you tell us about Steward Sneed's business dealings? We know he is holding Annie. We don't know why."

"Florrie…" Father John faltered and his voice broke. "Florrie is— was—the sister of Bailiff Crompton. The bailiff does Sneed's bidding and is deeply involved in his schemes. I do not believe the steward knew Florrie was involved in Ridley's death but I imagine she went to her brother for help this time. Sneed will do anything to keep Prior Gilbert from coming here and reports of Mistress Wistowe's niece being injured or dead would certainly cause an investigation. Perhaps Sneed panicked. Have no fear; he will be thinking up some sort of devious plan to wriggle out of his predicament."

Will's voice was sharp with impatience. "Forgive me Father; speed is of the essence. We know about Sneed's dealings with the smuggling. I'm sure he gets a big fat cut from the wool sales and for the wine. What else?"

"I know he sells wine to the inn at a huge profit. If you haven't received a reckoning yet, you will. He holds a lot of power here in the manor on behalf of Prior Gilbert. The villagers pay their tithes and rent each quarter, the last one being at Michaelmas in September, and the next one will be at Christmas. All the villagers, freemen or not, will gather at the Manor House and give ten percent of their income to the Church, that's the Augustine Order in this manor, either in coin or goods such as grain, wool and seeds. They pay their rent to the Lord of the Manor at this time, who happens to be Prior Gilbert. Sneed and the bailiff are responsible for the tally and keeping the accounts. As you can see, they have many opportunities for pilfering. I have no proof but Sneed is smart and I do not doubt that he is capable."

After such a long speech, the priest was exhausted and hung his head. "You finally have the truth that you have sought so diligently. Now I have to deal with this mess. If Florrie is proven to have committed suicide, I cannot bury her in consecrated ground."

"Who is to know?" Jack spoke for the first time. "It was an accident; she fell in the river while collecting water. That makes sense to me. You should know I came here looking for Annie when I found out she was missing. Florrie answered the door but I am sorry to say, looked inebriated. It could have happened easily. Father, name someone to be with you; we will bring him."

"Big John Braithwaite, the smithy, is a good man; he will assist me. Meanwhile, someone must go and tell Bailiff Crompton, he *is* Florrie's brother."

68

Annie slept after Ada left the room. She awoke to the sound of a key turning in the lock. Ada came in, carrying a scrap of parchment, a quill, and a pot of ink, wrapped in a piece of cloth.

"A've got these for thee. T'Steward keeps all 'is writin' stuff in 'is private quarters an' me mam keeps keys on 'er girdle. A told 'er a were goin' to sweep in there; it's me job anyway. T'Steward an' bailiff went out after visitors left so it were safe t'go in."

"Thank you, Ada. If I write the note now, can you take it to the Inn?"

"Aye. Am dun me work. What's tha goin' to say? A can't read an' write, more's the pity."

"You told me it's the pig killing day tomorrow, and everyone will be there, including you?"

"That's reight, but I 'ave to keep cummin' back to check on thee. Mek sure tha's not dead."

"So, I was thinking it would be lovely if my betrothed could sneak in and visit me. If I'm going to be taken to York it might be my last chance to see him."

Ada's eyes filled with tears. "Dunt seem fair, dus it? The thing is; a can't keep sayin' tha's unconscious for too much longer so it just might be last time tha'll see 'im. Trouble is, tha'd need keys, so tha can let 'im in an' out.

"That's alright. Leave the keys here. I'll never tell and after he leaves you can take the keys back. No one will ever know."

"It's like them stories of knights and their ladies, in't it, where she's trapped in a tall tower and t'andsome knight gallops up and rescues 'er. Except that tha won't be rescued. But I'd be the one bringin' thee both together, just like tha's doing for me and Nate."

Annie wrote her note:

I am ~~OK~~ well. <u>Both</u> come to M.H. tomorrow.
Jack to check Steward's records.
Ensure all at pig kill.
Annie

The version she read to an eager Ada differed in content.

Ada secreted the scrap of parchment down the bodice of her gown and left, looking excited at her role in bringing the lovers together for the last time.

Annie was pleased with her progress and tried to ignore the pangs of guilt she was feeling at deceiving a young, simple girl with a kind heart. Ada had unknowingly told her the steward kept his records locked in his private quarters and had agreed to leave the keys behind. Now, all she needed was Rosamund to help her pry open Sneed's secrets.

When Ada came back into Annie's prison, she had Rosamund in her arms.

"A found 'er 'angin' around outside. "'Ow did she know tha were 'ere? Anyhow, a took tha writin' to tha sweet'art. 'E'll see thee tomorra."

69

Will, Jack, and Meg went back to Meg's house to put their heads together. Meg informed them word had come from the slaughterer that the pig killing would take place the following day.

"It's a huge day; every single person from the village and the Manor House will be there. Once the pig slaughterer has done his work, the men cut up the carcasses. The women's job is to clean up after them and provide food and drink. Then the men pack the meat in barrels with layers of salt. It takes the whole day and goes well into the evening. A bonfire keeps the workers warm and rushlights around the green illuminate the space.

"I am guessing the Manor House will be empty of servants, including Sneed and the bailiff, although who knows what the bailiff will do with his sister's death on his mind. Sneed usually likes to watch over the proceedings. There are Manor House pigs to kill too."

"If the Manor House is deserted we should be able to get in and rescue Annie," said Will.

"And have a look at the manorial rolls," said Jack. "It's perfect. We'll come to the village green first; make sure Sneed and Crompton are busy, and then go up there. It's crucial to make sure the two bully boys are occupied too."

Will and Jack headed back to the inn feeling a little better now they had a plan. They felt a lot better after a young girl met them at the door and told them the young woman locked up at the Manor House had sent her. She handed a scrap of parchment to Will after asking his name.

"She's a witch tha knows. She's given me a luv spell to use. That's why I'm 'elping 'er. She'll let thee in. Me mam would kill me if she knew."

Will gave her some coins, which she took with alacrity and left with a smile on her face.

"It sounds as though Annie is well. According to this note, she is already thinking of a plan. This is interesting, Jack; she specifically mentions you and Sneed's records. It sounds as though Annie is thinking like us. She is smart: fancy pretending to be a witch to get the girl to help her."

70

Pig Killing Day dawned crisply. The sun rose into a clear sky promising fine weather, at least for now. The gloom of November forgotten, the village green buzzed with activity.

Will and Jack came down to watch for a while, after completing their morning chores. Bailiff Crompton had apparently stayed in the church all night keeping a vigil at the side of his sister's body. The news had spread about Florrie's death but did not appear to affect the atmosphere. People were determined to enjoy the day after looking forward to it all year.

Asne and Jobe walked up, down and around the village green, scowling and belligerent The villagers ignored them; the bullies had lost some of their fear power since the story of their meeting with Will, Sam, and Rob became common knowledge.

Pigs clustered together in the pigpen, shuffling and grunting softly as if they sensed the events to come. The most important person, the pig slaughterer, was already at work, his poleaxe stunning each pig before he cut its throat. The men then quickly hung the carcass to drain the blood. Other men were cutting up the carcasses and the women used buckets and bowls of water to clean the cutting areas.

Barrels of ale sat on trestles along with loaves of bread. Large steaming iron pots of pottage sat beside a fire pit dug the previous evening.

Sneed and his bailiff were present; Sneed enthroned on a chair brought from the big house and the bailiff standing behind him. They were not socializing, remaining focused on the pig slaughterer and his work.

The young girl who brought the note to Will yesterday evening walked by Will and muttered that all the inhabitants of the Manor House were here and he should go now. The two men left separately to head in a roundabout way to the Manor House. Meg stayed to observe Sneed and his bullyboys and watch for the bailiff's movements. She had her instructions: if any of them appeared to be leaving—delay them—even if she had to make a public nuisance of herself.

71

Annie awoke early and sat with Rosamund in her dark prison room, listening for external sounds. Not hearing any, she cautiously left using one of the keys Ada gave her. Nervously traversing the large, empty hall, following Ada's directions, she found the door to Sneed's private room.

Steward Sneed liked his home comforts. A solid oak bed dominated the centre of the oak-paneled room with carved posts at each corner supporting an elaborate wooden canopy. Heavy looking curtains hung from rails. Fine linens covered the mattress and plump pillows. After the thin mattresses Annie had been lying on since arriving in the fifteenth century she was tempted to crawl straight into this luxurious bed, but reminded herself of Goldilocks and the Three Bears—not a good idea!

A wooden chest and an interesting curved folding chair provided the only other furnishings other than a heavy oak desk, which sat beneath the only small window. The room was dark, the floorboards stained in a dark oak, and the wall hangings heavily textured. The space felt oppressively male to Annie. She realized she had never actually met her captor but could sense his energy. It was not a comfortable feeling.

Looking around, she reached for a disorderly pile of rolls sitting on top of the desk. Eagerly untying the leather strip securing the first roll, Annie found an ongoing record of the court leet, a court held every six months with the steward presiding. The court was responsible for punishing minor misdemeanors. Scanning the stitched parchment sheets, Annie looked for columns of numbers but saw only lists of names, offences and fines paid to the Lord of the Manor. She smiled seeing Sam and Rob's names appear frequently for poaching on the demesne lands.

Hearing a meow behind her, Annie turned to see Rosamund sitting on top of the wooden chest.

"Thanks, Rosamund, I would have got there eventually."

Digging into the chest, Annie found more rolls. Columns of numbers with headings, 'charge', and 'discharge' covered sheet after sheet. She presumed 'charge' was income and 'discharge' was monies paid out. As this was the sum total of her knowledge of accounting, she thankfully rolled up parchment sheets dating from the previous five years and took them out into the great hall to leave Jack to deal with the math.

The witch-in-training and her familiar, having sorted out the precious documents that might contain proof of the steward's perfidy, returned to the prison room. It was time to begin the next part of the plan. Rosamund began purring and Annie joined in with her humming. She found the resulting vibration caused her head to hurt but the pain slowly faded. The vibrations intensified until the walls of the Manor House were throbbing with the energy. Annie calmed her mind. Once in a theta state, the image of a woman in flowing white robes appeared. Each of her hands held a lighted torch and her tranquil face sent a message of hope and courage.

Annie spoke, an incantation coming unbidden to her lips:

The Goddess Hecate,
Bringer of Light
Keeper of the Crossroads
Patron of Magic
Bring me safe
May the truth I seek
Be revealed to me
May the truth come to light
So all can see.

Annie emerged slowly from the deeply meditative state. She looked around. The image of the woman had been so vivid she thought the Goddess must be present in the room.

"I saw the Goddess, Rosamund. She is real. Her name is Hecate. She gave me hope that all will be well."

Annie and Rosamund walked back to the great hall where a magnificent display unfolded before them. Iridescent light streamed through the window openings and dust motes spiralled in the shimmering air. In the great hearth, fiery red and yellow flames danced in a kaleidoscope of colour. The room shimmered with light and the high walls vibrated with energy.

"We did a good job here," Annie bent down to stroke her familiar. "This should shake free a few secrets and lies." She went to the window. "I see Will and Jack coming across the field." Unlocking the heavy oak door, she stood back, anticipation and hope growing inside.

A few minutes later, the door opened and both men stood there, mesmerized by the light display. They covered their ears against the throb of pure energy.

"What's going on?" cried Jack. "Is the place is bewitched?" He and Will looked at each other. Annie could read their minds. Perchance there was more to this witch naming than they had considered.

At the sound of Jack's voice, the light lessened and the pulsations decreased. Annie walked toward them escorted by Rosamund. Will ran to her and pulled her into his arms.

"I had thought you dead," he whispered, burying his face into her neck. He gently touched her darkly bruised forehead, and then held her face in his hands. "You look so pale, so fragile; yet you did not break."

Rosamund went straight to Jack. She walked in a high-stepping fashion with head and tail held high; signifying her pride in her expertise..

"I'm beginning to think you are much more than just a cat," Jack scratched behind Rosamund's ears.

"The rolls on the boards over here are the manorial records for the past five years. I believe we can prove Sneed is cooking the books," said Annie, once she had untangled herself from Will. Will and Jack lifted their eyebrows at the strange expression.

"If you mean he is defrauding Prior Gilbert of income and cheating on the villagers; we came to the same conclusion." Jack looked at Annie in astonishment.

"Then we are all of the same mind," Annie smiled sweetly. "By the way, what happened to your eye? Did you walk into a door?"

"Something like that, but your bruise beats mine."

Jack hurried over to the pile of leather wrapped roles and settled in to study them. Rosamund, following Annie's instructions, sat on the boards with her head close to Jack's head, purring from deep inside her chest.

Will, keeping Annie close by him, went to the window to watch for unwelcome visitors. While they stood there, Will told Annie about the death of Florrie Ridley. He told her people believed she fell into the river accidentally while fetching water. Another rumour—only whispered—inferred she had been drinking. Annie's brain flooded with the image of Florrie shouting at her and of her plunge into darkness. The scene was so vivid in her mind she felt as though it was happening all over again.

"Oh, my God!" she said, her hand coming up to her injured head, "I went to see her. I wanted to ask her about the relationship between the innkeeper and Father John. She became angry and started pushing me out of the house. She threatened me and when I turned around to say something, she hit me with something hard. I must have been unconscious. I have no idea how I finished up here. I hadn't remembered until now." More realization dawned. "Am I responsible for her death? Oh, how terrible. If I had not gone to see her she would still be alive. Poor Father John. But I believed he killed the innkeeper."

"Calm yourself." Will smoothed Annie's black curls away from her bruise. "You're not to blame. Florrie killed Ridley. Father John was protecting her, but her burden of guilt must have become too heavy for her to carry. Unintentionally, your questions caused her to break down. We believe she started drinking wine once Sneed's men took you away. Jack visited her to ask if she had seen you. He saw she was drunk. He could smell the wine on her along with her slurred speech and a staggering gait. Florrie was the bailiff's sister, which was why Sneed and Crompton protected her."

Annie's head swam, awash with guilt and with so much information coming so quickly. She stood quietly by Will's side trying to absorb it.

As dust motes settled and flames died down, Jack's scribbling, Rosamund's purring and the occasional collapse of a log in the hearth offered the only sounds in the now-quiet room. Jack methodically unwrapped each role, and, after copying what he wanted, rewrapped it. At length he stood and stretched. Scratching Rosamund behind the ears, he faced the couple standing by the window.

"I need to ask some of the villagers what they paid for tithes and rent, and, in some cases, what fines they paid out. I have copied lists of wages paid for labour. We will compare these numbers with what the villagers say. I have no way of knowing if these are accurate or altered amounts. I'm not looking at seeds, grain, or other food stuff, only coinage. I have what I need. It was so easy to know where to look, the numbers leapt off the pages. We can be off."

Annie allowed herself a tiny smile. She heard Rosamund rumble deep in her throat. The cat's job had been to stimulate Jack's mental acumen with her purring. She and Rosamund had covered all angles.

"Annie," Will held Annie by the shoulders, and looked deeply into her eyes. "I think you and Rosamund should come back to the inn where we can keep look after you, only until we have absolute proof of Sneed's cheating. The next few days could be dangerous. I'm sure Sneed will send out a search party. He can't afford to have you free to tell people what happened. We'll arrange for Meg to come and stay with you."

Carefully replacing the rolls on the desk and in the chest in Sneed's room, exactly as she had found them, Annie locked the door to Sneed's room. She stopped abruptly as they walked across the great hall. "There's one point I forgot about when I was planning this; I don't want young Ada to be blamed for my escape; she has been so helpful and kind to me."

Will looked around. "Where did they keep you? I was here with Father John. You must have been in another room."

Annie led them to her prison storage room. When Will saw the thin, dirty mattress Annie had been lying on, he swore an oath, "God's Bones, that man will pay for what he has done to you."

"It's alright, Will. It's over."

Jack was poking around in the various storage containers and searching the shelves. "This should do." Picking up a clay pot, he wrapped it in a piece of sacking and smashed the pot against a barrel. "Just the job." He chose a couple of long shards and showed them to Will.

"Good thinking, Jack, I'm with you." Will turned to face a puzzled Annie. "You have to break out of this room, so you need something to break the lock. It looks flimsy, anyway."

Jack began fiddling with the shard, trying to ease it between the door and the frame. After making a few scratch marks, he took out his knife and easily snapped the lock, dropping the shard on the floor. They went into the great hall and locked the main door.

"Show me the back entrance, please Annie." Jack held the second shard in his hand.

He did the same with the lock on the kitchen door, making scratches with the pottery shard, dropping it on the ground, and then prying open the lock with his sturdy dagger. Annie went back to her prison cell, placed the keys under the mattress, and then they all left by the back door.

72

The big day came to its conclusion. Many barrels had been filled with layers of salt and pork; meat required by the villagers to survive the winter and to pay the tithe owing to Prior Gilbert. The following day they would make sausages, pickle pork hocks, and scrape hides for later use. Not a piece of pig would be unused. All the villagers could now look forward to 'The Great Pig Feast' at the Manor House.

Meg and Annie settled in the innkeepers' private quarters. Meg brought clean clothes for Annie and a warm sponge down and fresh linen almost made a new woman of her. Meg also prepared a spell to protect the space and keep them from harm. Lighting a candle, she circled the room. Using salt and water to draw a five-pointed star, a pentacle, on each wall, she chanted:

> *"Evil, Harm, Negativity,*
> *From thy life banished be,*
> *By power of the five-pointed star*
> *I seal your aura from evil both near and far.*
> *Safe from harm, safe and warm, all within dwell safe"*

Annie knew what Will and Jack planned to do and was aware it was time to let go. She lay on the mattress, sandwiched between Rosamund tucked in the curve of her belly, and the comforting presence of Aunt Meg curled around her back. In the split second before sleep took over, Annie murmured, so quietly Meg had to strain to hear the words, "What was the name of your beautiful horse?"

"Wildfire," replied her aunt and gave her niece a hug.

Annie slept a lot over the next two days but when she was awake, Meg reported faithfully on what was happening. The two innkeepers were sleeping in the hall along with the staff. Will had told them his betrothed had been ill and would stay at the inn while being nursed by Mistress Wistowe.

"Will has promised them a bonus to keep quiet about you being here. Apparently, Jobe and Asne have been snooping around the outside of the inn, hoping for information, and Mistress Bagsworth said they had been door to door in the village asking people if they have seen you but no one knows anything."

Jack was working diligently on the records. Enlisting the help of Sam and Rob, he had asked them to go around the cottages asking the villagers what they had paid in rent and tithes over the last few years. They were to tell the curious villagers Father John was updating his records. As neither man could read nor write, Jack set up a system so they could make marks on a piece of slate with a nail. Sam and Rob reported to Jack that the villagers had no problem remembering every hard-earned penny they had given for rent and tithes, or, unfortunately, fines for various misdemeanors. The people expressed their willingness to contribute and used the opportunity to vent their anger at a system that sometimes left them without enough food to feed their families.

Jack tabulated the list of tithes, rents and fines, and then compared the figures taken from Steward Sneed's records. The difference between the two sets of figures indicated Sneed had been making a substantial profit over the years he had been in charge of Hallamby Manor by stealing from both the King, the Church, and, more shamefully, from the villagers, who had so little to begin with.

This larceny could have gone on for many more years without discovery, if not for the detective skills of Will, Jack, and Annie, supported by Meg, Rosamund, and Bea. This is what they told one another as they marvelled at Sneed's duplicity.

"He had his fingers in so many pies, it is unbelievable," commented a refreshed and livelier Annie.

"What an interesting expression," laughed Will. "Something like your 'cooking the books'. I haven't heard it said before. I presume it means he was involved in various crooked dealings?"

"It's a common expression in York," Annie responded, hiding the fact that, once again, she had used an expression from another time and place.

They were celebrating their success with a good French wine in the seclusion of the private quarters.

"How will we use this information?" Jack was sitting on the clothes chest with Rosamund on his knee.

"We have to give it to Prior Gilbert," said Will. "He is the one with the power. He employed Sneed. He can get rid of him."

"I have an idea," Meg rose from the mattress in her excitement. "We must get the information to the clerics in York. If we use a sealed pouch with Father John's seal, it will be sure to get to the Prior. We'll mark it 'urgent'."

"A brilliant plan, Aunt Meg," Annie toasted her aunt with her now empty wine goblet.

"'Brilliant'. There's another word I haven't heard before," Will shook his head. "They seem to be speaking a new language in York these days."

Annie vowed to keep her mouth shut. She was not sure if the head injury or the wine caused her loose lips. She remembered the old wartime saying, 'Loose lips lose ships,' and giggled.

Jack wrote the letter; laying out in detail, with evidence, the greed, and fraudulence of Sneed and his cohorts. Dick Radcliffe would take the package to York the following day.

"Everyone is used to Dick travelling to York so he will be less conspicuous than one of us leaving."

Jack volunteered to take the letter to Father John.

Meg wanted Jack to ensure Mistress Davey had kept her promise to call in every day to care for the priest. He also had instructions to talk about the much-neglected arrangements for his wedding.

Later, Jack relayed the conversation he had had with Dick about taking the package to York.

"Tha wants me to do what—go all t'way t'city wi' a package—no vegetables. Seems a bit daft t'me. Why dunt tha go thissen—on one o' manor 'orses?"

"It's a secret mission, Dick, a bit like the smuggling. We don't want anybody to know about it, especially anybody from the Manor

House, if you see what I mean. Everyone is used to you making trips into York."

"Is this summat t'do wi' yon Sam an' Rob asking questions in t'village? A thought that business were a bit queer."

"It is. I need the information in this pouch to get to Prior Gilbert, wherever he is, and as soon as possible."

Jack laughed as he told the story to Will and the others. "When Dick realized how important his mission was, he looked excited—well, as excited as Dick would allow himself to look. He didn't mind being given the purse of coins too for his trouble. He'll do right by us; he's a good man."

The sealed pouch contained the incriminating document as well as a petition from Master Jack Fletcher asking for the consent of the Lord of the Manor regarding his marriage to Mistress Jenet Bagsworth, particularly during Advent, and an invitation to the Pig Feast.

The funeral mass for Florrie Ridley took place in the church with a large attendance. Florrie would have expressed surprise at the number of villagers who came dressed in their Sunday Best as a mark of respect. Steward Sneed sat in the chair behind the chancel screen. Everyone else stood, including the grieving bailiff.

Jack accompanied Meg, Will having stayed back at the inn to protect Annie from any devious plots to recapture her. Father John offered a full mass for Florrie's soul. Even though the priest conducted the service in Latin, in words incomprehensible to the congregation, people paid attention to the sound of his voice. There was no idle gossiping on this sombre occasion. The heavy smell of incense followed the mourners into the churchyard as they gathered around the open grave. The sky appeared to share the mood of the mourners: heavy dark grey clouds, weeping with a light drizzle. As soon as the service ended, the people surrounded their priest, sharing their condolences and offers of help. Then people returned to their work: the preserving of the pork.

* * *

Will was in the kitchen watching Aggie prepare dishes for the Pig

Feast. Aggie explained that the *Pygge y-farsyd* (the Stuffed Roast Pig), the highlight of the feast, would be prepared in the Manor House kitchen by the Manor House cook. Aggie wanted to make her own special dishes. She pointed out the large bowl filled with pork pieces and a batter of eggs and milk.

"I just 'ave to add 'oney an' pepper and pour it into these bowls of pastry, then put a top on 'em," Aggie wiped her brow with a rag. "It's a pork pie in custard; fancy name is *doucettes* and everybody loves 'em. Sam and Rob promised me some rabbits. T'villagers are allowed to trap 'em 'cos they're for t'feast."

"Will you roast them?"

"Nay, I'll poach 'em in an ale an' wine sauce; dish is called *Conies in Hogepoche*. I alus liked its name."

Will nodded his head in appreciation. Aggie would easily be able to provide a fancier menu for the inn.

Village women soon arrived to help and the entire building hummed with activity. In the main hall, women lined up at the boards, plucking, beating and stirring, and laughing and joking with each other. Will had persuaded Annie to remain secluded in her protected space. She waited impatiently for her aunt to return and share the details of Florrie's funeral.

73

Annie listened intently to her aunt's description of Florrie's funeral service. She wanted to know who attended and what the locals had to say, still feeling responsible for Florrie's death despite the reassurances of her friends.

A gentle tap interrupted Meg's account and Jack's head peered round the door.

"Permission to enter?"

"Granted," Annie smiled fondly at him.

"I have something to share with you both." Jack moved to a corner of the room and began prying up a flagstone with a wooden bar he retrieved from behind the clothes chest. Annie watched with fascination as he carried a bundle back to them wrapped in a tightly woven wool cloth.

"I suspected Ridley kept a record of all of his various schemes—he employed such detail in his regular bookkeeping. Being involved in the wool smuggling and making money from it, he had to have a record somewhere, away from prying eyes—and here it is."

Jack unwrapped the leather-enfolded role of parchment with a flourish and showed them the pages filled with columns of numbers.

"He's been filching money for years and making a tidy profit for himself. It makes sense he must have hidden his hoard somewhere, but I've not yet found it."

Rosamund and Bea, being cats, were curious and walked over to the dirt exposed by the raised flagstone. They sniffed and simultaneously began scratching at the exposed soil.

"Stop it!" called Jack. "This is not the place for a privy."

Annie lay her hand on his.

"Leave them be, they are smarter than you think."

Dirt flew, the hole deepened. The cats stopped and walked back with tails held high. Jack went over to the hole to see what they had done. Another wool wrapped bundle lay revealed in the bottom of the freshly dug space, much larger than the first one.

"Annie, Mistress Wistowe, this must be it!"

Jack brought the heavy bundle over to the two women and unwrapped it carefully. They looked in amazement at a wooden box with a solid metal lock. Jack quickly took care of the lock with his dagger and lifted the lid. Silver coins filled the large cavity.

"It looks like we've found Ridley's hoard."

Vigorous meowing from both cats interrupted Jack's exclamation.

"Sorry Rosamund and Bea. These incredibly clever cats have found Ridley's hoard. Between smuggling, extortion, and your 'book cooking', he did extremely well. What shall we do with it?"

"It belongs to Father John, unless Ridley was bribing someone else we don't know about," responded Annie. "What a wonderful surprise that will be for him, after all, he has gone through."

"Go find Will, we must share this find with him." Meg's face flushed with excitement.

Will came into the room followed by the sounds of merriment in the hall. He closed the door quickly and the others gathered around him to tell him elatedly about the find. Rosamund and Bea meowed throughout the telling, just to make sure they received the credit they were due.

"It's all making sense, isn't it?" Will shook his head. "What a bunch of greedy villains they were. By the way, Annie, I forgot to tell you this with all that has happened. Did you know that your parents had not registered you when you were born? Father John and I searched diligently for the records but we couldn't find your name anywhere." He turned to Meg. "We found you, Meg, and your sister."

Meg responded quickly. "I believe Annie's mother was ill for a long while after the birth, I suppose it got missed with all the worry."

Will smiled. "That explains it. But the main point is that no record means no evidence of cousinhood, so we can proceed with our betrothal. Do you agree, Annie?"

"Let me recover first, Will, and then I can think more clearly."

Will looked dismayed when he heard his betrothed unexpected response. "I'm sorry to be so impatient. Of course, you must get well." He turned hastily to Jack. "Let's hope Dick Radcliffe is successful in his mission to obtain Prior Gilbert's permission for your wedding. Time is running out if you want to have the ceremony on the same day as the Pig Feast. Do you have thoughts on another day if word doesn't come back?"

Jack shrugged his shoulders. "I suppose we will have to plan a later day for the ceremony if we don't receive permission in time. I pray Dick will be successful. Combining the two occasions will create such a merry time with the whole village in attendance." Jack looked sad for a moment. "Someone will have to fetch your parents," he said to Will.

"We'll sort that out later." Will reminded himself of the death of Jack's parents. "Meantime, we'll hope for the best and make our plans."

74

The big day arrived: the Pig Feast, anticipated by all. It was also to be the wedding day of Jack Fletcher and Jenet Bagsworth. Father John sent word that Dick had been successful in his undertaking in York and had brought back a message from the Prior giving his permission for the wedding to take place, the legitimacy of baby Thomas being paramount. The marriage ceremony would take place in the Hallamby church at Nones, and then everyone would make their way across the fields to the Manor House in a procession led by the bride and groom.

Will, Jack and Meg held a meeting to discuss plans for the big day and afterwards informed Annie she would attend both events. Annie's heart rate immediately doubled. She found it hard to breathe.

"Your aunt and I will be close to you at all times," Will assured her; he must have seen the look of fear on her face.

Food preparation had gone on apace in the inn's kitchen. Now, the night before the Feast, all the dishes were loaded onto Dick's cart for transfer to the Manor House. Aggie, Cissie and Nettie chatted excitedly to Annie and her aunt about the day ahead. Aggie had prepared a huge pot of pottage, enough to feed a small army, for any travellers arriving at the inn. The cook and the two girls were to go over to the Manor House to help with the feast.

"They're not keepin' us frum weddin', though," Aggie told Annie. "We're leavin' Manor kitchen to watch it."

Will arranged for a small number of disappointed staff to remain behind at the inn along with Sneed's two bullyboys.

The special day dawned clear and cold, with everyone praying the temperature would warm up as the sun rose. Jack went into the wool packing room to have a good scrub down and to don his new clothes, all sewn by Meg and Mistress Davey. It had taken some doing, but Annie persuaded him not to wear his leather jerkin, a survivor of the French campaign with many mementos. Instead, Jack dressed in a cream linen shirt with a soft green wool tunic, most appropriate, as the colour green represented young love. After tucking his loose black pants into his soft leather boots and tying back his black hair with a black velvet ribbon, Jack returned to the women for inspection. They pronounced him to be 'the perfect groom'; even his now fading multi-hued eye gave his appearance a slightly dashing look.

At the Manor House, many hands prepared the great hall for the afternoon's festivities. The head table, built by Mistress Daveys' son, sat in place on a raised dais. Four long trestle tables occupied the full length of the hall.

Status usually dictated where people sat but because this was a wedding, the order changed. The important people, such as the bride and groom, would sit at the head table, along with both sets of parents, Steward Sneed and Father John. Lesser beings were to sit just below them at the long tables. These would include Bailiff Crompton, Will Boucher, Mistress Wistowe, Reeve Brighouse, and the other village trades and crafts people. Those of lowest rank would be below the salt, including freemen and their families as well as serfs and theirs. It was ironic that Tom Bagsworth, seated at the head table, had transformed from felon to important person in a matter of weeks. Annie did not have a seat placing as, just like the late innkeeper, she had vanished.

The Manor House kitchen held a mass of warm bodies, all busily plucking and chopping, boiling and roasting, stuffing, and carving, swearing and laughing. Ale flowed freely. They would remember this special day all year.

Church bells rang out into the clear December air. The sun had travelled past its zenith but responded to the prayers and graciously warmed the air during its journey. Father John stood outside the closed door of the church with the entire village gathered around, once again wearing their Sunday Best; this time for a more joyous occasion.

Annie looked forward to the day ahead, knowing Will and Meg would stay close by. She and her aunt enjoyed sorting clothes for the event. She caressed the soft burgundy wool surcoat she wore over a gown of rose-coloured linen. Her aunt had attempted to tame Annie's dark curls by weaving a ribbon through them: as a single woman, she could wear her hair uncovered. Meg wore a surcoat in deep red with a cream coloured gown beneath.

"I've been saving these clothes for years; waiting for an occasion to wear them. I do not go into York often, but when I do, I splurge on good cloth as well as my healing supplies. We look wonderful, if I say so myself."

Will must have agreed for when he saw them his mouth fell open.

They now stood at the front of the church door. Will had the honour of being Best Man. He wore his dagger conspicuously as his role was to keep the peace. Annie held baby Thomas, hoping he would not drool or spit up on her finery. She looked anxiously at the priest. His pale face and dark shadows under his eyes offered an austere contrast to his black tunic.

Master and Mistress Bagsworth stood beside Meg and Annie, looking worthy to be the mother and father of the bride. Master Bagsworth wore a new tunic, which hung off his bony frame. Mistress Bagsworth had put to good use the cloth Will brought back to her from York. Her yellow gown looked like a bright beam of sunlight and Tinny's face shone from a vigorous scrubbing.

A distinct rise in the level of conversation occurred when the villagers recognized Annie amongst the crowd. The women waved to her and offered shy smiles. She heard snatches of accounts by the men of the search they had undertaken on the night she disappeared. Words like wolves, drunk, the devil, and the innkeeper, floated over to her. She relaxed when the villagers moved on to other topics.

The conversational murmur increased again as the crowd parted and the bride and groom came toward the priest. Jenet wore a gown of soft blue wool, high in the waist and trailing behind her. A white linen veil secured with a blue band around her forehead covered her fair hair.

A surprising sound emerged from the gatherers—laughter. Annie gasped and shook her head. Rosamund and Bea were the brides-maids, walking proudly behind, tails in the air, and pretty ribbons around their necks. Cissie and Nettie had to have been responsible for that surprise.

Once the bride stood on the left and the groom on the right, fac-ing the church door, Father John began asking the couple a series of questions and in a loud voice so all could hear.

"Are you of age? Do your parents give consent? Do you have a common great grandfather?

After the questions had been answered to the satisfaction of the priest, the couple exchanged oaths, kissed, and Jack handed Jenet half of a gold coin, keeping the other half for himself.

They were married.

Father John led everyone into the church for a mass, the bride and groom having the privilege of kneeling in the chancel before the altar.

The mass ended with Father John saying the words, "*Ego conjungo vos in matrimonium in nomine Patris et Filii et Spiritus Sancti.*"

Jenet and Jack turned to face their family and neighbours who opened a path for them to pass through. Smiles, and a few tears from the women, greeted them as the newlyweds made their way down the nave. Father John walked behind them, followed by Jenet's beam-ing parents, Will and Annie. Baby Thomas, secure in Annie's arms, slept peacefully, having behaved impeccably throughout.

The bride and groom left the church through the ancient stone arch accompanied by a triumphant peal of bells then stopped in sur-prise as Dick and his horse were waiting to greet them outside the door. 'Arry even had ribbons in his mane and his bay coat shone.

"Cum on, jump up," Dick cackled. The crowd coming out of the church began converging behind the couple.

"We'll get 'er up there," called Red Rob, and he and his mate, Sam, with a minimum of dignity, bundled the squealing bride onto the seat beside Dick. Jack followed, laughing. The cart carried the new-lywed couple to the Manor House with children skipping ahead and singing to the beating of drums and the sweet sound of pipes. The local dogs added to the chorus enthusiastically. Will, Annie and Meg danced along with the others, Thomas now in the arms of his grandma. The musicians were locals and more enthusiastic than accomplished, yet the merry sound carried them all along triumphantly.

75

Steward Sneed stood outside of the large oak door waiting to welcome his guests. Following tradition, he greeted each one as they made their way into the great hall. This was Annie's first glimpse of the man who had caused her so much misery, and, as far as she knew, the first time he had laid eyes on her. She was impressed with Sneed's countenance when he saw her: his face did not change. He continued to portray the genial, welcoming host, but Annie, acutely sensitive to the energy of others, felt a rise in tension in him as the steward acknowledged her aunt and Will, while ignoring his former captive.

Annie had enjoyed the wedding ceremony of Jenet and Jack. She became tearful as she imagined herself and Will standing before the priest. Now she determined to relish her first medieval feast.

Jack and his bride proceeded to the head table, led by a proud Ada, dressed in a soft buttercup yellow gown, followed by baby Thomas and his grandparents. While Cissie and Nettie were showing the rest of the guests to their places, Jenet's first task as a newly married woman was to feed Thomas, who noisily announced his hunger. Steward Sneed joined Father John at the head table. The shuffling and murmuring ceased, and everyone looked expectantly at Father John, looking more relaxed with colour in his cheeks. The priest proceeded to give the benediction.

Ale and wine pitchers passed down the long tables hand over hand and eagerly poured into waiting cups. Then, the much-anticipated procession of cooks and helpers came in from the kitchen bearing the first course of the feast. Large trays and trenchers, born overhead by sweating and grinning men, piled with breads, cheeses, and broths of both hare and rabbit; sausages, pork pies, roast turnips and beets came to rest at the head table. Once the guests of honour took what they wanted, the platters travelled down the tables. The hubbub of conversation increased as the wine, ale jugs, and platters emptied.

Annie dare not drink any of the copious amounts of alcohol passing in front of her due to her head injury, having learned her lesson after she had imbibed at the celebration gathering where she got the giggles. She made up for the lack of drink with food.

The second course came in with pipes and drums offering musical accompaniment. The first large platter, carried by two men, held a spit-roasted suckling pig (the *Pygge y-farsyd*), complete with an apple in its mouth. Much cheering greeted that spectacular dish. Pork hocks, pork pies, pork sausages, and pork fillets in a spicy sauce followed it. A few rabbits and capons shared the bill, including Aggie's *Coney Hogepoche*. Smuggler Rob would finally get to enjoy his coney.

Annie nudged Will. "Sneed and the bailiff are refusing all of the pork dishes," she whispered. "They are only eating cheese and chicken. Do you think they are allergic to pork?"

"What's 'allergic'?" Will looked puzzled. "Or is that another new word from York?"

"I meant to say 'averse'. Why keep pigs if they refuse the meat?"

The feast continued. Trenchers of bread provided the plates and fingers did the rest, except for the more affluent who had eating knives. People shared drinking bowls at the lower end of the tables. Annie was amazed at how much food people could consume at one meal, even Aunt Meg tucked in with relish.

At first, no one heard the knocking at the big oak door. The banging grew louder and, eventually, one of the children went to fetch Matilda from the kitchen. She opened the door to find Prior Gilbert and two clerics standing there.

"Please enter, my Lord," she gasped, offering a curtsey.

The large room became silent as the Lord of the Manor swept in with his attendants. Prior Gilbert had dressed in vestments of embroidered silk. He clearly intended making a point of his high office and presented an impressive figure in contrast to his two attendants who were dressed in somber black.

Steward Sneed quickly stood, knocking over his heavy, carved oak chair. A crescendo of noise filled the room as everyone else pushed back their seats and stood to welcome the Prior.

When the noise died down Steward Sneed spoke. "My Lord, what a wonderful surprise… I… we… we did not expect you."

"Greetings, Steward. I apologize for being tardy. Thank you for the invitation."

Sneed looked nonplussed at this remark, his face showing clearly that *he* had not invited him. The Prior made his way to the head table.

"My blessing on your nuptials my children; I was pleased to allow a special dispensation for your wedding to take place during Advent. I shall take pleasure in breaking bread with you all."

Prior Gilbert sat on Steward Sneed's substantial chair; the steward moved to a bench. The Prior offered Father John a warm smile as the priest introduced a self-conscious Tom Bagshaw and his wife. The room settled again and the conversational level rose to its previous heights, yet all eyes were on the head table. Annie realized this was pure theatre and settled in to watch after nudging both Will and her aunt with unrestrained glee.

Steward Sneed appeared stunned at the sudden turn of events. He glared down at his bailiff as if to hold him responsible. Prior Gilbert's clerics had seated themselves further down the table and quietly conversed with the tipsy villagers. Ada served the Prior a silver trencher filled with various offerings from the multitude of dishes. Steward Sneed turned a slight shade of green as the Prior tucked into some of the suckling pig—a fact that did not go unnoticed by Annie, Will, and Meg, who were thoroughly enjoying the unfolding drama.

Prior Gilbert speared a particularly tender looking piece of pork onto his knife and turned to Father John. "Has there been any sign of the missing innkeeper, Father?"

"Er, no, Prior. We have heard nothing more. Is that not correct, Steward Sneed?" Father John turned to the steward and smiled at him. The steward's face turned even greener.

When the Prior had eaten and drunk his fill, he turned to the apprehensive looking Sneed.

"I plan on enjoying your hospitality for a day or two only. I have to return to Kirkham as Advent is such a busy time but my clerics are to stay for a few days. I believe it is timely to conduct an audit and they can be present for the quarterly tithes and rent session. I am sure all will be in order, Steward, there is no need to concern yourself."

Judging by the faces of Sneed and Crompton, there was much to concern them.

Although everyone looked stuffed to the point of bursting, the third course came in with more ceremony. Custards, marzipan, pears in wine, sugarplums, apple tarts, and more cheeses passed down the tables and, amazingly, disappeared.

Apart from enjoying watching the distemper of Sneed and his bailiff, Annie kept an eye on her rescuer, Ada, who had been busy most of the evening serving the mounds of food. She appeared full of vim and vigour and, whenever she had the opportunity, paused behind a tousle-haired youth sitting well down the table to brush her hand across his hair. Later in the evening, she came to Annie and whispered in her ear.

"Am glad tha escaped. There were a reight commotion when they saw tha'd broken out, but it were nowt t'do wi' me. They just thought tha were clever. A nivver did like t'thought of tha bein' burned. That spell tha gave me must 'ave been reight strong. I only 'ad to say it twice before Nate asked me to be 'is betrothed. It'll be our weddin' next. 'Ere's tha yellow 'eart back; it's too powerful for me to keep." She handed Annie a ripe plum and bounced off but not before offering Will a big smile.

The day of the Great Pig Feast and of Jenet and Jack Fletcher's wedding wound to a close and was considered by all (excepting Steward Sneed and Bailiff Crompton) to have been glorious, especially the surprise arrival of Prior Gilbert. Everyone agreed the Prior had honoured the village with his presence.

All made their weary way home. A riotous group bedded the bride, groom, and baby in the innkeepers' room at the inn with a sheepskin-draped box thoughtfully provided for Thomas. Annie and Meg made their beds in the main hall, along with the innkeepers, grandparents and staff. Two disgruntled cats fastidiously found a spot as close to the warm hearth as they could, making it clear they were too worthy to be sleeping with the hoi polloi.

76

The news spread around the village like wildfire. Bleary-eyed villagers went from house to house spreading the word. People began gathering on the village green. The news reached the inn by mid-morning.

"They've gone! The buggars 'ave tekken to their 'eels!" Sam and Rob were out of breath and red-faced after running all the way from the village.

More bleary-eyed people gathered around the two men in the hall of the inn, including Will, Meg, and Annie.

"What are you talking about, Sam?" Will grabbed Sam's shoulders, detecting the excitement in Sam's voice.

"Steward an' bailiff. They left durin' night sumtime. Took two 'orses as well."

Annie and Meg danced a little jig in the hall to the amusement of the staff.

When questioned, Jobe Cartwright and Asne Butts professed to know nothing about it. They had been at the inn, they said, on guard with the small staff remaining there during the festivities, and had stayed there all night. They neglected to mention they had been snoring drunkenly in the stables, a fact shared gleefully by the staff.

* * *

A thorough search of the Manor House had not revealed a hidden hoard of money so Prior Gilbert presumed their ill-gotten gains had gone with them. He had decided not to mount a chase. "Let them go. Someone else can have the trouble of their company."

Prior Gilbert made a mental note to pass on a description of the rogues to his fellow churchmen. They would mount a watch for the thieves throughout the country. He'd take great satisfaction in bringing them to justice as the missing money, belonging by right to his Order, had left with them.

He felt quite pleased with himself apart from the loss of the money. His opening gambit to the steward had paid off. He anticipated, that, given the evidence he had seen, the accounts would not stand up under scrutiny and Sneed would realize his criminal activity had been exposed. Now the Prior needed to replace both the steward and the bailiff as soon as possible.

He invited Father John to sit with him over a drink of wine in the newly cleaned great hall.

"How are you feeling now?" he asked gently. "The last few days have been quite turbulent for you, I understand."

"If you are referring to the accidental death of my housekeeper, yes, it came as a shock."

"My dear Father, I have known for a long time of your close relationship with Mistress Ridley. Very few of the happenings in my manors are unknown to me. I have an excellent reporting system in place. It is important that I do so with the number of manors to care for on behalf of our Order."

A reflective silence descended following this remark.

"Be that as it may," continued the Prior, "do you have any suggestions for the replacement of those two villains? I can search elsewhere. I do prefer to look locally. We need men with at least some education, which narrows the choices."

Father John sipped his wine. "From what I understand, Jack Fletcher has had a good education and, more importantly, he is an honest man who can add up a column of numbers. His friend Will Boucher is also of good stock and educated but not too interested in bookkeeping. They have both just returned from the French Wars so have done their duties as bowmen to our King. No villagers have more than rudimentary learning such as they have received from me."

"I understand they are both innkeepers at present?" queried the Prior as he refilled the goblets.

"Yes, they took on the roles temporarily when our innkeeper went missing."

"This village does seem to have had bad luck with its most prominent citizens." Prior Gilbert laughed. "Is there something in the air of Hallamby?"

"I believe there has been something corrupt affecting us for a number of years. It interests me that it was when the three young people came here that events moved rapidly. I am sure they have had something to do with the way things have evolved."

"You said three people. Who are they?"

"Jack Fletcher and Will Boucher arrived here at the same time as Mistress Annie Thornton—the same night, as it happens. She is the niece of our estimable Mistress Wistowe, who does so much good work in the village." He recounted to the prelate the story Will had told him.

"Apparently, Mistress Thornton came to replace Mistress Wistowe in her healing work as she made plans to leave the village for a while. They are aunt and niece. From what I can gather, the young people were curious about the disappearance of the innkeeper. The fact that the inn had no innkeeper worked in the former soldiers' favour as they planned to look for an inn to buy for themselves. They fell right in to the innkeeper's job, particularly Will. Now Jack has married a village girl and, I believe, Will and Annie are betrothed. Not that I have heard anything recently about that."

"It seems we owe the threesome much for their efforts. What do you think about Jack Fletcher for the job of steward, Father John? It seems to me he has the qualifications: ex-army, therefore one would think him to be organized, disciplined, competent at figures and a family man now, ready to settle down."

"I can't think of a better choice. It will be agreeable to have a family living at the Manor House."

The Prior stroked his chin. "I have to fill the bailiff's position; it is such an important job. Master Boucher, do you think?

"I do not know what is in the young man's heart."

"And Mistress Thornton, what do you know of her plans? Will she stay here in Hallamby?"

"As I said, it depends on whether she and Will become formally betrothed but neither has approached me about the matter."

"Well, the decision is made about the steward position. Shall you approach Master Fletcher or will I?"

"I suggest you do the honours, Prior Gilbert. It will add to the importance of the position."

"That's settled then. Top up your glass Father? Where did Sneed obtain this vintage? We must acquire more of it."

77

Meg and Annie moved back to Meg's cottage the following day.

"I believe I can look at my future more realistically now those terrible men have gone," she confided to Meg.

Meg had already told Annie how proud she was of her niece's actions in saving herself from the clutches of Sneed. She complimented her niece on her witchcraft and her perspicacity. "I see a real increase in your confidence," Meg told her. "You were able to apply many skills to help yourself and the village.

"Aunt Meg, what *does* perspicacity mean?"

"Oh, I thought you knew; you used yours so well." Meg let Annie off the hook. "It means cleverness, discernment, judgement, inventiveness, and so much more; all of the skills you used to extricate yourself from the Manor House and the threat of dying a terrible death, and help solve the village's woes in the process."

There was a knock at the door. Jack and Will stood there, both with big grins splitting their faces.

"Annie, Mistress Wistowe, we have come to collect you. We're taking the money to Father John."

The four detectives trooped along the village street, followed closely by both Rosamund and Bea.

Jack knocked on the church house door. Father John opened it and invited them in. When they sat and had an ale before them, Jack could not contain himself for one more moment.

"Father John, look what we have found!" He handed the heavy box to a puzzled Father.

"I don't understand. What is it?"

"This box contains the money Ridley extorted from you over the years as well as all the money he reaped from his various enterprises. We found it along with his own records of larceny. The man kept detailed records of everything. He had listed all of the money you paid to him under 'C'. I am presuming that letter stands for 'church'. So it's all yours to do with as you will. Consider the rest of his assets as interest paid."

Father John broke down. When he had recovered he said, "I told the Prior how clever you had all been in sorting out this mess and putting us back on the right path. God's hand guided you to us. Bless you. I shall use this money for the benefit of the villagers."

Annie smiled to herself at the priest's suggestion that God was responsible. She believed her Aunt Meg to be the original schemer.

The original schemer addressed the priest. "Father, why do you not ask Mistress Davey if she will be your housekeeper for now? I know she has been coming in to look after you. She will be lonely when her son and his family move to York. She needs someone to fuss over."

"Then I shall do that." The priest still looked shaken over the return of his profits from the trade in smuggled wool and wine that he had been obliged to give to the rapacious Ridley, but he visibly straightened his shoulders and cleared his voice. "By the way, Jack, has the Prior asked to see you?"

"No—is there a problem? I thought we solved them all."

Everyone laughed.

"Oh, it was just something he had mentioned to me." The Father turned to Will and Annie. "What about you two. Do you have any plans?"

Annie and Will both spoke at the same time, Annie saying, "Not yet," and Will responding, "Yes."

"Later, later, we can talk later," Father John murmured. "Time enough for everything."

78

"What is happening to us, Annie? Why do you keep avoiding the subject of our wedding? There is nothing left to stand in our way, nothing except you, it seems."

Will sounded both angry and bewildered. They had returned to Meg's home after leaving the church house. Meg and Jack tactfully left them alone and went to visit the Bagsworths.

"I've thought about us so much, Will. I love you, but it won't work."

"What won't work? Is it because you don't wish to marry an innkeeper? Fine, I'll do something else. You can continue with your work."

Annie shook her head; tears were starting to roll down her cheeks. "It's not that. I have to go back."

"Oh, that's it. Well, I have an easy solution. We'll both go back to York. We certainly don't have to stay here."

"You don't understand. When I say, 'go back' I mean 'go forward.'"

Will looked even more confused. "I have no sense of what you are saying. Go forward to where?"

Annie took his hand. "Do you remember the night you and Jack found Rosamund and me on the floor, unconscious? We had arrived in Hallamby from the future."

Will started to speak but Annie put her hand over his mouth.

"I am from a time in the future where your children's children live. In the world I live in, we flick on a switch to have light and turn on a tap to get water. Houses heat and cool themselves. We have wagons driven by engines and not pulled by horses. Giant machines harvest crops instead of men using scythes. You can look into the sky and see objects flying like birds but they have people sitting inside of them. In war, we can kill thousands of innocent people with rockets and bombs. We use machines to wash our clothes and giant machines to build roads…" Annie stopped. She was using words he had never heard before. She could see she had lost him. He must think her crazy.

"Did you fly here on one of those bird machines?" he asked bitterly. "Annie, you don't need to lie to me; if you don't love me just say so. Perchance you are a witch after all and you bewitched me for your own amusement." He turned away from her, his shoulders slumping.

Annie did not know how to make him understand. Nevertheless, she had to, for his sake, so he would know she loved him but it was impossible for them to be together because of their different centuries.

Would he understand more clearly, if she were able to show him a picture of her time? She would contact Mary and they could 'skype' as they had done before.

"Will, I will try to make it easier for you to see my world. Perhaps then you will understand."

Annie conferred with Meg about how she could show Will the difference between their lives.

"It's not that I want to show him what he might have. He has to see that the difference in our two worlds is too great."

"Is that what this is about, Annie? Or are you trying to convince yourself it is so?"

"I came here because you brought me. I had no control over that. I did not even know why I was here. We, I mean Will, Jack, and I did what you wanted us to do. We solved the mystery of the missing innkeeper and ousted the crooked Sneed and his bailiff. Mary, I presume, has written her novel. It is impossible for me to stay here. I want to have a shower or soak in a bath. I hadn't realized how much I miss having a constant supply of running water. I want to have a latte. I want to buy new clothes. Oh, God, I realize I sound so shallow. I want to see children live and not die from simple infections; I want women not to die in childbirth… I… I… don't know what I want."

"Do you want Will as your husband or is that not an issue?"

"Is it fair to make him give up all he knows for a life beyond anything he can imagine?"

"Don't you think it is his decision, his choice? Give him the opportunity to decide for himself."

Annie stared at her aunt.

She and Meg sat well into the night, planning how to show Will her world: Yorkshire in the twenty-first century. They needed the help of Mary. Annie would ask her to travel around Yorkshire with a video camera to create a picture of her time by showing the people with their cars, houses, trains and planes, games and gadgets. Then they would invite Will and 'skype' with Mary to provide a visual show. Will might never be the same again but he would be able to choose. They decided that Jack would not be part of this as his life was here and now in Hallamby with his new family.

All the preparations were now complete and the stage was set. Annie and Meg had conferred with Mary on a number of occasions. Mary was now so used to this weird 'magic skyping' that she took it in her stride and expressed excitement about her role as filmmaker. She revealed she brought Jonathon in as assistant cameraman, telling him it was a work project.

Meg, Bea, Annie, Rosamund, and Will were sitting in a circle at Meg's home, Will looking totally bemused. He had expressed some cynicism about this 'future thing'. After all, he had been in France he told them; he was a man of the world, but Annie had said this was about their future, either together or apart.

The cats began purring, Meg and Annie began humming, and the walls began vibrating. A beam of light materialized in the centre of the circle of people and cats. The light grew into a long column. Strands of different colours and textures floated like gossamer inside the column then slowly fused together forming the face of Mary, Annie's friend.

"Hello, Will, I've wanted to meet you for a long time."

Will leapt to his feet in preparation for fleeing. Annie's hand reached out and landed on his knee.

"Be still, all is well."

"And now for the show…"

Mary always enjoyed centre stage. Annie groaned.

"Okay. Will, this could be your life, if you so choose."

Annie groaned again.

Images started to form in the centre of the spiralling column: a mass of people cheering at men kicking a ball—fade out. A traffic jam, a line of cars and huge trucks, horns honking—fade out. Planes taking off and landing—fade out. A plane soared into a blue sky leaving a white feathery trail behind it—fade out. A woman entered a kitchen and turned on a tap; water splashed into a sink. She then turned a knob on a stove and a circle of blue flame erupted—fade out. A large public pool showed people swimming, diving, and popping out from a giant tube, the women in bikinis, the men in shorts—fade out. A car was driving through Micklegate Bar—a different looking Micklegate Bar, without a barbican—fade out. York Minster, stunning, soaring, completed—fade out. Again, a car, but the watcher inside, travelling through rolling countryside, passing trees, sheep, and winding stone walls. More sheep on open moors, the high peak of a ruined abbey outlined against the sky—fade out. The stark remains of castle ramparts atop a hill, the sea in the background—

"STOP! This is all trickery. I will see no more. I do not know how you created this fantasy but I say the devil must be part of it. How can any of those images be real? I will have none of it. Do you take me for a fool, Annie? How could you do this to me? I said this to you before: why not just tell me you no longer love me? I *will* have none of it."

Will shook off Annie and left the house, the door crashing shut behind him.

The silence was deafening.

Mary's floating face showed disappointment . "He didn't like the movie?"

79

Prior Gilbert smiled at Jack and his new wife.

"So we are agreed that you are to be Hallamby Manor's steward, responsible for all matters pertaining to the manor and reporting to me? You and your family will reside here at the Manor House in my stead. I still have to find a bailiff to support you. My clerics will review your duties and will be available to help you as you learn your new role. Congratulations, Steward Fletcher. By the way, please ask your friend, Master Boucher, to come and see me at his convenience. Do you have any questions at this time?"

"I do, my Lord. Thank you for this wonderful opportunity for me and for my new family. I would like my first action to be informing Masters Butts and Cartwright, hired ruffians of the recently departed Sneed—if we can find them—that they no longer have a position in Hallamby and must move on. I must add that it will give me great pleasure to do so."

Will arrived at the Manor House; shoulders still slumped, not even looking curious about why Prior Gilbert had asked for him.

"Master Boucher, thank you for coming. Is something wrong? You look quite forlorn."

Will, with tight jaw and downcast eyes, told him he and Mistress Thornton were not to be wed.

"I am sorry to hear that, but affairs of the heart, so I understand, can be of a fickle nature. I often think that marriages arranged by the parents provide a more stable beginning.

"I asked you here because I wanted to thank you for the work you did to expose our two villains here in Hallamby. Have you heard that your friend Jack has accepted the position of steward? No? Well, he has. How would you like to be the new bailiff?"

Jolted out of his misery, Will looked at the Prior in surprise.

"I am pleased for Jack. Thank you, but no, I want to have my own inn. I have set my heart on owning my own inn."

"Do you have an inn in mind?"

"Yes. I like 'The King's Head' but I know it is in private hands."

The Prior smiled. "It is in my private hands, or should I say, my family's private hands. Ridley invested a small amount, but as he has left the area, I will have our scribes write up something and put his share in trust in the event he reappears. I understand you may have access to some revenue. Might you be interested in investing in a share of the inn? Mayhap with you managing the inn we might make a profit."

Will's jaw dropped. "I would." His face lost its look of dejection and hope appeared in his eyes.

"Then you shall. I will have the papers drawn up; say fifty percent ownership?

* * *

Will invited Meg and Annie to 'The King's Head' for a celebration. As Annie had not seen Will since the 'movie night', she was apprehensive. Will, Jack, and Jenet greeted them at the door. Thomas lay in his mother's arms.

"Welcome to 'The King's Glove," Will's smile lit up his face. "May I introduce you to the new steward of the Manor of Hallamby?" He turned to Jack, "Steward Fletcher, in person."

"Are you truly the new steward, Jack?" asked Meg.

"Aye, and we're goin' to live at big 'ouse," Jenet, speaking for her new husband, nodded her head vigorously. "An' me mam an' dad an' Tinny can live there as well. An' me dad will be 'elpin' Jack."

"What did you call the inn?" Annie's curiosity overcame her discomfort. She knew there had to be a story behind the unusual name, but never guessed she would be part of the name change.

"'The King's Glove', do you like the name? The Prior and I are co-owners." He turned them around and pointed to the new sign, the smell of wet paint lingering. Portrayed on the hanging board was a leather glove with an embroidered crown on the large cuff: the letters H. R. sat on either side of the crown. The glove swelled with gold coins.

"This is all wonderful news." Meg clapped her hands. "We must celebrate, and it will be a goodbye party for Annie too as she is to return home."

A shadow crossed Will's face, but it quickly passed and everyone started to troop into the hall for a party to remember. Before Annie could enter with the others, Will took hold of her arm and gently pulled her to one side.

"I am so sorry for losing my temper the other evening. I want you to know that I will always love you." His lopsided smile broke Annie's heart. "If the vision you showed me was real, you must know I cannot live in that world, no matter how much I love you. I will stay here and run my inn. Can you not stay here, in *this* Hallamby?"

Annie's eyes brimmed with tears. "I must return to my time. I have family there. Perhaps our paths will cross again."

"Know you will always be in a corner of my heart. I will think of you often." Will leaned over and kissed Annie gently on her cheek. She squeezed his arm and they walked inside.

80

December 2015, Hallamby, Yorkshire

Home.

Annie had not anticipated feeling like this. Aunt Meg sent her and Rosamund on their way with some powerful incantations and the energy from a heavy snowstorm. They arrived back in Annie's kitchen with no fuss at all.

How easy was that? Annie now put to rest her earlier misgivings about her aunt's time travel abilities; however, the time travel had been the simplest part. Settling into the twenty-first century was proving much more difficult. Rosamund was moping and refusing to eat. Annie was so lethargic it was too much effort to get off the couch.

Mary came around to visit as soon as Annie contacted her. Her book was now in the hands of a publisher in York, she announced, although she still had to provide an ending. Annie stared at her friend. "An ending, you want an ending. We've had the ending. It's all over."

As soon as Annie arrived back in the twenty-first century, she jumped into a long, hot shower, followed immediately by a long, lazy soak in the bathtub, made aromatic with Bergamot essential oil, supposedly uplifting and re-energizing, but not working. Now clean and dressed in her favourite jeans, she felt a brief respite from the sadness of leaving her aunt, Will and the rest of her new friends. Grinding coffee beans and breathing in the aroma created a headiness that only lasted until she drained the mug.

When Annie contacted her team leader at work, her heart was beating rapidly. How would she explain her long absence? Once again, her aunt proved to be all-knowing. Time *is* illusory. Her team leader expressed concern about Annie's family, hoping all was well. "…and as you have only been away a short while, Bev picked up the one birth…"

The future loomed darkly. Christmas hovered around the corner. Christmas tree lights blinked rhythmically through windows while more lights sparkled around doorways and windows and along the eaves and gables of the cottages. Carols played constantly on the radio.

Annie supposed she should buy presents. She should go and visit her parents in York. She just could not find any energy to do anything, especially 'the shoulds'.

Her phone rang.

"It's me. Get dressed up. Jonathon and I are taking you to the 'Glove'. No! We will not take no for an answer. We'll pick you up in half an hour."

"God damn it, I do not want to go," Annie continued muttering to herself as she changed into something dressier and combed her shining, clean, sweet-smelling hair. Draping the shawl Mistress Bagsworth had woven around the shoulders of her winter jacket set off the tears once more. After drying her eyes, Annie checked her reflection in her hall mirror. Even that act seemed strange, seeing her face, not having access to a mirror while away.

Annie picked Rosamund up to give her a hug but the cat refused to be placated. The doorbell rang and Mary and Jonathon stood there.

"We thought we would walk to the inn and look at the lights. It'll get us into the Christmas mood," Mary's cheeks were rosy from the crisp air. "The inn has a new manager. He has the family name, Boucher, sounds French for butcher, doesn't it." She looked pointedly at her friend. "The same family have had the inn forever. He took over at the beginning of the month. The food's still as good as before."

Annie had no idea what Mary was babbling on about. As they walked up the main street and she caught her first sighting of the village church, she nearly burst into tears again. It had not changed at all in five hundred years. It was still the same solid grey stone building figuring so largely in her recent adventure. In her mind's eye, she could see Jenet and Jack standing outside the porch in their wedding finery and dear Father John giving his blessing. Had the newlyweds moved into the Manor House? Was Mistress Davey taking good care of Father John? They were the reality, not here, not now.

She had become familiar with the fields being on either side of her walk to the inn and now she had to get used again to houses making their sprawling way almost to the main road. At least the old rookery remained, the rooks remaining quiet as they passed, huddled together in their nests against the frosty cold.

They saw 'The King's Glove' from a distance. Every lintel and scantling displayed twinkling lights. The light from inside poured out to cheer the December evening. The inn's sign swung on its brackets; the upturned glove filled with crowns almost the same as she had seen it, then with wet paint, a brief time ago. Even though the sign resembled the original, the rest of 'The King's Glove' had undergone many changes over the centuries. The customers still entered through the archway to a cobblestone yard but no stables existed now. The main entrance was still low with a worn doorstep; people taller than Annie had to duck their heads. Annie caught herself looking for the gargoyle-faced Butts and Cartwright—she shook her head—please don't tell me I'm missing them too. A large Christmas tree almost filled the small lobby and its walls displayed old black and white photos of village life, but nineteenth century, not fifteenth. The trio left their coats in the foyer cloakroom and a young girl, probably the same age as Cissie, showed them to their table.

Annie felt more and more disconnected. This was the inn: the same inn where she had recently enjoyed the celebration with dear Aunt Meg and Jack and Will. Oh, Will…. The sudden shaft of pain in her heart made her gasp. A tear slid down the side of her nose. She heard Mary speak.

"Aha!"

She lifted her gaze from the floor to see a young fair-haired man coming toward their table. He looked achingly familiar. Shaking her head in confusion, a wild hope blossomed in her chest. Had Will changed his mind? Aunt Meg had sent him to her.

"Annie..." said Mary.

Annie swore she heard a drum roll, faintly, coming from a long way off.

"...I would like you to meet the new manager of The King's Glove'. Annie, this is Adam Boucher. This place has been in his family for generations. I believe you were acquainted with one of his family members in the not so distant past."

Author's Note:

"Sailing To Byzantium"

Meet Annie and Rosamund again when they travel back in time to Jorvik (Scandinavian York) in 942 A.D. A Viking King, Eiric Blood-axe, rules the city. Jorvik is a cosmopolitan centre of trade with routes going as far as Asia, Russia, and Europe. Annie, Aunt Meg, and their two cats join a group of irascible Viking traders as they travel through the Baltic into what is now Russia, and on to Byzantium, in their mission to solve a terrible crime.

GLOSSARY

The Yorkshire dialect derives from Old English and Old Norse. As I am from West Yorkshire I have tried to incorporate enough Yorkshire dialect to give a flavour of this unique heritage, while still keeping some legibility for the reader. I hope the glossary is of help to you

a	I
'adn't	had not
afor	before
alreight	alright
alus	always
amon'	amongst
any'ow	anyway
aye	yes
babby	baby
bairns	children
beck	stream
besom	broom
biddies	elderly women
bin	been
blubberin'	crying
buss, bussing	kiss, kissing
coney	rabbit
clout	hit
cud	could
cum	come
cummin'	coming
dithering	undecided
dotty	crazy
din't	did not
dun	done
dus	does

dunt	does not
'e	he
eeh by gum!	oh my god!
'ell fire!	my goodness!
'ere	here
'ey up!	greeting/ exclamation
faggots	a bundle of sticks or twigs
fair t'middlin"	fair, reasonable
fair clemmed	really thirsty
fettle	put in order, mend
flippin' 'eck!	exclamation of surprise
flummoxed	confused
gaffer	boss
ginnel	alleyway
gob	mouth
gorm	sense
in his cups	drunk
jiggered	very tired
keep tha trap shut	do not talk
kip	sleep
laikin'	playing
lass	girl, woman
lumpkin	clumsy, stupid
luv	love
luvly	lovely
mardy	moody
me	my
mek	make
mekkin'	making
mebbe	maybe

midden	rubbish dump
Minster	cathedral
mithered	bothered/upset
missen	myself
missus	mistress
nay	no
natter	chat
niver	never
nowt	nothing
'ow do	hello
owt	anything
'ow's tha doin'?	how are you?
pinny	apron (pinafore)
pottage	stew
put wood int'oyle	close the door
quiver	pouch for arrows
reight	right
rum un	odd person, thing
shut tha gob	keep quiet
summat	something
sup	drink
t'	the
tek, tekkin'	take, taking
tear-arsing	racing around
thee	you
tha/thy	thou, you, your
thissen	yourself
trencher	plate
tyke	Yorkshire born

un   one
utha   other

wi'   with
wimmin   women

Henry V was King of England from 1413 until his death at the age of 36 in 1422. In 1415, Henry embarked on war with France in the ongoing Hundred Years' War between the two nations. His military successes culminated in his famous victory at the Battle of Agincourt (1415) and saw him come close to conquering France.

Will Boucher is from my imagination but the original man came from the imagination of William Shakespeare who wrote Henry V around 1599. Michael Williams, a soldier and minor player, first appears in Act 4, scene 1, where he berates a disguised king and blames him for the death of his subjects. Following the Battle of Agincourt, King Henry gives Williams a glove filled with crowns as a reward for his honesty. I gave him new life as Will Boucher. Boucher is French for butcher: the profession of Will's father.

Jack Fletcher is not real but his father's trade produced the weapons, the longbows and arrows that helped make the medieval English Army so powerful. Fletcher was the original surname for someone who made arrows.

Hallamby Village does not exist but is modelled on studies of deserted medieval villages.

The Yorkshire characters are all imaginary but their humour is real!

The Yorkshire scenery is real, beautiful, and well worth a visit. York and its environs are real and magnificent.

York Minster is real. The Cathedral and Metropolitical Church of Saint Peter in York, commonly known as *York Minster*, is the cathedral of York, England, and is one of the largest of its kind in Northern Europe.

Kirkham Priory is real but now in ruins. It sits by the River Derwent and is still awe-inspiring and serene. Prior Gilbert is imaginary but the founder, Walter l'Espec and later, the de Ros family were real. Legend has it that Kirkham Priory was founded in remembrance of l'Espec's only son who had died nearby as a consequence of his horse being startled by a boar. The area was later used to test the D-Day landing vehicles of WW2 and was visited by Winston Churchill.

Wool Smuggling was real. Wool was the first contraband and English wool was highly valued abroad: it was tough, and the fibres were long, making them easier to spin. English fleeces made for good fabric, and the surpluses (smuggled) found ready buyers among the merchants of Holland and France.

Wade's Causeway is real. Also called Wheeldale Roman Road although new theories question the Roman connection.

Robin Hood's Bay is real and, no doubt still riddled with tunnels throughout the limestone cliffs.

Henry Scrope, 3rd Baron Scrope of Masham, whose head sat upon the top of Micklegate Bar, was real. Baron Scrope was a good friend of Henry V but became involved in a plot to kill him, and so lost his head.

The King's Glove Inn is not real but there are many pubs and inns still operating from medieval times in the U.K. The low doors and uneven floors usually give them away!

The 'Packman' packhorses, bred by the monasteries and churches of northern England during the Middle Ages, evolved into the Cleveland Bay. It is the oldest established horse breed in England, and the only non-draught horse developed in Great Britain.

Acknowledgements

The working title of this novel was 'The Book that Wrote Itself'; however, I quickly learned that a story does not write itself.

It all began when a member of my winter writing group, 'Weavers of Words', in Venice, Florida, told me I was a storyteller. Thank you 'Weavers' for your inspiration.

Once I started writing and lost half my manuscript into the black hole of my laptop, I had to thank Lorrie of Lorrie's Computer Services for rescuing me.

Thank you to my three gentle but brutally honest readers, Bruce Robinson, Karen Sharp, and Patti Acheson for their dedication to steering me in the right direction.

Thank you to my editor, Carol Sokoloff, who has taught me much about wordsmithing and plot. Heartfelt thanks to Ekstasis Editions for having faith in me.

Thanks to my family for their continued encouragement and never saying, 'you're too old for this!'

Thanks to Elinor Florence, author, who answered all my questions with generosity.

A warm hug to my husband, Jim, who did the gardening when I should have been digging alongside him; and for supporting me from the beginning.